MOST ELIGIBLE BACHELOR

BY
MARGARET WAY

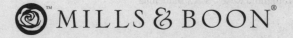

MILLS & BOON

DID YOU PURCHASE THIS BOOK WITHOUT A COVER?

If you did, you should be aware it is **stolen property** as it was reported *unsold and destroyed* by a retailer. Neither the author nor the publisher has received any payment for this book.

All the characters in this book have no existence outside the imagination of the author, and have no relation whatsoever to anyone bearing the same name or names. They are not even distantly inspired by any individual known or unknown to the author, and all the incidents are pure invention.

All Rights Reserved including the right of reproduction in whole or in part in any form. This edition is published by arrangement with Harlequin Enterprises II BV/S.à.r.l. The text of this publication or any part thereof may not be reproduced or transmitted in any form or by any means, electronic or mechanical, including photocopying, recording, storage in an information retrieval system, or otherwise, without the written permission of the publisher.

This book is sold subject to the condition that it shall not, by way of trade or otherwise, be lent, resold, hired out or otherwise circulated without the prior consent of the publisher in any form of binding or cover other than that in which it is published and without a similar condition including this condition being imposed on the subsequent purchaser.

® and TM are trademarks owned and used by the trademark owner and/or its licensee. Trademarks marked with ® are registered with the United Kingdom Patent Office and/or the Office for Harmonisation in the Internal Market and in other countries.

First published in Great Britain 2010
Harlequin Mills & Boon Limited,
Eton House, 18-24 Paradise Road, Richmond, Surrey TW9 1SR

© Margaret Way Pty, Ltd. 2010

ISBN: 978 0 263 87678 9

Harlequin Mills & Boon policy is to use papers that are natural, renewable and recyclable products and made from wood grown in sustainable forests. The logging and manufacturing process conform to the legal environmental regulations of the country of origin.

Printed and bound in Spain
by Litografia Rosés, S.A., Barcelona

Margaret Way, a definite Leo, was born and raised in the subtropical River City of Brisbane, capital of the Sunshine State of Queensland. A Conservatorium-trained pianist, teacher, accompanist and vocal coach, she found her musical career came to an unexpected end when she took up writing—initially as a fun thing to do. She currently lives in a harbourside apartment at beautiful Raby Bay, a thirty-minute drive from the state capital, where she loves dining *al fresco* on her plant-filled balcony, overlooking a translucent green marina filled with all manner of pleasure craft: from motor cruisers costing millions of dollars, and big, graceful yachts with carved masts standing tall against the cloudless blue sky, to little bay runabouts. No one and nothing is in a mad rush, and she finds the laid-back village atmosphere very conducive to her writing. With well over one hundred books to her credit, she still believes her best is yet to come.

LONDON BOROUGH OF HACKNEY LIBRARIES	
STANDING O	
Bertrams	22/06/2010
ROM	£4.99
	02/07/2010

PROLOGUE

Brisbane, State Capital, Queensland.
Three years earlier.

FOR Miranda in her hyped-up state, everything seemed to be *rushing* at her: cars, buses, cabs, pedestrians. Even her blood was whooshing through her veins. The city seemed incredibly noisy—the pulse and beat of traffic, the mélange of sight and sound. Just to top it off, there was the threat of a late-afternoon thunderstorm, routine for high summer. Heat was vibrating rapidly to and fro between the forest of tall buildings, bouncing down on to the pavements. This was the norm: expectation of a brief, hectic downpour, then the return of a sun that admitted no rival. The overhead sky was still a dazzling deep blue, but there were ominous cracklings in the distance, the odd detonation of thunder and a bank-up of dark, silver-shot clouds with acid-green at their heart on the invisible horizon.

She was abuzz with adrenalin. Almost dancing with nerves. The humidity in the atmosphere did nothing to bank her intensity. The crowded street was thick with voices. People were milling about, smiling and chattering, happy to be going home after a long day at work; others were laden with shopping bags, feeling slightly guilty about blowing the budget on things they didn't need; more held mobile phones glued to their ears, their side of the conversation loud enough to make the deaf sit up and take notice! Hadn't they woken up to the fact mobile phones were a potential health hazard?

Of course there were dangers everywhere—even crossing the busy intersection. She could see the born-to-take-a-risk oddballs and the habitual stragglers caught halfway across the street at the red light. Ah, well! She couldn't talk. Consider the dangerously risky move she was determined on making this very afternoon, given a stroke of luck? She only had one chance to get it right, but she had thought it through very carefully.

Over the last fortnight it had become routine surveillance, checking on the comings and goings of the Rylance men. Billionaire father Dalton Rylance, Chairman and CEO of Rylance Metals, one of the biggest metal companies in the world, and his only son and heir, Corin. Corin Rylance, twenty-five, was by all accounts the perfect candidate to inherit the Rylance empire. The Crown Prince, as it were. Super-rich. Super-handsome. Super-eligible. An opinion echoed countless times by the tabloids and gushing women's magazines. That didn't mean, however, the Rylances were nice people.

Anger merged with her constant grief. *Not* nice was starkly true of the present Mrs Rylance—Leila—Dalton Rylance's glamorous second wife. His first wife had died in a car accident when Corin Rylance was in his early teens and his sister Zara a couple of years younger. A privileged life cut short. A few years later Dalton Rylance had shocked everyone by marrying a young woman from the PR section at Head Office called Leila Richardson. A gold-digger and an opportunist, according to family and friends who didn't know anything about this young woman, however good she was supposed to be at her job. Collective wisdom had it she hailed from New Zealand.

Yet the marriage had survived. With all that money behind it, why not? Always beautiful, Leila Rylance, polished to within an inch of her life, had become over a few short years a bona fide member of the Establishment. She might have been born into one of the best families herself. Except Leila Rylance must live her glamorous life always looking over her shoulder. Leila Rylance wasn't who she claimed she was.

Leila Rylance was a heartless monster.

It took some nerve to tackle people like the Rylances, Miranda thought for the umpteenth time. She could get into very serious trouble. These were people who took threats and perceived threats very seriously. They had armies of people working for them: staff, bodyguards, lawyers, probably they even had the Police Commissioner on side. She had to think seriously of being arrested, restraining orders and the like—the shame and humiliation— only she was fired up by her massive sense of injustice. Seventeen she might be, but she was clever—hadn't that tag been hung on her since she was knee-high to a grasshopper?

"Miranda is such a clever little girl, Mrs Thornton. She must be given every chance!"

That from a stream of teachers—the latest, her highly regarded headmistress, Professor Elizabeth Morgan, reeling off her achievements. Professor Morgan had great hopes Miranda Thornton would bring credit on herself and her school. She had done her bit. She had secured the highest possible score for her leaving certificate, excelling at all the necessary subjects she needed for her goal: Mathematics, Physics, Chemistry, Biology. She had admittance to the university of her choice. She had the *brain* and the strong desire to become a doctor, but it would be hard, if not downright impossible, to get through the science diploma necessary for med school without *money*. She had long set her sights on Medicine.

"Where do you suppose that's come from then, Tom? Our little Miri wanting to be a doctor?"

Her mother had often asked her father that question, wonderment in her tone. There was no medical background on either side of the family. Just ordinary working-class people. No one had made it to university.

But she had things going for her. She was resourceful. She had a maturity beyond her years. She coped well under pressure. That came directly from having looked after her mother for the last three years of her life battling cancer. The agony of it! To make it much worse, her death had come only a year or so since her hard-working father had died of a sudden massive heart attack. They had not been a young couple. Miranda was, in fact, a mid-life baby. Her mother had been forty-two when she fell pregnant, at a time when both her parents had despaired of ever producing a living child after a series of heartbreaking miscarriages.

Her childhood had been a happy, stable. They'd lived in a glorious natural environment. There had never been much money, and few of life's little luxuries, but money was by no means essential for contentment. She'd loved and been loved, the apple of her parents' eyes. Her parents had owned and run a small dairy farm in sub-tropical Queensland—the incredibly lush Hinterland behind the eastern seaboard, with the magnificent blue Pacific Ocean rolling in to its shores and only a short drive away. The farm had rarely shown more than a small profit. But they'd got by, working very hard—she included—to secure the best possible education at her prestigious private school for her final four years.

She would never forget the sacrifices her parents had made. In turn she had been fully committed to looking after them as they aged. Only now they were gone. And her world was lying in great jagged piles of rubble around her feet.

Her parents hadn't been her parents at all.

They'd been her *grandparents*.

And no one had told her.

She had grown up living a lie.

Her heartbeat was as loud as a ticking clock, pumping so fast it was almost choking her. The sun flashing off windscreens temporarily blinded her. She blinked hard. Turned her head.

Then she *saw* him.

Eureka! She was close. Soooo close!

One had to fight fire with fire. She braced herself, lithe and as swift on her feet as a fleet fourteen-year-old boy. He was coming out of the steel-and-glass palace of Rylance Tower. The son. What a stroke of luck! She would know him anywhere. His image was etched into her brain. Who could miss him anyway? He was tall, dark, stunningly handsome with a dazzling white smile. The ultimate chick-magnet, as her friend Wynona would say. Could have been a movie star only for his layer of gravitas. Unusual at his age. But then he was a mining magnate's son and heir, with a brilliant career ahead of him.

Well, he wasn't the only one going places, she thought. Her whole body was shaking with nervous energy. She hadn't been exactly sure she could deal with the father anyway. He was a hugely important man and purportedly ruthless. The odd thing was she had no real desire to potentially cause a break-up in his marriage. The son would do, whiz kid that he was, by far the less problematic proposition. Sometimes you just got *lucky*!

She watched the silver Rolls slide into the loading zone outside the building as per usual. The grey-uniformed chauffer stepped out smartly— God, a uniform, in *this* heat?—going around the bonnet of the gleaming car to be at the ready to open the rear door for the supremo's son.

Couldn't he open it himself, for goodness' sake? Well, it did give the chauffeur a job. Every nerve in her body was throbbing with a mix of anticipation and a natural fear of the consequences. She had to get to him, speak to him, if her life was to go forward as she and her grandparents had planned. She watched Rylance dip his splendid crow-black head to get into the back seat of the car. This was the crucial moment. She seized it, taut as an athlete at the starter's gun. Before the chauffeur could make a move to close the door, she literally sprang into the vehicle in one excited leap, the wind lifting her skirt and showing the full length of her legs, landing in a breathless heap against the shoulder of her target, who was playing it very cool indeed.

"Hi there, Corin!" she cried breathlessly. "Remember me? The Beauman party? Didn't mean to scare you, but we have to talk."

Those kinds of words usually made young men sit up and pay attention.

The chauffeur, well-built, probably ex-army, leaned into the Rolls, concern written all over him. "You know this young lady, Mr Rylance?"

She smiled up at the grim-faced man, who appeared on trigger alert. "Of course he does. Don't you, Corin?"

Recognition didn't light up his brilliant dark eyes. "Convince me."

His speech was very clipped—blistering, really.

Before she knew what he was about his lean, long-fingered hand snaked out, ran deftly but with delicacy over her shoulder, then down over her bodice, sparking her small breasts to life. She was shocked to the core, her entire body flooded with electricity. Even her nipples sprang erect. She prayed he didn't register that. He continued to frisk her to her narrow waist, cinched as it was by a wide leather belt. Mercifully he stopped there. Not a full body search, then. She was wearing a short summer dress, well above her knees. Sleeveless, low-necked. Nowhere to hide anything. Nowhere decent anyhow.

He grabbed her tote bag and handed it over to the grim-faced chauffeur. "Check the contents, Gil."

"You're joking!" she railed. "Check the contents? What are you expecting, Corin? A Taser? I'm absolutely harmless."

"I don't think so." Rylance kept a firm hold on her while the chauffeur swiftly and efficiently searched her bag.

"Nothing here, sir," he reported with a note of relief. "Usual girly things. And a few old snapshots. Shall I send her on her way, or call the police?"

"And tell them what, Gil?" Her voice, which had acquired a prestige accent from school, was laced with sarcasm. "Your boss has been waylaid by a five-three, hundred-pound seventeen-year-old he doesn't seem to remember? Why, a twelve-year-old boy could wrestle me to the ground. Trust me, Corin." She turned a burning scornful glance on Rylance. "You don't want anyone else in on our little chat, do you? Tell your man to pull over when we're clear of the city. Then Gil here can go for a nice stroll. A park would be fine. There's one on Vine."

Women were always chasing him. Hell, it went with the territory. But never had one taken a spectacular leap into his car. That was a first. He couldn't believe it. Not even after years of being hotly pursued. It was the money, of course. Every girl wanted to marry a billionaire, or at the very least a billionaire's son. But this was a *kid*! She'd said seventeen. She could be sixteen. Not *sweet*. She looked a turbulent little thing, even a touch dangerous, with her great turquoise-green eyes and a fiery expression on her heart-shaped face. A riot of short silver gilt curls clung to her finely sculpted skull. She had very coltish light limbs, like a dancer; she was imaginatively if inexpensively dressed. Had he met her anywhere at all, he would definitely remember. No way was she *unmemorable*. And she had beautiful legs. He couldn't help but notice.

So who the hell was she and what did she want? He had a fleeting moment when she put him in mind of someone. Who? No one he knew had those remarkable eyes or the rare silver-gilt hair. He was certain the colour was real. No betraying dark roots. Then there was her luminous alabaster skin. A natural blonde. Then it came to him. She was the very image of one of those mischievous sprites, nymphs, fairies—whatever. His sister, Zara, had used to fill her sketchbooks with them when she was a child. Zara would be intrigued by this one. All she needed was pointed ears, a garland of flowers and forest leaves around her head, and a wisp of some diaphanous garment to cover her willowy body.

They rode in a tense silence while he kept a tight hold on her arm. No conversation in front of the chauffeur. Some ten minutes out of the CBD the chauffeur pulled up beside a small park aglow with poincianas so heavy in blossom the great branches dipped like the tines of umbrellas. "This okay, sir?" The chauffeur turned his head.

"Fine, thanks, Gil. I'll listen to this enterprising young woman's story—God only knows what that might be—then I'll give you a signal. I have a dinner party lined up for tonight."

"Of course you have!" said Miranda, still trying to recover from the shock of his touch and his nearness. She understood *exactly* now what made him what he was. He even gave off the scent of crisp, newly minted money.

The chauffeur stepped out of the Rolls, shut the door, then made off across the thick, springy grass to a bench beneath one of the trees. If Gil Roberts was wondering what the hell this was all about he knew better than to show it. He believed Corin implicitly when he said he didn't know the girl. He had been with the family for over twelve years, since Corin Rylance had been a boy. He had enormous liking and respect for him. Unlike a couple of his cousins, Corin was no playboy. He did *not* fool around with young girls, however enchanting and sexy. Maybe it had something to do with one of his cousins? A bit of blackmail, even? She had better not try it. Not on the Rylances.

"So?" Corin turned on her, his tone hard and edgy. "First of all, what's your name? You obviously know mine."

"Who doesn't?" she retorted, not insolently, but with some irony. "It's Miri Thornton. That's Miranda Thornton."

"Amazing—Miranda! Of course it would be." He didn't mask the sarcasm.

"What's that supposed to mean?" She stared at him with involuntary fascination. She was experiencing the weirdest feeling there was no one else in the world but the two of them. Imagine! Was she a total fool? She almost forgot what she was about with those dark eyes on her. God, he was handsome. The glossies were right. Up close and personal, his aura was so compelling it had her near gasping. It wasn't simply the good looks, it was the force field that surrounded him. It had picked her up with a vengeance. For the first time she felt intimidation.

"You're a smart girl," he was saying.

"Not a little twit?"

He ignored that. "Well educated, obviously. Miranda—Prospero's daughter?"

Deliberately she opened her eyes wide. "Got it in one. *The Tempest.* You know your Shakespeare. From whence did Corin come?" she asked with mock sweetness. "*Coriolanus?* Noble Caius Marcus?"

"Cut it out." His tone was terse. There was a decided glitter in his eyes, so dark a brown they were almost black. "I don't have time for this. What's it all about? You have exactly five minutes."

"Give me *one*," she retorted smartly, hoping she looked a whole lot more in control of herself than she was. "May I have my bag?"

He frowned at her. "What is it you want to show me?" He didn't oblige, but drew the tote bag onto his lap. Gil would have checked carefully, but there were always surprises in life. This extraordinary young woman didn't exactly look unstable or wired.

He could see the high intelligence in her face, the keenness of her turquoise-green regard. She was *nothing* like all the well-connected young women he knew. The pressure was on him from his father to pick out a suitable bride. Annette Atwood was highly suitable. But did he honestly believe in *love*?

"Photographs." Miranda's mind was momentarily distracted while she focused on his hands. He had beautifully shaped hands. Hands were important to her.

"That's nice!" He didn't hide the mockery.

"I'd hold the *nice* until you have a look at them," she warned. "Don't think for one minute it's porn. Good old Gil would have spotted that, and I don't deal in such things. I was very well brought up. Go on—pull them out. They won't bite you."

"The cheek of you!" he gritted. "You know what I'd really like to do with you?" He was uncomfortably aware his body was coiled taut. Why? She was pint-sized. No physical threat at all. What *did* he want to do with her? Why was he giving her the time of day? Actually, he didn't *want* to think it through. She was so *young*, with her life in front of her. Despite himself he felt a disturbing level of attraction.

"Throw me out onto the street?" she was suggesting. "You could do it easily."

"Maybe I will at some point." He withdrew

several photographs from a side pocket in her well-worn bag. They looked old, faded, turning up at the edges. He narrowed his dark eyes. "What exactly are these? Photographs of Mummy when she was a girl?" He was being facetious. Until he saw what he had in his hand.

God, no! This wasn't real. It couldn't be. It wasn't *her*. The girl in the photographs didn't just bear a strong resemblance to his stepmother. She *was* Leila—unless she had an identical twin.

"How clever of you, Corin," Miranda said, making an effort to conceal her own upset. "They're photographs of my mother when she was a year younger than I am now."

His expression turned daunting for so young a man. Shades of the father, Miranda supposed. "Just be quiet for a moment," he ordered.

Miranda knew when it was time to obey. She and Corin Rylance had polarised positions in life. She was a nobody. He was on the highest rung of society. Heir to a great fortune. He could cause her a lot of grief.

"So what's your game?" He shot her a steely glance, the expression in his fine eyes in no way benevolent.

"No game." She turned up her palms. "I'm deadly serious. We can keep this between the two of us, if you like. I'm certain from what I know of my birth mother—*your* stepmother—that she hasn't confided her sordid little story to another living soul. Least of all your father."

"You want money?" The stunning features drew tight with contempt.

"I *need* money," she corrected.

"Aaah! A big difference." The tone was withering.

"I think you can spare it."

"Do you, now?" His tone all but bit into her soft flesh. "So I'm to look after you indefinitely? Is that the plan? Well, let me help you out here, Miranda, as you're barely out of school. Blackmail is a very serious crime. I could turn you over to the police this afternoon. It would only take one call."

"Sure. I've risked that," she admitted. "But you won't be doing your family any favours, Corin. Don't think I'm not ashamed to have to ask you. I *have* to. My mother—*your* stepmother, your father's *wife*—owes me. I can't go to her. I loathe and despise her. She abandoned me when I was only a few weeks old."

"You can prove it?" His voice was harsh with unsuppressed emotion. "Or is this some highly imaginative ploy to make money?" The flaw in that was he could well see Leila doing such a thing. The only person Leila cared about was herself. Not his father. Although his father, business giant that he was, was in sexual thrall to her.

"I'm not stupid," Miranda said. "I'm not a liar or a con artist. Of course I can." She had to swallow hard on a sudden rush of tears. "I was brought up by my grandparents—my mother's parents—believing I was theirs. A change of life baby. Both of them are now dead. My grandmother very recently. She told me the truth on her deathbed. She wanted to make a clean breast of it. The last years of her life were terrible. She died of cancer."

His expression softened at the very real grief he saw in the depths of her crystalline eyes. "Miranda, I'm sorry, but your mother must have had a reason for doing what she did. That's if these photographs *are* of my stepmother. People do have doubles in life." Even as he said it he *knew* it was Leila.

"You know in your bones they are," Miranda told him bleakly. "I even look a teeny bit like her, don't you think?"

"Not really, no. Maybe the point to the chin—although Leila's is less pronounced."

"So I must have my father's colouring." There was a yearning note in her voice he picked up on. "Whoever he might be. She never would say. Anyway, I have a whole scrapbook if you want to see it. My birth mother was adored. My grandparents were lovely people. Yet she cut them—her own mother and father—ruthlessly out of her life. *I* didn't matter at all. Good gracious, no. I was just a huge mistake. You know how it is. She wasn't going to allow an unwanted baby to ruin her life. She ran away and never came back. Not even a postcard to say she was okay."

"You're sure about that?" he asked grimly. "Your grandmother mightn't have told you everything. People have secrets. Some they take to the grave."

"Tell me about it," Miranda countered with real sadness. "I loved Mum—Sally—my grandmother. I nursed her. I was with her at the end. She told me everything. Not a pretty story. I had to forgive her. I loved her. She was so good to me. Yet the person I had trusted more than anyone else in the world had lied to me. God, it hurt. It will always hurt."

"I imagine it would." He studied her downbent face. She had a lovely mouth, very finely cut. Leila's mouth was positively *lush*. This girl wore no lipstick. Maybe a touch of gloss. "I expect your grandmother thought it was best at the time. Then it all got away from her. Where did you live?"

She told him. "The Gold Coast Hinterland, Queensland."

"A beautiful area. I know it well. So your grandparents were farming people?" he asked with a frown. "According to Leila she was born in New Zealand."

"She was. And just look at how far she has come." Miranda gave a theatrical wave of her hands. "Married to one of the richest men in the country. You can bet your life she didn't want any more children. She's only thirty-three, you know. But children would only cramp her style."

True of Leila. "The woman you claim is your mother told my father she wasn't able to have children," he volunteered.

"I think you can take it she's a born liar. Anyway, your father has you and your sister. *You're* the heir."

"You bet your life I am."

"Don't look at *me*!" She slumped back against the rich leather upholstery. "*I* don't want to muscle in."

"I thought you did."

He had very sexy brackets at the sides of his mouth. "No way!" She shrugged, unsettled by his proximity. In a matter of moments this stranger had got under her skin. Definitely not allowed. "What I want—what I *need*—is to have the financial backing to get through med school. I'm clever. Maybe I'm even cleverer than you." She held up her hand. "Okay, joke! But I scored in the top one per cent for my finals."

"And there I was, only winning a few spelling bees."

"Not so." She sat straight. "You were awarded a university medal. You have an Honours Degree in Engineering. You also have a degree in Business Administration."

"Go on—what else?" he asked caustically.

"Listen, Corin. I did my homework. It was necessary. I'm not asking for a fortune, you know. I'll get a part-time job. Two if I have to. But I must attain my goal. It's what my par—my *grandparents* lived and worked for. I was the one who was to be given every chance. Only they both went and died on me. That's agony, you know."

He regarded her for a moment in silence, all kinds of emotions nipping at him fiercely. This girl was getting to him. And she had done it so easily. "Your story has to be checked out very thoroughly," he said. "You might tell me *how*, given there wasn't much money in the family, your mother got away? Everyone needs money to survive. She was just a schoolgirl. How did she manage?"

"I daresay she blackmailed my father," she said, bluntly rephrasing the explanation her grandmother had offered.

"So it runs in the family, then?"

She winced, her turquoise-green eyes flashing. "Don't make me hate you, Corin."

He laughed, very dryly. "That's okay. Hate works for me, Miranda."

Some note in his voice sent a shiver down her spine. "Miri, please."

He continued to scan her face. "I prefer Miranda."

She was locked into that brilliant regard. "You'll

find I'm telling the truth right down to the last detail. My grandparents didn't know who fathered Leila's child. But, whoever it was, his family must have had money. Someone must have given it to her. Although she took *everything* she could lay her hands on from her parents, including much needed money that was awaiting banking."

"It's a terrible story, Miranda, but not rare," he said. "Young people—girls and boys—go missing all the time, for any number of reasons. It must be heart-breaking for the caring parents."

"Leila obviously didn't care about *them*. There was no abuse, no excessive strictness, only love. You know, I've been thinking of you—your father and you, certainly Leila— as the enemy," she confessed. "*You're* not so bad."

"You don't know me," he said.

"I know you bear a noble name. The Corin bit anyway. I like it. I don't even mind being allied with you, or *your* part of the enemy. But you can't be slow about this, Corin. There are lots of things to be taken care of. I don't have another damned soul in the world to appeal to."

"And I'm supposed to care?" He was out to test her.

"But you *do* care, don't you?" She was looking into his eyes as if she was reading his mind. "Leila may have cast a spell on your father, but I bet she didn't cast any spell on you or your sister."

Nothing could be truer. They had disliked and distrusted Leila even before she had married their father. Now they hated her. "So you think this will give me an advantage?" Of course it would. But he knew he wouldn't use it. Not *yet*, anyway. His moment would come.

"Nothing so ugly," she said. "You may dislike Leila. But you love your father. That's it, isn't it?"

"You might well make a doctor, Miranda," he answered tersely. "You appear to have a gift."

She visibly relaxed. "I hope so. I want so much to do good in this world. I won't let my paren—" she corrected herself again "—grandparents down. I'm going to see this through and you've got to help me. I've even had a psychological assessment to determine whether I have the right stuff to become a doctor."

"And you passed?"

"With flying colours, Corin. Also the mandatory interview for selection into the MBBS course. You don't mind if I call you Corin?"

"Obviously you have a keen interest in getting me to like you."

"I like you already. Bit odd, really. But I believe in destiny, don't you? I was waiting for you— maybe your father. I got you. Far and away the better choice."

There was severity, but a touch of amusement in

his expression. "You can say that again. My father would have had you thrown out of the car. Right on your pretty ear."

"Is that so? You can tell a lot about a man by the way he treats a woman."

"I agree."

"Hey, you do love your dad, don't you?" She eyed him anxiously. There was something a bit *off* in his tone.

"Why do you ask that?"

"Unusual answer, Corin." She spoke in an unconscious clinical fashion. "I'd say textbook father-son conflict?"

"Sure you don't want to go for psychiatry?" he asked very dryly.

"I hit a nerve. Sorry. I'll back off. Anyway, even your father wouldn't have thrown me out. Not when I waved the photographs." His handsome face was near enough to hers to touch. "I have to be tough. Like you people. I know you can work this out somehow. I won't interfere. All you have to do is make it so I'm able to get through my first three years of training until I attain my BS, then I'll tackle my MB."

"An extremely arduous programme, Miranda," he warned her, shaking his head. Two of his old schoolfriends had dropped out in their second year, finding the going too tough. "Sure you're up to it?

I'll accept you have the brains. Maybe you can handle the ton of studying required. But there's a lot of evidence many students leaving high school with top scores fall by the wayside for any number of reasons. Happens all the time."

She nodded in agreement, but with a degree of frustration. She had been warned many times over how tough it was. "Listen, Corin, you don't have to tell me. I know how hard it's going to be. I know many drop out. But it's not going happen to me. I mightn't look it, but I'm a stoic. I've had to be. My grandparents' hopes and dreams will prevail. I'm up for it."

Everything seemed to point to it. "Where do you intend to study?" he asked.

"Griffith for my BS, then on to UQ. Why do you look like that? I promise you I won't ever bother you. You need never lay eyes on me again."

"Sorry!" He focused his brilliant dark gaze on her. "*If* you check out—and it's by no means a foregone conclusion—you'll be expected to take tests I'll arrange. Again, *if* you pass our criteria you'll be under constant scrutiny. You mustn't think you've got this all sewn up, Miranda."

"If you want references you can contact my old school principal," she suggested eagerly, her heart beating like a drum.

"You just leave that to me." He dismissed her

suggestion. "You'd be very foolish to try to put anything across me."

"Whoa...I gotcha, Corin." She held up her palms, her heart now drumming away triple-time. "So, you want to think it over?" She swallowed down her nerves, moistening her dry lips with the tip of her tongue.

"Of course I want to think it over." He spoke more sharply than he'd intended, but this girl was seriously sexy. God knew what power she'd have in a few years' time. "I may *sense* you're telling the truth. That's all. *If* you're Leila's daughter, as you claim, you could be an accomplished liar."

That made her heart swell with outrage. "What an absolutely rotten thing to say, Corin."

"Okay, I apologise." The glitter of tears stood in her beautiful eyes. Against all his principles, against rhyme and reason, even plain common sense, he had a powerful urge to catch that pointed chin and kiss her. Long and hard. A mind-body connection. It was almost as though he was being directed by another intelligence. Mercifully he had enough experience, let alone inbred caution, not to give way to an urge that was fraught with danger. Women had been making fools of men since time immemorial. Maybe this slip of a girl was trying to make a fool of *him*?

At first when she had made her mad leap into the car his mind had immediately sprung to his cousin,

Greg. Greg was forever getting himself into trouble with women, but not teenagers—at least not to date. He'd never thought in a million years this would have something to do with Leila.

"Do you drive?" He turned his attention back to the would-be doctor. That counted for a lot with him. He had the ability to read people. She was ambitious, which he liked, idealistic, and she appeared very sincere in her aim. Becoming a doctor was a fine goal in life. He should check out her driver's licence. If she had one.

"I *can* drive," she confided. "As good as your Gil. Bet he was in the army at some stage. I used to drive the ute around the farm all the time, but I don't have a car. I can't afford one. Listen, Corin, I'm dirt-*poor* at the moment."

"So where do you live now?" he asked. Gil *was* ex-army. She was very sharp.

"I share a flat with friends. A major downgrade for us all, but we have fun. My grandfather's dying was a nightmare, then my...grandmother. What money there was simply went in to the bottomless hole of medical costs. There's no licence for you to check. But you can check me out at my old school. I was Head Girl, no less Professor Morgan thought the world of me, which is as good a character reference as you're likely to get. You can check out my grandparents too. Needless to say everyone in the district believed me to be their mid-life child. I have more information on my birth mother if you want it. My grandmother knew all about her marrying your father. She read about it in the newspapers. Leila might be all dolled up, but she's the same Leila. Mum used to keep cuttings. Isn't that sad? A parent is always a parent. No matter what."

His father hadn't been much of one, he thought bleakly. Not much of a husband either. In fact, the powerful and ruthless Dalton Rylance was a major league bastard. But he was still madly infatuated with the very much younger Leila. Obsessed with her, really.

"It's all sad, Miranda."

He gave way to a dark sigh. He and Zara had been devastated when their mother had been killed. Their father's infidelities and lack of attention had brought great unhappiness to their beautiful, gentle mother. His maternal grandparents, the De Laceys, major shareholders in Ryland Metals, had positively loathed their son-in-law as much as they loved their daughter's children. He, as his mother's only son, had been extremely protective of her—ready to tell his father off at the drop of a hat, no matter the consequences. And there were quite a few he'd had to suffer along the way. The reality was he and Zara had looked to their mother for everything. Love, support, long serious discussions about life—where they were going. It was she who had taken them on numerous cultural outings. She'd been the source of joy in their so called privileged life. Their father had never been around. Jetting off here, off there. Legitimate business concerns, it had to be said, but it had never occurred to him to try to make up for his many absences when he returned. In his way Dalton Rylance had betrayed them all: his wife, his son and heir, and his daughter—the image of their beautiful mother.

And he punished her for it. Zara, the constant reminder. His hands tightened until his knuckles showed white.

"So what are *you* in the grip of?"

Her voice, which amazingly showed concern, brought him out of his dark thoughts.

"What do you mean?" She was way too perceptive, this girl.

"Don't bite my head off, Corin. It can't be *me*. It's someone else you're thinking about. What did you and your sister think when Leila turned up in your life? You couldn't have lost your mother long? You must have been grieving terribly?"

"Miranda, we're not talking about *me*," he told her curtly, shaken by her perception. "We're talking about you."

"So *you* say!" she responded, undeterred. "Where did I get my brains from anyway? My maths gene, for a start. I was always very good at maths. My grandparents were lovely people. Full of good practical common sense. My grandfather could fix any piece of machinery on the farm. My grandmother was a great cook and a great dressmaker. But they wouldn't have called themselves intellectuals. Neither of them read much."

"Of course you *are* an intellectual," he said, not sparing the dry-as-bone tone.

"No need to be sarcastic. I *am*. Fact of life, and I don't take the credit. I inherited what brain I have from the boy—the man—who was my father. Leila can't be too bright if she didn't think I was going to track her down one day."

"But there's no way you want to meet her?" He trapped her gaze. God, wouldn't that be an event to be in on?

"What? Show up unannounced? No way! I might tackle her to the ground and start pummelling her. Not that I've ever done anything like that before."

"Miranda, don't underestimate the woman you say is your mother," he rasped. "It's far more likely she'd seize you by the hair and have you thrown out. That's if you could get *in*. My stepmother isn't your normal woman."

"Now, isn't that exactly what I've been telling

you?" she cried, her turquoise-green eyes opened wide. "She's a *cruel* person. She broke her loving parents' hearts. My grandmother died without her only child by her side. I don't really care that Leila didn't want *me*. Who the heck do I look like anyway?" She tugged in frustration at a loose silver-gilt curl. "What's with the hair? The colour of my eyes? There's my father out there somewhere. I might go looking for him. Did he even know about me? Actually, I've got a few doubts about *your* father. Given he's the big mining magnate, how come he fell for Leila hook, line and sinker? What got into him?"

"Let's not go there, Miranda," he said tersely.

"Okay, she's beautiful. She's gorgeous. And she must be great in bed."

And as dangerous as a taipan. "Are you done?" he asked, amazed. This seventeen-year-old girl was a total stranger, yet already they had made a strong connection.

"Don't get angry with me, Corin," she urged gently. "I could be worse. I could be out to make trouble, but I'm not. I don't want to stress this— it's a bit embarrassing—but look at the big picture. Aren't we related by marriage?"

"I only have your word for it," he answered, very sharply indeed because he was rattled. "Plus a few old photographs as some sort of proof."

"Please...I don't want you to be angry and upset. You might be keeping it well under wraps, but I think you have...difficulties in life."

He didn't care he sounded so cutting. "You're a very special person, Miranda." She had to be. Every cell in his body was drawn to her. It was an involuntary reaction. But sometimes one had to be cruel to be kind.

"You believe me, though, don't you?" The glitter of unshed tears was back in her eyes at his harshness. "You believe *me* more than you would believe the woman you've known for years. I bet she's been no friend to your sister. You *do* love your sister?"

He gritted his teeth. "Do you expect me to sit still for this interrogation?"

"Okay, okay!" She pressed her hands together as though in prayer. "I shouldn't have said it. Let's get back to what I need to get me through med school. I promise I'll work harder than I ever have in my life. Back me and I won't let you down. I'll even try to pay you back once I qualify."

He was driven to dropping his head into his hands. "Miranda, just stop talking for a moment. I'm going to check out your whole story. Or have my people do it for me. Don't worry. They're professionals. It will all be very confidential. None of the information they supply to me will get out. Where is this flat of yours?"

She was so nervous, excited, upset, her hands were shaking. "Look, I'll write it down for you. And my mobile number. I hope I didn't seriously ruin your day?"

"I can't pretend you haven't stunned me." He shot back his cuff to check his watch. "I have a very tedious dinner party tonight I can't get out of. I'll get Gil to drop me off first at my apartment, then he can take you home."

She became agitated. "No, no, don't bother. I don't want to put you to the trouble. Besides, I can't possibly arrive back at the flat in a Rolls."

"Gil can stop and let you out a short distance away," he said shortly. "Anyway, it will be dark by the time he gets there." He lifted his hand to signal the chauffeur, who now turned their way, walking down the path.

"So, will you let me know?" In her agitation she reached out to grip his hand hard, feeling the little shock wave of skin on skin. "Can I trust you, Corin? I *do* need help."

"Have you told anyone else about this? Your friends?"

The brilliant gaze seared her. "Gosh, no! I promise you I haven't told a living soul."

"A smart move, Miranda, for a smart girl. You'll hear from me within a few days. We'll do this thing legitimately."

"Legitimately, how?" She perked up.

"I'll tell you when I judge it time for you to know," he said dismissively. "But if you've dreamed up some story—"

"Then you're free to go to the police." She spoke with intensity. "It's no story, Corin. That's why you've been giving me a hearing. Even if your stepmother did lay eyes on me she wouldn't recognise me."

"On the other hand she might," he answered her bluntly. "There is such a thing as genetics. You said it yourself. How did Leila produce a child with silver-gilt hair and turquoise-green eyes? It has to be your father's legacy."

"Or it could be any number of complex interactions." She frowned in concentration. "So many variables—enzyms, proteins, biological phenomenon. I'm greatly interested in genetics and genomics, molecular biology. Why wouldn't I be? I don't even know who I am. That should put me at a serious disadvantage psychologically."

He saw humour in that. "I don't think so, Miranda. You appear pretty well integrated to me."

"Gee, thanks!" She flushed with genuine pleasure. His good opinion meant a great deal. "Trust me, Corin," she said earnestly. "Leila has totally forgotten she ever had a child."

He swallowed his caustic retort. Hadn't Zara

always said there would come a time Leila, their stepmother, the central figure in their father's life, would be caught out?

And so it began.

CHAPTER ONE

The present.

THE top floor of the immense glass-and-steel monolith, the command post of Rylance Metals, housed the multibillion-dollar corporation's hierarchy. As Miranda rode the elevator to Corin's office she had an overwhelming feeling she shouldn't be in this building. Not that she would have to duck if she saw anyone. She had been inside Rylance Tower on isolated occasions over the past three years and no one had taken the slightest notice of her. Why would they? Her status of university student would have been obvious to them from her classic student dress. Besides, the Rylance Foundation sponsored a number of gifted students. They came and went. On those occasions she had been careful to maintain her camouflage. On campus she was a lot more flamboyant. Some of her girlfriends laughingly called her a *fashio-*

nista. Amazing what one could do on a low budget, given a bit of flair. She had inherited that flair from someone. Leila? Leila was renowned for her style.

She had long since learned from Corin that Leila had been given a position on the board by her besotted husband. Corin had become so important to her she could recognise the fact he deplored his father's decision. Not that he spoke about it. Only once, and then briefly. Corin played his cards very close to his chest. Mercifully today there was no chance of running into the woman who had abandoned her soon after birth. Leila only ventured into Rylance Tower for board meetings. Right now, she and her husband, Dalton Rylance, were in Singapore—a mix of business and pleasure, the newspapers said. Corin said *business*. It was always *business*. But Leila would get the opportunity to spend lots of money to make up for the time she had to spend on her own and so prevent herself from getting bored.

As Miranda stepped out into the hushed corridor, thickly carpeted and lined with architectural drawings—the corporation had its own architectural as well as engineering departments—she checked her watch. Ten minutes until Corin would see her. She was always early, never late for Corin. It was pleasant to make a little light conversation with his secretary, the beautifully groomed, forty-something Clare Howard, who was devoted to him and exceptionally good at her job. As she would have to be.

Afterwards, Miranda took a seat on one of the sofas facing a granite-and-chrome coffee table neatly stacked with trade magazines and financial papers. She picked up one, flipping through it without actually seeing anything. Today she had allowed herself a little more pizzazz with her dress. Ms Howard had kindly made a comment on how lovely she looked. Her dress *was* pretty. The yellow silk background was splashed with tiny daisy-like flowers in deep blue, violet and turquoise, with a fine tracery of green leaves. A sale coup. All the major department stores were running them in the recession. New turquoise sandals and a turquoise tote bag that looked a whole lot more expensive than they were completed the outfit. Her hair she continued to wear short, cutting her bubble of curls herself, sometimes enlisting a girlfriend's help for the back of her head. She didn't have the time or the money to go all-out with a glamorous new hairstyle. She had maintained her part-time job—waitressing at city restaurants, three nights a week—but that money was stretched to the limit. She had been given assistance by the Rylance Foundation to rent her inner-city flat, which was in a good, safe, very convenient area.

With two minutes to go she could feel the rise in her blood pressure. One's blood pressure always rose when in the company of someone one was attracted to. Fact. She ached over her reasons. At least she felt confident she looked good. Healthy, eyes bright, skin glowing, despite the endless hours of burning the midnight oil.

Over the past three years she had grown close to Corin. She told herself it was in a quasi *professional* way. Mentor-protégée sort of thing. He always appeared pleased to see her at any rate, and was always willing to take the time to listen to her accounts of student life. A friendship had been established, but they both took good care to keep within the proper framework. Wealth could open doors for people. Corin had opened a door for her. She was immensely grateful. So much so she had gone all out to top her graduating class. Corin had actually taken the time to attend, clapping enthusiastically after she had given her speech.

"I knew the moment I laid eyes on you, you were a girl with enormous potential." This with a mocking sparkle in his dark eyes.

By now she knew his every expression, every nuance of his resonant voice. She knew she had to be extremely careful to control her feelings. Her career was mapped out. She had to concentrate on her studies. She couldn't allow emotion to get in the way. A show of emotion—however slight—could jeopardise her standing with Corin. There was a definite etiquette involved. She could not overstep the mark. Fortunately she had mastered the art of masking her deepest feelings. She might not appear vulnerable. But vulnerable she was. Privately she had run out of making excuses for herself. The truth was she had a huge crush on Corin Rylance.

Get real! You're madly in love with him.

No one must ever know.

They shared their dark secret about Leila, but they rarely allowed it to come to the surface. From time to time she weakened in her discipline, always when she was in bed at night, allowing herself to wonder what Corin was doing. Who he was doing it with. Lately there had been rumours of an impending engagement that made the muscles of her stomach clench at every mention. Corin—married! Yet it seemed to her Corin didn't have the look of a man in love. The young woman in the spotlight was one of his circle. Annette Atwood. An extremely attractive brunette of imposing height, with a great figure. A real figure. Naturally Ms Atwood was asked everywhere. Photographed wherever she went. Lately the paparazzi had taken to following her as though they *knew* she was a strong contender to become the heir apparent's wife. Corin himself never spoke of her. But then, since she had met him Corin hadn't spoken of any particular woman. Except his sister, Zara, who was working in London at a big financial institution. Zara had a Masters in Business. She had an excellent head on her shoulders and was also very artistic, like their mother and her side of the family. Zara was a gifted artist, but their father had been totally against her trying to make a career as a painter.

"A hobby, girl. Just a hobby! Live in the real world. Can't abide dabblers."

The image Miranda kept getting was that Dalton Rylance wasn't a nice man at all. No comfort to his children—especially his daughter. No wonder Dalton and her mother were inseparable. They were creatures of the jungle. Power was all that counted.

"Hi, Miranda!" Corin looked up from something he had been reading to give her his irresistible smile. It was impossible not to smile back. "Take a seat, won't you?" He gestured towards the leather armchairs arranged companionably on the opposite side of his desk. It was a huge space, his office, beautifully and comfortably furnished. Hundreds of leather-bound volumes gleamed through the antique English mahogany cabinets. A neat pile of files sat to one side on his desk; one was open before him. No disorder whatever. Everything in its proper place. There was a splendid view over the city towers and the broad, deep river to his back. "Clare is organising coffee. We have a few things we need to discuss."

"Oh, Corin, like what?" She was feeling a little giddy at the sight of him—he looked so vibrant, impossible not to stare—so she quickly took an armchair opposite, folding her hands with a commendable show of calm in her lap.

"You look well," he sidetracked. In fact, she looked enchanting. He had never seen her in so pretty or so feminine a dress. She was such an intriguing combination of inner strength and physical delicacy. No doubt she had picked the dress to suit her rare colouring. She probably knew her eyes were the exact colour of the turquoise flowers. He wanted to tell her. Thought he'd better not. Miranda kept her own space.

"So do you." She stared back at him with a little worried frown. "Why is it I think you're about to persuade me to take a gap year?" He had raised the subject before, but had since let it drop. She should have known better.

"Well, it *is* a good idea," he said mildly.

She glanced away. A large canvas hung on the far wall. It depicted a lush rainforest scene with the buttressed trunk of a giant tree of extraordinary shape in the foreground. The magnificent tree was surrounded by a wide circle of copper-coloured dry leaves, and ferns of all kinds, fungi and terrestrial white orchids sprouted everywhere in the background. His sister, Zara, had painted it. Miranda, who had a good eye for such things, loved it. The scene looked so real—so immediate—one could almost walk into it. "I can handle the studying, Corin." She looked back slowly.

He held up an elegant, long-fingered hand. "Please, Miranda, don't look so crestfallen."

"How can I not be?"

"You push yourself too hard. I worry about you."

"You worry about me?" Her heart gave a quick jolt.

"Why look so surprised?"

"You don't *have* to," she said, trying to hide her immense gratification. He *worried* about her?

"Of course I do," he confirmed. "You're virtually an orphan. We share a history."

She didn't say she worried about *him* when he went off on his field trips to inspect various corporation mine sites.

With every passing year he had become more handsome and compelling. She watched with a mix of fascination and trepidation as he stood up, then came around his desk to perch on the edge of it. He was always impeccably dressed. Beautiful suits, shirts, ties, cufflinks, supple expensive shoes. The lot! How could she not fall in love with a man like that?

"I know you can handle the mind-numbing workload," he said. "You've demonstrated ample proof of that. But you're still very young, Miranda. Only twenty. Not twenty-one until next June, which is months off. I don't want you totally blitzed."

She drew in a long breath, preparing to argue. "Corin—"

Again he chopped her off with a gesture of his hand. "A gap year would give you time for personal development. Time to develop your other skills. You need to get a balance in life, Miranda. Believe me, it will all help in your chosen profession. You could travel. See something of the world. Do research if you like."

She couldn't hold back her derision. "Travel? You must be joking."

"Do I look like I'm joking?" He lifted a black brow. "I'm very serious about this, Miranda. You're not just another brilliant student we're sponsoring. The two of us have a strong connection. Your mother is married to my father. Many people thought it would be all over within a year or two, but they were wrong. She knows *exactly* how to handle him."

"It has to be sex," she said with a dark frown. "Razzle-dazzle." Leila Rylance was famous for her beauty and glamour, her parties. From all accounts she had made herself knowledgeable about the political and big business scene. Even the art world, where she was fêted by gallery-owners. Leila was right at the top of the tree when it came to social-climbers.

"Don't knock it," Corin was saying dryly. "It's important. Dad is still a vigorous and virile man. Besides, Leila has numerous other wiles at her disposal. She runs his private life and the house— indeed the houses all over the world—with considerable competence. She's no fool. She's appears very loving, very loyal, very respectful. She hangs on my father's every word."

"But is it for real?" Miranda demanded with a good deal of fire. "She obviously didn't win you and Zara over."

There was a flash in his brilliant dark eyes. "He brought her frequently to the house before our mother died, like she was a colleague and not an employee well down the rung. Fooled no one. At one stage I thought our housekeeper Matty was planning on poisoning her over morning tea. Matty adored our mother. Leila spent a lot of time trying to charm us. We were only children, but *thinking* children. We could see she posed a real threat to our parents' marriage. Dad lusted after Leila long before she got him to marry her."

She studied his handsome, brooding face, seeing how it must have been for him and his sister. "So hurting people didn't concern her? Between the two of them they must have broken your mother's heart."

His expression was grim. "It was pretty harrowing for all of us. My beautiful mother most of all. I can't talk about it, Miranda. I'll never forgive either of them."

"Why would you? I'd feel exactly the same. I *do* feel the same. The thing is, do they *know*? Does your father know? You're his heir."

He gave a brief laugh. "My grandparents, the De Laceys, are major shareholders. My grandfather Hugo still sits on the board. It was he who staked my father in the beginning—a lot of money, I can tell you. I have my mother's shares. And Zara and I will have our grandparents' eventually. Dad couldn't overthrow me even if he wanted to. Which he doesn't. In his own peculiar way he's proud of me. It's Zara, my beautiful, gifted sister, he endeavours to avoid. I look like *him*, except his eyes are a piercing pale blue and mine are dark."

"They're beautiful eyes," she said without thinking.

"Thank you." He smiled, thus lightening the atmosphere. "But I still say yours are the most remarkable eyes I've ever seen."

"Someone has them," she said. "My biological father? Some member of his family? Even you with all your resources couldn't find out who my father was."

"We couldn't, and Lord knows my people tried. But we don't know if it's a good or a bad thing. Some people don't want to become involved—not many years after, when the pattern of their lives is set. No one in the area where your grandparents and Leila lived fitted the bill or the time frame. It could have been someone she just happened to meet—"

"Like a one-night stand?" Miranda said sharply. "Barely sixteen, and Leila was taking lovers? Or was she raped? I can't bear to think about that." She shuddered. "My grandmother was convinced from the way Leila acted and spoke that wasn't the case."

Corin's eyes never left her face. "There's no way to tell, Miranda. I'm sorry. Only Leila knows. One day you might get the opportunity to ask her—" He broke off at a discreet tap on the door, calling for entry. A young woman Miranda had never seen before wheeled a trolley into the office.

"Thank you, Fiona. We'll take it from here."

"Yes, Mr Rylance." Fiona flashed him her most dazzling smile, at the same time managing to give Miranda a comprehensive once-over.

Fiona left. Miranda stood up. "I'll pour. No milk? Teaspoon of sugar?" She remembered.

"Fine." His mind was clearly focused on something else.

"Want one of these sandwiches and a Danish?"

"Why not?" He went back to sit at his desk.

They were both settled before he spoke again. "This coffee is good."

"Nothing less than the best." It *was* very good. So were the neat little chicken sandwiches and the freshly baked mini-pastries. She was hungry. She'd only had fruit for breakfast. Papaya with a spritz of lime.

"Money would be made available for you to travel," Corin said, setting down his coffee cup.

She looked at him in amazement. "You can't be serious, Corin! Why would you do that? I'm taking enough. Can I say no?"

His brilliant eyes burned into her. "Better to say yes, Miranda."

"Oh, Lord!" She took another hasty swallow of the excellent coffee. "You're worried about burnout. Is that it?"

"There *is* such a thing. We both know that. The sheer drudgery of study. Your friend Peter almost died from an overdose."

Her head sank. "Poor Peter!" Peter—her friend, the brilliant class geek. She had looked out for him from the start. When other students had tended to mock his extreme shyness and his bone-thin appearance she had been his constant support. Peter's appearance at that stage of his life hadn't matched up with his formidable brain.

"You were devastated," Corin reminded her. Did she *know* poor Peter idolised her?

"Of course I was devastated," she said, lifting her head. "We were supposed to be friends, but he never *told* me how bad he felt. Why didn't he? I could have helped."

"You can't blame yourself, Miranda. You were a good friend to Peter, but his depression got the better of him. He was the classic square peg in a round hole."

"Wasn't he just?" She sighed. "I'm so grateful you were there for me that night." Not knowing what else to do, she had called Corin from the hospital and he had come. "I'll always remember that. And what you did for Peter afterwards. You spoke to his family. They listened. They'd been blind to the fact Peter wasn't meant to be a doctor. With the family medical background they more or less forced him into it. Peter desperately wanted to become a musician. His ambition wasn't taken at all seriously until you spoke up."

"I wanted to help."

"Well, you did." These days Peter was studying the cello at the very prestigeous Royal College of Music in London.

"Still hearing from him?" Corin asked.

"All the time."

She smiled. A sweet, uncomplicated smile. Peter was her friend. No more. He would never be her lover. He was glad about that. He didn't stop to question why. But emotions had such intrusive, pressing qualities. Sometimes they had to be pushed away.

"I love Zara's rainforest painting," she said, gesturing to it.

"So do I. Zara keeps up her painting. I'll find one of hers for you. I have quite a collection. But we're not talking about Zara. Or Peter—though I'm very glad to hear he's doing so well. We're talking about *you*, Miranda. I firmly believe you'll benefit from a gap year."

Her fingers laced themselves together.

"Don't argue. You wanted to fast-track science, remember?"

She looked across at him with pleading eyes. "I could have done it in two years had I worked through the long vacations."

His tongue clicked with impatience. "Why won't you admit you were *glad* when I made the decision for you? I'm on your side, Miranda. I'm simply not going to allow you to crash and burn. Two years was far too gruelling for a three-year science course and you know it. No time at all for a personal life."

"Who needs a personal life?" she asked discordantly, stretching her slender arms along the sides of the armchair. "*You're* a workaholic, though rumour has it you're going to marry Annette Atwood. She's stunning."

He let the silence build. "So she is," he agreed eventually. "But you appear to know more about it than I do."

"You're *not*?" It came out far too intensely. Damn, damn, *damn*.

"Let's get back to you," he said smoothly, aware she hadn't meant to show such interest. "Professor Sutton shares my view you'd benefit from a gap year. And *there's* a man who thinks the world of you."

Her expression softened. "The Prof would like me to stick to science. He's told me many times. He thinks I have a future in medical research. When you think about it, nine of our ten Nobel Prize winners have been medical scientists, or doctors of medicine. And Patrick White, of course, for Literature. I know at some future stage the Prof would like me to be in a position to make his team. I'm sure he's told you he's enormously grateful for the funding he receives from the Foundation?"

"He's doing great work," Corin acknowledged, as though that said it all. "Research doesn't appeal to you?"

She ran her fingers through her short glittering curls. "I'd be honoured. But I have to get my MB first, Corin." Her brain was ticking over at a million miles a minute. Travel? See the world? She felt exhilarated. And shocked.

"No reason to believe you won't. I applaud your ambition. But taking a gap year will work out to be a distinct advantage. The more experienced and the more cultivated you are as a human being, you can only enhance your chosen career."

"So I'm to do what I'm told? Is that it?"

He could see the mix of emotions in her eyes. "I've mapped out an agenda for your perusal."

"Not my approval?" she commented wryly.

He ignored that. "Zara will be happy to keep an eye on you in London. I know the two of you will get on like a house on fire. Dad splashed out and bought a house in London when our mother was alive—an 1840s house in Holland Park. Rather run-down at the time, but in a superb location of beautiful tree-lined streets and gardens, and of course the park itself, which was once the grounds of a vast Jacobean Manor. Anyway, my mother and her English decorator transformed it. Zara is living in the house now. But there's a basement apartment which I had turned into a very comfortable *pied-à-terre* for whenever I'm in London. You could live there. It will give you the feeling of independence. You can come and go as you please, but Zara would still be around for you. There's a very elegant apartment in Paris too, typically Parisian, but Leila doesn't go there often. She much prefers the villa she talked Dad into buying on the Côte d'Azur. It has a spectacular view of the Mediterranean."

"So in the years of her marriage Leila has lived like royalty, greedily soaking up all the luxury your father's billions can buy?"

"It's not a new phenomenon. There have always been courtesans."

"You hate her, don't you?"

"I hate what she did to my *mother*," he said tautly. "And how shamelessly. That's when it all began. She worked to alienate Zara from Dad. These days I'm…indifferent to her."

Miranda had to wonder about that. Only eight years separated Corin and Leila. "She must have to work very hard to be indifferent to *you*!" She spoke without thinking.

His handsome face tightened and his whole body tensed. "What's that supposed to mean?"

She reined herself in quickly. "Leila likes to charm wherever she goes. Men, that is."

"Well, she doesn't charm *me*!" His voice was heavily freighted with hostility.

"Okay, don't be angry."

"Maybe you should start thinking about psychiatry?"

She met his dark eyes. "You've said that before. I've got good instincts, Corin. I let them work for me. Are you going to show me that agenda of yours?"

"I've got it right here." He picked up a sheet of paper, then passed it across the desk to her. He must have been checking it when she arrived. "A bank account will be opened for you. You'll have all the money you need to travel. See the great art museums of the world, study a language if you like. Go to the opera, the theatre, the ballet. Zara loves the ballet. Buy clothes. I want you to make the best of this time, Miranda. You'll have a long, hard slog ahead of you."

Her eyes ran dazedly down the page. "Look, I can't do this, Corin," she said eventually. "I'm not family. Yet you're treating me like family."

"Oh, for God's sake, you *are* family—in a way. Your mother is married to my father. That's family. Besides, I'm fond of you, Miranda. You must know that. We clicked from the very first moment you near landed in my lap. Your welfare has become important. It's the least I can do for someone who has taken more than her share of blows. We're both caught up in this, Miranda, so you *must* do as I say. This gap year will work wonders. Just see how quickly it goes."

She closed her eyes briefly. "So a girl's gotta do what a girl's gotta do? Is that it?"

"I want your promise right now," he said.

Her eyes opened. Her head flew back. "What if Leila and your father decide to visit London, or the Paris apartment or whatever?" she queried with sharp concern. "I see there's another apartment in Rome."

"You wouldn't need to have contact should they visit. Leila likes the great hotels. Claridges in London, the Ritz in Paris are favourites. Dad does what she wants. She's an expert manipulator. Anyway, I'll always know their movements. Leave it to me."

"Leave it to you?" She drew in a stunned breath. "I'm shocked by all this, Corin. I knew you might spring the gap year on me again, but never an agenda like this! Zara still doesn't know about me and Leila?"

"I don't think she could handle it," he said sombrely. "Not without speaking out. She knows about my clever protégée Miranda Thornton. She knows nothing about the family connection. It'll have to wait."

"Until you're good and ready, Machiavelli. Do protégées usually get world trips and a hefty bank allowance?"

"My sister knows I have a reason for everything I do," he answered smoothly. "She won't question it, or you. All she needs to know is that I consider, as does Professor Sutton, you'll gain a great deal from a gap year."

Her beautiful eyes glittered like jewels. "I think I knew from the start it might end up like this. You changing my life."

His mouth twisted sardonically. "Cheer up! Didn't you once call it destiny?"

"You believe in it?"

Their eyes locked. For the longest moment. "I do," he said.

CHAPTER TWO

IT WAS more like a fairy tale than real life. She was living a glittering lifestyle, like the most impossible of dreams. She had to remind herself every day that she couldn't allow such a life to seduce her. Not that there was any real chance of that. Zara was the heiress. She most assuredly wasn't. The practice of medicine would be *her* role in life. But for now she was enjoying herself immensely—just as Corin had wanted her to. Days, weeks, months simply flew by in a whirl of pleasure and excitement. She was learning a new way of life, acquiring much knowledge along the way.

She loved London—perhaps not the climate, not after the blue and gold of Queensland, but she worked around that like everyone else. London was one of the great cities of the world. It embraced her. It allowed her to trace its illustrious history, to see its magnificent historic buildings, the art galleries, the wonderful antiques shops, markets, to shop at the legendary Harrods, visit the beautiful parks. She was doubly blessed by being billeted in very swish Holland Park, just west of Notting Hill. More than anything she loved living in Corin's elegant apartment, with its French Art Deco furniture and a basic colour scheme of brown, bronze and white enlivened by cinnamon and gold. It was definitely a male sanctum, but it welcomed her.

Though fourteen thousand miles separated them, she somehow felt Corin very close. That could have had a lot to do with the fact that she was sleeping in *his* huge Art Deco bed!

Zara was largely responsible for the lovely time she was having. She had quickly found Zara was the most beautiful, gracious creature on earth. And the kindest. A true lady. Miranda knew from the photographs of their mother—Corin had one lovely silver framed study he kept on his desk—Zara was fashioned in her mother's image, but she did see a lot of Corin in her. The sharpness of intellect, the generosity of spirit, the sense of humour that happily they all shared. Just like Corin, there was something utterly irresistible about Zara. Yet Miranda sensed a deep sadness that lay in Zara's heart. From time to time it was reflected in her huge dark eyes. Zara had some pretty serious stuff stacked away in the background.

Over the months Zara had taken the place of the

big sister Miranda had never had. She had been so lonely for siblings that had never arrived. How could they? Her real mother, Leila, had fled, desperate to get away from her parents and her child. She now claimed she couldn't bear children. Maybe, just maybe, it was true. Leila would surely have wanted to cement her new position by producing a male child? It was possible it was Dalton Rylance who didn't want or need any more children. He had Corin and his daughter, even if she so painfully brought to mind his first wife. Was his cold disregard a by-product of his guilt? Miranda found herself both fascinated and repelled by the whole story.

Kathryn Rylance had died when she'd crashed her car. Had it been an accident? She would never dare ask. But surely such a loving mother would never have deliberately left her children? Not to such a father. Or the covetous young woman waiting in the wings. The potential stepmother. There could have been a single moment when Kathryn had become careless and lost control of the wheel. She could have been blinded by tears. Miranda realised she wouldn't be the only one to ponder such things. There were the grieving grandparents, the De Laceys, and Kathryn's clever, perceptive children, her close friends. Talk must have been rife!

But no one knew what really happened. Nor would they ever.

Often she wanted to break her own silence and confide in Zara, but she had given her promise to Corin. *He* would decide when it was time. In the meantime, Zara was always on hand with support and advice. She took Miranda everywhere—parties, functions, art showings—and introduced her to many highly placed people who seemed to like her. She was now included in many invitations. Zara arranged weekend trips to Paris, the fabulous City of Light, where they crammed in as much sightseeing as they could. All for her benefit, of course. Zara had visited the city many times before.

Back in London they lunched together whenever Zara could make it from work, went shopping together, loving every moment of it. But Zara never interfered or asked too many questions. It was as if she knew Miranda wasn't too sure of the answers. The great thing was they had become the best of friends. Miranda valued that friendship greatly. For a young woman with a billionaire father Zara was remarkably down to earth. But Miranda, acutely attuned to Corin and now to his sister, knew Zara wasn't happy at heart. It wasn't as if she brooded or was subject to mood swings, nothing like that, but Miranda felt right in her judgement. Beautiful, privileged Zara, for all the money behind her and a long list of admirers, wasn't happy or fulfilled. A melancholy lay behind the melting dark eyes that those who looked beyond the superficial clearly saw.

Miranda had written to Peter well in advance of her arrival. He had been thrilled to know she was coming. He thoroughly agreed with Corin, whom he referred to as his saviour, a gap year was an excellent idea.

"You don't want to end up a burnt-out old wreck like me."

These days they met up frequently for coffee and conversation, took in a concert or a movie. On good days, like today, when the sun was shining, they packed a picnic lunch and sat on the grass in either Hyde Park or St James's, with its wonderful views of Buckingham Palace in one direction and Whitehall in the other. There was just so much history to this great city! Currently Peter's teacher had entered him in a big European competition and convinced Peter if he worked hard and continued to show progress he would make his mark in the world of music.

"You're in your element at last, aren't you?" Miranda said, glancing over at her friend with affection. Peter had made a complete recovery now that he had been granted his wish to pursue a musical career.

"Absolutely!" Peter lolled on the green grass, tucking into a ham and salad roll. "I've never felt so at home in my life. I love London. All the action is here. And there's no culture gap to contend with. Even the family has settled, knowing I'm making a success of myself over here. Life's strange, isn't it? I wouldn't be here except for Corin. My parents actually listened to him. But then he has enormous presence and—what?—he's not even thirty."

"Twenty-eight." Miranda took the last bite out of her crunchy apple.

"Still in love with him?" Peter leaned on an elbow to peer into her face.

"Why ever would you say that?" She feigned nonchalance though her heart had started to hammer. Was she that transparent?

"Come off it, Miri," he scoffed gently. "I'm super-observant when it comes to you. Heck, I don't blame you. I could fall in love with him myself and I'm not gay. Corin has more going for him than the law should allow. It's a wonder some determined young woman hasn't snaffled him up."

Carefully Miranda wiped her hands, putting the apple core into a disposable bag. "There *is* one determined young woman on the scene. But no announcements as yet. Annette Atwood. You know the family?"

"Of course!" Peter nodded. His best feature, his

mane of thick golden-brown hair, gleamed in the sun. He was growing it artistically long, as Miranda had suggested. The look suited him and added a certain panache. "Dad's a big-time lawyer turned property developer?"

"That's the one."

"Think they'll make a go of it?" Peter asked, sensitive to how Miranda might feel about that.

"Corin has never come close to telling me about his love life," Miranda returned very dryly.

"What about *your* love life?" He turned questioning blue eyes on her. Corin's sister, who was a really lovely person and a great beauty in the classic style, was making it her business to introduce Miri to a lot of high-flying guys.

But Miranda smiled as though she didn't have a care in the world. "I have a powerful reason to stay on course, Peter. So do you. We have careers lined up."

"That we do. I've often wondered where your driving interest in medicine and medical research came from, Miri. Your background isn't like mine, with so many doctors in it. They say genius is random. Dad says it has to be in your genes."

"Then it must be a very long way back." She laughed. "I come from a line of small farmers."

"So it's just as they say. Genius is random."

"And we're *both* geniuses!" She lightly punched

his arm. "Better get going. Haven't you got a master class at three-thirty?"

Peter started. "Hell, I almost forget. It's so lovely being with you, Miri." He stood up, all of six-four, dusting his jeans off. "So, what are you going to do about your birthday? It's coming up. I suppose Zara will have something arranged?"

"No, no!" She shook her head vigorously. "Zara doesn't know anything about it. And you are *not* to tell her. I don't want any fuss. No presents, except a little one from my best mate—and that's you!"

"But you *should* celebrate!" he insisted. "You're only twenty-one once."

"It's no big deal."

"Of course it is! What say we get dressed up and have dinner at some posh hotel? I have money. The parents are very generous these days."

Miranda handed over the picnic basket, then took his arm. "That will suit me just fine."

Peter felt so happy he could have shouted with joy.

The best laid plans could always go awry, and circumstance forced them to move her birthday date forward to mid-week. Peter had been selected at short notice to replace the cellist in a highly regarded quartet, who had fallen ill. With a new member on board, intensive rehearsals would have to take place all over the weekend.

"No worries, Peter," she reassured him, thrilled he was getting such a lucky break. "New horizons are opening up for you. Wednesday evening will be fine."

And so it eventually turned out that Miranda's early twenty-first birthday dinner with the young man who would become her life-long friend proved a special treat.

The following day Zara and three of her colleagues, all foreign-exchange traders, led by her boss, Sir Marcus Boyle, were to fly off to Berlin for a series of top-level business meetings.

Zara eased her tall, elegant body into the jacket of her Armani suit, picked up her briefcase, then walked to the front door that led onto its own private patch of emerald-green lawn and blossoming flowerbeds. Miranda was holding the door open for her, waving acknowledgement to the London taxi driver who had just arrived to take Zara to Heathrow. At twenty-six, Zara was very good indeed at her job. Miranda had learned that from one of her colleagues at a recent party.

"Tremendous flair. Not afraid of taking risks. She's a star turn. In the genes, I suppose, as a Rylance. Rival banks regularly try to lure our Zara away. So far no luck!"

"I'll be back Tuesday." Zara smiled at the girl she had come to regard as the nearest thing she would ever have to a younger sister. "Be good. Don't accept any solo invitations from Eddie Walton. He's really keen on you, but he's too old and too much the playboy. As I told you, he was involved in a rather high-profile scandal not all that long back. Likes the ladies, does our Viscount Edward."

"Don't worry, I can look after myself," Miranda assured her. "Besides, I'm immune to Eddie's mature charms. Though he does have them."

"That he does," Zara agreed wryly. "Well, look after yourself, Miri." Zara bent to give the petite Miranda a real kiss on the cheek. "You don't mind watering the plants, do you? There are rather a lot of them."

"It'll be a pleasure."

"Thank you," Zara said gratefully. "Oh, yes, that reminds me. You're set for the charity do Wednesday evening?"

"Looking forward to it." Miranda gave Zara a final hug. "Go on, now. The taxi is waiting. Have a safe trip and wow them in Berlin."

Zara's answer came in a fluent flow of German that sounded perfect to Miranda's ears. She continued to stand on the doorstep of the handsome pristine white terrace house, watching until the taxi had disappeared.

You'll be alone, all alone, on your twenty-first birthday, girl.

Not that she minded being alone—she was fully aware how blessed she was being taken on by Corin and Zara—but it was her twenty-first birthday after all. She hadn't dared tell Zara about it. Zara would have done her utmost to organise something—even try to get out of the scheduled Berlin meetings.

With a little sigh, she shut the glass door of the big beautiful house and leaned against it.

Be happy, Miranda. It's not so terrible, is it, to be alone on your birthday?

Of a sudden her eyes filled with emotional tears. She blinked them back, feeling ashamed of herself. She had been handed a marvellous London sojourn on a plate. Trips to Paris. A luxurious lifestyle. The ease and affection of Zara's company. Most young women could only dream of being offered such an experience.

Buck up!

She breathed deeply. Corin knew it was her birthday tomorrow. No card had arrived. Maybe he thought a card might have alerted Zara? Flowers perhaps tomorrow? A possibility. She made a real effort to brighten up, wondering if she would ever find anyone in the world to fall in love with after Corin Rylance.

It was after midnight before she finished reading the latest novel by a writer she always enjoyed,

Laura Lippman. She set the book down on the bedside table before turning off the light. The beautifully laundered sheets and pillowcases had a lovely fragrance of mimosa. Zara would have asked for it especially, as a reminder of home. Mimosa, or wattle to Australians, the national flower.

With practice Miranda had mastered the knack of putting herself into some lovely serene place to enable her to drift off to sleep. These places were always near water—the ocean, a lake, a river—with lots of blue and gold, a background of leafy trees, spring green…

She didn't know how long she had been asleep, but she awoke with a great start and a swiftly muffled cry of fright in her throat. There were movements—soft, muted sounds—coming from upstairs in the house. She sat up, straining her ears, while the atmosphere in the apartment settled like a heavy blanket around her. She knew perfectly well she had set the state-of-the-art security system just as Zara had shown her. Who or what could have de-activated it? Should she ring the security people? Hastily she turned on a bedside lamp, checking the time: *1:30 a.m.* She had never been more aware of how exposed a lone woman could be. She said a quick prayer—not at all convinced there was really someone up there to hear her, but prepared to give it a shot.

Stacks of valuable things were in the house. Paintings, antiques, silver, Oriental porcelain, rugs. Heart thudding, she slid out of bed, pulling on the turquoise silk kimono Zara had insisted on buying for her.

"It exactly matches your eyes, Miri. You must have it!"

She took several deep breaths. Held them. An exercise in slowing her heart-rate. Then very quietly she let herself out of the apartment into the staircase hall that connected the apartment to the house proper. For the first time since arriving in London she felt very much alone. The area lay in intense darkness. She reached out her fingers, seeking the bank of switches. She pressed one and a single low-level light came on, gleaming against the teal-blue-painted wall with its collection of miniatures in gilded frames. Now she could find her way up the curving internal staircase. A good twenty-four oak steps. Before leaving the apartment she had taken the precaution of arming herself with one of Corin's golf clubs, which for some reason she had kept handy: an iron, a lethal weapon. God forbid she would have to use it. Maybe wave it about threateningly. Her mobile was in the pocket of her embroidered silk robe. She could ring the police.

Why don't you do it now?

What if it's Leila with Corin's father?

She very nearly went into a panic at the idea. Surely Zara would have told her of their impending arrival in London?

That was if Zara even knew they were coming.

A whole world of problems opened up. Corin had been adamant Leila favoured the great hotels of the world when she was traveling, even though her husband maintained residences in various capital cities. Besides, Zara was in residence, and there was no love lost between Zara, her father and his second wife. None of them would have wanted to come into contact.

What a dysfunctional family! Leila the stepmother was at the root of it all. Leila, her birth mother. She had a hard time with that. If Leila ever laid eyes on her what reaction would she get? She had to closely resemble *someone*, in her colouring alone. Probably Leila would deny she had a daughter with her last breath.

Silently she edged up the staircase to the first landing, her bare feet making no sound. Halfway up she fancied she could smell coffee.

Of course she could smell coffee. The marvellous aroma was unmistakable. What sort of burglar would make himself coffee? It had to be some member of the family. A distant member, perhaps? One of the male cousins? That playboy, Greg?

Just as she was hesitating, full of uncertainty, she heard footsteps in the long, spacious entrance hall with its marble tiling. Light, but simply not light enough to be a woman's. It was a male. Intruder or relation?

Her stomach contracted and her head went into a spin. Adrenalin pumped into her blood, otherwise she thought she wouldn't have been able to go a step further. As it was, she continued upwards. Someone was punching numbers into the security system. Why? They were already in. Or were they leaving? She felt a sharp ache at her temples, swayed a little, dropped the golf club.

You idiot!

If one accepted Murphy's Law, if anything could go wrong, it would. She did. The club landed with a clatter, the stick pinging off the shining brass balustrade of the wrought-iron staircase. A thousand miserable damns! She backed down a step or two, in a great hurry to retrieve the golf club. The noise of its falling would have alerted the intruder. Silence now roared at her.

Breathe in and out. Slow your pulse.

She readied herself. She didn't rate herself as fearless, but if something bad was about to overtake her she wouldn't let it pass without a fight.

Only, like a benediction came a voice. A deep, vibrant, sophisticated male voice. She would recognise it anywhere in the world. Probably even if she were out moon-walking.

"Miranda, is that you?"

Louder footsteps struck the marble tiles. She stood electrified. Panic thinly plastered over with stoicism gave way to an excitement so thrilling it was impossible to contain it.

It's me…it's me…it's me! She wanted to shout it from the rooftops.

Corin! Was that a birthday present or what?

"God, I thought I was being as quiet as the proverbial mouse," he called down to her.

"I'm here." She was practically whispering now, her mouth had gone so dry. Corin was *here*. She'd had only a forlorn hope he would even remember her birth date. But he was here! She didn't think she could climb the rest of the stairs, she was starting to shake so much. She had to take a moment to settle, to compose herself.

Corin!

This was the nearest she had ever come to euphoria. It was making her quite woozy.

"Where are you? On the stairs?" His footsteps were moving closer. "I'm sorry I woke you." His tone held both concern and apology. "I thought you'd be fast asleep."

Pull yourself together, silly. Think of your next move. No way can you act the gauche girl.

Only she couldn't seem to get her head around the fact Corin was here in the house. There had been no advance warning. Just his electrifying presence. Had Zara known, she would have told her. So that meant Zara didn't know either. She felt so unnerved, so totally off balance, she was almost ready to scuttle back down the stairs. She knew she looked perfectly presentable, with the kimono tied tightly around her, but the shock and wonder of his arrival was so enormously extravagant it was emotional agony.

All at once her knees gave way. She collapsed in a silken huddle on the step.

Corin appeared, taking in her small crumpled figure. "Oh, for God's sake, Miranda!" He hurried down to her, bringing with him the force field that always zoomed in on her. He was wearing evening dress. Black trousers, white pin-tucked shirt. The black bow tie was undone and left dangling. "I can't apologise enough!" He spoke very gently, getting an arm around her and lifting her to her feet. "I frightened you?"

"I have to say you did." From chills of fright, she was now bathed in the glorious heat of contact. It seared her lightly clad body that was pressed so alarmingly close to his. "Why didn't you let us know you were coming?" She ventured to lift her head, staring into his brilliant dark eyes.

"But that would have spoilt the surprise. Though I was taking a risk, wasn't I?" His expression went wry. "Surely that's one of my golf irons on the step?"

"I was hoping I wouldn't have to use it." She stayed within the curve of his arm and shoulder, for the moment physically unable to stand straight. The warmth and scent of him was the most powerful aphrodisiac.

"Oh, poor you!" he groaned. Still with his arm around her, he steered them up the rest of the stairs and from there along the corridor into the entrance hall. Once there, he dropped a kiss on the top of her silver-gilt curls. "A very happy birthday, Miranda. I can say that, as it's gone twelve."

"Thank you." The thrill of his presence was so *keen* it was like exquisite little pinpricks all over her skin. Plus there was the fear she would betray herself. "But you surely didn't fly into London to say that?" She managed to make it sound as though she was well aware he hadn't.

"Why not? You're twenty-one only once in your life." His dark eyes moved slowly, steadfastly over her. "You look well." Marvellously pretty would have said it better. Not a skerrick of make-up on her heart-shaped face, her mouth a delectable rose, and the lovely blue-green of the silk kimono matching her eyes, turning them to jewels. The silver-gilt curls still clung to her head, but he thought they were a little longer and expertly styled. Zara would know all the right places to take her. "I've made coffee. Would you like a cup, or do you want to go back to sleep?"

"Won't the coffee keep you awake?" She could only stand, staring at him. His white dress shirt was a wonderful foil for his deep tan.

"Who cares?" he said lightly, finding himself with a battle on his hands. He wanted to reach for her and draw her back into his arms. She fitted perfectly. At least take her hand. Frustrating, then, to have so many obstacles in the way. "I feel like one. Come along. You weren't really going to hit me with that golf club, were you?"

"I was going to ring the police."

"I'm so glad you didn't." He led the way into the large, beautifully designed kitchen. She and Zara had had many a meal here. Often she had done the cooking.

"You're so much better than I am!" Zara had declared.

True. Only unlike Zara she'd had years of helping prepare meals, in the end taking over the job completely for her mother, who had morphed into her grandmother.

God rest her loving soul.

"They wouldn't have been too happy, coming out this time of night—and for what?" Corin was saying, pulling her out of her thoughts. "It's all my fault. I take full responsibility. It's just that I remember you once told me you were out like a light as soon as your head hit the pillow."

"That's when I was studying hard," she admitted with a faint smile. "These days I'm doing little but enjoying myself. I've got used to the sounds of the house as well, and Zara is in Berlin."

"Yes, I know."

"So she *did* know you were coming?"

"No, she didn't." He glanced across at her, a delicate figurine wrapped in turquoise silk. She had no idea how alluring she was. Which was just as well. "I told you. It had to be a surprise. I knew about the Berlin meetings, however. She'll be back Tuesday anyway."

"Yes."

"So sit down."

This was one of those kitchens that didn't look like a kitchen. It looked more like an exceptionally inviting living area, big sparkling chandelier and all. The space was so large it could easily accommodate the marble-topped carved wood table, painted the same off-white as all the cabinetry and surrounded by six comfortable be-cushioned chairs.

She took one, conscious he was looking at her. She glanced up. Their eyes met. Married. Or was she imagining it?

"Hello!" he said, very gently.

Whatever it was, she could hardly speak for the force of her emotions. "And greetings to you." Even her voice shook, as though she had lost much of her habitual control. There was *something* in his tone; in the depths of his brilliant dark eyes.

Eyes say more than words ever can.

What were hers saying? That she wanted to leap up, go to him, hug him, tell him she had missed him *dreadfully*, for all the wonderful times she'd been having.

Common sense won over. This was Corin Rylance. Dalton Rylance's son and heir. A family worth billions. These were important people who mattered. Corin was way out of her league. For all she knew he could be about to tell her he was getting engaged when he went home. To the Atwood woman.

"What am I thinking of?" he asked himself with a quick frown. "Champagne is more in order than coffee. There's a bottle of Dom in the fridge. I think we might crack it. What do you say?"

"I guess it *should* be champagne," she agreed. She sounded so *polite*! No easy feat, when the level of excitement was rising at an alarming rate. She saw it as a flame that if only lightly fanned could turn into a dangerous blaze. Formality seemed as good as any defence mechanism.

Keep your deeper emotions out of it.
Sound advice.

"Twenty-one and don't you forget it," Corin said.

"So where have you been?" She inspected his tall elegant frame. "The evening clothes?" He looked so wonderful it made her feel strangely fretful, her legs restless.

"I spent the evening with old friends. I actually arrived in London from Rome late yesterday. Needed to catch up on my sleep. Had a business meeting this morning that lasted until lunch. I let Zara get away on her trip to Germany so I could move in."

She thought of something to distract her attention away from him. "Let me get the glasses." She rose swiftly on her small bare feet. "Zara and I often eat in here. In fact, we've had many an enjoyable late-night supper."

"She tells me you get on wonderfully well together." He lowered his handsome dark head to look into the well-stocked refrigerator.

"She's my honorary big sister."

He turned back, champagne bottle in hand, black eyes glittery. "Just don't make me your big brother."

She was surprised by his tone. "Why not?"

"I don't *feel* like your big brother."

His body language confirmed it. She felt a rush of emotion that was the equivalent to a huge jolt of adrenalin.

How can he possibly look at you like that if he doesn't like you?

Get real! Don't you mean he's attracted?

In the past few months, with all the socialising she had been doing, she had been made aware men found her very attractive. Viscount Walton, the famous ladies' man, for one. Now, for the first time, was there a tension and an *intimacy* between them? Maybe it was the lateness of the hour? The months of separation? All she knew was there was a star-bright, bursting sensation in her chest, as if sparkling, spinning, Catherine wheels were going off.

So what role does he want?

Don't invite disaster.

She tried to ignore her voices, reaching up to grasp two beautiful crystal flutes. They were kept on the shelf above other crystal wine glasses of varying sizes. Sheer nerves and a surfeit of emotion made her fingers uncharacteristically clumsy. To her utter embarrassment, the flute she had just barely grasped fell from her hand onto the tiled floor. The long stem remained intact, but the bowl shattered into glittering fragments that covered a surprisingly wide area.

"Oh, *no*! Sorry, sorry—I'm so sorry." She apologised over and over. Emotion was her undoing. "How could I have been so clumsy?"

Corin moved in very quickly. "Stand right where

you are," he instructed. "The glass has gone everywhere. Amazing how it can do that! You'd think the chandelier had fallen."

"I'll replace it."

Corin sounded totally indifferent to the damage. "Forget it, Miranda. It's only a glass."

"A very expensive glass." Her voice conveyed her distress and agitation.

"I said forget it," he responded rather tersely, as though her evident upset was getting to him. "Rather a broken glass than you cut your pretty feet. No slippers?"

"Extra quiet on the stairs," she explained shakily. "You could have been a burglar. Anyway, I'm fine. I'll get the broom." She unfroze, determined to sweep up the fragments, only Corin shocked her by reaching out for her and lifting her clean off her feet.

"I *said* stay put."

Her breathing had escalated to such a pitch it was darn nearly a whistle. "No need to turn cranky."

"I'm *not* cranky." He laughed.

"All the same, I was clumsy."

"You and clumsy don't go together."

It was precisely then that the silk sash of her kimono slid out of its knot and unfurled, making its sinuous way to the tiles, thus exposing Miranda's flimsy nightgown: fine white cotton caught by a deep V of crocheted lace that was threaded with blue satin ribbon. She had never felt so naked in her life.

"You *can't* hold me." Her nerves were coiled so tight they were about to snap.

"Does holding you change things, Miranda?" The amusement had gone out of his voice. It was oddly taut, as were the muscles in his lean, powerful body. Even his eyes were filled with a daunting yet exciting masculine intensity.

"I mean I must be h-heavy."

"You're a featherweight." He hoisted her higher, to prove his point, carrying her back to the table. "There—you can relax now!" He set her atop it, with a big blue pottery bowl filled with fat, juicy lemons just to her right. "Stay there. That's an order. I've opened the champagne. We're going to have a glass or two each. It's your birthday. I'm not going to allow anything to spoil it."

With his height, he reached easily into the top shelf, taking down two exquisite flutes while glass crunched beneath his gleaming black dress shoes. "Right! I'd better sweep this little lot up."

The odd tension between them resonated in the large room. She watched him sweep up the glass with a few swift, efficient movements, then push it into a pile, clearly sticking to his plan of pouring the champagne. That done, he handed her a frosted flute, his strong, elegant fingers closing momentarily around hers.

The pleasure was so sharp it was a wonder she didn't cry out.

"Congratulations, Miranda, on your twenty-first!" He toasted her. "May you have a long, happy, healthy and fulfilled life."

"And may I always know you and Zara," she returned emotionally. "The two of you have come to mean the world to this orphan."

"Listen to you!" he said gently. "Drink up. This is a great year."

She savoured the fine vintage wine, first in her mouth, experiencing the burst of delicious bubbles, then in the flavour, letting the wine run down her throat in a cold rivulet until the flute was empty. "Beautiful!" she breathed, her tongue retaining the cold, crisp after-taste.

"Then how come there's a little heartbreak in your voice?" he asked, finding her far more of an intoxicant than the most superb wine.

"I don't know, Corin. The significance of the moment?"

So many unsaid things were suddenly between them.

And then his hand came out. He touched the satin texture of her cheek.

She couldn't help it. She *moaned*. "I feel like I've known you all my life."

"So look at me."

She obeyed, looking directly into his brilliant eyes. Dark as they were, they couldn't hide the gleaming sensuality.

No distance at all now divided them. Both seemed possessed by the moment. "It's your birthday, so I believe I should be allowed to kiss you," he murmured, already dipping his head. "One kiss. That's all. On this very special occasion we might find it permissible to go out on a limb." He managed to speak lightly, affectionately, even, but in reality he was driven by pure desire that had to find at least some degree of release. Time to confront the repressed knowledge that his desire for her had begun the moment he had first laid eyes on her years before.

He wanted to run an urgent hand down the column of her throat to her delicate breasts. To his captive eyes they resembled pink-tipped white roses, not long out of bud. He wanted to feel her heartbeat beneath his palm. If only she were older, more experienced, more along the way with her ambitions, he would kiss her and caress her before carrying her to bed.

But this was Miranda. He couldn't allow his control to slip. He had vowed to look after her and her interests. She was *young*, when his experience of life and living had gone far beyond even his own age group.

From long practice Corin reined himself back to a pace he thought they both could handle. He set down his wine glass before taking hers out of her hand.

"Happy birthday, Miranda." His voice was low, and to Miranda's ears heart-stoppingly deep and romantic. Even before he touched her she felt as if she was being possessed. Gently he took her face between his hands, inhaling her sweet fragrance.

There can be no future in this.

Her warning voice tolled like a bell.

All you stand to gain is heartbreak.

At that moment she couldn't bring herself to care. She had to seize this one breathless instant. One kiss, then everything would go back to normal. They would return to their respective roles.

It doesn't work that way.

"Come here," he whispered.

All there was was a deep hunger. She moved her upper body into him, her spine curved, while he held her face and kissed her as if he had never in his life known a woman he wanted to kiss more. He kissed her not like Corin her mentor. He kissed her like the most ardent lover. It was a brilliant, beautiful, incredibly *real* kiss, as if for those short moments out of time he was declaring love for her. This was no quick flare of pleasure-seeking. None of the male's driving sex urge was on display. All control wasn't lost. The kiss was *contained*. A decision acted upon. But deeply, deeply erotic for all that.

One of you will get hurt. It won't be him. It will be you.

Corin found he had to pull his mouth away. Even with his exercising of strict control, the level of excitement had surged so high he thought it would take a long time to subside. "Has no one told you how beautiful you are, Miranda?" He gazed down on her face. It looked dreamy, almost somnolent, as though she had been transported to another place.

It took her long moments to answer. "If they have, I haven't taken much notice."

As an answer it was very revealing. Careful now, Corin thought. He would do nothing to threaten her well being. One kiss had proved more than enough to handle, luring him on while staying his hand. He moved his body back a little, deliberately lightening his tone. "Zara has mentioned many times how charming people find you. There's some old roué—what's his name? Walton?"

Her heart was racing so hard and fast it was moving the lace at her breast. "Eddie *is* quite a player." With an effort she summoned up a smile. She had taken their kiss in her stride, hadn't she? There was wisdom in caution. "There are many women in his life."

"But he wants to spend time with you?"

"Maybe he does. But I'm not anyone's passing fancy, Corin. I avoid danger and damage."

"Good." He turned away from temptation. "One more glass, then I must let you go back to bed. I need to turn in myself. We're off to Venice in the morning."

She was so startled she gave a little cry. "*What* did you say?"

Venice? Magic in the air.

She wished she was sitting in a chair, so she could ease back into it for support. As it was, she thought she might topple off the table.

"Venice. Probably the most fascinating city ever built by man," he said, busy refilling their sparkling flutes. "I have us booked into a first-class hotel. Tons of atmosphere. It's on the site of the orphanage church where Vivaldi probably dreamed up the Four Seasons. I think you'll love it. It's the quintessential Venetian luxury hotel and its position is superb. Our respective suites overlook the Lagoon, and it's only a few minutes' walk from the Piazza San Marco. It'll be a great experience for you. You're just the sort of young woman to fully appreciate it. The heart of a pure romantic beats beneath this Bachelor of Science."

She was perilously close to bursting into tears. "Corin, you don't have to do all this for me."

"What have I done for you really?" He held her with his compelling eyes.

"What no one else has done! You overwhelm me."

"What? Feisty little you?" he scoffed. "The teenager who launched herself into my lap? If that wasn't initiative, what is? Risky too, as you very well knew. Here—drink this down, then off to bed. A cab will be here at eight sharp to take us to the airport. Ninety minutes or so on we take off to Marco Polo International. We return to London Monday afternoon. I'll wait to see Zara when she comes back, then I'll be heading home for a few days before I head off to meet up with my father in China. Business, needless to say."

"This is like a fairy tale," Miranda breathed, accepting the crystal flute from him with visions of the legendary Serenissima she had seen only in books and films rising before her eyes.

"Well, your life hasn't exactly been a fairy tale up to date. This is by way of balance. Besides, even if we're not related by blood we do have a strong connection."

A shadow crossed her small heart-shaped face. "I want to tell Zara," she confessed. "We've become close. I don't like keeping my true identity from her."

"Only there might be quite a price to pay," he offered rather tensely. "For the moment anyway. I know how you feel. I don't keep secrets from my sister. I love her. After our mother was killed we were so *alone*, except for one another and our grandparents when we were allowed to see them. Dad did his best to isolate us, but he didn't succeed. A life of wealth and privilege doesn't guarantee happiness, that's for sure. The occasion *will* present itself. You just have to be patient."

"Until the timing fits in with *your* agenda, Corin?" There was just the tiniest hint of challenge in her tone.

"Trust me," he urged. "Right at the moment I'm most concerned with protecting you from what could be a very unpleasant experience."

"You feel contempt for Leila, don't you?" she said, sadly aware this woman was her mother.

He gave a nonchalant shrug, but the expression on his handsome face had darkened. "Leila is a very destructive woman. My father can't see it, but Leila's whole being is centred on *self*. Valiant as you are, clever as you are, you'd be no match for her. You see life very differently from your mother, Miranda. You want to *serve*. Leila only wants to *take*."

"Does she want to take *you*?" The instant it was out of her mouth she felt a great spasm of shock. *Why* had she broached such a highly dangerous and emotive subject? Could it have been acute feminine intuition at work? There *was* such a thing. Corin's father was still a very handsome man. But Corin was young. He was much closer in age to Leila than his father. And Corin was *blindingly* sexy.

"Only *you* could get away with saying that." He turned her face to him, fingers closing around her pointed chin.

"So forgive me." She was actually appalled at herself. "But you make her sound such a rapacious woman."

His hand dropped. "She makes my father happy. Zara and I might wish she had never come into our lives, but she did. My father is a business giant, a brilliantly clever man, but in some respects he's completely under Leila's domination."

"And this is the woman who bore me?" she said, a dismal note in her voice.

"You are *you*," he replied with strong emphasis. "All your admirable characteristics come from a different source."

"Oh, I hope so," she gasped. "My grandparents were fine people. They formed me. But then they would have done their best to form Leila. Perhaps my father, whoever he may be, made some sort of a contribution?" she suggested with some irony. "There are many mysteries in life, aren't there? A lot of them I would think unsolved."

His expression had turned brooding. "I agree. It's possible that whoever your father was he didn't know Leila was pregnant."

"So where did she get the money to run away? My grandparents didn't have anything. She didn't rob a bank. Someone gave it to her."

"Someone who might have been appalled by the whole situation. It could be a real grief, Miranda. Anyway, we won't talk about it any more. It's your birthday."

"Do you think Leila will remember?" she asked with a twist of bitterness.

"If she does she won't flail herself." His answer was full of contempt. "Promise me you'll put Leila out of your mind. I'm planning a long festive weekend. Promise?"

She threw up her shining head. "I promise," she said.

"Then drink up and we'll go to bed."

If only! If only! If only!

CHAPTER THREE

THERE followed the most glorious day of her life. The word *dazzling* should be kept for the rarest occasions, Miranda thought. A private mini-bus was waiting at Marco Polo airport to take them to their water taxi, which again had to be private, because they had it all to themselves. What it is to be rich! Miranda mused, all but mesmerised by this whirl of luxury and dream trips to fabled locations. With her particular mind set, another thought inevitably struck her. One would need to be sprightly when visiting Venice, with all the getting in and out of water craft. She had to think of the elderly, and people with back and knee problems. Mercifully, at the grand old age of twenty-one, her body was wonderfully flexible.

In a haze of unbounded pleasure and excitement she moved ahead of Corin into the cabin, and from there into the sunshine at the rear of the *vaporetto*. There was so much to take in. So much to capture the imagination. The triumph of Venice, a city built on water! At times like this she would have given almost anything to be an artist. She could scarcely believe she, Miranda Thornton, raised by ordinary country folk, the people who had loved her the most, yet who had kept secret from her the fact she had been abandoned by her mother as an infant, was now entering upon the most glorious street in the world. A street that had been immortalised by some of history's truly great artists. Canaletto immediately sprang to mind. And the great English painter J. M. W. Turner. She had adored Turner's work on her gallery trips with Zara, who was very knowledgeable about art. Turner had really spoken to her. Then there was the American John Singer Sargent, who had painted many scenes of Venice. And why not?

The sheer grandeur was breathtaking: the splendid frontages of the magnificent palaces—Venetian Byzantine, Gothic, Renaissance—that lined either bank of the famous waterway with a hot sun beating down. She felt as though she was absorbing the palpable sense of history—of a city founded in the fifth century—through her pores, though it was near impossible to absorb the totality of the scene, so much splendour was on show.

The water was an indescribable blue-green. Not sparkling, like the waters of home, but with a kind of lustre like oil spreading out over the surface of the great canal, thus picking up marvellous reflections. She wondered what Venice would look like at night. And she was *here*! It made one have faith in miracles.

"Well?" asked Corin, studying her enchantingly pretty face. From the moment he had met her he had found her fascinating—not just her highly distinctive looks, but her manner, her speech, the sense of purpose that even at seventeen had emanated from her. He and Zara had visited Venice, a favourite city of their mother's, many times before, but this time with Miranda, brandnew to the fabled Serenissima, he found his own pleasure expanding by the minute.

She turned to him eagerly with a spontaneous smile, turquoise eyes glittering. "It's beyond—way beyond—my expectations. The extraordinary light!"

"The golden glow of Venice," he said.

"The colour of the water is indescribable!"

"From a height it shimmers," he told her. "Anyone familiar with our waters in Australia speaks about the dazzling blue sparkle, but the Grand Canal—indeed all the waters of Europe—have a different palette and a different character." He studied her flawless white skin with the luminosity of alabaster. "Are you wearing sun block?"

She shook her head almost guiltily. "No." She

had meant to put some on. Not that she had needed it so far in London.

He tut-tutted. "And you a doctor in the making. It's very hot, and it will get hotter as the day wears on. It's a different heat from ours, as I'm sure you've already noticed. Come back inside. Don't worry. We'll see everything. Take a gondola ride. The gondolas can reach the narrowest and most shallow canals. It's the best way to get around. These days it costs an arm and a leg, but you learn the city from both sides of the canal. There's a tremendous amount to see, but we have to make the best choices to fit in with our time. We might manage a visit to the island of Murano."

"World-renowned for its glass-making. I do know that." She had a girlfriend whose parents had brought her back a beautiful necklace and earrings set from Murano.

He nodded. "For centuries they were the only craftsmen in the whole of Europe who knew the secret of making mirrors. They held on to the technique for all that time."

"I'm not surprised." She laughed. "It would have brought in a great deal of money as well as prestige."

"Exactly. There's a very fine museum on the island called Palazzo Guistinian. Thousands of pieces cover the entire history of glassmaking from the ancient Egyptians to the present day."

"Wasn't there some Bond movie when they sent a cabinet toppling?" She frowned, trying to remember. Was it an older movie, with a marvellously handsome Roger Moore?

"Wouldn't be a bit surprised," he said wryly. "They sent a *palazzo* toppling into the Grand Canal for the first one featuring the new James Bond, Daniel Craig. If you like I can arrange a water taxi so we can go over on our own. Only a short trip."

"That would be wonderful, Corin. But I must admit I'm a bit worried about how much money you must be spending." A fortune already, in her reckoning.

"Don't feel guilty. I've got it. One of the perks of being a Rylance."

She watched him closely. He had only been standing in the sun a short time, but she could have sworn his golden tan had deepened. "It's sad and strange, isn't it, that you and Zara, brought up with such wealth, haven't had a happy life?"

"And you all of twenty-one!" He gave her a smile.

"Okay, okay!" She drew in a quick breath. "But please let me tell you I'll never forget this birthday if I live another eighty years." It came out with enormous gratitude and a tiny quiver of sob.

Instantly, he enfolded her in a brief hug, as if

she was his favourite cousin. "So why do you think I brought you?" he said.

Her suite overlooked a great breadth of the luminous waterscape, looking towards the island of San Giorgio. She could see its magnificent church, San Giorgio Maggiore with its Renaissance façade, gleaming white in the sun, and the imposing *campanile*—the bell tower. The bedroom's décor was like no other she had ever seen. Sumptuous, seductive, otherworldly in its way, with antique furniture, fine art, fragrances on the air—and she thought a delicious touch of spookiness. But then she did have a great deal of imagination.

As she stood there, marvelling, Corin turned to face her for a moment, with amused and indulgent dark eyes. "I don't like to drag you away, but I must. A quick lunch, then as much as we can comfortably fit in of a grand tour, before dinner here. The hotel has a very fine restaurant and chef. Then we take in the city by night. Don't forget the sun block."

"I wish I could say in Italian your wish is my command."

"Then let me say it for you."

She applauded as he broke into fluent Italian. "*Non parlo Italiano,* I'm afraid," she smiled.

"Apart from the usual one liners. *Arriverderci, addio, ciao,* and the like—and what I've picked up from Donna Leon's Venice-based books. I really enjoy her charming *Commissario Brunetti.* I studied Japanese at school, but I had to concentrate on Maths, Physics and Chemistry. Not much time available for languages, I'm sorry to say."

"You've got plenty of time to learn," he said casually. "This won't be your last trip to Italy, Miranda. This is your *first.*"

She couldn't help it. She clapped her hands. "Prophecies already? Marvellous!"

"Don't mention it," he said.

She knew she would be having flashbacks of this fabulous trip to Venice for the rest of her life. In a single afternoon and evening they had packed in as much as they possibly could see of what had to be the most fascinating and mysterious city on earth. The fact that Corin spoke fluent Italian and knew the city so well proved to be an enormous advantage. She was free to soak up so many dazzling sights and scenes, buildings and churches. The famous Basilica of San Marco the focal point of the great *piazza*, Santa Maria della Salute. She loved the art, the sculpture—it was like partaking of a glorious banquet. Corin kept up a running commentary. She listened. They took a gondola ride.

When they walked it was hand in hand. She knew he was keeping her close to his side, but they might have been lovers. Except they weren't. Nor could they be. Theirs was no conventional friendship, yet Miranda had never felt more close to anyone in her life.

When they met up for dinner he greeted her with a low, admiring, "*Come sei bella*, Miranda!"

Although he had adopted the lightest of tones, something in his expression made her throat tighten and tears prick at the back of her eyes. *Did* he find her beautiful? She had tried her hardest to be. For him. She had packed a short glittery silver dress, little more than a slip, but she was slim and petite and it did touch in all the right places and show off her legs. She well remembered the lovely day shopping with Zara, who had picked the gauzy dress out for her.

"It's you exactly, Miri!"

Pleasures! Ecstasies! She had allowed them to enter her life. Now she began to fear their power. She realised with a degree of shock that she didn't know herself very well. She had thought herself as a calm, contained person, well in control. A young woman with a brain perfectly designed for study: taking in reams of information and retaining it. She had a serious purpose in life. What she had to confront now was the fact that beneath the containment, her serious ambitions in life, she had a very passionate nature. And it was Corin who had unlocked it.

Dinner was absolutely brilliant; the *sala da pranzo* richly appointed. Wherever her eyes rested it was on something beautiful. The hotel was renowned for its collection of artwork, all on display for the pleasure of their guests. They had a table for two looking directly across the lagoon at San Giorgio Maggiori. To her delight it was all lit up for the night.

Dishes materialised as if by magic. A superb mingling of flavours, combinations and textures; the finest, fresh ingredients; the presentation a work of art. In the background soft harmonious chamber music added to the ambience. Vivaldi, most likely. His famous church the Pieta was just next door. Her choice of dessert was a bitter chocolate mousse with coffee granita and ginger cream. It simply melted in her mouth. Corin's choice was a classic *tiramisu* she thought had to be carried to the highest level of perfection.

"This has been so groaningly delicious I think we'll take a stroll before bed," he suggested. They had finished coffee, and now he motioned to their discreetly attentive *cameriere*.

"Yes, of course. Good idea!"

She didn't want the night to end. But Corin had

arranged a tour of the Grand Canal in a private *vaporetto* in the morning, including a trip to the Guggenheim, the great heiress Peggy Guggenheim's former home, right on the Grand Canal, now one of Europe's premier museums devoted to modern art. This might have been Miranda's gap year, but no gap was being left unfilled. She was having a wonderful time. Small wonder the children of the wealthy were granted their finishing year in Europe. It added a fine polish. And there was nothing in the world like first-hand experience.

Outside the door of her suite, Corin tucked a breeze-ruffled curl behind her ear. "Sleep well. Lots to do tomorrow."

They had returned from their stroll around the great *piazza*, along with the summer tourists enjoying the warmth and beauty of their surroundings, her arm tucked cozily in his. Now it was time to say goodnight.

"I can't thank you enough for this trip, Corin." She looked up to meet those brilliant, intense eyes. He had such an aura. She could only imagine it would increase with the years. "You and Zara have been wonderful to me."

"You don't think it's because you're easy to be wonderful to?" he asked with a smile. "You're so receptive to new experiences, Miranda. You undoubtedly have an eye. I know you've added a considerable lustre to *my* stay. Now, goodnight. Breakfast at eight. Okay?"

"Fine. My first night in a huge canopied Venetian bed. This is such an alluring place!" She threw up her arms.

Did she know just how alluring *she* was? Corin thought as he moved resolutely away. All those fascinating changes of expression! Every minute he spent with her bound him closer and closer. It had taken all his resolve to walk away, pretending light affection, when he hungered to pick her up, take her to her Venetian bed and make endless love to her. She was twenty-one. Was she still a virgin? Had the usual experimentation gone on? Not with her Peter. He was sure of that. But with another intelligent, caring young man? Miranda wouldn't settle for less. She was now very much a part of his life. He had no intention of letting her get away. But it would take time. Such was his high regard for her and her ambitions he was prepared to wait.

Only he was human, and he wanted her so much it was *pain*.

The bathroom of her suite was magnificent, lavishly covered in Italian marble. The finest bath and body products were to hand, and robe and slippers. Miranda took a quick shower and emerged glowing. She dried herself off, slipped on her nightdress and her own satin robe, then padded into the bedroom with the panoramic tiny terrace beyond. Truth be told, she felt too keyed-up to sleep. She had thought the warm shower followed by a quick cool blast would quell all the stirrings in her body. But just the opposite. This intense awareness of herself as a woman, the awareness of her body, had been brought about by Corin. His brilliant dark eyes as he had said goodnight had been hooded—just the broad, high sweep of his cheekbones. Was that to hide his thoughts? They had connected on many levels, but the physical one was definitely there. She had *seen* it. She had *felt* it when he took her face between his hands. So much was transmitted by touch. Whatever he felt, however, he wasn't going to do a thing about it. In his position he would be weighing up the consequences. She wasn't the only one with defence strategies. Did he consider a sexual relationship with her taboo? Technically she was his stepsister, wasn't she? Was there a liability attached to having a physical relationship?

Feeling a wave of sweet melancholy, she picked up her crystal-backed brush to give her hair its ritual thirty strokes. Forget one hundred. Mentally she had long dreamed of Corin as her lover.

Incredibly stupid of anyone to hanker for someone out of their reach. Her past lovers had been infrequent. Two, actually. Both fellow students, both in love with her, both very tender in their ministrations. She had wanted to know what making love was all about. She hadn't found much of an answer in either short-lived experience. She had considered at those times she mightn't be capable of giving herself completely to anyone. Look what had happened to her mother. She didn't understand her mother's life. It was crucial she understood her own.

That was when she casually looked up, glancing into the ornately carved pier mirror in front of her.

A man was staring back at her, his body as solid and impenetrable as a stone statue.

The level of shock was bottomless. She drew in a sharp breath that quivered like an arrow in flight. A judder racked her spine. Yet not a single word burst from her throat. No scream. No cry at all.

Somehow she kept upright, determined to stay that way. He was dressed very *oddly*. He might have stepped out of another century. Could it be some sort of fancy dress? Venice was famous for it. But even as she considered that she had to reject it.

Push back the panic.

He remained eerily still. Where had he sprung from? The terrace? Had he been hiding out there?

Had he slipped in earlier in the night when the maid came in to turn down the bed?

"What are you *doing* here?" she cried as she spun to confront him. Aggression seemed the best way to go, though some part of her brain had signalled he meant her harm.

She required an explanation.

Only she was by herself.

Quite, quite *alone*.

How could that be? A kind of dread started cold in her veins. She had a well-organised mind. She was certain she wasn't losing it. Her eyes darted all around the room. This was alarming. He'd had no time to get anywhere within a framework of seconds. There had to be a logical explanation. Yet her view of life as she had known it started to waver. The parameters were suddenly blurred. She leaned against the canopied bed. Had he stepped out of a parallel universe? Was there any such thing? Many people believed there was, but she was far too rational to believe in—

Ghosts?

The word presented itself, only it was seriously weird. She'd had more than a glimpse of her visitor. It couldn't have been a trick of the light. More than a touch of dizziness beset her. The air had definitely chilled around her. Indeed, the opulent room was filled with an impenetrable thick silence, as if she had cotton wool stuffed into her ears. Except she could distinctly hear the tinkling of the chandelier above her head. Something had set the lovely crystal lustres in motion.

There was no breeze.

Sometimes life can depart from the easily explained.

It had to be a trick of the light. Her imagination. The legendary mystique of Venice at work?

She made a big effort to get control of herself. None of those explanations would wash. What she saw, she *saw*. No way was she crazy or mildly intoxicated. The walk after dinner had cleared her head in any case. Already a strong suspicion was with her. There just could be a paper-thin wall between this world and *that*. The majority of the population managed to keep it at arm's length. But many learned people, academics and the like— one had to discount the fanciful—had theorised that ghosts *did* exist. And they were notorious for hanging around castles and palaces.

She was fairly sure now what her visitor was.

An apparition.

One she had done nothing to summon up. Her mind's eye retained a snapshot of that long, narrow face, the black beard, the shoulder-length dark hair, the strange dress like a priest's cassock. His hands, as white as his face, had been quietly folded. A glinting medallion hung around his neck. He hadn't appeared hazy. Quite the contrary. He'd been substantial. Someone strong enough to materialise if only for a moment. Energy, perhaps? Something of a person that lingered in the atmosphere? She was striving to rationalise what she had seen.

Only she was certain she wouldn't be able to sleep here. Imagine if he came back again? Imagine if he sat down on the side of the bed?

If anyone had asked her that morning if she believed in ghosts she would have laughed and quoted some lines from *Hamlet*:

"There are more things in Heaven and Earth, Horatio,
Than are dreamt of in your philosophy."

She wasn't laughing now. She was a quaking bundle of nerves.

Corin answered the phone almost immediately. *"Pronto!"*

"It's me," she said at a rush, ashamed of the tremor in her voice. "Can you please come down to my suite? *Now!*"

His answer was sharp. "You're okay? What's happened?"

"I'll tell you when you arrive."

She needed his strong arms to enclose her. His powerful presence. At least whatever she had seen was long gone. How did ghosts come by their clothes anyway? she pondered weakly. Did they have access to communal wardrobes? She began to feel mildly hysterical. Jewellery pools? How did he manage to hold onto the medallion he wore around his neck?

What she had so briefly experienced had opened up a nest of snakes. She didn't feel at all foolish. She had her wits about her. She had seen what she had seen for long enough to be sure.

Vast relief swept her as Corin strode in. His thick, lustrous hair was tousled into deep waves. He wore a white T-shirt and jeans, hurriedly pulled on.

"For God's sake, Miranda, you're as white as a sheet. What's happened? Did something frighten you?" He looked at her, then beyond her, obviously searching the room, and then just as she had hoped he reached for her and drew her into his arms, clamping her close. "It's okay. I'm here." Solid warm flesh, strong arms, vibrantly male. She could feel the strength and power in him. The dizziness eased.

"And am I glad!" she muttered into his warm chest. "Listen, I don't want to make an issue of it— wake up the manager, demand an exorcism—but I think I've had a visit from Signor Vivaldi." She was capable now of attempting a joke.

He drew back a little so he could stare into her eyes. "What are you talking about? Did someone get in here?"

She shook her head. "Trust me. It was Signor Vivaldi. Only he wasn't carrying his violin. Don't let go!" she cried out as his grip slackened in his surprise.

"I won't." He sounded gentle, but perplexed. "Come and sit down." He led her, still with his arms around her, to the sofa, upholstered in rich scarlet, amber and gold brocade to match the bedspread and the hangings around the canopied bed.

"Do *you* believe in ghosts, Corin?" she asked, staring into his eyes. "Serious question, here. And please don't laugh."

"Who's laughing?" he answered soberly. Indeed, there was no trace of a laugh in his face or his voice. "Are you telling me you saw a ghost?"

"Right there in the mirror," she said. "Go on. Take a look. You're so tall and strong you'll probably frighten him off."

"More like he'd frighten *me*!" Corin rose to his feet, moving position so he could stare into the ornate antique pier glass.

"I confess I'm only getting a reflection of you," he said. She looked profoundly shaken, but it was obvious to him she was trying hard to keep herself together. That impressed him. "The brain does funny things sometimes. Miranda," he said very gently. "Both Zara and I saw our mother in all sorts of places for ages after she'd gone. On the landing. The stairs. The end of the hallway. The rose gardens especially. It's grief. It's trying to come to terms with it. The sense of loss drives you to conjure up the loved one's presence."

Her eyes filled with tears. "Of course, Corin. I understand about you and Zara. I've had my own moments with my grandparents, but I knew them for what they were. I don't know this guy. I'm pretty clear-headed. Strong-minded, if I say so myself. I wasn't hallucinating. I'm not losing my marbles. I know what I know. I saw what I saw."

Corin resisted any attempt to convince her she had to be mistaken. "Well, it wasn't Vivaldi. He had *red* hair. He was called the Red Monk."

"Then it was one of his cronies. The whole place is intrinsically spooky. It wasn't my imagination. The whole experience was beyond eerie. He didn't look particularly dangerous, but I don't fancy seeing him again."

"I bet you don't !" Corin agreed on the instant. The weird thing was he believed her. Or believed her enough not to contradict her. "We'll swap suites."

Miranda reacted fast. "How do I know he won't follow me to yours?"

"I wouldn't blame him if he did." His answer was wry.

"This isn't a joke, Corin," she told him sharply. "You have to stay with me."

"What? Share the bed?" He had to try to inject some humour into a situation that was threatening to get out of hand.

"*You* can have the bed," she said magnanimously. "I'll sleep on this sofa. It's big and it's very comfortable. We might shift it closer to the bed, though."

"So we can hold hands?"

"Do you believe me or not?" she challenged. "Or do you think this is some kind of idiotic ploy to entice you here?"

"Never occurred to me." He kept his voice serious.

"If he'd been real I would have attacked him with my hairbrush. But there was no one. I suppose the fascination of Venice, apart from its beauty, mystery and exoticism, is that it's tantalisingly spooky. Part of the mythology, isn't it?"

He fetched up a sigh. "So my mother always said. As for me, I keep an open mind about ghosts. I have to admit it would take a lot to convince me. I do believe, however, *you* are convinced. Now, I have a suggestion. Why don't I take you down to my suite? Let you see what you think?"

"No way!" She rejected the offer. "You have to stay here with me. The air changed, you know. It was like I had wads of cotton wool stuffed in my ears, except I could hear the tinkling of the chandelier."

"It isn't tinkling now," he said somewhat dryly.

"Of course it isn't!" She struck his arm. "He's *gone*. Buzzed off. Maybe he has a full roster tonight? Some people are into the paranormal big-time. The thing is he looked just like he would have looked in life. Not some ectoplasm I could walk through. Stay with me, Corin. This is the most beautiful place in the world, but it *is* scary."

He released a long groan, feeling the onset of a raging torrent of emotions. "How can I possibly sleep in the bed and leave you on the sofa?"

"The bed's big enough for both of us," she said, trying to persuade him with the appeal in her turquoise eyes.

He groaned louder. "Miranda, there's not a bed in the world big enough for both of us. What do you think's going on here? You're a beautiful girl, and I'm as frail as the next guy."

"No, you're not," she said. "Not once you make up your mind. And you *have* made it up, haven't you?"

He gave a soundless laugh. "How do you know my best intentions won't fall into ruins?"

"If they do, it's *our* secret," she said. "We have secrets, don't we, Corin?"

"Boy, are you full of surprises!" he exclaimed. "You're saying you'll sleep with me?"

"I'm desperate."

He laughed aloud. "Miranda, I can't sleep on the

sofa. I'm too big. You can. We can't share the bed. You know as well as I do that's pushing it too far. My job is to look after you."

"Well, I didn't say you have this terrible aching longing for me, did I? You're not by any chance getting engaged when you go home?"

"Miranda, engagements are the last thing on my mind." The expression on his handsome face turned severe.

"Me too. So take it easy. Can you sleep in your jeans?"

"You bet I can."

"Thank you for coming, Corin," she said. "I'm not making this up. I'm sure of what I saw."

"Then you're a very lucky girl!" he offered darkly. "You'll be dining off the experience for years." He rose to his six foot plus, giving vent to a disturbed sigh. "Okay, I take the bed."

"I'll just curl up here on the sofa," she said, immensely grateful for his presence. The force in him overrode all sense of trepidation. The worst of the trembling had stopped. "You can throw me the silk throw, if you would."

"Anything, my lady." He picked it up and passed it to her.

"Can we keep a light on in the sitting room?" she asked, settling herself with the luxurious silk throw over her.

"I don't see why not." He moved into the other room, switching on a single lamp, with its golden pool of illumination. "I just knew in my bones this was going to be a memorable stay. Shut your eyes and go to sleep now, Miranda. Your ghost will know better than to return."

CHAPTER FOUR

SOMETHING drew him out of a tormented sleep. His body was still vibrating, unable to shut down. It had taken him ages to settle into a doze, but at least Miranda had lapsed into sleep almost immediately. Shock, of course. She was a highly intelligent, level-headed young woman. He had to believe she had seen *something*. Whatever it was, it wasn't about to bother him. Or he sure as hell wasn't worried. What worried him was that sex was very much on his mind. Sex with Miranda. God knew it was normal enough to want to make love to a young woman who held him in thrall. But not now—not like this. It seemed to him too much like taking advantage. That he could not do. But try telling that to his powerfully aroused body.

Decency must override desire, Corin.

He was getting a bit tired of his conscience blasting him.

Only the unthinkable had happened. Miranda

had crept into bed beside him and now rolled lightly against his back, her petite body with its soft curves and light bones nestled up against his flesh. Tension tore through him. His heart set up a loud tattoo, beating in his ears with the volume turned full on. He turned very carefully, fighting not to give a strangled moan. He was lying beneath the coverlet. She was lying on top of it.

My God, what do I do next?

His whole body was throbbing, stirred into flaming life. He could barely stay in his skin. Desire was a burning fever. He would have coped with half a dozen Venetian ghosts far better than this intensely desirable young woman curled up against him. The lightness of her! The fragrance! A man could drown in it. The only course open to him was to retreat, slide out of the other side of the bed. He could prop himself up on the sofa for the rest of the night. Get comfortable somehow. See it out until morning. Ghosts didn't hang around in the light of day. They were too tired out from their nocturnal excursions. Or was that vampires? Either way, he didn't care. Miranda was the real problem.

"Corin?" Just to make the problem near unsolvable, she suddenly sat up, twisting her shining head towards him. Her voice was hushed, but filled with urgency. "Don't go away. Please don't. I didn't like the sofa much. I wanted to be closer."

"Miranda, stop it," he begged.

You're losing it, Corin!

"I can't stay here in this bed with you," he said tautly. "You're nobody's fool. My whole body is hurting. I'll make love to you. Nothing surer!"

"Then do it!" she burst out, sounding as though she knew far better than he did. "Ease the pain. This is *life*! I've decided I want to live it. None of us knows how much time we have, do we? Why waste what we've got? You're alive. I'm alive. If you like, when we wake up we can pretend it was all a dream."

"And you think there's going to be a lot of comfort in that?" he demanded, aghast. He reached for her, took hold of a bare delicate shoulder where her robe had fallen off. He could see the silver shimmer of her hair, like radiant moonlight. "Are you or are you not a virgin?"

"Will that improve or detract from my status?" she challenged. "Technically I'm not, but I *can* say in all truth the earth has never moved for me. I've had two lovers. Really nice guys. Fellow students. Smart, good-looking. Not untried either. But I couldn't for the life of me see what all the fuss was about. Perhaps you can tell me? I'm sure you've had plenty of experience."

"And you'd like me to share it with you?" he asked acidly. "Does this give me the go-ahead?"

A golden glow was spilling out of the sitting room. She could easily make out the hard tension in his face. "Oh, God, that's up to you!" she moaned, embarrassment welling, but not enough to drown the yearning. "I've had more thrills from your touching my cheek than ever I got from my previous experiences. You can multiply that by one thousand. Such are your erotic skills. Once I thought I couldn't give myself to anyone. Not after my mother. Not after her falling pregnant as a schoolgirl. Abandoning me. It altered my life. Maybe altered me in a radical way. Do you understand?"

"No, I damned well do not." He was merciless. He had to be.

"You're weighing up the consequences?" she asked.

"Miranda, this is madness," he groaned. But then, hadn't it been madness from the moment she had literally catapulted into his life?

"There are always consequences, I suppose. One or both of us could be hurt. But you're not married. I'm not married. Neither of us is in any great rush."

He gave a harsh laugh. "Either you go back to the sofa or I do."

"No, stay. *Please*. I'm not asking you to love me. I'm asking you to *make* love to me. There's a big difference. You said you wanted to, so just *do* it."

"And perhaps make you pay for it?" He showed

the full heat of his anger and arousal. "I don't walk around with condoms in my pocket. Oh, my God, Miranda, what are we talking about?" he asked in an agonised voice. Never in his life had he faced such temptation.

"Making love. You may not care to hear it, but I'm on the pill. I believe in being prepared. I'm not saying with you. I never dreamt we'd be here together like this. But I could have met someone. You never know. I'm a modern girl. This is right. For tonight, Corin. I know it in my soul. I didn't set out to seduce you. You had no intention of seducing me, such are your stringent scruples and code of morality. The ghost actually did us a favour."

"Oh, be quiet! Truly, *be quiet!*" He pulled her across him, wrapping his arms around her. She had to know what she was doing to him, but she didn't seem to care. "This is madness!"

"But splendid madness!" She let her head fall against his chest. She would remember this extraordinary night in the last dying seconds of her life.

"To put yourself in my hands?" His vibrant voice turned steely.

"Yes, yes, and *yes*! Put it down to shock. Shock has made me shameless. *'My heart, by many snares beguiled, Has grown timorous and wild!'* Some poet said that. Can't think who."

She allowed her body to spread out over his:

fantastic feeling, utter abandon. Then she locked her bare, slender arms around his neck. She wasn't herself at all. She was a Miranda she had never known. Had her otherworldly visitor put a sensual spell on her? Maybe that was what he'd come for?

The agony of it! Corin felt every muscle shift in his lean body. His head was nearly bursting with conflicting emotions. Should he? Shouldn't he? The truth was he was already lost. He let his crow-black head fall back against the piled-up pillows like a man defeated. Such extreme sexual agony demanded release. There could be no ease without action. He wanted her. God, how he wanted her! Yet for a split second he faltered. Was it possible this perfect creature with her beautiful turquoise eyes was after *revenge*? Did she count this the right time? Had she *really* seen anything? Or was she winding him up? It could all be an elaborate scam. Some kind of weird payback? She was extremely intelligent. Highly rational. Very possibly an accomplished actress. Was she indeed playing him for a fool? If so, it was working!

Momentarily maddened, he turned her onto her side. That too was dangerously erotic, increasing the sexual tension. Then he put a hand to her tender neck, his fingers on that pulsing vein. Her flesh was like lustrous satin, as warm and as flushed as a rose. He wasn't *her* captor, though. That was the trouble, he thought with a tiny stab of hostility. She had captured *him*. Delilah bringing another Samson to his knees.

"Look at me. Kiss me," she whispered. "Before I dissolve right away."

Her little sigh was quite audible in the deeply shadowed room. He answered darkly. "What man can resist such witchcraft? Okay, Miranda, if this is what you want."

With one wrench, he had the coverlet on the floor, and then he pulled her to him, never more excruciatingly aware that passion was heedless of anything but itself. Such was his appetite, his mouth crushed hers…covered its sweetness completely…his tongue making triumphant entry into the moist apple-fresh interior. The kiss was punishing at first, ruthless, explosive, raw in its conquest. As he'd intended it to be. A futile show of male superiority? Only very quickly the fierceness gentled into something miraculous…utterly voluptuous… undreamed of rapture!

She was working her magic, turning the key to a heart he had thought locked safely away.

He paused for a moment, holding her hips, his head bent above her. He could see that her jewelled eyes were tightly shut. Her limbs were wound around his like tendrils, curved and curled. She was beautiful to him. Beautiful beyond belief. He could no more have stopped kissing her, no more stopped his hands from moving to shape and caress her small perfect breasts, than he could have stopped his own breath.

She was right. This was living. This was *life*!

They were entering into it together. No matter the consequences.

The moments of astonishing sensuality spun on and on, until he could no longer tolerate a shred of clothing to separate skin from skin. He had to unwrap her from her robe—it had almost fallen off her—then her nightgown, flinging both garments away. He looked back for the switch on the lamp. She seemed to shake her head, but he took no notice.

"Don't refuse me." He turned back to her, fully exposed to his sight; she was beautifully, delicately nude, like some lovely painting, showing lustrous skin tones. In one sweeping movement he slid his hand in a widening circle around her taut but pliant stomach, stopping to within an inch of the sensitive delta between her legs. "I want to *see* you. I want to kiss every inch of you. I want you to know you're exquisite to my eyes. And you *wanted* this, Miranda, remember."

Wanted it? She was half mad with longing. Pelted with it. She made a soft, helpless sound that was like a wail. He cut it off with his mouth.

Every cell in Miranda's body was a live wire of

sensation. It was impossible not to respond to such mastery. She might never have been kissed or touched in her life before now.

He placed her exactly as he wanted her. Then he began to play her like a superbly crafted instrument. Perfect for a man's hand, its pitch exact, and capable of displaying a glorious range of emotions. He had never had a woman respond to his love-making with such passion and urgency. He had never felt within himself so wild an elation. He found he was shaping words, *saying* words—what were they? She had him totally in her power. Did it matter? All he knew was this was ecstasy, as fabulous as it was strange to him.

She could be your downfall.

He was more than willing to risk it. He needed to throw off his own clothes. Naked, he returned to the bed, where she pulled him down to her, glittery tears standing in her eyes.

"No—oh, *no*, Miranda, don't cry." Her tears stayed him. He leaned over her, supported by his strong arms, overtaken by a powerful sense of protectiveness.

"I'm *not* crying," she protested, reaching up to sink her fingers into his thick hair, all tousled waves and curls, tugging at it in her passion. "I'm on fire!"

Any glimmer of uncertainty vanished into thin air. Air that seemed scented by hundreds of glowing, unimaginably beautiful flowers. None of this had been premeditated, he thought, yet he had the absolute certainty both of them were in their rightful place. Slowly, voluptuously, on a surge of exultation, he covered her smooth-as-silk body with his own, still controlling his far more substantial weight with his arms while she clutched his naked back, her voice an emotional little sob.

"Love me!"

"For hours. Hours and hours on end." He was confronted with a searing truth. He wasn't just in love with Miranda. He wanted her with him for as long as he lived.

That in itself presented intractable problems.

But not tonight.

Tonight a miracle had been offered.

Miracles demanded they be grasped with both hands.

For the rest of their stay problems became irrelevant. Time out of mind. They both knew it. For those few precious days they lived their lives in a glorious conflict-free zone. Conflict would come later. There could be no avoiding it. There was always Leila. Leila had to be regarded as a most serious threat. She could potentially end the emotional journey they had embarked upon. But for now even the ghost was invited to come back if he so wished. He declined. No doubt he had a full book of hauntings.

Their golden days in Venice came as a revelation. Miranda knew she was living a fairy tale. Even her ambitions seemed fuzzy, such was her emotional awakening. There was only Corin. The shimmer and heat of summer. A backdrop of the most beautiful and mysterious city in the world with its grand canal and streets of water.

The flight back to London came much too quickly. Reality set in, as it inevitably did. Already she was steeling herself to face Corin's impending departure for Australia. After which he had a follow-up trip to Beijing to meet up with his father. So separation from this man she had fallen passionately in love with would be her fate.

For long months? Or something far more permanent?

Zara had been home for several hours when they arrived. "Well, you two! Talk about secrets!" She greeted them with open arms, her great dark eyes alight with pleasure and more than a touch of mischief.

Corin had texted his sister, informing her he had taken Miranda to Venice for the long weekend, and given her an approximate time when they would be arriving home. Now Miranda thought an apology was in order. "Zara, I must tell you I never had the faintest idea Corin was coming to London," she explained. "And I didn't tell you about my birthday because—"

"You thought I'd want to arrange something and bow out of my trip?"

"Exactly." Miranda smiled. "Anyway, now you know. I've come of age. I've had the most breath-taking time!"

"I can see that!" Zara turned to search her brother's handsome face. He was tanned an even dark gold. She had never seen him look more stunning or so vibrantly alive. She had long since formed the opinion Corin had a very special interest in Ms Miranda Thornton, though she had intuited there had been no romantic involvement.

Until now.

Body language expressed so much: love, hate, joy, sorrow, pity, contempt. In this case it expressed the heart. The two of them had that magic aura—the extraordinarily attractive intensity that drew a circle around them and caught the beholder's eye with pleasure, nostalgia or just plain envy. For her part Zara prayed that each had truly found a soul mate in the other. God knew she had forfeited *her* chance at lasting happiness years ago, back home in Australia. But that was another story. She never talked about it, even to Corin. It was buried under many layers.

Already she was very fond of Miranda. One couldn't ask for a sweeter, more harmonious sister-in-law. Could it possibly happen? Miranda was almost eight years younger than Corin, but with an impressive maturity of her own. Corin had huge responsibilites, especially for so young a man. And they would only increase. Miranda had set her sights firmly on becoming a doctor. She knew Corin would support her all the way. Two clever, ambitious people.

But alas, there was their all-powerful, all-interfering father to contend with. At least he loved Corin. He did not love her. She had long accepted that. She had been forced to cope with all the pain and personal havoc her father had caused. Internalise it. Her father, even if he didn't love her, had made it his business to rule her life. He had deliberately altered its course, going out of his way to destroy her chance at happiness with the young man she had loved with all her heart.

Garrick Rylance. A kinsman.

Why had her father done it? He had nothing against Garrick, had he? Garrick was a splendid young man by anyone's reckoning. Yet her father had taken all necessary steps to sever their relationship. Didn't he *want* her to be happy? He had stoutly maintained that wasn't the reason for his ordering her home from Cooranga, the ancestral home of the Rylance cattle barons. Threats would have been more like it. He father was good at threatening people. Perhaps it was her strong resemblance to their dead mother that had closed her out of his affection. His twisted sense of guilt? Whatever it was, she had lived on the periphery. But she had always had her brother as her champion. Yet from time to time the love and pride their father felt for his brilliant son was heavily overlaid by a species of jealousy. A competitiveness. The old lion and the young lion, just waiting to take over the pride.

She couldn't bear to think how their father would react if he thought for one moment that Leila had romantic daydreams about his son. He would probably kill her. Their father was a man of very strong passions. Worse, he had been rich and powerful for so long he acted like a man who was a law unto himself. Despite his children's aversion to his second wife, their father was still deeply in love or lust or both with her. She had dazzled and hypnotised him. Leila—the omnipresent figure who excelled at manipulation.

To Zara's acutely sensitive eye Leila had shown every sign of being secretly infatuated with Corin. God help her if their father ever stumbled on to it. But Leila was smart. And she would do everything in her power to undermine any young woman who

sought to play a key role in Corin's life. She had
done it in the past. As highly intelligent as Miranda
was, she would be a mere innocent in competition
with a feline mastermind. If the relationship continued at this level Miranda would have to be told
the risks. Leila Rylance was a dangerous woman.
Miranda would never have had contact with such
a woman in her entire life.

Or so Zara thought.

Corin took them out to dinner. A quiet but exclusive restaurant where they were well-known and
their privacy was protected. There was always
some member of staff on hand to report that paparazzi were out at the front, looking for some celebrity or other. In that way, if they had to, they could
leave by the back door.

Zara spoke of her trip over dinner, telling them
a little of her group's dealings and her meeting
with a certain high-ranking businessman of
renowned wealth: Konrad Hartmann.

"Hartmann? Heard of him, of course." Corin
was frowning hard, as though what he had heard
wasn't good.

Zara confided, rather diffidently for such a beautiful woman, that Hartmann had taken quite a shine
to her. Twice divorced, in his mid-forties, he was a
man who enjoyed enormous prestige, but her boss,

Sir Marcus, who had a legendary "nose" about these things, was concerned about where all the mountains of money were coming from. So far Hartmann—and he was under close observation—was clean.

"He wants to see me when he comes to London," Zara told them with a faint flush.

"And will you see him?" Corin asked crisply.

Zara took another sip of her wine. "Probably not." A hesitation, then, "He's a very attractive man."

"Better listen to Sir Marcus," Corin clipped off.

Miranda took note of Corin's formidable expression. She knew he was very protective of his sister. "You're a beautiful woman, Zara," Corin said. "You can have anyone you want. One time I thought— Anyway that's another story." He broke off as though on dangerous ground. "Look, this guy might appear up front, but with all that unexplained wealth he's uncharted territory. I'll have him checked out more thoroughly."

"You won't find anything." Zara shook her head. "No one can up to date. And they're looking. It's just one of Sir Marcus's hunches."

"Sir Marcus Boyle is renowned for his hunches," Corin said.

"But you felt an attraction?" Miranda intervened. She knew by now Zara could indeed take her pick of any number of highly eligible men on the social scene. Yet she had taken no more than a passing interest in any of them. Her heart didn't appear to be in it. Miranda was certain Zara had her secrets as well.

The flush still stained Zara's magnolia cheeks. "I did, I suppose. I'm used to powerful men. At the same time it was a bit threatening."

"I think I know what you mean," said Miranda.

Corin's brilliant dark eyes swept over her. She looked radiant, her colouring—the silver gilt hair and turquoise eyes—a wonderful foil for Zara's sable hair and huge dark eyes. To think he had such an intimate tactile knowledge of her body! It was something he regarded as a revelation. "So who has threatened you?" He gave her his fullest attention.

"What if I said *you*?"

"*Me?* Threaten you?" He fell back in disbelief.

"Well, you *are* a member of an important family." She hastened to explain. "You're Corin Rylance, your father's heir. It's easy for the rich not to touch base with ordinary folk like me. Financial worries hound a lot of people to death. You've always been rich. You've probably never even caught a bus."

"I beg your pardon! If I didn't know you better, Miranda, I'd think that was a cheap shot."

"Not at all. A plain statement of fact. Throw in a train."

Corin gave a wry laugh, but Zara looked at

Miranda with understanding. "I was the one who went to and from school in the Rolls."

Corin drew Miranda's gaze with the power of his own. "I have caught a bus, Miranda. I can't say a train. The school bus used to take our teams off to cricket, football, swimming carnivals and the like."

"Just tongue in cheek." Miranda smiled. "So don't look so affronted." She had good reason to know by now the rich really were different. They had their problems. Big problems too. But worry about blowing the budget wasn't one of them.

"I think Miranda means some old-style snobs might perceive a gap in the social pecking order." Zara tried to help Miranda out. She knew for a fact their father had the daughter of one of his biggest and most influential business partners in mind for Corin. Their father always got what he wanted. Split up one of his children from the love of her life. Marry off the other.

"What rot!" Corin said mildly. "You'd fit in anywhere, Miranda. You fit better than anyone I know. Outside my beautiful sister, of course." He reached out to grasp both young women's hands.

"Let's drink to that!" Zara suggested with her lovely smile.

Zara had left only the lights on in the entrance hall when they had left for the restaurant. When they returned by cab, a little over two hours later, the whole house was ablaze.

An apprehensive frisson shuddered the length of Miranda's spine. From the moment they'd got into the cab she had a sense life was about to change. Some *difference* in the air. A disturbance.

Danger lurking.

Maybe she really did have a sixth sense? She couldn't feel the way she did for nothing. A fissure in her happiness was about to open up. Could happiness ever last? She knew she had broken out of the social confines of her life. That itself presented big problems.

"Could it be your father?" she asked Zara, trying to hide her agitation. Where Dalton Rylance was, so too would be her mother.

"I don't know!" Zara made no attempt to hide her own unease. Both stood watching as Corin, leaving the young women behind, swiftly mounted the few steps to the front door to check things out. "I doubt it." Nevertheless her voice wavered. "It's as I told you, Miri. I don't get on well with Leila, though she's convinced my father that is entirely *my* fault. Despite all she's supposedly done to reach out to me I continue to regard her as the enemy. To be honest, I have to admit our relationship was doomed from the start. Father showed no understanding. He blames me. Better me than him. I was never in the right, no matter what I did. If they're here, I don't know why. Leila likes to stay at Claridges when she's in town. I would have thought if they were calling in, however briefly, they would have left a message. That's what has happened in the past."

"Then who else could it be? An intruder wouldn't turn on every light in the house."

"No." Zara took hold of Miranda's hand, as if divining they were in need of mutual support. Indeed, they were acting like a couple of robots, Miranda thought.

What sort of woman is my mother that Zara, a beautiful and accomplished woman, fears her? And Corin loathes her?

Did she have some of her mother in her? God forbid. Was she about to find out? No wonder she felt deeply troubled. How would Zara react when she found out she was Leila's daughter? Not only that, she had deliberately kept that knowledge from her? Okay, she had done as Corin wanted. Would that make a difference to Zara? Or would she feel betrayed by both of them? Zara appeared to have trodden a difficult path in life. Her resemblance to her dead mother was only part of it. There was more. She was sure of it. And that *more* involved her mother. Mistress before stepmother? Deeply disturbing.

"Corin's inside." Zara was gasping in air. Her fingers tightened on Miranda's. "We'd better go in. And to think we were all so happy!"

"It must be them." Miranda firmed up her backbone. She was becoming as protective of Zara as Corin.

Think hard thoughts, Miranda. You're not prepared, but if it's Leila she won't know it's you. Leila abandoned you without a trace of memory. The willed amnesia syndrome. No need to slip away to the basement. Zara needs you.

There was the inner voice again, like a non-stop voice-over.

Corin's tall figure had disappeared into the entrance hall. Out of sight. They began to mount the steps, with no option but to do otherwise. Miranda had already arrived at the most unwelcome conclusion. For some reason Dalton Rylance and Leila were in the house. It belonged to them anyway.

They paused to the left of the top step, just out of sight of anyone inside the marble-tiled entrance hall. "Good chance to see who it is!" Miranda muttered under her breath.

"It's Father and Leila, of course." Zara sounded shattered. Something that wasn't lost on Miranda.

The two of them stood mesmerised as they were made witness to the grand entrance of the beautiful, statuesque woman descending the staircase, calling out Corin's name as she came.

He might as well have been deaf, Miranda thought, because he didn't respond.

Undeterred, the woman threw out pale, slender arms in welcome, much as a famous diva might, supremely confident of herself and her adoring audience. She was dressed in a slinky ankle-length dress, a lovely shade between peach and bronze. It suited her perfectly. Her long, thick superbly styled bronze-coloured hair swirled around her shoulders. Her golden-brown eyes, offset by arching black brows, shimmered in the light from the great chandelier. She looked no more than late twenties.

A good ten years younger than she was.

"So that's Leila!" Miranda had to work hard to suppress a sick combination of rage, shock and an involuntary stomach clenching excitement. This, at long last, was her *mother*. Albeit a personage invented. It didn't seem possible. Yet she herself had set the wheels of fortune in motion. Now she felt not triumph—*I've found her at long last*—but a continuing sense of loss. Leila was a head-turner. No doubt about that. Ultra-glamorous. Streamlined seduction coming off her like a powerful incense.

"Corin, dear!" She spoke in a husky, cultured voice, acquired over time. "What a shock it was to hear you were in London!"

Corin remained where he was, remote, stunningly handsome, keeping his distance. "Shock? How would it be a shock, Leila?" he challenged. "You seem intent on following my movements."

"Well, you *are* my stepson!" A low amused gurgle deep in the throat.

"We should go in," Zara whispered, still rooted to the spot. Both had registered that Corin spoke in his coldest, hardest voice.

"Give it a minute." Miranda held tight to her vulnerable friend. She truly believed Leila had tried to break the young Zara. No female competitors for her husband's time and attention. Least of all one who was the mirror image of his first wife. "I want to see something." Indeed she did. There was a tremendous tension between Corin and the outwardly smiling Leila. She couldn't ignore it.

"She's in love with him," Zara confided in an intensely unhappy voice.

"No question!" All trace of their pleasant evening had been wiped clear. "He must know it at some level."

Of course he does, said the warning voice in Miranda's head. *But he's hidden it from you.*

"He won't *have* it." Zara was adamant. "Do you blame him?"

"It would bring great shame to the family."

Miranda stared at the tableau before them. Leila had entered her life. There was no going back.

There she is—your mother. A serial adulteress?

"It would!" Zara breathed.

"Then God knows how it will end." Miranda transferred her gaze from her mother to the man she loved. His tall, handsome figure emanated hostility. But it was a man-woman thing. The two of them were locked in confrontation. Was it possible they had shared some secret moments Corin, at least, was desperate to forget? Miranda turned the burning question over and over in her mind. Here was a very beautiful, seductive woman. Such a woman would always have the advantage over a young man susceptible to a woman's beauty. It didn't bear thinking about. On the other hand, she might never be able to *stop* thinking about it.

Women were lied to all the time. Betrayed. She ought to remember she was no woman of the world. She was twenty-one years old. Leila, on the other hand, was the walking, breathing epitome of ancient wisdom and womanly allure. A born seductress. She shook her head as if to clear it. "Your father is a proud and arrogant man. Not a man to cross."

"Not unless you're tough enough to pick yourself up and put the pieces together again." Zara shuddered. "Few are. Me included. Corin brings the ball right to him. Truth to tell, Father is somewhat in awe of Corin, though he'd rather die than admit it. Our father is profoundly unforgiving. I speak from long experience."

Great wealth appeared to make for dysfunctional families! "Oh, Zara!" Miranda locked a protective arm around Zara's waist. How easy it would be to traumatise a young girl. Especially one who had lost the love and support of her adored mother. "Come on, now," she said bracingly, putting her own fears aside. "Let's get it over. Bring Leila's movie-star efforts to fascinate Corin to an end."

Zara responded with a strangled laugh. Together they *swung* rather than moved quietly into the entrance hall.

Their arrival stopped Leila in mid-flight. She turned from devouring Corin with her golden tigress's eyes to address Zara and whoever it was with her. Perhaps with a few subtly mocking words. Nothing Leila could say would lack a certain sting.

Except it didn't happen that way.

Leila stood transfixed. All colour drained out of her face. *"What—?"* Her voice cracked on the solitary word. She looked pole-axed, robbed of all confidence. Her almond eyes opened wide. Full of *fear*?

"I'm sorry." Zara made a little perplexed gesture, looking swiftly to her silent brother for guidance. "This is Miranda—a friend of ours, Leila. We've all been out to dinner. Miranda, this is my step-mother, Leila Rylance."

Pull out all the stops, Miranda. You've served a long apprenticeship. You can do it. You can cope.

Her inner voice came through, unusually fierce. It was beginning to sound more and more like her grandmother. So many currents in the sea of life! Miranda stepped forward, an enchantingly pretty young woman, with exquisite colouring, wearing a short fuchsia silk dress. "How do you do, Mrs Rylance?" She couldn't for the life of her order up a smile, but she found herself able to speak calmly, politely. A well brought up young woman.

Hang tough. This is your mother and she's only a few feet away. The closest she has been in twenty-one long years.

Leila for her part seemed totally incapable of finding her usual brilliant smile. She might have been looking at an apparition, and a nightmare at that.

"Leila, you've gone very pale." Corin's words were solicitous enough, but his tone was far from warm. "Are you all right?"

Leila didn't answer. She backed away, grasping behind her for the scrolled end of the balustrade. When her long, elegant fingers, flashing a fortune in diamonds, found it, she gripped it tight. Consummate actress that she was, she couldn't collect herself, though she was clearly involved in some extremely harrowing thought processes.

"The long trip, I expect," Zara offered kindly, because kind was the way she was, trying to fill in the gap. Leila was feeling unwell for some reason. *No.* That wasn't it. Leila, always in command of herself, appeared to have gone into extreme shock. Zara had no idea why. She had now taken to hugging her bare arms, as though the air had turned icy. How extraordinary! Something to do with Miranda? Zara cast about for a reason, however unlikely.

Corin and Miranda had no doubts whatsoever. Whoever Leila was seeing, it wasn't Miranda. It was Leila's girlhood lover. The father of her child. The child she had been desperate to leave behind. As if she had never been born.

This could be my first meeting and my last, Miranda thought somberly.

So here I am, Mother dear. A threat. Only I don't propose to threaten you at all. Your life is your life. I won't disturb it. My life is mine.

Corin was making some comment when a deep, markedly authoritative voice called from the gallery. The voice of a dictator, a tyrant. One who must be obeyed. "So they're home at last, are they?"

Ah! The magnate billionaire was in their midst. *You don't bother me at all.*

Miranda had to wonder why she felt like that.

Very many people went in fear and trepidation of Dalton Rylance. It was common knowledge. There was no such fear in her. Her mother *knew* her. Knew her instantly. How elemental was that?

At the sound of her husband's dark, sonorous tones Leila made a supreme effort to pull herself together. Perhaps before it was too late? It had to be an ongoing ordeal, getting into bed with one man while longing for another, Miranda thought without pity. Keeping it from an adoring, jealous husband would stretch the nerves to breaking point, surely?

"They have a young friend with them, darling," Leila called, though her voice, compared to the way Miranda had first heard her speak, sounded thin and weak. Not the voice of a practised seductress at all.

Dalton Rylance appeared at the top of the stairs, an imposing figure in evening dress. He was very tall, very fit, still an extremely handsome man in his late fifties, with a thick dark plume of hair, silver wings, penetrating light blue eyes. He didn't ask for a name. His entire focus was on his wife. "Is anything wrong, my darling?" In an instant he had reacted to the reedy sound in his wife's voice.

If anyone upsets my wife, I'll destroy them.

He might as well have shouted it aloud, Miranda thought. No wonder sensitive Zara trod warily with this man. He might be her father, but he wasn't her friend, let alone her protector. Miranda took a violent dislike to Dalton Rylance on the spot.

"Why would anything be wrong, Dad?" Corin lifted his head, his voice very smooth and self-assured. Corin obviously didn't share his sister's qualms. But then, Corin was the heir. "Leila was just saying she's a little tired from travelling."

"My dear, why didn't you tell me?" Quickly, as though he were at fault, Dalton Rylance descended the staircase. Obviously in thrall to her, he went to his wife's side, staring with great concern into her exotic face, at her golden-olive complexion turned to parchment.

Immediately, no doubt for cover, Leila held a hand to her temple, as though to contain the pain. "I don't like to worry you, darling. You know that. I've been perfectly all right up until now. But it seems to have hit me all at once." Suddenly she sounded very sober. And dangerous. A tigress under threat.

"Then we'll go back to the hotel immediately." A deep frown creased the area between Dalton Rylance's black brows. He pressed his greatest treasure—his wife—against his side. Only then did he notice Miranda.

"Friend of Zara's are you, young lady?" He shot the question at her, giving her a comprehensive once-over. Then, miracle of miracles, he smiled. A very attractive white smile that highlighted the strong resemblance between father and son. Dalton Rylance obviously had quite an eye for a pretty woman.

"Miranda Graham, Mr Rylance." Swiftly she improvised. To say *Thornton* would have confirmed Leila's worst fears. The nightmare of her past was here to haunt her. Most probably to blackmail her. People had been killed for less. "It's an honour to meet you, sir." Graham was her grandfather's Christian name. It was the best she could do on the run. Out of the corner of her eye she saw Zara's head turn wonderingly towards her, but mercifully Zara said nothing.

"We must meet again when my wife is feeling more like herself," Dalton Rylance promised, his manner turned suave. Miranda had very obviously passed muster. "We only popped in for a few moments to say hello. It was Leila's idea, actually, to have a few days in London. Didn't intend it at all. Quite out of the way. But naturally Leila wanted to catch up with Corin and Zara. She's a very caring woman."

Wouldn't it be great to put him straight?

"I'll call a cab for you, Dad." Corin had already pulled his mobile out of a pocket, dialling the number.

"Thank you, son." Dalton Rylance turned belatedly to his only daughter. "How are you, Zara?"

There was a terse edge to his tone. To Miranda's ears it was almost as though he felt *obliged* to speak to Zara—something he preferred not to do. She had rejected his darling wife, for a start. Dalton Rylance from all accounts had only become isolated from his daughter since the untimely death of his first wife, his children's mother—or perhaps from the moment it became apparent to his very perceptive children that Leila was a cunning and ambitious young woman who would stop at nothing in her determined pursuit of their father. Certainly their mother had seen Leila for what she was. A woman consumed by the desire for wealth and social status.

"I'm fine, thank you, Father," Zara answered composedly. Zara the classic beauty. A young woman of charm, understanding and high intelligence. In short, a daughter any man would be proud of. Yet here was a man who fended such a daughter off.

"That's all right, then," he huffed. "Getting along well enough with Boyle? No problems?" He turned back to his wife, as though uninterested in the answer. A wife counted far more than a daughter.

"Sir Marcus thinks the world of her," Corin broke in suavely. "Cab's on the way, Dad. You'll be back to the hotel in no time. A good night's rest will help enormously, Leila." He addressed his stepmother, his brilliant gaze black, fathomless. "We all hope so."

How could his father miss the lick of sarcasm?

Miranda was beset by anxiety, but oddly enough Dalton Rylance took his son's words at face value. "My angel!" He bent to kiss the top of his wife's golden-brown head. "Come with me, now. Corin's right. It's sleep you need, dearest girl."

One had to hand it to Leila, her daughter thought. She was making a phenomenal recovery, though her cheeks were still colourless. "We'll catch up," she assured them all sweetly, with a brave little wave of her hand. But her gaze hit on Miranda with the force of a bullet. A warning Miranda was smart enough to catch. Leila, her long-lost mother, pretty much wanted her dead. "I didn't see any of your things lying around, Miranda?" Leila delivered another bullet sheathed in velvet.

So she's been poking around? Checking in rooms. Despicable.

Mercifully, not even Zara had the key to Corin's apartment. Otherwise Leila would have been down there like a shot.

"I'm very neat, Mrs Rylance," said Miranda. "I hope you have a restful night."

"I will. I have my darling husband." Leila lifted her head to bestow on Dalton Rylance a shimmering, conspiratorial smile.

Obviously sex was on the agenda. Leila had to be terribly good at it. Here was a man dazzled on the outside, without bothering to get to know the woman on the inside.

Corin closed the front door, then leaned back against it, releasing a long drawn-out breath. "Damn, damn, damn!" He spat out the words, as though choking on his feelings. The cab had left, taking his father and Leila back to their hotel.

"My angel? Dearest girl?" Miranda questioned with some irony. If proof were ever needed, it was evident one of the toughest businessmen in the world was putty in Leila's hands.

"And who are *you*, dearest girl?" There was a catch of laughter in Zara's voice, but an edge of perplexity too. "Miranda *Graham*?"

"I'll be darned if I know why I said it." Miranda stalled for time, the muscles of her stomach badly knotted. "Motive unclear." Zara was no fool. This looked very much like crunch time.

"You didn't want them to know who you are?" Zara looked at her searchingly. "That's it, isn't it? We saw Leila when she was talking to Corin. She was herself—the *femme fatale*, absolutely secure in her powers. But as soon as she spotted you she turned into a totally different women. It had to be *you*, Miri. The sight of you stunned her. I thought she was going to pass out."

Miranda looked pointedly at Corin, who shrugged, his brilliant dark eyes full of a simmering anger. "I just want to know who the mole is back home. Someone who passes on my itinerary. Work itinerary, that is. Whoever it is, they're sacked. Let's go into the drawing room."

Zara took Miranda's arm. "There's something you two are keeping from me? I knew it. What is it?"

"Sit down, both of you," Corin said, though he remained standing, the dominant figure, obviously tense.

And now you're going to lose Zara. Most probably the two of them. You don't belong here. Leila has seen to that.

Zara was watching her brother very closely now. "You didn't know Father was coming to London?"

"Zara." He groaned. "Do you honestly believe I wouldn't warn you? Of course I didn't know."

"I'm sorry," Zara apologised. "It's just that woman upsets me so. I'm perfectly all right when I'm fourteen thousand miles away from her. She's turned Father against me. For all we know she drove our beautiful mother—"

"I don't see that, Zara." Corin stopped his sister from saying more. "I *have* been keeping something from you. But it was to protect you. I didn't know how you would handle it then. I don't know *now*."

"Oh, God, Corin. Tell me," Zara begged. "It has something to do with Miri, doesn't it?"

Miranda thought it high time she spoke up for herself.

Take what comes on the chin.

"Leila and I are related, Zara," she said.

Zara almost jumped out of her skin. "Related? In what way?" Her great eyes locked onto Miranda's. "I can't think of anyone less like Leila than you."

"Thank God for that!" Miranda said gratefully. "I have no official standing in your stepmother's eyes. She doesn't know me. You know I've become very fond of you, Zara. You've been so kind to me. I look on you as a close friend. Someone I can turn to. It hasn't been easy keeping my story to myself. You must believe that. I don't think I could bear it if you didn't."

"Let me tell it, Miranda," Corin said, coming to sit beside her. "Miranda has only been following orders, Zara," he explained. "My orders."

Is following orders a valid excuse? Miranda now asked herself.

"I intended to pick the right time," Corin explained, "but Leila showing up like that tonight— you're quite right. She believes herself all-powerful. Dad backs her in everything she does and wants. Now she's pulled the rug out from under our feet.

But she didn't get off scot-free. She's been administered one almighty shock."

"I *saw* that, Corin." Zara matched his terseness. "Move on."

Again Miranda intervened. She was her own person. She should speak for herself. "I'm sorry you had to learn it like this, Zara, but Leila is…no easy way to say it, so here it is…my *mother*."

Zara blanched. She shook her head in seeming bewilderment, then jumped up, looking in a stricken fashion to her brother. "*Mother?* Did Miri really say that, Corin? Did I hear right? Leila, our stepmother, is Miranda's *mother*?"

So much depends on how Zara takes this.

"Please don't upset yourself, Zara," Corin begged his sister quietly. "Miranda didn't even know herself until a few years back."

"*Years?*" Zara's voice soared. She looked at them both, obviously incredulous and deeply distressed they had kept such a thing from her.

"I was brought up by my grandparents, believing them to be my parents," Miranda explained, desperate for Zara to understand. "I nursed my dying grandmother. That was almost four years ago. Only then did she tell me the true story. My mother abandoned me as an infant. She was only sixteen when she had me. Starting out in life. She didn't want a baby to drag her down."

Zara was all flashing dark eyes. "Dear heaven! This is shocking—*shocking*! So why, on reflection, doesn't it surprise me? Leila had a child. You. Miri." She collapsed into an armchair, shoulders drooping under the weight of this new knowledge. "We've been so *close*, Miri, and you didn't *tell* me."

"I'm sorry." Miranda bowed her head, she too showing her upset. "So sorry. I might have lost you. I could lose you now."

Corin took Miranda's hand in his, tightening his grip. "Miranda did as *I* asked, Zara. Blame me if you want to blame anyone. Miranda was all for telling you, but it wouldn't have done you a bit of good. The knowledge wouldn't have given you any rest. You'd have come out with it some time. And who could blame you? All those years of provocation, of Leila's conniving, her malice, behind the scenes stripping you of Dad's affection. She kept you away. She lied all the time: concocted stories, complained of your stubborn refusal to meet her halfway. What do you suppose would have happened had you known about Miranda and confronted her?"

Zara stared back at him, then gave a wild little laugh. "I'd have *murdered* her, like she murdered our mother."

"No, no, Zara." He felt pain like a twisting knife inside him. Whatever he and Zara believed, he wasn't going to lay that charge against Leila at Miranda's feet. "I'm not having that."

Zara shook her head again, trying to rid herself of shock. She realised Corin didn't want to her to go on with her suspicions. Of course she shouldn't have said what she had. The last thing she wanted to do was add to Miranda's heartbreak.

Only Miranda sprang up, as though divining the truth. "I can't help my mother, Zara. Any more than you can help your father. We don't get to pick our parents. You can't think I *want* to talk about this woman? This woman without a heart? I've only laid eyes on her for the first time tonight. I used to think I could fall from the sky and land on top of her and she wouldn't acknowledge me. But she *does* know me. We saw the evidence of that tonight. You're shocked? Consider *my* shock. And it hasn't even hit me yet. Leila's whole history is mind-blowing. Far better my grandmother never told me."

Corin responded sharply. "Then you'd never have come into our lives." He rose, drawing Miranda back to the sofa. "None of us wants that."

Zara slowly lifted her head, her beautiful face full of a heartbreaking poignancy. "So how *did* you and Corin get to meet?" she asked.

"Pretty much as Miranda told you." Corin regarded his sister with compassion. "She approached me for a Rylance Foundation scholarship. She was a very promising candidate. A top-level student. She explained who she was."

"Not quite true." Miranda decided to intervene. Set the record straight. "Corin is putting the best possible spin on it, Zara. What really happened was that I told him Leila *owed* me. I had already checked her out. Checked out your family. I lay in wait for Corin, more or less cornered him, forced his hand."

"Very enterprising too," said Corin, with the first trace of amusement.

Miranda wasn't to be distracted. "My life's ambition, Zara, is to become a doctor. It's what my grandparents worked so very hard for. They were everything in the world to me, but even they didn't tell me the truth. I have to see it as protection, not betrayal. Just as Corin believes he was protecting you by not telling you what he had learned."

Zara sat motionless, head bent, locked in thought.

Miranda was strong by nature, Corin thought. Zara was far more fragile. Miranda had the price-less advantage of being brought up by loving, dedicated *parents*. He and Zara had experienced more than their share of trauma after their mother's death. He had been scarred to a degree. But never to the same extent as Zara. He was the son, the heir. He was *male*. That made a huge difference. To his father and, sickeningly as it was to turn out, to Leila. His scars had healed over. He was forging ahead in life.

So was Zara. Up to a point. It was any additional damage to Zara's psyche that was in the balance. The *wicked stepmother* didn't simply exist in fiction. She made her presence felt the world over.

Miranda hadn't enjoyed being party to keeping the truth from his sister. He was well aware of that. She hadn't refused because she trusted him. That was all-important. Up to date Zara had trusted him too.

But now Zara remained quiet.

Please, oh, please, Zara, don't see it as a betrayal, Miranda prayed.

Second by second dragged on. Miranda counted them with her heartbeats. Then Zara lifted her head, her lustrous dark glance embracing them both. "Start at the beginning," she said.

Some note in her voice calmed Miranda's trembling heart.

CHAPTER FIVE

THEY were in the apartment. Miranda had put distance between herself and Corin, her thoughts chaotic. The realisation that she had actually met her mother was starting to hit punishingly home. It wasn't as though Leila, whatever her regrettable actions in the past, had transformed herself into a loving, caring person. Leopards didn't change their spots. Leila was stuck with hers.

So where did that leave her, Leila's biological daughter? She had studied the history of genetics, the chemistry of the genes. The word *heredity* referred to the way specific characteristics are transmitted from parent to child, from one generation to the other. Now she found herself dreading the thought that there could be traits of Leila lying dormant in her. Traits could express themselves at any time. Or had she escaped the major flaws in Leila's character?

What did Corin think when he looked at her? Did he have nagging concerns at the corner of his mind? Who could blame him if he did? She knew sexually they were in perfect accord. But at some point he had to have fully registered she was Leila's flesh and blood. Leila—his stepmother, the woman he loathed. Was it conceivable he was waiting for something beneath the surface in her to suddenly emerge? Tonight she had seen with her own eyes that Leila lusted after Corin. That was already gnawing away at her. It raised terrible questions. Had Corin at some time been caught in some taboo situation? No one could deny such things did happen when an experienced adult manipulated someone much younger.

Shame could encourage hatred.

Zara, before she had retired to bed, had turned to announce prophetically, "She'll be back. You know that."

"Nothing surer," had been Corin's response.

Corin's greatest concern was to spare Miranda what was to come! Protective strategies had already begun to dominate his mind. Miranda, like his sister, was going into self-protective mode. He empathised with Miranda's powerful experience of the night. Her encounter with her long-lost mother. She had been totally unprepared for such deep emotional upheaval. All things considered, she was handling it remarkably well. It only added to his admiration for her. Miranda had real character.

"Is there any way she could mount some attack on me?" she asked now, holding on to the back of an armchair as if for support. "Undermine me? Pre-warned is pre-armed. Will she get rid of me out of your lives?"

"Over my dead body," Corin countered grimly. "Why are you over there, when I'm *here*?" he questioned tautly. He wanted her in his arms, but her mood was very sombre, warding him off.

Leila was no nice everyday mum. If Leila got so much as a hint he had a romantic interest in Miranda she would immediately turn to formulating ways to separate them. After all, she was mistress of that infamous art form. Though he did everything in his power to block it from his mind, he'd had plenty of experience of Leila's seeing off anyone she saw as competition. Sick as it was, Leila still held hopes she could lure him into her bed. She'd been trying it on for years. Even now she wasn't about to give up. She had no sense of honour. Worse, such was her colossal arrogance she thought she had only to catch him off guard. Arrogance was Leila's defining characteristic.

"What sort of woman *is* my mother that she ties everyone in knots?" Miranda begged of him.

He looked back, brows knotted. "The straight answer? She's a born manipulator. She breaks up families. She's cunning. She's cruel. She'll stop at nothing to get her way. Dad is blind and deaf to all this. He's mad about her."

"That could stop if he ever knew the truth." Miranda saw the strain in Corin.

"I doubt it," he answered crisply. "She would come up with something. Some pathetic story. She wanted to tell him so often, but she loved him so much she couldn't bear to lose his trust. She was so young, et cetera, et cetera... Sixteen. It was rape, of course. Or near enough. Overpowered by a man she knew and trusted. Her parents agreed to take her baby and rear it. She sent them all the money she could raise for years. Oh, she's *good*, Miranda. Don't underestimate her. Already she'll be working on her case."

"I don't intend to inform on her. I must make that plain. I thought I would hate her, but in a way I feel sorry for her."

"You *won't*," Corin predicted bluntly. "I can guarantee that. Are you going to come here? Sit with me?" How many times would he have to tell her she was the best thing that had ever happened to him?

"I think better over here," she said with a shake of the head. "It's all changed, hasn't it, Corin?" She lamented. "Simple and sad as that. Our golden days, our *stolen* days, are over. I'll never forget them. But we're back to *real* life. The way things actually *are*. I confess I'm disappointed in you. I never thought I would be. It really hurts."

"Hurts?" That stung him. Purposefully he closed the distance between them. Loomed tall over her. "You think I should have told Zara?" He took her by the shoulders. "You don't know how badly traumatised Zara was as a young girl. She's fought out of it, but a big reason for that is having Leila out of her life."

"All right. I accept that." She stared up at him, seeing the muscle working along his chiselled jawline. "I can see how it happened with Zara and with *you*. I don't want to read more into this than I *saw*, Corin, but I watched you and Leila together tonight. I'm not stupid. I'm a trained observer. You *know* she's in love with you. Why do you deny it? It couldn't be more obvious."

"Well, it's not *obvious* to me," Corin exploded, sick to death of the noxious Leila. "Leila does the big come-on on rare occasions when we're alone. If Dad caught her at it, God knows what would happen."

"Take a guess," she lashed out. At Corin! But she *loved* him.

No matter what?

"Would he throw her out?" she suggested, with a forced little laugh. "Alternatively, would he throw *you* out? God, it could all end in tragedy. At the very least a huge scandal."

"And you think I don't *know* that?" Corin rasped. "Zara knows it. Leila knows it, but doesn't seem to care. Now *you* know. For the record, I'd never for a single second think you stupid. You're as smart as they come. Incidentally, Dad *can't* throw me out. Zara and I have our mother's shares, and my grandparents stand very strongly behind me. Even Dad can't risk that sort of internal fight. Besides, I have the backing of the board. I'm regarded as top man to replace Dad. My position in that regard is quite safe. Dad *needs* me. Our investors are happy dealing with me if Dad is not around. I'm his Number One man."

"And it would appear you're also Leila's Number One man," Miranda said with a trenchancy that shocked her.

His glittering regard gave fair warning. "Don't talk like that, Miranda. I don't like it."

"I don't like it either." She threw up her head in challenge. "Leila has already tried something on, hasn't she?"

No, no, no. Don't let it be true.

Corin's handsome features tightened into a mask. "Miranda, please accept once and for all I have no tender feelings for Leila."

"But I'm not talking about *tender* feelings," Miranda said very crisply. "Leila is one dangerous, over-sexed woman."

"No argument there. But to put it bluntly I *loathe* her. She's a viper. She did her best to cripple my mother emotionally. She succeeded in alienating my beautiful sister from Dad. But, as you so correctly identified, Leila *is* a very sexual person."

"So are *you*!" It was out before she could call it back.

"And so are *you*," he retaliated, his hands tightening on her shoulders. "Maybe I'd better remind you." He took her face between his hands, held it still, then kissed her hard, like a brand. "I want to lead you to bed. I want to make love to you for the rest of the night. Instead we're embroiled in an unsavoury family drama. Leila wants what she *can't* have. Some people are like that. The chase is everything. She went after Dad. She got him. Only he wasn't enough for her. As the years passed, she turned her attention to me."

She tried to break away, but he wouldn't allow it. "Well, it would have been a temptation, wouldn't it? You would have been remarkable even then. A brilliant, sexy young man. I'm sorry if I'm making you angry, but I want the truth. I need it. Maybe it was all a grand illusion, but we've been as close as two people can be. That doesn't mean I believed it was going to last. Or be *allowed* to last. We control nothing in life. We just think we do. This woman, this catalyst in our midst, is my *mother*. There's no physical resemblance. She's much taller than I am. More lavishly built. Her colouring is totally different. I have to be the living image of my father or someone in my father's family. Someone with *my* distinctive colouring. The resemblance is so strong Leila recognised me immediately. She probably thinks I'm up to something. A go-getter like her? Who knows? I could have some of her characteristics in me, just waiting to break out. Ever thought of that?" She held his eyes.

"You're *nothing* like Leila." His black eyes smouldered in his dynamic face.

"Maybe you've only seen me at my best?"

"Don't do this to yourself, Miranda," he said. "Leila is a one-off. Meeting her tonight, so unprepared, has been a big shock for you."

"More than a shock, Corin," she said. A torrent of emotions was racing through her. "Have you ever slept with her?"

"What?" Corin's expression turned very daunting. "I can't believe you said that!" He held her so tightly she winced. Instantly his grip relaxed. "I'm going to *forget* you said that."

"But you *can't* forget." Her beautiful blue-green eyes glittered with unshed tears. "You'll always think of it now. I asked the question. Perhaps you might consider I have a right to. *Have* you?"

"Don't cry. *Don't.*" He wiped a tear clear of her luminous cheek. "This is the last time I'm going to say it. I loathe Leila."

"You *could* very easily loathe her. That's perfectly understandable. She tempted you against your will. It might have been years back. She's seductive enough to make the head of a male of any age swim."

"Never *mine*!" He released her as though all his former feelings for her were dissolving. "I adored my mother. There's a sacred principle involved here, Miranda. A son's love for his mother. My mother didn't deliberately leave us. She loved us too much. When her car went flying off the Westlake Bridge, it was at a time when she was in terrible distress. She was at the wheel of a powerful car. Perhaps blinded by tears. She really did love my father. Then she had to confront the fact he had fallen in love with another woman, many years younger. He had brought her into the house. Forced her upon us all. His mistress. I'm sure she was. Even then. When I was seventeen, nearly eighteen—" an unmistakable note of outrage entered his voice "—Leila came to my room. Dad hadn't arrived home. They were going to a party. She needed someone to fix the zipper on her evening dress. Zara was just down the hall. But she wanted *me*."

"Of course she did!" Miranda released a long shuddering breath.

He'll hate you for making him remember. He'll hate you for making him recount an ugly, disturbing incident.

"You needn't go on if you don't want to."

His brief laugh cut her off. "You *wanted* to know, didn't you? Kindly let me finish. Weigh up the evidence, Miranda, before you sit in judgment."

"I'm *not* judging you," she protested. "I can understand this, Corin. I've *seen* Leila in action."

"You *are* judging me," he corrected flatly. "I can see it in your eyes. Eyes are the windows of the soul. So don't back away from it. You started this. Let me finish it. I have nothing to feel guilty about in relation to Leila. She engineered it so her dress—a slip of satin—all but fell from her. Her breasts were uncovered. She wasn't wearing a bra. Most of her body was exposed. I was supposed to be turned on. Instant arousal. Instant disgust, more like. I was supposed to be the callow boy, about to lose control. But she had it all wrong. Even without my love for my mother, my aversion to Leila, I would never betray my father. The whole situation was appalling. I remember yelling at her to get out. *Get out! Get out!* She wasn't such a fool she didn't pull up her dress and make a bolt back to her bedroom. *Their* bedroom—the master suite."

"And that was the only time?" Miranda wasn't shocked. She had *seen* her mother the sexual predator, seen the overweening confidence in the way she stood. Head up, back arched, hand on hip. She'd probably seduced the man who had fathered her. Not the other way around. Her grandmother had admitted Leila had been very *mature* for her years.

Mature? One could define maturity in a number of ways.

"Need I say more?" Corin spoke coldly, as though deeply disappointed in her and her reactions.

"But she hasn't let you alone, has she?" Miranda persisted.

"Okay, let's have this out," Corin retorted in an abrasive voice. "Leila is an extraordinary woman. A man-eater. A home-wrecker. She's very motivated."

"Like me?"

"Let me finish." He cut her off. "Leila thinks sooner or later it's going to happen. She and I *will* eventually have sex."

"Instead it happened with *us*." Solid ground had turned to shifting sand. "Some of that loathing has to wash up on me? If not now at some future time?"

"Now you really are being ridiculous. And unforgivably insulting," he said. "Both to me and to yourself."

"So I should be disgusted with myself?" Miranda asked, low-voiced. "Well, I feel like I'm being pulled apart, Corin. Try to understand that. I *am* my mother's daughter. There's a lot of twisted emotion going on here. In you. In me. Even in Zara."

He rounded on her. "Don't get into the psychobabble, Miranda. Where has our sense of *belonging*, our depth and balance gone?"

"No psychobabble," Miranda said sadly. "A conclusion based on hard evidence. I take the scientific approach. Leila has badly affected your family. Affected me, the abandoned child. We all bear testament to that. She's that kind of woman."

"Ah, to hell with her!" Corin threw up his hands. "We lose the good people in life. The devil looks after his own." What he desperately needed was to hold her, but at that moment it seemed impossible. It was obvious she needed time. As for him—he accepted the fact he had fallen deeply and irrevocably in love with a young woman whose life story was drastically entwined with his own.

But love was a form of armour. Wasn't it? He *had* to believe that.

"If Leila thinks there's anything between us she'll become even more of an enemy," Miranda said. "I think I should go home. Get a job for the rest of the year. I've had almost seven months of luxurious living. I've learned a great deal. I'll never forget it. But it's imperative I keep my feet on the ground. I'll miss Zara, but she has her job and good friends here. You'll be joining your father in Beijing. He'll have Leila with him. So far as she's concerned I'm *Zara's* friend. Which I desperately hope I still am." She paused, watching Corin slump dejectedly into an armchair. "I should take some of my clothes upstairs. Leave most of them here, if I may. Leila obviously doesn't have a key to your apartment."

"I hope that's not a question?" he shot back, his expression dark and forebiding.

"Don't be angry with me, Corin." She was careful to keep her tone level. "I know she doesn't. If she had, she'd already have checked." She gave a humourless laugh. "I called myself Miranda Graham."

"She wasn't fooled."

"Of course not. At least she knew I wasn't about to bring her immediately unstuck. Your father didn't know her as Leila Thornton?"

"Got it in one. Leila Richardson. That's if he even bothered to look at any documents."

"I would never have taken him for a fool."

"He's obsessed with her," Corin said. "Makes fools of us all. I want you to stay with me tonight, Miranda. We'll take some of your clothes up tomorrow. I suggest you go out for the day. I have a meeting I can't put off in the morning. Otherwise I would. Should go on for hours, then I'll be taken out for the obligatory lunch. But I'll be back no later than 3:00 p.m. Leila will make a rush to get at you. She's probably raised all sorts of possibilities in her mind."

"Blackmail, most probably," Miranda said

soberly. "She'll be sure I want to blackmail her. Take her for all she can manage to get from your father. I blackmailed you in a way, didn't I?"

Corin came to his full height—a very formidable young man. He went to her, pulling her tightly into his arms. Hunger, anger, a counter-balancing protectiveness blazed out his eyes. "Let's go to bed," he said roughly, putting his mouth to hers.

Immediately, touch leapt across the barriers between them as if they were of no consequence. The kiss lengthened, deepened. Physically, they were in perfect accord. "We must stick together," he muttered passionately when he lifted his head. "Trust together. If we do, all the Leilas in the world can't hurt us."

At that moment Miranda, fathoms deep in love, believed him.

She wasn't sure exactly why she did it, but Miranda elected to remain in the house the following morning.

Zara looked worried. "I can ring and say I won't be in to work," she offered, thus validating their closeness. "I'll make some excuse. No one will mind. I pull my weight."

"I'm sure you do, but I don't want you to do that, Zara," Miranda said, showing her gratitude for the offer. "Even if Leila does turn up I'll be okay. It's not as though she would physically attack me. She might come off second best if she did. A few of my girlfriends and I undertook a course in self-defence a year or so back. I was the shortest, the slightest and the best of the lot." She laughed at the memory. "For months on campus I was called Mighty Mouse. Besides, this is something deeply personal between us. Leila is the mother who abandoned me. Not only me, but her own mother and father, who never got over her defection. My grandmother spoke about it on her deathbed. This won't be a one-way thing. It works two ways. I'll let Leila tell me her side of the whole sorry story."

"Leila never tells the truth," Zara warned. "If you need me I'm only a phone call away. And Corin will get away from his meeting as soon as he can. You love him, don't you?"

Miranda's beautiful eyes were on fire. "At first sight," she admitted. "It was the most powerful connection of my life. Neither of us ever talked about it. That side of our friendship went unmentioned. I had my degree to get through. Corin was always under pressure. Venice was the happiest time of my life." She paused before adding quietly, "But things change, don't they, Zara? You know that. Therefore I must be prepared."

"Don't you *let* them change!" Zara advised. "I did—to my cost. One day I'll tell you all about it. How I lost the love of my life."

* * *

Miranda was sitting in an armchair in the sumptuous drawing room, with its antiques, fine art, glorious chandeliers, gilded mirrors, Aubusson carpet, golden yellow silk drapes falling from the ceiling to floor French windows, when a cab drew to a halt outside.

You knew she'd come.

She had to be channelling her grandmother. That was her voice. She could handle the paranormal now.

She stood up, facing the quiet, leafy crescent, as Leila, dressed in a black-and-white two-piece suit—unmistakably Chanel—emerged from the back seat, turning to pay the driver. She looked up at the grand white stucco building, then walked purposefully towards the short flight of front steps.

Don't forget there's a caged tigress inside.

Miranda believed she was locked into celestial wisdom. She went to the front door, opening it just as Leila was about to press the buzzer.

"Ah, Mrs Rylance. How lovely to see you. This *is* a surprise." Miranda stood back as the much taller Leila swept by her, leaving a delightful trail of Chanel No. 5.

"Where have you come from and why are you here?" Leila bypassed all the niceties. She had control of her voice, but her right hand was clenching and unclenching.

Does she mean to sock you?

"Why don't we go and sit down?" Miranda gestured towards the drawing room.

"Don't tell me what to do in my own home!" Leila shot back in the most hostile voice possible. "Who sent you?"

"I think *I* should be the one asking questions here." Miranda surprised herself with her own calm in the face of a storm.

Courage under fire.

Her grandmother again. She was having a lot to say today. Miranda waited for Leila to be seated before she resumed her armchair by the tall French windows. Who knew? She might have to jump out.

"I repeat—who sent you?" Leila was really angry, her golden-brown eyes lit like a bonfire. "What are you up to?"

"Why don't we cut to the chase?" Miranda suggested. "I know you. You know me. Like any mother and daughter. I assume you're not here to ask my forgiveness?"

Leila looked stunned by Miranda's response and her composure. "What is it you want?"

"Good question." Miranda sat back, finding the whole situation the stuff of fiction. Here was her *mother*. A total stranger.

"Money?" Leila sneered. "It's always money.

So just how much is it going to take for you to go away? Not just go away. *Stay* away."

Miranda studied her mother's impeccably made-up face. It had an underlying *scream* behind it. Leila was like a wild animal caught in a trap. But even in the golden light pouring into the room she still looked a good ten years younger than her age. Her long, lustrous hair was arranged in a smooth pleat. Her accessories were perfection. She had lovely legs, an ultra-slim, ultra-toned body.

"Gran loved you to the end," Miranda told her in a saddened voice. "You can't even ask about her. Or your father. Gran died a very painful death. Cancer. My grandfather preceded her by a few months. Lovely man—so gentle and kind. Both of them scrimping and saving to provide the best for me. You really deserve to be exposed, Leila. Afterwards there was just Gran and me, although I called her *Mum* all my life. I thought I was a change-of-life baby, you see. You might redeem yourself in a very small way if you told me the name of my father. Clearly you've never forgotten him. I must be his spitting image."

Leila's face froze. And it wasn't due to Botox. She didn't answer for a minute. "You have no father. He abandoned me."

Miranda followed her instincts. She didn't wait for the celestial voice to break in. "I don't believe that for a minute. Maybe you never told him you were pregnant. Maybe you told him you were on the pill. Maybe you went very privately to his parents—mother most likely. Some mothers will do anything for their sons. His mother—my grandmother, God help me—paid you to get out of town. She wasn't going to have her son's life destroyed. How am I doing so far?"

"You could hardly do better." Leila gave her a mirthless smile. "I wasn't good enough to become part of *that* family, my dear. We're lower class, you see. Farming stock as opposed to big sheep station owners. Therefore I didn't belong in one of the richest families in New Zealand. A family that had produced the country's best doctors and academics as well. I was nothing and nobody. She made that very clear. I waited too long to abort you. I was forced to go through with it. If you must know, your father is dead."

That touched a deep, sensitive nerve. The pain was intense. "May I ask how?" Miranda asked quietly.

Leila shrugged an elegant shoulder. "The last time I saw him he was the picture of health. Killed in a skiing accident years later. A mountain of snow got dumped on him, poor man. Can't say I was sorry to read it."

True or false? You have to find out.

"Did you feel anything at all for him, or was it just another sexual thrill?" Miranda asked on impulse.

Leila made a small grimace. "Come on—it was a lifetime ago."

"And haven't you moved on! Could I have a name, please?"

Leila gave her a look sharp enough to cut to the bone. "Don't even *think* of looking the family up. They won't want to know you any more than they wanted to know me. Your grandfather is a big-time professor. Revered."

"Well, then, it will be easy enough to track him down from what you've already told me."

"More fool you!" Leila said scornfully, her face if not her voice tightly controlled. This was a woman never stricken by remorse. A woman who would never admit to the gravest mistakes. "Take my advice," she said. "Let sleeping dogs lie."

"I'm sure they'll recognise me," Miranda continued, as if Leila hadn't spoken. "The sight of me stupefied *you*."

For a second Leila looked as though she had been hit between the eyes all over again. "Oh, they'll recognise you, all right," she said, sounding more and more furious. "You look just like his sister. And him too, of course. That silver hair and the turquoise eyes. Very few people have eyes like that. I'm pleased in a way that you've turned out so well. That's something that has come on me unawares. Good looks in a woman are a tremendous advantage. But what I have to know before we can talk any deal is this—who put you up to it? It was Zara, wasn't it? You contrived a meeting with her back home. I would have done it. It was no accident of fate. A woman has to take fate into her own hands. It was your heaven-sent opportunity to spill the beans. Get revenge. I'd have played it that way. Zara's your friend, isn't she? Though she's years older. Zara hates me. She'll do anything to damage me with Dalton and...and Corin. She's tried to poison her brother against me. It hasn't worked. Of course she blames me for her saintly mother's death."

Some aspect of Leila was corrupt. "Well, it *did* happen after you became her father's mistress," Miranda came back.

Leila blinked, clearly shocked. "The woman's death had *nothing* to do with me," she cried angrily. "It was an accident. Pure and simple. Dalton was going to divorce her anyway. He fell madly in love with me, you see."

Miranda stared back at her glamorous, youthful-looking mother.

Nothing good can come of this.

Miranda had come to the same conclusion. "Looks like he still is," she said. "But I'm thinking you're not and never have been in love with him?"

Leila's answer was a languid, super-confident

drawl. "My dear, you could never convince him of that. Outside of Corin, I'm the only person Dalton does care about."

"Then it sounds like you're a good pair. No heart, either of you. Just a high sex-drive." Miranda's tone was strongly condemnatory.

Leila wasn't in the least perturbed. "Don't, my dear, be fool enough to knock sex. It's all most men think about. I should know. Dalton and I will remain a good pair for as long as it takes." Her smile was very cold. "What I don't understand is what you are doing in London. Got Zara to invite you, I suppose? *Money* is enormously seductive. Even being around it."

There was a lot of truth in that. "Zara and Corin were born to wealth," she said. "You and I weren't. I have none of your illusions or ambitions, Leila. Zara and I *are* friends. I'll be going home soon in any case."

Leila made a derisive sound in her throat. "A whole lot richer, you're hoping. What do you do, exactly? You're very pretty, in a highly individual way, but you're way too short to model."

"Perish the thought! You're not going to believe this, but I'm on my way to becoming a doctor," Miranda said. "I already have my BS. That's Bachelor of Science. Now I need my BM."

Flickers of admiration appeared in Leila's eyes.

"Well, good for you!" she said, with as much warmth as she could ever muster.

"Thanks, *Mum*!"

"Spare me." Leila waved a dismissive hand. "I was never cut out to be a mum. But you've turned out better than I thought. Seems it's true, then. Blood will out." She paused, her gaze sharpening. "But where's the money coming from? My poor old mum and dad had nothing."

Miranda's eyes shone with an inner light. "They had nothing when they had *you*. But they worked their fingers to the bone so I could have a first-class education. You'd know nothing about that." Somehow she managed to inject a cool touch of irony. "Actually, I won a scholarship with the Rylance Foundation."

"What?" A dark cloud passed slowly across Leila's face. "Zara has nothing to do with the Foundation. You surely didn't approach *Corin*?" Her lush lips were pressed into a tight line.

"What would be wrong if I did?" Miranda assumed an artless voice and lied. "Zara put forward my name. The rest was easy. I had all the qualifications that were needed."

Leila was putting two and two together, making the inevitable five. "How well *do* you know Corin?" Her voice was a lot harder now. There was a near demonic look in her golden-brown eyes.

"I'm sure I don't need to answer that."

"Don't play games with me, girlie," Leila warned, her voice hinting at impending physical action.

"Who's threatening who here?" Miranda asked, getting ready to defend herself and unafraid. She was still Mighty Mouse and she had her celestial gran on side. "You're the one in the hot seat, Leila. Not me. I should tell you Zara knows you're my mother."

Leila looked as though she was about to faint.

"She had to be told," Miranda said. "She's my friend. We're related in a way, thanks to you. Put your head down and take a few fortifying breaths," she said, feeling pity despite herself. "In, out. In, out. Calm yourself."

For a wonder, Leila obeyed. It took a few moments, then she lifted her head, looking as though all her defences had abruptly been swept away.

"That's better. I don't want to harm you, Leila," Miranda said, knowing it to be true. "I'm not like you, you see. You need have no fear. Zara won't say one word to her father. It's agreed what action is to be taken—if any—will be taken by me. *I* am the victim here. The abandoned child."

Leila gave the queerest laugh. "Suppose I have you killed? It could be arranged. An accident crossing the road…"

"Wouldn't do you a bit of good." Miranda's

glance slid over this beautiful woman with sick resignation. "It's all on the record," she improvised. "Anything untoward happens to me, the finger points right at you. So don't talk foolishly. And, incidentally, criminally."

Leila's tight smile was more a sneer. "You think I'm fool enough to trust you? You could change your mind at any time. So could that step-daughter of mine. So let's come up with a solution. How much?"

A wave of anger swept Miranda, but she didn't allow it to show. "How does ten million sound?"

"Ten million?" Leila sat back grimly, as if she was already deciding on the right hit man.

"That's sterling, of course," Miranda said. "Roughly double in the Aussie dollar. I'd be set up for life. You understand that, don't you, Leila? That would have been your very thought the moment Dalton Rylance's roving eye fell on you. *I can get this man. Be rich!*"

Leila stared back in genuine disbelief. "How could I get hold of that kind of money?"

"Sell a few jewels?" Miranda suggested. "You can't ask your husband. I understand that. We could do it in stages, if you like. The odd million here, a couple of million there…"

"You're *unbelievable*!" Leila spat.

"You astonish me, Mother," Miranda said.

"Look at yourself. What *you've* become. My role model. Your husband isn't looking beyond the beautiful face and body. The acquired polish. What happens if and when he does? The most beautiful, seductive women have to age. None of us can escape the process. Once past their use-by date, they're not wanted any more. Some men only want trophy figures, after all."

Leila jerked up in volcanic anger. Outraged. And outflanked. "Cross me and you put your life on the line. You'd better know that."

"At long last I've met my mother," Miranda breathed. "A woman who considers she has never done anything that requires explanation. You broke your loving parents' hearts. You've haunted me, but I've managed to keep my heart intact. No, Mother dear. No need to go back to the hotel and rifle through your little black book for a hit man. I want to make it perfectly clear to you I don't want *anything* from you. So you can sit down again and relax. You have your life. I have mine. I'm not going to simply vanish, like you. I might pop up from time to time. But your former life—the life you've secreted away—is safe with me. Gran saw nothing of you in me. Thank God for that. Most women would find their only child the crowning glory of their life. Not you. It might strike me as shocking, but I accept it. Gran loved you to the end, you know? But she knew in her heart you weren't worth a bumper."

Leila stood for a moment, apparently numb. "I can trust you?"

"Would that be your first experience of trusting? Maybe your husband doesn't trust you? That's why he takes you with him wherever he goes. You *can* trust me. The mother-daughter relationship is a powerful and unbreakable bond. I don't want to see you come a cropper. I'm really not a vengeful person."

Leila stared into her daughter's crystal-clear turquoise eyes. "Don't feel sorry for me, Miranda," she said bitterly. "I have everything I want."

Everything? I don't think so. She wants the man you love.

Point taken, Gran.

Leila appeared to brighten. "Well, that's it, then!" She gathered up her expensive designer bag. No doubt worth thousands of dollars. "I'm taking it Corin knows none of this?"

"*Zara* is my friend," Miranda offered by way of an answer.

"Keep it that way," Leila said. "You're smart enough to realise it would do you no good at all to expose me. Corin and I are close. I would strike back. There are always ways."

Miranda stood up. "You have my word, Leila.

On your mother's grave. She wouldn't want me to destroy you. Your life is your own. By and large it always has been. It's never been mine."

Leila started to head towards the door. "Dalton was rather taken with you, in an avuncular sort of way. You're extremely attractive, but you really ought to let your hair grow. He wants to take us all out to dinner before we leave, which is at the end of the week. Both Dalton and Corin have to be in Beijing for a round of business meetings. What say tomorrow evening? You can't refuse."

"Like I don't know that!" Miranda said very dryly. "Could I bring a friend?"

Leila turned, smiling. A real smile. "A boyfriend? Of course you've got one."

"His name is Peter. Australian. He's a brilliant young cellist. I've known him for years. He's studying at the Royal College of Music here in London. He's been assured he has a future."

"Fine, fine," Leila said, putting up a hand to her immaculate hairdo. "Call me a cab, would you? I'm meeting Corin for lunch."

Now that was silly!

Miranda cast off the suspicion.

"Bring your Peter by all means," Leila said, as though a burden had been lifted off her. "I think we'll dine in. We're at Claridges. Wonderful hotel.

It suits us perfectly. Even *you* will have heard of Gordon Ramsay's restaurant there."

"We've all heard of Gordon Ramsay, Leila."

"Now, I *can* give you some money, you know," Leila offered. "I guess I owe you that much."

Miranda shook her head. "It's not about money, Leila. I'm going to get ahead. I'm going to become a doctor. Just like my father's family. That's one mystery you've solved."

Leila showed a shadow of concern. "I'm just enough of a mother not to want you to get hurt. Like me. I can't stop you from finding out who they are. I can see you're a very smart girl. But I can warn you to keep well away. Your paternal grandmother, my dear, unlike me, is a total bitch."

Leila sounded as though she truly believed she was basically a good person.

"How old was he? My father?" Miranda asked quietly. She wasn't showing it, but inside she felt deeply wounded. A father she would never meet. As an individual, she was very short on relations.

"The same age as me," Leila admitted carelessly, as though they were talking ancient history. "He'd never had a girl before. Not that I was a virgin. *He* was. He was head over heels in love with me. Not the only one, I can tell you." She walked to the door, then turned back for a moment. "Until tomorrow evening, then, *Miranda*. Where did

Mum rake up *that* name? Blue-green eyes, I suppose. I only saw them as navy. Dress up. Tell your friend black tie."

CHAPTER SIX

AFTER she was gone, Miranda curled back in her chair like a young woman in pain. She felt very strange, as if severely dehydrated. Why not? Leila had all but drained the life out of her. Where was this mystical love that was supposed to exist between mother and child? Certainly her lovely grandmother had loved the daughter who had turned her back on them all to the end. And she, herself, had been the central figure in her grandparents' lives. They had lavished their love on her. They had been so proud of her. Going on the evidence, Leila had no need whatever for any mother-daughter relationship. She had been biologically capable of giving birth. Tragically, she was mentally and morally incapable of nurturing that child. To her, motherhood was only a commitment that dragged a woman down.

Corin arrived back earlier than expected, at 2:30 p.m. She watched him bound towards the front steps, reinforcing the impression he was very anxious to get home to her.

No need to be volunteering information. Let Corin do the talking.

She didn't know at this stage when her inner voice started and her grandmother's stopped.

Because you're part of me. We're part of one another.

Corin was inside now, devastatingly handsome in his elegant city clothes, the pristine white collar of his blue-and-white striped shirt accentuating a deep golden tan that could never came out of a bottle. He drew her into his arms without saying a word. So easy to take refuge. So easy to dissolve into him, to feed off his blazing energy. So easy to suspend deep concern.

He tipped up her face to kiss her, long and lingeringly. "Got away without much trouble," he murmured, when he lifted his head. "I hear you've had a visit from Leila."

She looked directly into his eyes. What was she looking for? Deception from Corin? Leila had really undermined her confidence. "How did you know?"

He reacted to the strain in her voice. "She rang my mobile, of course. What else? Leila lives to alienate people. It would serve you well not to forget that. She sounded super friendly. She's the ultimate con-woman. Seems we're all invited out to dinner tomorrow night. Dad, apparently, took to you. Never could resist a pretty woman."

"When was it she rang you? You didn't see her?"

"Hey, what is this, Miranda?" His tone was different from before. Anger was stirring. "Listen to what I'm saying. I refuse to be put under suspicion. I refuse to have my integrity questioned. I'm an expert at evading Leila. I'd been tied up with the meeting. Which went well, thank you for asking," he added crisply. "She caught me about two minutes before I flagged down a cab. She said you were bringing your boyfriend along. I take it she meant Peter?"

"I don't think Leila would care to hear my boyfriend is *you*." Miranda knew she was on dangerous ground. Throwing down the gauntlet, as it were. But he had to pick it up. "I *was* getting around to asking about your meeting, but my priorities seem to be all screwed up."

He turned her to face him. "So why don't you tell me about them? I'm here now. Peter is a smokescreen. I've got that, although I know you're very fond of him. What did she have to say to you?"

"Actually, *I* did a lot of the talking."

"Which seems to have exhausted you. Are you going to let me in on the conversation?" His dark eyes were trained on her face. It would be a disaster if he lost her trust.

She lifted her head to him, seeing herself reflected in the brilliance of his eyes. "I must repeat I'm not going to expose my mother, Corin. Not for you. Not for anyone. Deep down I think she's a very unhappy, driven person without any real self-esteem."

Corin's hands dropped away. There wasn't just disapproval in his voice, there was outright disgust. "Even if it were true, Miranda, I couldn't care less. She's caused too much harm to my family. She's failed to be any sort of a mother to you. For the record, as it appears I'm under investigation, I don't believe I've ever said I *was* going to expose her."

"So what *do* you intend?" Discord was growing between them like a malignant plant.

"Why sound so ominous?" he challenged. "It means we'll leave it alone. Zara and I care too much about you, Miranda, to override your wishes. You don't want to reveal Leila's history. That's it!"

"You'll keep your word?"

His expression toughened. "With one proviso. Leila must swear not to further upset you or interfere in your life. Should she do that, the position will change. She knows Zara and I know?"

"She thinks only Zara knows. That's all. She did ask if you knew. My answer was ambiguous, but she took it at face value. I told her Zara was my friend."

"So you and I are not supposed to be close?"

She stared back at him, wanting the discord to

cease, but unable to stop its escalation. "I played it that way, Corin. Safer, don't you think?"

"Only for a time." There was a brooding expression on his dark, handsome face. "All we have is a breathing space. I won't let you go out of my life, Miranda. You can't think for one moment I will."

She gave a broken laugh. "Well, we *are* related by marriage."

"Oh, stop it!" He drew in a tense, frustrated breath. "Leila has only just arrived on the scene and already she's causing trouble. You can't let her get to you, Miranda. Bad enough she's started to erode your trust in me. There will be difficult times ahead. Leila would like nothing better than to see you out of the way."

"I realise that," she said quietly, averting her head.

"Don't let it weigh you down. Zara and I have had years and years of Leila. You've only had a matter of hours. Yet she's messed up your thinking, hasn't she?"

"Give me time, Corin."

"Of course." He drew her into his arms again, his own expression softening. "Don't let Leila come between us, Miranda," he begged. "She's so good at that sort of thing. I wish I didn't have to leave you, but Dad and I have the China trip."

That was the hardest part. "Leila's going along?"

"She always does," he clipped off.

"She can't want to go all the time—be on her own for hours on end. Doesn't he trust her?"

Corin gave a bitter laugh. "Would you? It's just as well billionaires aren't all that thick on the ground, or Leila would be running off with a younger one."

Her unspoken *like you* hung in the air.

Insight into her thoughts sharpened his tone. "I'm not a billionaire yet, Miranda. I won't be until my father dies, and I want him to last for another twenty-five years. He hasn't been much of a father, but he's all I've got. He does give me due credit as a fitting heir. In his own strange way he loves me. He has need of me as a business confidant. He keeps things so close to his chest, and I'm sure I'm the only one he truly trusts."

"And he has some suitable young woman lined up for you?" Miranda continued to look questioningly at him. "Annette Atwood, isn't it?"

"Are there no limits to gossip?" He sighed. "There's no chance in the world, Miranda. I can't marry a woman I don't love with all my heart. I had thought that was *you*. Now I have to ask. Do you *want* me to love you with all my heart, or does that frighten you? Were our days and nights in Venice just too perfect, too unreal? You can't believe in what we had now you've hit the first obstacle? I refuse point blank to allow a woman like Leila to destroy our relationship."

She stared blindly at a landscape on the wall. "I'm not holding you to anything, Corin. I care too much to bring more trauma into your life. Leila mightn't want to have anything to do with me, but I can never escape being Leila's daughter. It's like a stain."

The melancholy note in her voice pierced his heart. He drew her against him, his arms steely strong, the muscles rigid. "I won't allow you to see it like that," he said forcefully. "You're lovely, inside and out. When you think about it, you escaped your mother. Instead, you were blessed with your grandparents. They brought you up. As for me, I refuse to let you go. You've given yourself to me of your own free will. So I'm keeping you, Miranda. God knows, I've had to resist every temptation so you could get on with your studies undistracted. You have your science degree in your pocket. That's the first step. I'm very proud of you and your sense of commitment. I'll support you every inch of the way in your ambitions. But you're twenty-one now. I want more of you. You've seen Leila. You've felt her destructive power. Don't let her reach you."

"In her way, she's the one who should fear," she said, taking great comfort from his words and his arms around her. "She has so much to hide."

"Indeed she has!" Each word was flattened, as though weighted down. "But don't let's waste any more time talking about Leila. I want to take you shopping."

The dazzling change of topic brought out a flicker of a smile. "Do you really?" She was picturing the two of them together. "I thought men hated shopping?"

"Well, we shopped in Venice, didn't we? You have that beautiful gold-shot glass horse from Murano."

"And I treasure it," Miranda said. "Are you going to tell me what we're shopping for?"

There was unrestrained ardour in his dark eyes. "A dress for you to wear tomorrow night. I want you to knock Dad and our dear Leila dead."

Peter, giddied to be invited, presented very well in a hired dinner suit. He had the height, the wide shoulders, and he had put on much needed weight.

"Peter, you look great!" Miranda reached up to kiss his cheek.

"Bought the dress shirt and the black tie—rented the suit." He grinned. "You look out of this world!" He fell back theatrically, gasping with unfeigned admiration. "If I were wearing my glasses they'd be steamed up. The dress is fabulous! You look a million dollars. Surely they're not *diamonds* dripping off your pretty ears?"

She smiled impishly, fingering one of the diamond-studded drops. "Real, absolutely! On loan from Zara. Come on in. Zara and Corin will be down soon. Both of them are so pleased you're coming along tonight."

"To be honest, I'm blown away to be invited," Peter said, moving farther into the entrance hall and glancing up the grand staircase to the art-lined gallery. "Word is Mrs Rylance is a real knock-out."

"Well, you can make your own mind up."

"Goodness, how intriguing!" Peter looked quickly back at her, but her silver-gilt head was turned away.

Whatever did Miri mean?

To his perfectly tuned ears it sounded as though she hadn't taken to the second Mrs Rylance at all. He reminded himself he had always respected Miri's judgment...

Miranda was glad she had become familiar with the full on dazzle of Claridges black-and-white marble front hall, with its tall mirrors and superb Art Deco ironwork, so her head wasn't swivelling like Peter's. The hall led on to the sumptuous foyer, where she and Zara had enjoyed afternoon tea on several memorable occasions—once when a famous movie star had been seated at a table only a few feet away. She might have been reared on a small farm in rural Queensland, but she was taking the glittering London night life in her stride. This was a time to be enjoyed. A time to capture and relive in memory.

She and Zara had planned their outfits to complement one another. Like a magician pulling a bouquet of flowers out of a hat, Zara had taken from her wardrobe a deep emerald silk-satin dress with a short sparkly bolero that harmonised beautifully with Miranda's dress, which was the gorgeous shade of a blue-purple iris. The bodice was tiny, strapless, the short, flirty, tiered skirt cinched with a wide satin diamante-clasped belt to show off her enviably small waist.

Beautiful dresses were powerful confidence-builders. Zara, born into wealth, had been wearing beautiful clothes all her life. It was all very recent for Miranda. As a student she'd bought cheap, but her petite figure and inherent good taste had turned cheap into stylish. Her girlfriends had thought so anyway. They had often enlisted her aid—down to actually borrowing an outfit when they were going out on a special date.

Corin had picked the dress out of several, all of them beautiful. His choice had been so wickedly expensive she had tried to talk him out of it. And then there were the accessories to complete the exclusive image!

"It's terribly, terribly *you*, my dear," the saleswoman had told her, looking very expensive and sophisticated herself. She had turned on the charm for Corin from the moment they had walked through the door. And Corin had played up to her, Miranda was sure. He had a streak of devilment.

When Leila first caught sight of Miranda, she gave her the blankest stare—as if in no way had she expected Miranda to look so exquisitely and so expensively turned out.

Miranda now knew with certainty she was looking her absolute best.

She's not happy!

Miranda, who had been lightly holding Peter's hand, as her evening date, felt him squeeze it. Perhaps letting her know a light had been switched on in his head.

It had been. So *this* was the second Mrs Rylance! Peter regarded her, fascinated. A stunning woman, a bit on the dangerous side. Facing down the competition probably dominated her life. Sad, that! He could just imagine her on the rampage. She was wearing black, intricately draped, off the shoulder, showing a generous amount of golden cleavage. Her thick, burnished hair was swept smoothly back from her high forehead and coiled at the back, no doubt to showcase her bedazzling diamond jewellery: earrings like chandeliers, which swung with every movement of her head, and a necklace that danced and glittered with light.

It must have set her very imposing magnate husband back millions.

Ah, well, what was a million or two? A billionaire needed a wife who could dazzle. The second Mrs Rylance without question did that.

"What do I do? Bow down on one knee?" Peter whispered, head bent, shoulders hunched, so Miranda could hear him.

"Just hope she likes you."

Was that a warning?

Cocktails were served in the bar, with its deep red leather banquettes and silver-leafed ceiling. Every drink available was on the offer—the classics and the latest concoctions—all served perfectly chilled in crystal. Each table was decorated with a single red rose at its centre, but they found their way over to a reserved banquette.

"Sit here," murmured Corin in Miranda's ear, settling her deftly between him and Peter. Leila, thank the Lord, was busy saying something to his father, so missed the smooth manoeuvre. "I'd suggest a champagne cocktail."

"Lovely!" Miranda smiled, sinking into the seat. She had been extremely careful not to let her eyes rest on Corin over-long. This wasn't the time to invite catastrophe. He looked strikingly handsome, his resemblance to his father apparent. The Rylances were one good-looking family. Zara had to be one of the most beautiful women in a room full of glamorous and beautiful women, Miranda thought.

Dalton Rylance's first act on greeting Miranda had surprised even his children, and brought a glint to Leila's eyes that had been veiled in a second. Even so Peter had caught it, and felt like ducking. Rylance hadn't taken Miranda's small extended hand, as expected, but had bent to kiss her on both cheeks, clearly enjoying the sensation of satiny smooth young skin against his lips.

"You look exquisite, my dear." He straightened, smiling down into her eyes. "Your young man here must be very proud of you."

"Oh, I am, sir!" Peter spoke up, playing his part to the hilt. "And may I say how happy I am to be invited?" He sounded it, but not overwhelmed. Peter, since his exceptional musical gifts had been acknowledged, had come a long way in confidence. Besides, he came from a prominent family back home—though they certainly weren't swimming in the Rylances' ocean of money.

"Good. Good," Dalton Rylance clipped off, his attention not to be diverted from Miranda, who was looking irresistibly young and sexy. He had given his daughter, Zara, just one perfunctory kiss on the cheek.

What an act of kindness!

Playing to the public, of course.

Gran had come along for the evening, apparently having no difficulty in moving between parallel universes.

Miranda couldn't help but be aware that many eyes had strayed in their direction. Dalton Rylance and his ultra-glamorous wife were frequent guests of the hotel, and the small party with him tonight included his strikingly handsome son and his very beautiful daughter, who was a regular on London's social circuit, along with two young guests—all of them a treat for the eye.

The very generously sized restaurant featured more of the Art Deco for which the hotel was famous. Miranda loved the bronze-and-gilt metal doors, the mirrored murals and the lighting. The food was predictably superb, and Dalton Rylance ordered the finest wines to go with the successive courses from the French menu. The hotel had an outstanding cellar. It was being given a real workout that night.

Miranda was surprised at how much Leila drank, although she didn't appear affected. Zara drank sparingly, but she clearly enjoyed the beautiful wines, as did Miranda. Neither young woman had any intention of matching Leila, or they would have slipped under the table.

The extraordinary thing was, the evening went

very well. Dalton Rylance, as host, was in excellent form, as was their hostess, and his clever, sophisticated son carried a good deal of the wide-ranging conversation. Indeed, Leila turned frequently to Corin, smiling, begging him to cap off some story. Family solidarity. Here was a stepmother everyone might long for. But to those who knew her she was playing a role for which any major actress would have taken home an Academy Award. Not once did Leila slip. She laughed. She talked. She revelled in her beauty, power and position of prestige. Such things were what she lived for. It was her destiny.

But beneath the façade Leila Rylance was stewing in a white-hot fury. Practised as she was in concealing her emotions, she was fighting hard to contain them. Now, of all times, the daughter she had given birth to all those years ago had appeared on the scene to *ruin* things. Her daughter's ability to catch her husband's eye was one thing. Nothing could possibly come of that. Dalton had always had an eye for a pretty woman. Only there had been a fleeting moment when she had intercepted a glance between Corin and Miranda.

A split second to a woman like Leila was all it took. It had turned her warm, glowing flesh to ice. Even her vision had darkened. Yet with a tremendous effort of will she'd managed to choke down the shocked gasp in her throat—but not the tidal wave of jealousy. She was forced to sit there, holding down her explosive feelings with all her strength.

Corin had had a number of affairs. They had never lasted. But, to her infinitely keen eye where Corin was concerned, she had accepted in a nano-second that he found Miranda, the daughter she had abandoned, powerfully attractive. She had seen desire in too many men's eyes not to be able to recognise the faintest glint. Corin wanted Miranda. Had he already had her? Of course he had. They were lovers, the devious little bitch. Though God knows didn't that prove Miranda was indeed her child? she thought bitterly. Both of them were born schemers.

With her obsessive mind-set she had convinced herself that one day Corin would surrender to the forbidden attraction between then. The day would come when he allowed himself to be lured into her bed. She lived for it. Her very nature had as its bedrock *sex*. Sex with Corin would be fabulous! It had to be experienced.

The young man Peter was simply a blind. He and Miranda were friends. No more. The young man loved her, of course, but Miranda simply treated him with affection. How different was the relationship between Corin and Miranda! She couldn't miss the depth of desire in Corin's brilliant dark eyes, the fleeting but profoundly revealing response from Miranda. Miranda was head over heels in love with him. Every bit as much in love with him as *she* was.

How had it all happened? When? What was the game they were playing?

She wouldn't tolerate it. It had to be stopped. No way could she allow the glittering life she had built up for herself to fall apart. If anyone was going to get hurt, it wouldn't be her. When the timing was ripe she would expose Miranda as a nasty little blackmailer. *She* had set up the whole thing. Used Corin and Zara for her own ends. It would have to be sooner rather than later. Dalton might be in sexual thrall to her now, but how long was that going to continue? She was in her prime. But even she couldn't hold back the hands of time. Her husband's passion for her would pass. Before that she had to save her own skin.

Corin had booked a limousine for the evening. They were to drop Peter off first, at the flat he shared with three other very promising students from the Royal College.

"She *knows*!" Peter grabbed the opportunity to whisper in Miranda's ear.

The limousine was sliding to a halt a few feet away, Corin and Zara were moving towards it, waiting for them to catch up.

"Knows what?" She spoke sharply, because she had already intuited the answer.

"About you and Corin. The fact you're in love. Tread carefully, Miri," he warned, kissing her cheek. "That's one dangerous woman, in my opinion. How the hell doesn't her husband know?"

"None so blind as those who refuse to see," Miranda answered, very sombrely. "Thank you for being so supportive, Peter. I love you dearly."

"Ditto!" said Peter, flashing her a sympathetic smile.

She and Corin might have Leila Rylance to contend with, but in his view Miranda and Corin would make a wonderful couple. Maybe it was time for him to work on his increasingly friendly relationship with Natalia, one of his flatmates. Natalia Barton was a brilliant young pianist. She had acted on several occasions as his accompanist, and a fine job she had done too. They were very much in harmony—as musicians and as people. Music was to be their lives.

CHAPTER SEVEN

WHEN the three of them arrived home, they all headed into the drawing room to go over the evening's events. Corin mixed himself a single malt Scotch and ice. Zara and Miranda settled for mineral water.

"Do you hate your mother for what she did to you, Miri?" Zara asked presently, setting down her glass on a little giltwood marble-topped table.

"I can't forgive her, Zara, but I don't hate her. I can't forgive her for the terrible hurt and worry she inflicted on my grandparents. She doesn't appear to have any remorse."

"God, no!" Corin agreed bluntly. "Leila doesn't trouble herself with such things. Everything begins and ends with her. She truly believes it was her destiny to have power and money. She must have dreamt about it, hungered after it from girlhood, determined she would get it."

"So what does she say about your father?" Zara asked in her lovely gentle voice.

Miranda's turquoise eyes glittered with inner disturbances. "That he was very young, like her. That she didn't even tell him she was pregnant. He never knew. Now it turns out he's dead," she added starkly. "A skiing accident in New Zealand."

Corin's black brows drew together as he felt a searing stab of hurt. "You could have told me."

"I wasn't hiding anything, Corin." Miranda turned to him quickly, seeing his reaction. "I wanted a little time to take it in myself. It also appears my paternal grandfather is a highly respected medical man."

"Now, why doesn't that surprise me?" he said. "It'll be easy enough now to trace your father's family. That's if you want to?"

"*Do* you want to, Miri, dear?" Zara asked, sadly aware a new tension had arisen between Miranda and her brother. One needn't wonder why. Leila had brought so much unhappiness on them all. Hadn't she felt the virulence in her stepmother all through the evening? The venom behind the practised charm? Miranda wasn't a long-lost daughter. Miranda was a challenger—the stand-in ready to oust the star.

"I don't know, Zara," Miranda confessed. "Leila said they wouldn't want to know me any more than they wanted to know her. It was my father's mother—*my grandmother*—that she spoke to. She was the one who gave Leila money. Some grand-mother!" she lamented. "How could she ignore *me*?"

Corin took her hand, soothing the palm with his thumb. "At that time the woman was thinking only of her son and the impact on his life. A lot of mothers are like that. He was very young. He had his whole life in front of him. She wouldn't have allowed him to be burdened with a pregnant girl-friend and a child. It's very possible she has deeply regretted her actions through the years. Especially as her son lost his life."

"So why didn't she try to find me?" Miranda asked, showing painful emotion.

"Maybe secrecy is her creed? Just like Leila." Corin struck a sombre note. "Don't upset yourself, Miranda. It will be easy enough to find out every-thing you need to know about your paternal grand-parents. Only then, I think, will you be in the position to decide what you want to do."

Zara went off to bed a short time later.

"So, what was Peter whispering about?" Corin asked.

Anxiety spiked. "He warned me that Leila *knows*."

"Peter doesn't miss much, does he?" Corin observed dryly, moving about to turn off lights.

"He's very observant. And to think I'd been con-centrating on not looking at you for over-long."

"Then Leila intercepted a glance. She has a

genius for that." He allowed his gaze to rest on her. "You look wonderful tonight. Small wonder Leila was flooded with jealousy. And you got Dad's attention. He was captivated."

"I don't think that worried Leila." She looked up at him as he stood above her. There was usually such pleasure in studying every aspect of his striking face—broad forehead, high cheekbones, sculpted chin, the brilliance of his dark eyes. Now she felt like a pinned butterfly, unable to withstand that dark scrutiny. She hadn't properly taken on board that Corin was already a powerful personality, and that power would only increase. Right at that moment she felt hopelessly outmatched. Yet she persisted. She needed to push for answers. "She's going with you to China. A lot can happen in a week."

"Like what?" He stared at her, his expression pure challenge.

Now she felt thoroughly flustered. Didn't reply.

"I thought we'd been over this, Miranda." His gaze eased. "What bothers you, exactly?"

Tell him.

"I have this premonition of trouble. So ominous! It makes me feel like I'm lost at sea. I don't know where all of this will ultimately lead. Leila is a powerfully sexual woman. She never stops trying. I'm frightened your father will suddenly whip off his blindfold and see what's been right in front of his eyes."

Corin started to circle the room like a big cat on the prowl. "Then he'll see I have no liking—let alone *love*—for Leila." Miranda's concern, the worry in her eyes, were driving him to strengthen his case. Only *what* case, for God's sake? He had done nothing wrong. But he knew he had to deal with Miranda's fears. She was handling an extraordinary situation remarkably well, but she was clearly in a state of crisis, trying hard to keep her feelings under control.

Leila, the mother she had never known, was suddenly on the scene. A *major* player. Leila, the stepmother for whom he and his sister felt only contempt, the woman who had deliberately gone about destroying his parents' marriage and ultimately their mother's life. He had long divined what was eating away at his father. It was *guilt*. With Zara, a constant reminder, fourteen thousand miles away, his father had been able to shuffle off the burden for much of the time. But many people outside family were still deeply troubled by the way his mother had died.

Miranda's voice brought him out of his tormented thoughts. "I hate liars," she said. "They're such dangerous people. Leila is not unlike a wild animal. If she's cornered, she'll lash out."

"Or move in for the kill." Corin spoke with a contemptuous rasp. "Leila is a stalker. There are women like that. Women who want vengeance for being scorned. Please let me deal with her. Don't forget she has a lot to hide."

"She does indeed," Miranda agreed, quietly intense. "I'm not forgetting anything, Corin. But neither of us can hide from the fact I came out of my mother's body. No matter how dark her journey through life, I don't want to hurt her. She's my *mother*. It's very strange how life works out. I'm not a vindictive person. My ambition is to be a healer. As for Leila, so much depends on just how long your father will remain captive to her. He is at the moment. So Leila could well concoct a story he might well fall for. She could claim I've threatened her with exposure. Demanded money from her. Blackmail, no less. She could be doing it right now for all we know."

He made a very impatient slicing movement with his hand. "Guesswork is tiring and unproductive. I don't like to see you so upset. Come down to the apartment now. I'm sick to death of hearing about Leila. You were so happy, so hopeful. I hate to see that change. No one is happy with Leila around, Miranda. Not even Dad. Our being separated even for a week doesn't sit easily with me," he confessed.

* * *

Corin closed the apartment door as if he was closing out the world. "If Leila is going to make some move she'll wait until the Beijing trip is over. I don't think it would be wrong to do some threatening myself." He shrugged out of his dinner jacket, undid the black tie. "It might even be a pleasure. Trying to make Dad see me as someone who desires her would be absolutely crazy, even for Leila. My father *knows* me. He knows better than anyone his children think Leila should burn in hell."

Miranda couldn't prevent a sick moan. "Burn in hell? She's my *mother*, Corin! I feel more pity for her than anger or a thirst for revenge." She went to stand in front of one of Zara's shimmering landscapes, hoping it would calm her. "Do you see anything of her in me?" she turned to ask.

The anguish in her beautiful sparkling eyes made Corin move with swift, unleashed power. He pulled her into a long kiss. Not gentle. A kiss of craving that contained a high degree of emotional frustration. "No, no, a thousand times *no*! I refuse to allow you to distance yourself from me with these worries," he muttered, his mouth still pressed against hers. "Leila erased you from her life. You must do the same to her. I have such *need* for you, Miranda. Can't you feel it? I can't *stand* to be apart. I want to bind you to me in marriage."

Marriage?

Shock left her momentarily speechless. For a minute she thought she was weightless. Ready to take wing. She all but lost her breath. Hot blood rushed to her face. She felt wildly elated, astonished, wanting to follow wherever he went yet fearful of the consequences. She put trembling fingers to his lips. "Corin, *no*!" she whispered, as though their futures were already in jeopardy. "You must think of the fall-out!" His was no ordinary family. Dalton Rylance was an industrial giant. Corin was his son and heir. Her heart was beating so fast she might have been running…running…running.

But Corin wanted to marry her! She wanted to give herself up to the ecstasy, but terror stripped it back.

"Do you love me or don't you?" He gripped her shoulders, very much the dominant male.

She heard the hard challenge in his tone. She took a deep breath. "You know I love you. It's just that I can't keep seem to keep up with all the shocks! I'm thrilled out of my mind you want to marry me. I'm honoured. But you must see better than I how talk of marriage right now might affect Leila? When it comes to you, I don't think she's quite sane."

"Ah, to hell with Leila!" he cried, near violently. "She might go after what she wants, but so do *I*. I want *you*."

"You have no *doubts*?" It was almost impossible to centre herself, so high was she soaring.

"None whatsoever!"

"When we know Leila is the enemy? One who will stop at nothing? She made her position very plain to me. If she is to suffer any consequences, she'll make sure we all do. She could hurt the people I love as a way of hurting me. There could be public scandal. A huge rift in the family. And what of your standing in Rylance Metals? Could that be undermined? We're dealing with a woman who would lie and lie and lie. The most outrageous lies are often believed. I believed all my life my grandparents were my parents."

A wave of anger for what had been done to *all* of them swept him. "Your grandparents were good people, doing everything they could to protect you. You had a happy, stable childhood. It shows. You might consider I'd suffer much more if I heeded your concerns about Leila. If secrets are to come out, let them. Hold them up to the light of day. There's nothing and no one who could make me give you up."

She felt like weeping at the depth of emotion in his face, in his voice. Love from Corin, when her mother was spitting hate. "Maybe it's best if I go home."

"Well, yes, I want you home," he confirmed strongly. "But of course Leila has the greatest chance of tracking our every movement there. Not that I care. We have to deal with her sooner or later. She might be crazy mad, but not mad enough to risk having her story come out. Dad isn't a man to privately let alone publicly humiliate. Leila could well get more than she bargained for."

"Would you like to unmask her?" She lifted her eyes to him, loving him with all her heart, but knowing Leila had caused a shift in the landscape.

"Yes," he said with certainty. "But I want *you* more than I could ever want to bring Leila unstuck. It's as Zara and I have told you. We abide by your decision. The fact that Leila is your mother is ir-remediable. We can't change it. We can work around it. She's not a fool. She's got very used to being rich. The houses, the clothes, the jewellery, the travel."

"So we lie to your father?" She broke gently away. She couldn't think clearly with his arms around her. "You want me to live a lie? I suppose I have to. I can imagine the effect on him if I told the truth. It could destroy their marriage!"

"Forgive me if I don't think it a tragedy," Corin said caustically, fuelled by frustration. He wanted Miranda desperately, yet knew she was withhold-ing some part of herself. "You can't have it both ways, Miranda. You can't protect your mother *and* not suffer some harm to yourself."

"But think what a huge target I'd make if we suddenly announced our engagement." Her turquoise eyes dominated her small face. "*Think* of it. You're a Rylance. Dalton Rylance's heir. The press would want to know everything about me. They'd send some hotshot reporter to check on me and my background."

He had given that situation plenty of consideration. If Leila overnight suddenly revealed she had been triumphantly reunited with her long-lost daughter, all hell would break loose.

"Corin, you *must* listen." Her eyes had been truly opened to her mother. She was chillingly self-centred.

He lifted a quelling hand. "Let me work it out, Miranda. There has to be a resolution. You don't want your mother brought to account. So be it. The press side of it can be handled. We have people whose job is to take care of that. No one has unearthed any story on Leila, for a start. Very likely my father saw to that. Any story can be killed if enough influence is brought to bear. My father is a very powerful man. You really don't know how powerful. He's an industrial giant. God knows what fairy tale Leila told him, but if he didn't entirely swallow it he certainly took care of it. I'll take care of this."

He gave her a little space of time, then he went to her, drawing her into his arms. "I think I'd die without you." He bent to kiss her, the touch of his mouth exquisitely tender.

She felt its imprint right through her body. He kissed her under the chin, along her neck, making every pulse jump and her eyes glisten with tears.

"Do you believe, as I do, there's only *one* person for us in life, Miranda?" He laid a tender hand on her breast. "*One* person out there for us to find. Some never manage it, no matter how hard they search for their soul mate. The *blessed* do. That's how I feel about you. You're my *one* person. We can and will marry. And no one will be allowed to stand in our way."

CHAPTER EIGHT

THE Peninsula Beijing was his father's five-star hotel of choice when in the great city on business. It boasted everything he wanted. Understated elegance, top-notch amenities and an English-speaking staff. To keep Leila happy there was a luxury shopping arcade where she could spend his money to her heart's content. His father never set a limit on her.

Queensland's vast mineral resources and its mining boom had earned mining magnates like his father enormous wealth. Dalton Rylance's total preoccupation was making money. Huge profits for Rylance Metals. Corin had been arguing strongly for some time now for the industry to tackle other issues that needed to be acted on. Like promoting a higher standard of living for their mining communities for a start. God knew, enough money was being generated. He had been speaking on an off to other members of the board, taking the issue right to them, and been gratified to learn they weren't turning a deaf ear like his father. Such a high level of prosperity demanded the big players like Rylance address problems within the industry. When his day came—hopefully before then—that would certainly be the case.

China was a monolith. A great power and a most highly valued trading partner. Their negotiations with one of its leading corporations had spun out for several additional days. There were difficulties, always difficulties, trying to arrange a "marriage", but finally they had an outcome that both parties could agree on. A significant mining investment in Rylance Bauxite would be made. A decision that had brought a hugely satisfied smile to his father's handsome face.

"Great idea of yours, son, learning Mandarin like our PM," he said proudly, punching Corin's shoulder. "By the way, Lee wants to take us in his private plane to the Anhui Provence. We haven't been there. The landscape is supposed to be magnificent—lots of scenic wonders Leila might enjoy. Great men were born in the province, I understand, and it's famous for its arts and crafts—that sort of thing. I'd like you to come. Liang wants you along as well. He's formed a very high regard for you."

"And me for him," Corin said sincerely. "I'll think about it, Dad."

"Do," Rylance urged. "Regular flights shuttle around, of course, but Lee loves piloting his own plane. He knows the whole province like the back of his hand. I'd like us all to enjoy it—and his hospitality."

Leila carried her burning rage with her to the ancient city. It was a rage that she had never experienced before. She had watched Corin sidestep any number of the suitable young women that inhabited his privileged circle. She had used to congratulate herself on how she had helped see them off. Now everything had changed.

Miranda had entered their lives. Miranda—her own daughter. The turn of events defied belief. She suddenly saw Corin, the object of her long-held sexual desire, being taken away from her. Her infatuation for him had never diminished. It had only grown stronger over the years. Corin had matured into the whole man: brilliant, stunning good looks, charm, impressing everyone who came his way. She hated the way she felt sometimes. Hated it. It was like being held in bondage. The very fact she was dealing with her own daughter demanded she show mercy, but she had to be a monster, because she couldn't manage a flicker. It was Miranda who had captured Corin's attention. Miranda who had come between her and her fatal obsession. Miranda needed punishing.

For some little time now she had felt Dalton's desire for her lessening. It had been *years*, after all. She counted on maintaining her beauty unimpaired until at least forty-two, forty-three. There were so many aids. But youth, unmatchable youth, never to be regained, was on her daughter's side. Miranda was exquisitely pretty. How ridiculous, then, was her ambition to become a doctor? That lofty profession was very much part of Jason's family.

There—she'd thought it. *Jason!* She had hardly given him a thought in twenty years, until that shocking night in London when she had turned around to see him reincarnated in his daughter. There were, after all, genes. It was to be expected. Miranda was so much like him, and his sister Roslyn. The resemblance was amazing. It had struck her dumb with fear.

Leila forced herself to take several deep breaths. Dalton was full of this trip to the Anhui Province. She was expected to go. They did everything together. And Dalton wanted Corin to accompany them. In many ways, Dalton idolised his son. He was enormously proud of him. When the time came Dalton was convinced Rylance Metals would be in safe hands.

Leila made a snap decision. She pivoted on her

stiletto heels, going to the door of the suite. Dalton had gone for drinks with a couple of his American cronies, also in Beijing on business. With any luck at all Corin might still be in his room. Only one way to find out. Pay him a visit.

Corin answered the light tap on the door, only to find Leila, of all people, hovering with every appearance of nervousness. That was a first.

"Dad's not here, Leila," he told her briskly. "That's if you've come to find him and not corner me? He's having a drink with Hank Gardner and his business partner."

"I know." She expelled a quick breath. "May I come in?"

Corin's smile was faintly twisted. "What? Aid and abet a designing woman? I'm sorry, Leila, I'm just about to go out. What is it you want, anyway?"

"It's about Miranda," she said, actress that she was, managing to force tears into her eyes. "I may have deserted her, but I do care about her, you know."

"Yeah, right! Give me a break, Leila!" Corin continued to mock, his sexual presence so strong, so exciting, she wanted to throw herself at him, be gathered up in his arms. His youth—he was not yet thirty—his devastating good looks and the enormous energy that radiated off him only underscored the fact her husband was ageing.

"Please, please, just let me inside for a moment," she pleaded. "We have to talk. Really it's for the best." She managed to push past him, hurrying into the room, where she settled herself in an armchair, pressing down on its sides because her hands were shaking so much. This was her last-ditch stand. "Are you serious about my daughter?"

"Your *daughter*?" Corin scoffed. "That's right—so she is. You've been a great mother, Leila. All that money you sent to help out. Well, listen, and listen up well. I'm madly, deeply and irrevocably in love with Miranda. I intend to marry her."

Leila reacted as if he had shot a deadly arrow that had hit its mark. "You *can't*." A look of extreme pain crossed her face. *Real* pain. He hadn't known she was capable of it. "I won't allow it."

"How can you possibly stop it?" He gave her a long, challenging look.

"I'll go to Dalton," she said, throwing up her burnished head. "I'll confess my past."

"What? Version Two? He might well ask how many versions there are. I know you enjoy your power over him, Leila, but do you really believe you can sell him another sob story?"

Leila glanced about wildly. "I know how to handle your father, Corin. Miranda may look like butter wouldn't melt in her mouth, but she's a born schemer. She went after you like I went after your father. She freely admitted it to me. Proud of it, actually. We're two of a kind, you see."

"Quite sure of that, are you?" Corin remained standing, looking down at her with a vestige of Miranda's pity.

"She wants ten million to go away," Leila announced with great intensity. "That's sterling, would you believe? I told her I couldn't possibly put my hands on an amount like that. She then started to talk increments. She was relishing her power over me, her own mother. She said she would go to Dalton and give him the true story. How I abandoned her and my parents. Left them to rear her. No word from me. Ever. I told her in return for the money she would have to give you up completely. I have to be able to trust her, you see."

"Takes one sinner to know another," he mocked.

"True." Leila's face brightened. "She's quite the little con-woman."

"Is she, now?" Corin gave her a hard stare. "Leila, *I'm* worth a great deal more than ten million in any currency. Wouldn't she do better sticking with me?"

"But she doesn't *love* you, my dear!" Leila's voice rose, verging on hysteria. The room was swimming before her eyes. "She told me. She used you. She's been planning her revenge all these years. She wants to ruin me. Surely you realise that? You have to trust me, Corin. I care too much about you to see you get hurt. You would have no future with Miranda. It wouldn't take you long to see her in a different light. She would repulse you. No, don't shake your head. You should have been there when she was talking to me. It was a revelation. She *enjoyed* seeing me suffer."

And there it was, he thought. What he hadn't considered. Leila *was* suffering as she had made others suffer. He could *almost* find it in his heart to feel sorry for her. Only there was his mother. And Zara. And her attack on Miranda. "Leila, the last thing Miranda wants is to see you suffer," he said, his expression grave. "You're far too self-centred, too self-absorbed to see that. Miranda is a creature of the light. She's beautiful, tender, capable of giving great joy. I'm going to marry her. You need to accept that."

But Leila couldn't accept it. She had allowed her obsession to grow and flourish. "I never will!" She shot to her feet, her tortured expression showing the full depth of her futile passion.

"Leila, you know you have to drop this matter," Corin said urgently. "For your own sake. I've seen Dad turn on people. It's like watching a guillotine come down. You must get over this stupid infatuation, whatever it is. I am *not* and never have been attracted to you. What we have to do now is get a handle on the whole situation. Miranda refuses to see your life destroyed. You're her *mother*. *Your* mother continued to care deeply about you to her dying day. Miranda is respecting her grandmother's wishes as well. She must have been a fine woman, your mother. She brought Miranda up beautifully."

"But you've got entirely the wrong idea of Miranda!" Leila cried fiercely, not to be swayed. "Revenge has dominated her life. I'll tell you this, Corin, and mark my words—I'll break up my own marriage before I let you marry Miranda." Her golden-brown eyes glittered with real tears. "You won't come out well over this. We both know your father's temper. The way it bubbles up in him, then explodes. He won't let his plans for you go by the board. He has his mind set on that Atwood girl. He would never accept Miranda. You could be doing yourself and your career great damage."

Corin shook his head. "I don't think so. But that's a risk I'm prepared to take. Nothing in this world will stop me. I love Miranda. I honour and respect her. I loved her from the moment I laid eyes on her. Which you should know was nearly four years ago. Miranda could have gone to my father then. She didn't. She came to me. She wants to be a doctor. She will be a doctor. She has what it takes. As for me, I'll be very happy to have a doctor in the family. You should know I'm going to track down her father's family. It's up to Miranda, of course, if she wants to make contact."

Leila's face turned ashen. "You fool! Men are such fools!" She rose, then stalked past him, head up, her bronze eyes filled with anger and loathing. "You may not believe me yet, Corin, but my daughter is playing you for all she's worth. It happens. I should know. I played your father."

"And you contributed to the death of my mother." Corin's voice was a whiplash across her back. "Get out, Leila. Do your worst. I assure you, it won't be half good enough."

It was just after ten in the morning London time when the news came through.

Australian mining magnate Dalton Rylance killed in a light airplane crash in China.

The newsflash posted on the Internet went on to report that Mr Rylance, his wife, Leila, and two other passengers, one believed to be Rylance's son Corin, had all been killed, along with the experienced pilot, the greatly respected Dr Lee Zhang, CEO of CMDC, a leading Chinese resource and development company.

Miranda was having coffee with Peter and his

friend Natalia when Zara texted a message for her to go home immediately, where she would soon join her.

"What's that all about?" Peter asked, his high forehead creasing with worry. "Must be serious for Zara to send you a message like that."

Miranda, who had been enjoying Natalia's account of her accompanying a budding young diva, suddenly lost all colour. For long moments she was panic stricken, with streams of images flowing through her mind. None of them good. "It must be something to do with the China trip."

Peter thought so too. "We'll come with you," he said instantly. "At least see you home."

"I'll fix this." Natalia pushed back her chair, ready to make her way into the coffee shop to pay the bill. "There could be other reasons, Miri." She tried to offer comfort.

"I don't think so," Miranda answered. "I know this isn't good."

"Wait until you speak to Zara," Peter advised. "You don't really have any idea."

"I'm so afraid I do, Peter." Miranda's small white face was very still.

Zara had already arrived back at the house when Miranda arrived. She opened the door to them, her beautiful face, like Miranda's, pale and stricken.

"No—oh, no!" Miranda tried to ward off what was surely coming. She stood on the top step as though petrified. Peter and Natalia were frozen behind her. Clearly the news was very bad indeed.

"Come in. Come in," Zara urged. Her slender figure was swaying. "You too, Peter, and your friend." She tried to smile at Natalia.

"What is it? What's happened?" Peter asked, aghast, keeping one eye on Miranda. She looked as if she was about to faint.

Zara didn't answer. She didn't have the strength. She beckoned them into the drawing room, where she gave them the news.

"Father has been killed in a light aircraft crash in Anhui Province in China," she told them, chilling them through. "A distinguished Chinese businessman was the pilot. Leila was with Father, as usual, and there were two other passengers. The plane came down in the hills. No survivors."

"God!" Peter blurted out, flinching with shock.

"But this is dreadful news!" Tears of sympathy sprang into Natalia's green eyes. "Miri?" she cried out in alarm. "Miri?"

Galvanised, Peter got an arm around Miranda before she hit the floor. He held her for a moment, then settled her into an armchair. "Put your head down, Miri. There's a good girl. Nat—" he appealed to his friend "—can you make us all tea? You can find the kitchen."

"Don't worry." Efficient in all things, Natalia moved off, controlling her own shock. Did this mean Zara's father, stepmother *and* her adored brother Corin had all been killed? It was too horrible to contemplate. Miranda looked as badly affected as Zara. Peter hadn't said much, but she had gained the impression Miranda and Corin Rylance had a strong connection. That had to be so.

An hour later Zara's mobile rang. They had stopped answering the incessant landline phone calls. It was always the press, avid for news and hopefully some comment from family on the other end.

"*Who?* Who is it?" There was a fearful catch in Miranda's voice. The shock was so violent even tears wouldn't come. Peter and Natalia, on call for rehearsal, had left some time earlier, still reeling with dismay, leaving the two distraught young women to try and comfort one another.

Under Miranda's stunned gaze, Zara's grief-stricken expression eased. She looked as though the worst had been averted. Faint colour returned to her cheeks. With her great dark eyes fixed on Miranda's face, she passed across her mobile.

And, with that, Miranda spoke to Corin.

* * *

Corin brought his father's and Leila's bodies home in a corporate jet, and they rested overnight in the Rylance family mansion.

The morning of the combined funerals dawned in glorious sunshine. A State funeral had been graciously declined by the family, although mourners dressed in black, with Dalton Rylance's colleagues all wearing black armbands, came from near and far to fill the cathedral to capacity, so it might as well have been. Everyone, right up to the State Premier, was filled with shock. The terrible suddenness of it all—the unexpectedness. Dalton Rylance had been only fifty-eight, a man in his prime, and his beautiful wife Leila some twenty years younger. They had been such a devoted couple. Dalton Rylance had strode the business scene like a colossus. No one had been prepared for it.

Such a tragedy! Now all eyes were on his son and heir, Corin, formidable in his iron-clad grief. His beautiful sister, Zara, back from London for the funeral and to be close to her beloved brother, stayed by his side. As did a young woman called Miranda Thornton, understood to be a Rylance Foundation recipient. Not a classic beauty, as was Zara Rylance, but immensely pretty. Neither Corin nor Zara Rylance did anything to hide their ease with her. Indeed, both appeared as though they were trying to protect her. She might well have been family.

It was something that alerted a lot of people. Indeed, many turned to stare after Miranda. She would be difficult to miss with her eye-catching head of silver-gilt curls.

Decisions, pressures and obligations came upon Corin from all directions. The responsibilities that accompanied being a Rylance. He scarcely had a minute to mourn.

Zara stayed on for a month, before she had to return to London to hand in her notice. There was no longer any need to live and work fourteen thousand miles away. She could come home. There was plenty for her to do. It was agreed she would wind up her affairs in London, then return.

Miranda elected to remain in Australia. Her mother's death had hit in her unexpected ways. The what *ifs?* Although at the same time she knew those "what ifs" would never have happened. Leila had taken what she had really wanted out of life. Not her daughter. Leila had craved the rich husband, the social prestige. She'd had it all for a while. Still, Miranda found herself grieving. Death was so final. No chance to work things out. She realised she *had* entertained a glimmer of hope.

Never mind, Miranda! that familiar voice said inside her head. *You were kind to her when other daughters mightn't have been. You chose to let Leila keep her secrets. She died with them.*

One increasing difficulty since the funeral was that the media had decided to take an interest in Miranda. Something she hadn't been looking for. It was worrying. Now she was linked to the Rylance family, they might start to concentrate their attention on her. What could they learn? She'd been born and raised on a small country farm. Her parents had been respectable community people. She had always been clever, an exceptional student. She had been awarded a scholarship by the Rylance Foundation to study for her Bachelor of Science degree, which she had attained with high distinction. In the year to come she was to take Medicine. Her ambition was clearly to become a doctor. Well, good doctors were desperately needed…

Harmless enough stuff surely? Only some reporters chasing a good story were unstoppable. That very morning, when she'd left Zara's riverside apartment where she was staying, it had been to find a member of the press camped outside.

"Staying in Miss Rylance's apartment, are you, love?" A cheeky-looking young man wearing a press badge swiftly closed in on her as she went to her small car, parked on the street.

"Is that any of your business?" She swung on

him, so frazzled she wanted to hit him with her handbag.

He held up his hands. "Be reasonable now, love. Only asking a simple question."

Miranda faced him, a warning sparkle in her eyes. "First of all, I am not your *love*. Zara Rylance is my friend. I'm looking after the apartment for her. Does that answer your question? You might step out my way. There are laws against harassment."

"Hang on. Hang on. Who's harassing you? I don't much care for that."

"And *I* don't much care for your hanging about outside," she responded sharply. "I'm nobody you could be interested in."

"Can't be a *nobody*, love, and a friend of the Rylances." He smirked. "Could Corin Rylance have an interest in you, by any chance?"

Miranda forced a peal of laughter. Never again would she be caught off guard. "You've got to be joking!"

The reporter pulled back. "You're saying he isn't?"

"I'm saying you're on the wrong track, pal." She managed another derisive laugh. "Bye, now!"

It might be wise for Corin to stay away from her altogether. He had more than enough to contend with. As always her first thought was for him.

* * *

Corin had left it late, using a different car from his own Mercedes and parking in Zara's double spot in the basement car park. No one was around. In the car park, or in the lift that took him to the penthouse level. There were two apartments. One belonged to a prominent businessman and his wife, well-known to the family and trusted, the other was Zara's. There were all sorts of problems he had to face, then somehow solve. Prioritising took precious time and there was more to come. A long-time member of the board had been so upset by the death of his father he had given notice of his retirement. That meant finding the right replacement. He had his eye on someone. Young, like himself, but with the intellect and the business acumen to take him far.

The weeks following the death of his father had been so labour intensive he'd scarcely had a minute to dwell on his grief. And grief it was. He had no idea, nor would he ever know, if Leila had carried out her threat to blacken Miranda's name and thus save her own. His father had appeared only mildly irritated by his decision not to join them on the Anhui Province trip, so he'd known nothing then. Corin prayed he never had. His father had failed him and Zara in many ways— certainly he had broken their adored mother's heart—but he had loved him and greatly admired his razor-sharp brain.

This current invasion of privacy was hard to take,

but it was one of the hazards of public life. Miranda had already told him she didn't want the media anywhere near her. He knew she feared her whole sorry story would come out, but he had his PR people controlling the flow of information. The last thing either of them wanted at this point was press speculation on a possible love affair. Worse, a love-nest. He couldn't bear the thought of Miranda being hounded. Anyone in the extended family who had raised doubts about his stepmother in the distant past had been told very firmly to keep their mouths shut. His grandparents *had* to know, but to his eternal relief after the first resounding shock they'd rallied. If there was a price to pay for Leila's deceptions they were united in their belief her abandoned daughter shouldn't have to pay it. Genealogy had to be put to one side.

His grandparents had met Miranda at the reception held at the house after the funeral. They'd had no idea of her true identity then. At the time they had confided they found themselves "quite taken" with Zara's little friend—indeed felt curiously protective of her. They didn't know exactly why. Miranda really was a child of light, Corin thought. His grandparents had had no difficulty seeing it. If anything, they were full of good will. Miranda might be Leila's daughter, but over and above that she was *herself*.

* * *

Corin moved Miranda into the living room before he took her in his arms. Every time he hugged her it was to realise she had lost weight. It wouldn't do for a featherweight like Miranda.

"I've a suggestion." He had lost much of his tension in one single kiss. "A friend of mine has a great hideaway on the Gold Coast. I can't send you to our place, obviously. You wouldn't have any peace or privacy. Dave and his wife are in Los Angeles at the moment. They'll be away for six months or so. They're more than happy to let you stay in their beach house. Secluded, a short walk to the beach."

Miranda turned up her face, her sombre mood lightened just with his presence. "Sounds good to me."

"You need the break."

"I do. Life is so fragile, isn't it? Sometimes it seems as though it's hanging by a mere thread. What would I have done, Corin, if you had gone on that fatal trip? The very thought is a terror."

He clasped her tighter. He had picked up on her depressed mood the instant he had walked through the door. She really did need to get away. "It's been an ordeal. That's why the beach house seems like the answer. Somewhere quiet and beautiful, tranquil, where you can shut down all the images that are passing through your head. I share those images. Both of us have lost a parent. It's a milestone in life. And this was a particularly bad way for them all to go. Dr Zhang was an experienced pilot, in apparent good health. No one could have foretold he would have a stroke at the controls."

"There's no total security anywhere," she said. "You can be in the wrong place at the wrong time. He would have survived had he been back in Beijing. They all would."

"No one can control fate, Miranda," he said gently. "Profound fears for the safety of our loved ones are part of life. Those fears, at least, we can and must control. You need peace and quiet. No one to bother you like they're starting to bother you here. You'll have the sun and sea, dazzling white sand. We have it all at our doorstep there. We've known its healing power since we were kids. It's a glorious spot. You can surf, go for long walks, read, drive up to Marina Mirage to shop. I'll call you every day. I'll come to you at the weekend. You look exhausted." Very gently he touched the mauve shadows beneath her beautiful eyes.

"Not sleeping," she confessed, pressing her mouth against his hand. "Not eating much either. Not hungry. First time ever. I've always had a good appetite. The accident killed it. And those horrendous moments when Zara and I thought you were on the plane too. Maybe we shouldn't love too much," she said in an unsteady voice. "To love is to risk losing. The more intense the love, the greater the risk. I never knew my mother, Corin, yet I'm mourning her. I'm mourning your father. The only way I can describe it is to say I feel…*hulled.*"

He pressed her silver-gilt head against his chest. "Oh, Miranda! If only I could go with you, but that isn't possible," he groaned.

"I know. I'm not asking."

He held up her chin. "You take too much on yourself. You can't carry your natural capacity for caring beyond certain boundaries. You'll have to do it when you're a doctor."

"I know! But such a lot has happened. Losing my grandparents—especially my grandmother—was a terrible experience. Then Leila and your father. What if I'd lost *you*?" Her voice broke in anguish.

"Well, you didn't. I'm here." He gathered her against his heart. She clung to him. His Miranda. He lowered his head to kiss her, this young woman he cherished. "Love you. Love you. Love you."

The fervent admission was deeply thrilling. Within moments all the sadness that had beset Miranda vanished like morning mist. Heat ran through her veins. Soon an overwhelming desire lapped them in a ring of fire. She was transported to another world, a world with only the two of them in it.

"I'm not going anywhere either," Corin muttered against her parted lips. "You're stuck with me."

She lay on the sofa, where he had carried her. He sat at her head, quite comfortable on the floor. Her hand was delicately tracing the outline of his face. "I love you so much it frightens me, Corin. I feel ashamed, too, for showing my weakness. I know the demands on your time. No demands are being made on me."

He made a little scoffing sound. "Carrying around multiple griefs is a demand. You've had a series of powerful shocks, Miranda. Dad's end was so sudden and violent we're all affected. Even the staff are traumatised. Everyone is walking around in a near trance. Dad always appeared indestructible. Now he's gone. Just like that! God knows, I'm finding it difficult to keep my mind ticking over."

"Of course. I'm sorry, Corin." She turned her head, bolstered by a few silk cushions, towards him. "Do you think she told him? That question haunts me."

"We've been over that, Miranda. The answer is *no*!" He spoke firmly, catching her fingers and holding them tight. No point whatever in dwelling on the possibility that Leila might have, he thought.

"It's hard coming to terms with death, isn't it?" she said very quietly.

Love for her pierced his heart. She had known too much sadness. He was going to change that. "We have one another now, Miranda. That means *everything*!"

"Everything to me too," she whispered, her voice very soft.

"I want Zara back home as soon as possible. She's given in her notice. Her colleagues are sorry to see her go, but they understand."

"She's coping," Miranda said, glad that was so. She and Zara were in frequent contact. "One loves one's parents even if they don't always treat us kindly. Why don't I get you a drink?" she asked with haste. She would have got him one long before this, but their lovemaking had taken precedence over all else. "I've got plenty of food in the fridge. Salmon fillets, scallops, fresh crab meat. Everything we need for a salad. I thought we could sit out on the balcony." Miranda sat upright, straightening her short, loose dress, a lovely water-colour print that tied on the shoulders like a little girl's dress. It was a style back in fashion.

She swung her legs to the floor. A beautiful breeze was blowing in from the balcony. She walked to the open sliding doors, looking out across the plant-filled area at the night-time glitter. City towers on the skyline, apartment blocks, wonderful old buildings, bridges that spanned the broad, deep river, the City Kats moving passengers smoothly from the inner suburbs to the city, rippling dark waters shot with multicoloured reflected light—blue, orange, red, gold and silver. The breeze coming off the water was as soft as a silk banner against her bare skin.

"I'm staying the night." Corin joined her, sliding his arms around her, his breath warm against her cheek.

"Marvellous!" She didn't think she would ever get enough of him. Her guardian angel must have been watching over her the day she met Corin.

His warm mouth burnished the tender skin of her nape.

"You don't think we should be cautious?" she asked very quietly, always concerned for him.

"Right now I'm beyond caution," he murmured. "I'm *passionate* for you. I can't let you go."

She spun in his arms. "You're not worried someone will spot you when you leave? You do rather stand out," she smiled. He was a *prince*!

"A small risk. I don't want to walk alone any more, Miranda," he said very seriously. "I need you with me. Every step of the way."

She wanted to cry. "Then that's a miracle, Corin." Her heart was in her eyes.

"A miracle that humbles me. Can I just say this—and I don't want you to be cross—?"

"Say whatever you want. Don't keep anything to yourself. No secrets. Not any more."

She swallowed on a little dry patch in her throat. He *had* to know. She had no choice. "I know you've tried to reassure me, but I can't help agonising over whether you're shoving my true identity to the back of your mind? You must give me a truthful answer, Corin. Do you think it possible it could surface over time?"

"Miranda!" He released her name on a long, agonised exhalation.

"Let me finish. Time brings changes. We both know that. You're taking me into *your* world. It's a vastly different world from the one I grew up in. We must be clear on this. I know you love me. Lord knows I love you. The magic of it has kept me safe. And sane, I should tell you. There has been a lot to handle. It's just that I can't help feeling—actually *knowing*—your life would be so much easier, less problematic, without me."

"Stop it, Miranda!"

"But it's eating at me. What if someone tracks me down? Don't they always say the truth will out?" She held his glittering, dark eyes. "You could be letting yourself in for a lot, Corin. It's a bizarre story—like something out of a movie—and we can't escape it."

He lifted a hand to silence her. "We can and we

will!" he said with great authority. "No more of this, Miranda. With you at my side, nothing is beyond me. I would want you whatever the cost. Surely you know that? At its worst what would it be? A nine-day wonder? If Leila left any tracks, Dad covered them. I can do the same. Besides, it's *me* you're worrying about, not yourself. I won't have it. You're everything in the world to me. There's no going back. There's only *forward*!"

He sounded so strong, so utterly sure of himself and *her*, and her own waning courage was restored. She wasn't physically like her mother. Her nature was very different. What more was there to know?

"Come to bed," Corin urged in a deep, desirous voice. "Just holding you in my arms is the most perfect feeling in the world." Gently he pulled at the ties on her shoulders. Her loose dress, a series of ruffles, landed gently in an iridescent pool at their feet.

"You're beautiful, so beautiful!" He cupped her breasts, letting the pads of his thumbs encircle the nipples.

The merest touch and she was aflame, her body flooding with sensation.

His voice had dropped to a deep, yearning pitch. "You're like some exquisite figurine wrought out of alabaster. You're more than I deserve, Miranda."

"No, that isn't so!" Such a tumult of emotion

rose inside her it was like a starburst. Against the catastrophe in their lives, they could set the miracle of their love.

It was the wheel of fortune in motion. If she hadn't found her mother she would never have found Corin. So in the end it was Leila who had brought Corin into her life. There was grace in that.

Her arms trembling, Miranda reached up to lock them around his neck. "I give myself into your hands completely," she said with such fervour it became a vow. "You are my love. My lover. My life!" It was the ultimate expression of trust. And with the giving came a hitherto unattainable *peace* and acceptance. Corin had made his choice in life. He wanted *her* for his wife. That was the greatest honour of all.

The radiance of her expression made Corin's breath catch in his throat. He swept her up into his arms, in that moment no mere man but a god, exultant. He stood for a moment, locking in the memory of her at that precise moment. Then he carried her down the hallway to the quiet of the master bedroom, where he would peel from her what single garment remained, spread her alabaster body on the bed, silver-gilt head against the pillows, before he sank onto her.

Kissing would pass to prolonged caresses... little whispered endearments to moans...soon the rapture would become too intense for them. It wasn't simply a matter of two people becoming physically one. It was an exchange of *souls*. Corin knew deep within himself he could surmount any and every problem that might confront them. It was the *future* that beckoned, luminous with light, rich with promise.

Life was a tapestry composed of many strands: love, loss, sorrow, happiness, success, failure. There was only one way to handle it—take up the tapestry with both hands. Miranda had given great depth to his existence. He considered himself truly blessed. No greater gift could a woman give to her man than her *heart*.

No one in this world would look after Miranda's tender heart better than he.

THE BRIDESMAID'S SECRET

BY
FIONA HARPER

MILLS & BOON

DID YOU PURCHASE THIS BOOK WITHOUT A COVER?

If you did, you should be aware it is **stolen property** as it was reported *unsold and destroyed* by a retailer. Neither the author nor the publisher has received any payment for this book.

All the characters in this book have no existence outside the imagination of the author, and have no relation whatsoever to anyone bearing the same name or names. They are not even distantly inspired by any individual known or unknown to the author, and all the incidents are pure invention.

All Rights Reserved including the right of reproduction in whole or in part in any form. This edition is published by arrangement with Harlequin Enterprises II BV/S.à.r.l. The text of this publication or any part thereof may not be reproduced or transmitted in any form or by any means, electronic or mechanical, including photocopying, recording, storage in an information retrieval system, or otherwise, without the written permission of the publisher.

This book is sold subject to the condition that it shall not, by way of trade or otherwise, be lent, resold, hired out or otherwise circulated without the prior consent of the publisher in any form of binding or cover other than that in which it is published and without a similar condition including this condition being imposed on the subsequent purchaser.

® and TM are trademarks owned and used by the trademark owner and/or its licensee. Trademarks marked with ® are registered with the United Kingdom Patent Office and/or the Office for Harmonisation in the Internal Market and in other countries.

First published in Great Britain 2010
Harlequin Mills & Boon Limited,
Eton House, 18-24 Paradise Road, Richmond, Surrey TW9 1SR

© Harlequin Books S.A. 2010

Special thanks and acknowledgement are given to Fiona Harper
for her contribution to The Brides of Bella Rosa series.

ISBN: 978 0 263 87678 9

Harlequin Mills & Boon policy is to use papers that are natural, renewable and recyclable products and made from wood grown in sustainable forests. The logging and manufacturing process conform to the legal environmental regulations of the country of origin.

Printed and bound in Spain
by Litografia Rosés, S.A., Barcelona

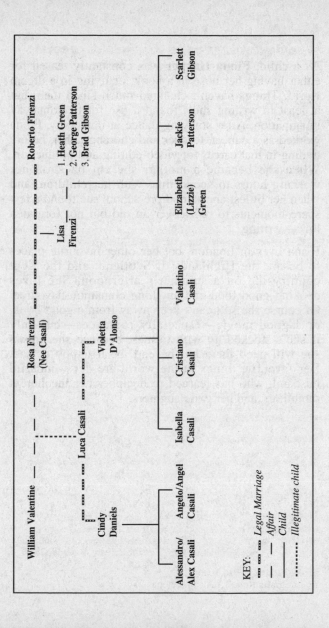

William Valentine — — — Rosa Firenzi
(Nee Casali)
‖
Luca Casali

Lisa
Firenzi

Roberto Firenzi

Cindy
Daniels

Violetta
D'Alonso

Elizabeth
(Lizzie)
Green

1. Heath Green
2. George Patterson
3. Brad Gibson

Alessandro/
Alex Casali

Angelo/Angel
Casali

Isabella
Casali

Cristiano
Casali

Valentino
Casali

Elizabeth
(Lizzie)
Green

Jackie
Patterson

Scarlett
Gibson

KEY:
— — — — *Legal Marriage*
— — *Affair*
———— *Child*
·········· *Illegitimate child*

As a child, **Fiona Harper** was constantly teased for either having her nose in a book, or living in a dream world. Things haven't changed much since then, but at least in writing she's found a use for her runaway imagination. After studying dance at university, Fiona worked as a dancer, teacher and choreographer, before trading in that career for video-editing and production. When she became a mother she cut back on her working hours to spend time with her children, and when her littlest one started pre-school she found a few spare moments to rediscover an old but not forgotten love—writing.

Fiona lives in London, but her other favourite places to be are the Highlands of Scotland, and the Kent countryside on a summer's afternoon. She loves cooking good food and anything cinnamon-flavoured. Of course she still can't keep away from a good book, or a good movie—especially romances—but only if she's stocked up with tissues, because she knows she will need them by the end, be it happy or sad. Her favourite things in the world are her wonderful husband, who has learned to decipher her incoherent ramblings, and her two daughters.

PROLOGUE

No one else must see the contents of this letter, Scarlett! Give it only to Romano.

Her older sister's words echoed through her head as Scarlett ran through the woods on the outskirts of Monta Correnti, her long dark hair trailing behind her. Jackie would be cross if she knew Scarlett had peeked at the sheets of the scrawled, tear-stained writing, but one corner of the envelope flap had been a little loose and it had been too tempting.

Before she went to the piazza to find Romano and give it to him, she had to show Isabella, her cousin and partner in crime. This was way too big a secret to keep to herself. Although she and Isabella were both the same age, Isabella was the eldest in her family and always seemed to know what to do, how to take charge when anyone needed her.

It was totally different in Scarlett's family. She was the youngest of the three sisters. The one who

was always left out of important discussions
because she 'wouldn't understand'. She was fed up
with it. Just because Jackie was four years older
she thought it was okay to boss Scarlett around and
make her do her errands, which wasn't fair. So just
this once Scarlett was going to do things her way,
to *make* it fair.

There were too many hushed voices and whispered insults in her family already, and no one
would tell her why.

She was heading for a small clearing with a
stream running through it at the bottom of the hill.
No one else knew about this spot. It was her and
Isabella's secret. They would come here to talk
girl-type stuff, when Isabella could get away from
looking after her nosey little brothers. They would
build camps out of branches and leaves, and make
up secret codes and write in their diaries—which
they always let each other read. Sometimes they
would whisper about Romano Puccini, the best-
looking boy in the whole of Monta Correnti.

That was another thing that wasn't fair!

Just as Scarlett had decided she was old enough to
notice boys and develop her first crush, Jackie had got
in there first—as always. Jackie had been seeing
Romano for weeks and weeks! Behind Mamma's
back as well. Just wait until Isabella found out!

Scarlett's breaths were coming in light gasps

now and the small sigh she let out was hardly noticeable. So Romano only had eyes for bossy old Jackie! Scarlett hated her for it. At least she did when she remembered to.

A flash of pink sundress through the trees told Scarlett that Isabella was in the clearing already. They'd whispered their plans to meet earlier, in the piazza outside their parents' restaurants.

As Scarlett burst into the clearing Isabella looked up. Her raised eyebrows said it all. *What are you in a flap about this time, Scarlett?*

Scarlett just slowed to a walk and held the letter out to Isabella, her arm rigid.

Isabella shrugged as she took the envelope and pulled three sheets of paper out of it. But she wasn't sitting and shrugging and rolling her eyes at Scarlett for long. Once she'd read the first page she was on her feet and joining in the *flapping*.

After all the exclamations, they stood and stared at each other, guilty smiles on their lips.

'Oh, my goodness!' Isabella finally whispered. 'Jackie and Romano! Really?'

This was the reaction Scarlett had been hoping for. She nodded. She'd hardly believed it herself when she'd read all that mushy stuff Jackie had written to Romano! Okay, some of it hadn't exactly made sense, but she'd got the general gist. She nodded to Isabella to keep reading.

Isabella didn't need much encouragement. She quietened down and carried on, stopping every now and then to ask Scarlett to decipher her sister's handwriting.

When she'd finished she looked up. This time there were no guilty smiles. There was no *flapping*. The look on Isabella's face wiped away the giddiness Scarlett had been experiencing and the spinning feeling moved swiftly to her stomach.

'What are you going to do?' Isabella asked.

Scarlett frowned. 'Give the letter to Romano, of course.'

Isabella shook her head. 'You can't do that. You need to show this to Aunt Lisa!'

A noise of disbelief forced its way out of Scarlett's lips. 'Do you *know* what Mamma will do if she finds out? Jackie will be in *so* much trouble!'

Isabella looked at the sheets of paper between her fingers, now looking less than pristine and just a little crumpled. 'It's too big a secret.' The letter made a crinkling noise as she tightened her grip.

Scarlett suddenly had a nasty feeling about this. Isabella wouldn't, would she? She wouldn't take the letter to Mamma herself? But then she saw the glint of determination in her cousin's eyes and knew that Isabella just might take the matter into her own hands.

If that happened, not only would Jackie suffer

their mother's wrath, but Scarlett would be in big trouble herself. Jackie had a temper every bit as fiery as Mamma's. Scarlett snatched for the letter.

Isabella was fast, though, too used to dealing with a pair of rambunctious younger brothers to be caught off guard, and Scarlett only managed to get a grip on one bit of paper. They pulled at either end of the sheet. Isabella was shouting that Scarlett needed to let go, because she wasn't going to tell. Just as the words were starting to make sense to Scarlett, as the page was on the verge of ripping in two, Isabella released it. The sheets of pink writing paper and matching envelope flew into the air.

Both girls froze and watched them flutter slowly towards the ground.

Just before it landed in the dirt, one wayward sheet decided to catch its freedom on a gust of air. It started to lift, to twirl, to spin. Suddenly Scarlett was moving, jumping, reaching, trying to snatch it back, but it always seemed to dance out of her fingers just as she was about to get a hold of it.

Now Isabella had finished collecting up the rest of the paper, she was trying to get it too. The wind heaved a sigh and the piece of paper fluttered tantalisingly close. Scarlett jumped for it. Her fingers closed around it.

But then Isabella collided with her and she found herself crashing onto the damp earth of the stream bank. She hit the ground hard and every last bit of air evacuated from her lungs, and she momentarily lost the ability to control her muscles. The page saw its chance and eased itself out of her hand and into the waiting stream.

Isabella started to cry, but all Scarlett could do was watch it float away, the ink turning the paper a watery blue, before it disappeared beneath the surface.

She pulled herself up and brushed the dirt off her front. 'Stop it!' she yelled at Isabella, who was sobbing. And before she could dampen the rest of the pages with her silly crying, Scarlett pulled them from Isabella's fist and tried to smooth them out.

'Page three is missing! Page three!' She glanced back towards the stream, her face alive with panic.

Oh, why couldn't it have been page two, with all the love-struck gushing and rambling? Romano would never have noticed. But it had been page three—the one with the *really* big secret.

'What are we going to do?' Isabella said quietly, dragging a hand over her eyes to dry her tears. More threatened to fall, but she sniffed them away.

Scarlett shook her head. 'I don't know.'

The icy fear that had been solidifying her limbs suddenly melted into something much warmer, much hotter.

This was all Jackie's fault! Why couldn't she have taken the letter to Romano herself? Why had she involved her baby sister in the first place? Didn't she know that was a stupid thing to do? According to everyone else, Scarlett couldn't be trusted with anything!

She turned to Isabella, her mouth pulled thin. 'We can't give the letter to Romano like this.' Jackie would just have to do her own dirty work and talk to him herself. 'And Jackie will kill me if I tell her what I did. There's only one thing we can do.'

Isabella started to sniff again, mumbling something about it all being her fault, but Scarlett wasn't listening; she was staring at the gurgling waters of the stream.

Slowly, she walked back to the very edge of the bank. Between thumb and forefinger, she lifted another page high and then, in a very deliberate motion of her fingers, let it go. Another page followed, then the envelope. It seemed an almost solemn procedure, as if she were scattering dirt on a coffin. Thick, funereal silence hovered in the air around them as they held their breath and watched Jackie's secret float downstream.

No one else must see the contents of this letter, Scarlett.

Now no one ever would.

CHAPTER ONE

THE air conditioning of the limo was functioning perfectly, but as Jackie stared out of the tinted window at the rolling hills, at the vineyards and citrus groves, she could almost feel the sun warming her forearms. It was an illusion. But she was big on illusions, so she let it slide and just enjoyed the experience.

The whole process of coming home would also be an illusion. There would be loud exclamations, bear hugs, family dinners where no one could get a word in—not that it would stop anyone trying—but underneath there would be a wariness. There always was. Even the siblings and cousins who didn't know her secret somehow picked up on the atmosphere and joined in, letting her keep them at arm's length.

They became her co-conspirators as she tried to deny her Italian side and laced herself up tight in Britishness—the one thing her father had given her that she treasured. She had learned how to shore herself up and keep herself together, but then Jackie always excelled at everything she did, and this was no exception.

She hadn't called ahead to let the family know what time she was arriving. A limousine and her own company were preferable at present. She needed time to collect herself before she faced them all again.

It had been a couple of years since she'd been home to Monta Correnti. And when she did come these days, it was always in the winter. The summers were too glorious here, too full of memories she couldn't afford to revisit. But then her older sister had chosen a weekend in May for her wedding celebrations, and Jackie hadn't had much choice. It seemed she hadn't been able to outrun the tug of a big Italian family after all, even though she'd tried very, very hard.

She turned away from the scenery—the golds and olives, the almost painful blue of the sky—and picked up a magazine from the leather seat beside her. It was the latest issue from *Gloss!* magazine's main rival. Her lips curved in triumph as she noted that her editorial team had done a much better job of covering the season's latest trends. But that was what she paid them for. She expected nothing less. The main fashion caught her attention.

Puccini—one of Italy's top labels. But she hadn't needed to read the heading to recognise the style. The fashion house had gone from strength to strength since Rafael Puccini had handed the design department over to his son.

With such a man at the helm, you'd expect the menswear to outshine the women's collections, but it wasn't the case. Romano Puccini understood women's bodies so well that he created the most exquisite clothes for them. Elegant, sensuous, stylish. Although she'd resisted buying one of his creations for years, she'd succumbed last summer, and the dress now hung guiltily in the back of her wardrobe. She'd worn it only once, and in it she'd felt sexy, powerful and feminine.

Maybe that was why the house of Puccini was so successful, why women stampeded the boutiques to own one of their dresses. Good looks and bucket-loads of charm aside, Romano Puccini knew how to make each and every woman feel as if she were as essentially female as Botticelli's *Venus*. Of course, that too was an illusion. And Jackie knew that better than most.

She frowned, then instantly relaxed her forehead. She hadn't given in to the lure of Botox yet, but there was no point making matters worse. Although she was at the top of her game, Editor-in-chief of London's top fashion magazine, she was confronted daily by women who wore the youthful, fresh-faced glow that she'd been forced to abandon early. Working and living in that environment would make any woman over the age of twenty-two paranoid.

Her mobile phone rang and, glad of the distraction, she reached into her large soft leather bag to answer it. The name on the caller ID gave her an unwanted spike of adrenaline. Surely she should be used to seeing that name there by now?

'Hello, Kate.'

'Hey, Jacqueline.'

Her own name jarred in her ears. It sounded wrong, but she hadn't earned the title of 'mother' from this young woman yet. Maybe she never would.

'Is there something I can help you with?'

There was a pause. A loaded sixteen-year-old pause.

'Are you *there*? In Italy?'

Jackie's gaze returned to the view beyond the tinted windows. It whipped past silently, the insulation of the limousine blocking out any noise from outside. 'Yes. I left the airport about twenty minutes ago.'

There was a sigh—which managed to be both wistful and accusatory—on the other end of the line. 'I wish I could have come with you.'

'I know. I wish you could have too. But this

situation…telling my family…it needs some careful handling.'

'They're my family too.'

Jackie closed her eyes. 'I know. But it's complicated. You don't know them—'

'No, I don't. And that's not my fault, is it?'

Jackie didn't miss Kate's silent implication. Yes, it was her fault. She knew that. Had always known that. But that wasn't going to help calm her mother down when she announced that the child she'd handed over for adoption sixteen years ago had recently sought her out, that she'd been secretly meeting with that daughter in London for the last few months—especially when it had been her mother's iron insistence that no one else in the family should ever know. To a woman like Lisa Firenzi, image was everything. And a pregnant teenage daughter who'd refused to name the father of her baby didn't fit in the glossy brochure that was her life.

Jackie hadn't even been as old as Kate when it had happened. Back then, every day when she'd come down the stairs for breakfast, her mother had scrutinised her profile. When she hadn't been able to disguise the growing swell of her stomach with baggy T-shirts, she'd been quietly sent away.

She'd arrived in London one wet November evening, a shivering fifteen-year-old, feeling lost and alone. The family had been told she'd gone to stay with her father, which was true. He'd been husband number two. Lisa had managed to devour and spit out another husband and quite a few lovers since then.

So, not only had Jackie to reconcile her mother to the fact that the dirty family secret she'd tried to hide was now out in the open, but she had to break the news to her uncle and cousins—even Lizzie and Scarlett, her sisters, didn't know. She was going to have to handle the situation very, very carefully.

Lizzie's wedding would be the first time she and all her sisters and cousins had been together in years and she couldn't gazump her sister's big day by turning up with a mystery daughter in tow, and it wouldn't have been fair to drop Kate into the boiling pot of her family's reactions either. Jackie had absolutely no idea how they were going to take the news and the last thing her fragile daughter needed was another heap of rejection.

She drew in a breath through her nostrils, the way her Pilates instructor had taught her. 'I know, Kate. And I'm sorry. Maybe next time.'

The silence between them soured.

'You're ashamed of me, aren't you?'

Jackie sat bolt upright in the back seat. 'No!'

'Well, then, why won't you let me meet my uncles and aunts, my cousins—my grandmother?'

There was no shyness about this girl. She was hot-headed, impulsive, full of self-righteous anger. Very much as her biological mother had been as a teenager. And that very same attitude had landed her into a whole heap of trouble.

'Family things…they're difficult, you know…'

A soft snort in her ear told Jackie that Kate didn't know. That she didn't even *want* to know. Jackie only had one card left to play and she hoped it worked.

'Remember how you told me your mum—' Your mum. Oh, how that phrase was difficult to get out '—found it difficult when you told her you wanted to find your biological mother, even though you weren't eighteen yet? It was hard to tell her, wasn't it? Because you didn't want to hurt her, but at the same time it was something you needed to do.'

'Yes.' The voice was quieter now, slightly shaky.

'You're just going to have to trust me—' Sweetheart. She wanted to say *'sweetheart'* '—Kate. This is something I need to do first. And then you can come on a visit and meet everyone, I promise.'

Just like every other girl of her age, Kate was rushing at life, her head full of the possibilities ahead of her, possibilities that dangled like bright shiny stars hung on strings from the heavens. They tempted, called. If only she could make Kate see how dangerous those sparkly things were…how deceptive.

Something in her tone must have placated her newly found daughter, because Kate sounded resigned rather than angry when she rang off. Jackie slid her phone closed and sank back into the padded leather seat, exhausted.

She hadn't realised how hard the reunion would be, even though she'd been waiting for it since she'd put her name on the adoption register when she'd been twenty. When she'd got the first call she'd been overjoyed, but terror had quickly followed. She and Kate had had a tearful and awkward first meeting under the watchful eye of her adoptive mother, Sue.

Kate had been slightly overawed by Jackie's high-fashion wardrobe and sleek sports car. Sue had taken Jackie aside after a few weeks and warned her that Kate was dazzled by the fact her 'real' mum was Jacqueline Patterson, style icon and fashion goddess. *Don't you dare let her down,* Sue's eyes had said as she'd poured the tea and motioned for Jackie to sit at her weathered kitchen table.

Jackie was doing her best, but she wasn't convinced she could make this work, that she and Kate could settle into a semblance of a mother-daughter relationship. They'd gone through a sort of honeymoon period for the first month or two, but now questions and emotions from the past were starting to surface and not everything that was rising to the top was as glossy and pretty as Jackie normally liked things to be.

Once she told her mother, Kate's grandmother,

the cat would be out of the bag and there would be no going back. But Jackie had no other option. She wanted…*needed*…to have her daughter back in her life, and she was going to do whatever it took to make a comfortable space for her, no matter how hard the fallout landed.

The limo swung round a bend in the road and Jackie held her breath. There was Monta Correnti in the distance, a stunningly beautiful little town with a square church steeple and patchwork of ter-racotta tiled roofs seemingly clinging to the steep hillside. It was currently a 'hot' holiday destination for Europe's rich and notorious, but it had once been Jackie's home. Her only *real* home. A place filled with memories, yellow and faded like old family photographs.

Before they reached the town centre, the limo branched off to the left, heading up a tree-lined road to the brow of the hill that was close enough to look down its nose on the town but not near enough to feel neighbourly.

The road to her mother's villa.

Jackie tided the magazines on the back seat, made sure everything she needed was in her handbag and pulled herself up straight as the car eased through gates more suited to a maximum-security prison than a family home.

* * *

Romano opened the tall windows of his drawing room and stepped onto the garden terrace. It all looked perfect. It always looked perfect. That pleased him. He liked simple lines, clean shapes. He wasn't a man who relished anything complicated or fussy. Of course, he knew that perfection came at a cost. None of this happened by accident.

In his absence, the low hedges of the parterre had been clipped by an army of gardeners, the gravel paths raked and smoothed until they were perfectly flat and unsullied by footprints. The flowers in the vast stone urns had been lovingly weeded and watered. And the attention hadn't been confined to the garden. Every inch of the Puccini family's old summer home was free from dust. Every window and polished surface gleamed. It was the perfect place to retreat from the grime and noise of Rome in the summer months. And Romano enjoyed it so much here he'd recently decided to keep it as his main residence, even in winter, when Lake Adrina was filled with waves of polished pewter and the wind was less than gentle.

Palazzo Raverno was unique, built by an ostentatious count in the eighteenth century on a small island, shaped like a long drawn-out teardrop. On the wider end of the island Count Raverno had spared no expense in erecting a Neo-gothic

Venetian palace, all high arches and ornate masonry in contrasting pink and white stone. It should have looked ridiculously out of place on a tranquil wooded island in the middle of a lake— but somehow the icing-sugar crispness of the house just made it a well-placed adornment to the island. From what he knew of the infamous count, Romano suspected this had been more by accident than design.

And if the palazzo was spectacular, the gardens took one's breath away. Closer to the house the gardens were formal, with intricate topiary and symmetrical beds, but as they rolled away to the shore and reached to the thin end of the island they gave the impression of a natural Eden.

Romano could resist it no longer. His wandering became striding and he soon found himself walking down the shady paths, stopping to listen to the soft music of the gurgling waterfall that sprang out of a rockery. He didn't plan a route, just let his feet take him where they wanted, and it wasn't long before he arrived in the sunken garden.

The breeze was deliciously cool here, lifting the fringes of the drooping ferns. Everything was green, from the vibrant shades of the tropical plants and the dark glossiness of the ivy, to the subtle sponginess of the moss on the walls of the grotto.

It was all so unbearably romantic. The island was the perfect place for a wedding.

Not his wedding, of course. He smiled at the thought. Nobody would ever be foolish enough to think the day would come when he'd pledge his body and soul to one woman for eternity.

A month or two, maybe.

He sighed as he left the leafy seclusion of the sunken garden and walked into the fragrant sunshine of a neatly clipped lawn. From here he climbed a succession of terraces as he made his way back towards the house. The days when this island had been a playground for the idle rich were long gone. He had work to do.

However, he was whistling when he headed into the ground-floor room he'd converted into a studio to collect the paperwork for his afternoon appointment. When a man had a job that involved dressing and undressing beautiful women, he couldn't really complain, could he?

Before Jackie's stiletto-heeled foot could make contact with the driveway, her mother flew out of the front door and rushed towards her, her arms flung wide.

'Jackie! There you are!'

Jackie's eyes widened behind her rather huge and rather fashionable sunglasses. What on earth was going on? Her mother never greeted her like this. It was as if she were actually overjoyed to see—

'You're late!' Her mother stopped ten feet shy of the limo and her fists came to rest on her hips, making the jacket of her Chanel suit bunch up in a most unappealing manner.

This was more the reception Jackie had been anticipating.

Her mother looked her up and down. Something Jackie didn't mind at all now she knew her mother could find no fault with her appearance, but once upon a time it had sent a shiver up her spine.

'I don't believe I mentioned what time I—'

'The other girls arrived over an hour ago,' her mother said before giving her a spiky little peck on the cheek, then hooking an arm in hers and propelling Jackie inside the large double doors of the villa.

What girls?

Jackie decided there was no point in reminding Mamma that she hadn't actually specified a time of arrival, only a date. Her mother was a woman of expectations, and heaven help the poor soul who actually suggested she deviate from her catalogue of fixed and rigid ideas. Jackie had come to terms with the fact that, even though she was the toast of London, in the labyrinthine recesses of Lisa Firenzi's mind her middle daughter was the specimen on a dark and dusty shelf whose label read: Problem Child.

Although Jackie hadn't seen her mother in almost a year, she looked the same as always. She still oozed the style and natural chic that had made her a top model in her day. She was wearing an updated version of the classic suit she'd had last season, and her black hair was in the same neat pleat at the back of her head.

The excited female chatter coming from her mother's bedroom and dressing room alternated between Italian and English with frightening speed. Three women, all in various states of undress, were twittering and cooing over some of the most exquisite bridal wear that Jackie had ever seen. In fact, they were so absorbed in helping the bride-to-be into her wedding dress that they didn't even notice Jackie standing there.

Lizzie, who was half in, half out of the bodice, looked up and spotted her first, and all at once she was waddling across the room in a mound of white satin. She pulled Jackie into a tight hug.

'Your sister finally deigned to arrive for the dress fitting.'

Jackie closed her eyes and ignored her mother's voice. Dress fitting? Oh, that was what Mamma had her knickers in a twist about. She needn't have worried. Jackie had sent her measurements over by email a couple of weeks ago and she knew her rigorous fitness regime would not have allowed for even a millimetre of variation.

'We all know Jackie operates in her own time zone these days, don't we?'

Ah. So that was it. Mamma was still irritated that she hadn't fallen in with her plans and arrived yesterday. But there had been a very important show she'd needed to attend in Paris, which she couldn't afford to miss. Her mother of all people should understand how cut-throat the fashion industry was. One minor stumble and a thousand knives would be ready to welcome her back as a sheath.

She wanted to turn round, to tell her mother to mind her own business, but this was neither the time nor the place. She wasn't about to do anything to spoil the frivolity of her sister's wedding preparations. She squeezed Lizzie back, gently, softly.

'It's been too long, Lizzie!' she said in a hoarse voice.

As she pulled away she tried to file her mother's remark away in her memory banks with all the others, but the words left a sting inside her.

'Here, let me help you with this.' She pulled away from Lizzie and walked round her so she could help with the row of covered buttons at the back. The dress was empire line, gently complementing Lizzie's growing pregnant silhouette. And true to form, the bride was positively glowing, whether that was the effect of carrying double the amount of hormones from the twins inside her or because she was wildly in love with the groom Jackie had yet to meet, she wasn't sure. Whatever it was, Lizzie looked happier and more relaxed than she'd ever been. If it was down to Jack Lewis, he'd better know how to keep it up, because Jackie would have his hide if he didn't.

'Thanks. I knew there was a reason why we had a fashion expert in the family,' Lizzie said, smiling as she pulled her long dark hair out of the way.

Jackie concentrated on the row of tiny silk-covered buttons that seemed to go on for ever. 'This dress is exquisite,' she said as she reached the last few. Which was amazing, since it had to have been made in mere weeks.

Jackie stood back and admired her sister. Getting a dress to not only fit somebody perfectly, but complement their personality was something that even cold, hard cash couldn't buy, unless you were in the hands of a true artist.

Isabella and Scarlett came close to inspect the dress and mutter their appreciation. Jackie turned, a smile of utter serenity on her face, and prepared herself to greet her fellow bridesmaids.

Isabella first. They kissed lightly on both cheeks and Isabella rubbed her shoulder gently with her hand as they traded pleasantries. Jackie kept her smile in place as she turned to face her younger sister. They kissed without actually making contact and made a pretence of an embrace.

She and Scarlett had been so close once, especially after Lizzie had gone to university in Australia, when it had just been the two of them and she'd felt like a proper big sister rather than just Lizzie's deputy. She'd even thought vainly that Scarlett might have hero-worshipped her a little bit.

But that had all changed the summer she'd got pregnant with Kate. Scarlett had never looked at her the same way again. And why should she have? Some role model Jackie had been. Who would want to emulate the disaster area that had been her life back then—Jackie in tears most of the day, Mamma alternating between ranting and giving her the ice-queen treatment?

Not long after that Scarlett had moved away too. She'd followed in Lizzie's footsteps and flown halfway round the world to live with her father. They'd never had a chance to patch things up, for Jackie to say how sorry she was to make Scarlett so ashamed of her. No more late-night secret-sharing sessions. No more raiding the kitchen at Sorella, one of them rifling through the giant stainless-steel fridge for chocolate cake, one of them keeping guard in case the chef spotted them.

Now they talked as little as possible and met in person even less. Jackie released Scarlett from the awkward hug and took a good look at her. They hadn't laid eyes on each other in more than five years. Scarlett hadn't changed much, except for looking a little bit older and even more like their mother. She had the same hint of iron behind her eyes these days, but the generous twist of the mouth Jackie recognised from their childhood tempered it a little.

Of course, Lizzie was far too excited to notice the undercurrents flowing around amidst the tulle and taffeta.

'Come on, girls! You next. I want to see how fabulous my bridesmaids are going to look.'

Scarlett and Isabella had already removed their dresses from their garment bags. They were every bit as stunning as Lizzie's. She'd been told that all three dresses would be the same shade of dusky aubergine, but she hadn't realised that they would vary in style and cut.

Isabella's was classic and feminine, with a gathered upper bodice, tiny spaghetti straps and a bow under the bustline, where the empire-line skirt fell away. Scarlett's was edgier, with a nineteen-thirties feel—devoid of frills and with a deep V in the front.

Jackie appointed herself as wardrobe mistress

and zipped, buttoned and laced wherever help was needed. When she'd finished, Isabella handed her a garment bag.

Jackie hesitated before she took the bag from her cousin. It had been a bad idea to help the others get dressed. Now they had nothing else to do but watch her strip off. She clutched the bag to her chest and looked for the nearest corner. Isabella and Scarlett just stood there, waiting.

Then she felt the bag being tugged gently from between her fingers. 'Why don't you use Mamma's dressing room?' Lizzie said as she relieved Jackie of the bag and led her towards a door on the other side of the room. 'You can freshen up a little from your flight, if you need to.'

Jackie sent her sister a grateful look and did exactly that.

Lizzie had been the only one she'd confided in about her body issues. It had started not long after she'd given Kate away. At first, eating less and exercising had been about getting her shape back before she returned to Italy, removing all evidence that her body had been stretched and changed irrevocably. Mamma had been pleased when she'd met her off the plane, had complimented her on her self-discipline. But back in Italy she'd been confronted with the sheer pleasure of food, the sensuality of how people ate, and she'd shied away from it. Somewhere along the line the self-denial, the discipline, had become something darker. She'd sought control. Punishment. Atonement.

She'd liked the angles and lines of her physique and, when she'd finally escaped Monta Correnti at eighteen and moved to London to take the position of office assistant at a quirky style magazine, she'd fitted right in. Her new world had been full of girls eating nothing but celery and moaning that their matchstick thighs were too chunky.

It had taken her quite a few years to admit she'd had a problem. To admit that the yellowish tinge her skin had taken on had been more than just the product of her Italian genes, that the sunken hollows beneath her cheeks weren't good bone structure and that it hadn't been natural to be able to count her ribs with such ease.

Quietly she'd got help. Putting the weight back on had been a struggle. Every pound she'd gained had been an accusation. But she'd done it. And now she was proud to have a body that most women her age would kill for. It was meticulously nourished on the best organic food and trained four times a week by a personal trainer.

Even though she knew she looked good, she still didn't want to be gawped at without her clothes on. It was different when she was in her cutting-edge designer suits. Dressed like that she was *Jacqueline*

Patterson—the woman whose name was only uttered in hushed tones when she walked down the corridors of *Gloss!* magazine's high-rise offices. Remove the armour and she became faceless. Just another woman in her thirties with stretch marks and a Caesarean scar.

With the dressing-room door shut firmly behind her, Jackie slipped out of her linen trouser suit and went through the connecting door to Mamma's en suite to freshen up. As she washed she could hear her cousin catching Lizzie up on all the latest Monta Correnti gossip, especially the unabridged story of how Isabella had met her own fiancé.

When Jackie felt she'd finally got all the traces of aeroplane air off her skin, she returned to the dressing room and removed her bridesmaid's dress from its protective covering.

Wow. Stunning.

It reminded her of designs she'd done in senior school for the class play of *Romeo and Juliet*. Like the other dresses, it was empire line, with an embroidered bodice that scooped underneath the gathered chiffon at the bust and then round and up into shoulder straps.

Not many people knew enough about fashion design to see the artistry in the cutting that gave the skirt its effortlessly feminine swell. Nor would they notice the inner rigid structure of the bodice that would accentuate every curve of a woman's torso but give the impression that it was nature that had done all the hard work and not the fine stitching and cutting. She took it off the hanger and undid the zip. As she stepped into the dress there was a knock at the door that led back out into the bedroom.

'Everything okay in there?' Lizzie's voice was muffled through the closed door. Jackie smiled.

'Almost ready,' she yelled back, sliding the dress over her hips and stopping to remove the bra that would ruin the line of the low-cut bodice.

She'd been right, she realised as she started to slide the zip upwards. If her instincts were correct, this dress was going to fit like the proverbial glove. She doubted it would need any alteration at all.

As she got to the top she ran into problems with the zip. Despite all the yoga and Pilates, she just couldn't get her arms and shoulder sockets to do what was necessary to pull it all the way up.

'Lizzie? Isabella? I need a hand,' she yelled and dipped her head forwards, brushing her immaculately straightened hair over one shoulder so whoever rushed to her aid had easy access to the stubborn zip.

There was a soft click as the door opened. The thick carpet hushed the even footsteps as her saviour came towards her.

'If you could just…' She wiggled her shoulders to indicate where the problem was.

Whoever it was said nothing, just stepped close and set about deftly zipping her into place. For a second or so Jackie let her mind drift, wondering if it would look as dreamy as it felt when she raised her head and looked into the full-length mirror, but then she realised something was out of balance.

The fingers brushing her upper back as they held the top of the bodice's zip together didn't have Scarlett's long, perfectly manicured fingernails. Lizzie was already getting too big with the twins to be standing quite this close and, at five feet five, Isabella was a good inch shorter than she was. This person's breath was warming her exposed left ear.

Jackie stilled her lungs. Where fingers touched bare back, the pinpricks of awareness were so acute they were almost painful.

The person finished their job by neatly joining the hook and eye at the top of the bodice and then stepped back. Jackie began to shake. Right down in her knees. And it travelled upwards until her shoulders seemed to rattle.

Even before she pushed her hair out of her face and straightened her spine, she knew the eyes that would meet hers in the mirror would be those of Romano Puccini.

CHAPTER TWO

HIGH in the hills above Monta Correnti was an olive grove that had long since been abandoned. The small stone house that sat on the edge of one of the larger terraces remained unmolested, forgotten by everyone.

Well, almost everyone.

Just as the sun's heat began to wane, as the white light of noon began to mellow into something closer to gold, a teenage girl appeared, walking along the dirt track that led to the farmhouse, a short distance from the main road into town. She looked over her shoulder every couple of seconds and kept close to the shade of the trees on the other side of the track. When she was sure no one was following her, she moved into the sunlight and started to jog lightly towards the farmhouse, a smile on her face.

She was on the way to being pretty, a bud just beginning to open, with long dark hair that hung almost to her waist and softly tanned skin. When she stopped smiling, there was a fierce intensity to her expression but, as she seemed to be joyfully awaiting something, that didn't happen very often. She rested in the shade, leaning against the doorway of the cottage, looking down the hill towards the town.

After not more than ten minutes a sound interrupted the soft chirruping of the crickets, the gentle whoosh of the wind in the branches of the olive trees. The girl stood up, ramrod straight, and looked in the direction of the track. After a couple of seconds the faint buzzing that an untrained ear might have interpreted for a bee or a faraway tractor became more distinct. She recognised the two-stroke engine of a Vespa and her smile returned at double the intensity.

Closer and closer it came, until suddenly the engine cut out and the grove returned to sleepy silence. The girl held her breath.

Her patience ran out. Instead of waiting in the doorway, looking cool and unaffected, she jumped off the low step and started running. As she turned the corner of the house she saw him jogging towards her, wearing a smile so bright it could light up the sky if the sun ever decided it wanted a siesta. Her leg muscles lost all tone and energy and she stumbled to a halt, unable to take her eyes from him.

Finally he was standing right in front of her, his dark hair ruffled by the wind and his grey eyes warmed by the residual laughter that always lived there. They stood there for a few seconds, hearts pounding, and then he gently touched her cheek and drew her into a kiss that was soft and sweet and full of remembered promises. She sighed and reached for him, pulling him close. Somehow they ended up back in the doorway of the old, half-fallen-down cottage, with her pressed against the jamb as he tickled her neck with butterfly kisses.

He pulled away and looked at her, his hands on her shoulders, and she gazed back at him, never thinking for a second how awkward it could be to just stare into another person's eyes, never considering for a second what a brave act it was to see and be seen. She blinked and smiled at him, and his dancing grey eyes became suddenly serious.

'I love you, Jackie,' he said, and moved his hands up off her shoulders and onto her neck so he could trace the line of her jawbone with his thumbs.

'I love you too, Romano,' she whispered as she buried her face in his shirt and wrapped herself up in him.

Jackie hadn't actually believed that a person could literally be frozen with surprise. Too late she discovered it was perfectly possible to find one's feet stuck to the floor just as firmly as if they had actually grown roots, and to find one's mouth suddenly incapable of speech.

Romano, however, seemed to be experiencing none of the same disquiet. He was just looking back at her in the mirror, his pale eyes full of mischief. '*Bellissima*,' he said, glancing at the dress, but making it sound much more intimate.

She blinked and coughed, and when her voice returned she found a sudden need to speak in English instead of Italian. 'What are you doing here?'

Romano just shrugged and made that infuriatingly ambiguous hand gesture he'd always used to make. 'It is a dress fitting, Jacqueline, so I *fit*.'

She spun round to face him. '*You* made the dresses? Why didn't anyone tell me?'

He made a rueful expression. 'Why should they? As far as anyone else is concerned, we hardly know each other. Your mother and my father are old friends and the rest of your family thinks we've only met a handful of times.'

Jackie took a shallow breath and puffed it out again. 'That's true.' She frowned. 'But how…? Why did you…?'

'When your mother told my father that Lizzie was getting married, he insisted we take care of the designs. It's what old friends do for each other.'

Jackie took a step back, regaining some of her

usual poise. 'Old friends? That hardly applies to you and I.'

Romano was prevented from answering by an impatient Lizzie bursting into the room. Still, his eyes twinkled as Lizzie made Jackie do a three-sixty-degree spin. When she found herself back at the starting point he was waiting for her, his gaze hooking hers. *Not old friends,* it said. *But old lovers, certainly.*

Jackie wanted to hit him.

'It's beautiful!' Lizzie exclaimed. 'Perfect!'

'Yes. That is what I said,' Romano replied, and Jackie had to look away or she'd be tempted to throttle him, dress or no dress.

'Come and show the others!' Lizzie grabbed her hand and dragged her outside for Isabella and Scarlett to see. Isabella was just as enthusiastic as Lizzie but Scarlett looked as if she'd just sucked a whole pound of lemons. What was up with her? She just kept glowering at Jackie and sending daggers at Romano. Somebody or something had definitely put her nose out of joint.

The fitting was exhausting for Jackie. Not because her dress needed any alterations—she'd been right about that—but because she kept finding herself watching Romano, his deft fingers pinching at a seam as he discussed how and where he would make alterations, the way his brow creased with intense concentration as he discussed the possibilities with the bride-to-be, and how easily he smiled when the concentration lifted.

She'd spent the last seventeen years studiously avoiding him. It was laughable the lengths she'd gone to in order to make sure they never met face to face. Quite a few junior editors had been over-joyed when she'd sent them on plum assignments so that she wouldn't have to cross paths with that no-good, womanising charmer.

How could she chit-chat with him at fashion industry parties as if nothing had ever happened? As if he'd never done what he'd done? It was asking too much.

Of course, sometimes over the years she'd had to attend the same functions as him—especially during London fashion week, when she was expected to be seen at everything—but she had enough clout to be able to look at seating plans in advance and position herself accordingly.

However, there was no avoiding Romano now.

At least not for the next twenty minutes or so. After that she needn't see him again. Her dress was perfect. No more fittings for her, thank goodness.

Her mother chose that moment to sweep into the room. She gave Romano an indulgent smile and kissed him on both cheeks. Jackie couldn't hear what he said to her mother but Mamma batted her eyelashes and called him a 'charming young man'.

Hah! She'd changed her tune! Last time Lisa Firenzi had seen her daughter and Romano Puccini within a mile of each other, she'd had no compunctions about warning Jackie off. 'That boy is trouble,' she'd said. 'Just like his father. You are not to have anything to do with him. If I catch you even *talking* to him, you will be grounded for a month.'

But it had been too late.

Mamma had made Jackie help out at Sorella that summer, to 'keep her out of trouble'. And, if her mother had actually had some hands-on part in running the restaurant rather than leaving it all to managers, she would have known that Jackie and Romano had met weeks earlier when he'd come in for lunch with his father.

Of course she'd paid him no attention whatsoever. She'd seen him hanging around the piazza that summer, all the girls trailing around after him, and she hadn't been about to join that pathetic band of creatures, no matter how good-looking the object of their adoration was. But Romano had been rather persistent, had made her believe he was really interested, and, when she'd noticed that he hadn't had another girl on the back of his Vespa in more than a fortnight, she'd cautiously agreed to go out on it with him.

She should have listened to her mother. 'Like father, like son,' Lisa had said at the time. Jackie had always known that her mother and Romano's father, Rafe Puccini, had known each other in the past, but it wasn't until she'd moved to London and heard all the industry gossip that she realised how significant that relationship had been. By all accounts they'd had a rather steamy affair.

Look at her mother and Romano now! They were laughing at something. Her mother laid a hand on his upper arm and wiped a tear from under her mascara, calling him an 'impossible boy'. That was as much as Jackie could take. She strutted off to the dressing room and changed back into her trouser suit, studiously ignoring her reflection in the mirror. She didn't even want to see herself in his dress at the moment.

Keep a lid on it, Jacqueline. In a few minutes he'll be gone. You won't have to see him again for another seventeen years if you don't want to.

When she emerged, smoothing down her hair with a hand, her mother was just finishing a sentence: '…of course you must come with us, Romano. I insist.'

Jackie raised her eyebrows and looked at the other girls. Scarlett stomped off in the direction of the en suite, while Isabella just shrugged, collected up her clothes and headed for the empty dressing room.

'Give me a hand?' Lizzie asked and turned her back on Jackie so she could help with the covered buttons once again. As she worked Jackie kept glancing at her mother and Romano, who eventually left the room, still chatting and laughing.

'What's going on?' she muttered as she got to the last couple of buttons.

Lizzie strained to look over her shoulder at her sister. 'Oh, Mamma has decided we're all going to the restaurant for dinner this evening.'

Jackie kept her focus firmly on the last button, even though it was already unlooped. 'And she's invited Romano?'

Lizzie nodded. 'He's been spending a lot of time at the palazzo in the last few years. He comes into Monta Correnti regularly and eats at both Mamma's and Uncle Luca's often.'

Jackie stepped back and Lizzie turned to face her.

'Why?' Lizzie said, sliding the dress off her shoulders. 'Is that a problem? That she's invited Romano?'

Jackie smiled and shook her head. 'No,' she said. 'No problem at all.'

She looked at the door that led out to the landing. Would her mother be quite as welcoming, quite as chummy with him, if she'd known that Romano Puccini was the boy who'd got her teenage daughter pregnant and then abandoned her?

She'd always refused to name the father, no matter

how much her mother had begged and scolded and threatened, too ashamed for the world to know she'd been rejected so spectacularly by her first love. Even a knocked-up fifteen-year-old had her pride.

Jackie picked up her handbag and headed for the door. It still seemed like a good plan. There was no reason why her mother should ever know that Romano was Kate's father. No reason at all.

Refusing an invitation to dine with five attractive women would not only be the height of bad manners but also stupidity. And no one had ever accused Romano Puccini of being stupid. Infuriatingly slippery, maybe. Too full of charm for his own good. But never stupid. And he'd been far too curious *not* to come.

He hadn't had the chance to get this close to Jackie Patterson in years, which was odd, seeing as they moved in similar circles. But those circles always seemed to be rotating in different directions, the arcs never intersecting. Why was that? Did she still feel guilty about the way their romance had ended?

That summer seemed to be almost a million years ago. He sighed and took a sip of his wine, while the chatter of the elegant restaurant carried on around him.

Jackie Patterson. She'd really been a knockout.

Long dark hair with a hint of a wave, tanned legs, smooth skin and eyes that refused to be either green or brown but glittered with fire anyway.

Yes, that had been a really good summer.

He'd foolishly thought himself in love with her but he'd been seventeen. It was easy to mistake hormones for romance at that age. Now he saw his summer with Jackie for what it really had been— a fling. A wonderful, heady, teenage fling that had unfortunately had a sour final act. Sourness that obviously continued to the present day.

She had deliberately placed herself on the same side of the table as him, and had made sure that her mother had taken the seat next to him. With Lisa Firenzi in the way, he had no hope of engaging Jackie in any kind of conversation. And she had known that.

Surely enough time had gone by that he and Jackie could put foolish youthful decisions behind them? Wasn't the whole I'm-still-ignoring-you thing just a little juvenile? He wouldn't have thought a polished woman like her would resort to such tactics.

And polished she was. Gone were the little shorts and cotton summer dresses, halter tops and flip-flops, replaced by excellent tailoring, effortless elegance that took a lot of hard work to get just right. And even if her reputation hadn't preceded her, he'd have been able to tell that this was a woman who pushed herself hard. Every hint of the soft fifteen-year-old curves that had driven him wild had been sculptured into defined muscle. The toffee and caramel lights in her long hair were so well done that most people would have thought it natural. He'd preferred it dark, wavy, and spread out on the grass as he'd leaned in to kiss her.

Where had that thought come from? He'd seen it in his mind's eye as if it had happened only that morning.

He blinked and returned his attention to his food, an amazing lobster ravioli that the chef here did particularly well. But now he'd thought about Jackie in that way, he couldn't quite seem to switch the memory off.

The main course was finished and Lizzie's fiancé appeared and whisked her away. Isabella disappeared off to the restaurant next door and when Lisa was approached by her restaurant manager and scuttled off with him, talking in low, hushed tones, that left him sitting at the table with just Jackie and Scarlett. He made a light-hearted comment, looking towards his right at Jackie, and saw her stiffen.

This was stupid. Although he didn't do serious conversations and relationship-type stuff, there was obviously bad air between them that needed to be cleared. He was just going to have to do his best to show Jackie that there were no hard feelings, that he could behave like a grown-up in the here and now, whatever had happened in the past. Hopefully she would follow his lead.

He turned to face her, waited, all the time looking intently at her until she could bear it no longer and met his gaze.

He smiled at her. 'It has been a long time, Jackie.'

Jackie's mouth didn't move; her eyes gave her reply: *Not long enough.*

He ignored the leaden vibes heading his way and persevered. 'I thought the March issue of *Gloss!* was particularly good. The shoot at the botanical gardens was unlike anything I'd ever seen before.'

Jackie folded her arms. 'It's been seventeen years since we've had a conversation and you want to talk to me about *work*?'

He shrugged and pulled the corners of his mouth down. It had seemed like a safe starting point.

'You don't think that maybe there are other, more important issues to enquire after?'

Nothing floated into his head. He rested his arm across the back of Lisa's empty chair and turned his body to face Jackie, ready to engage a little more fully in whatever was going on between them. 'Communication is communication, Jackie. We have to start somewhere.'

'Do we?'

'It seemed like a good idea to me,' he said, refusing to be cowed by the look she was giving him, a look that probably made her employees perspire so much they were in danger of dehydration.

Now she turned to face him too, forgetting her earlier stiff posture, her eyes smouldering. A familiar prickle of awareness crept up the back of his neck.

'Don't you dare take the high ground, Romano! You have no right. No right at all.'

He opened his mouth and shut it again. This conversation had too much high drama in it for him and, unfortunately, he and Jackie seemed to be, not only on different pages, but reading from totally different scripts. He looked across the table at Scarlett, to see if she was making sense of any of this, but her expression was just as puzzling as her sister's. She looked pale and shaky, as if she was about to be sick, and then she suddenly shot to her feet and dashed out of the restaurant door. Romano just stared after her.

'What was that all about?' he said.

Jackie, who was obviously too surprised to remember she was steaming angry with him, just frowned after her disappearing sister. 'I have no idea.'

He took the opportunity to climb through the chink in her defences. He reached over and placed his hand over hers on the table top. 'Can't we let the past be the past?'

Jackie removed her hand from under his so fast he thought he might have a friction burn.

'It's too late. We can't go back, not after all that has happened.' Instead of looking fierce and untouchable, she looked very, very sad as she said this, and he saw just a glimpse of the young, stubborn, vulnerable girl he'd once lost his heart to.

'Why not?'

Suddenly he really wanted to know. And it wasn't just about putting the past to rest.

She looked down at his hand on the tablecloth, still waiting in the same spot from where she'd snatched hers away. For a long time she didn't move, didn't speak.

'You know why, Romano,' she whispered. 'Please don't push this, just…don't.'

'I don't want to push this. I just want us to be able to be around each other without spitting and hissing or creating an atmosphere. That's not what you want for Lizzie's wedding, is it?'

She frowned and stared at him. 'What on earth has this got to do with Lizzie's wedding?'

Didn't she know? Hadn't Lizzie or Lisa told her yet?

'The reception… Lizzie wanted to have it at the palazzo. She thought the lake would be so—'

'No. That can't be.' She spoke quietly, with no hint of anger in her voice, and then she just stood up and walked away, her chin high and her eyes dull, leaving him alone at the table, drawing the glances of some of the other diners.

This was not how most of his evenings out ended—alone, with all the pretty women having left without him. Most definitely not.

Back at the villa, Jackie ignored the warm glow of lights spilling from the drawing-room windows and took the path round the side of the house that led into the terraced garden. She kept walking, past the fountains and clipped lawns, past the immaculately groomed shrubs, to the lowest part of the garden, an area slightly wilder and shadier than the rest.

Right near the boundary, overlooking Monta Correnti and the valley below, was an old, spreading fir tree. Many parts of its lower branches had been worn smooth by the seats and shoes of a couple of generations of climbers.

Without thinking about the consequences for her white linen trousers, Jackie put one foot on the stump of a branch at the base of the trunk and hoisted herself up onto one of the boughs. Her mind was elsewhere but her body remembered a series of movements—a hand here, a foot there—and within seconds she was sitting down, her toes dangling three feet above the ground as she stared out across the darkening valley.

The sun had set long ago, leaving the sky a shade of such a deep, rich blue that she could almost believe it possible to reach out and sink her hand into the thick colour. The sight brought back a rush of home-sickness, which was odd, because surely people were only supposed to get homesick when they were away, not when they came back. It didn't make any sense. But not much about this evening had made sense.

She'd expected Romano to be a grown-up version of the boy she'd known: confident, intelli-gent, incorrigible. But she hadn't expected such blatant insensitivity.

She closed her eyes and tried to concentrate on the sensation of the cool night breeze on her neck and cheeks.

Thank goodness she hadn't given into Kate's pleading and let her daughter come on this trip. If Romano could be so blithe about their failed rela-tionship all those years ago, she'd hate to think how he might have reacted to their daughter.

If only things had been different…

No. It was no good thinking that way. Time had proved her right. Romano Puccini was not cut out to be a husband and father. The string of girlfriends he'd paraded through the tabloids and celebrity magazines had only confirmed her worst fears. Maybe, if he'd settled down, there would have been some hope of him regretting his decision to disown his firstborn. Maybe a second child might have melted his heart, caused him to realise what he'd been missing.

A huge sigh shuddered through her. Jackie kicked off her shoes and looked at her toes.

And Romano had made her miss all of those moments too. Without his support she'd had no choice but to go along with her mother's wishes. How stupid she'd been to believe all those whispered promises, all those hushed plans to make their parents see sense, the plotting to elope one day. He'd said he'd wait for ever for her. The truth was, he hadn't even waited a month before moving on to Francesca Gambardi. One silly spat was all it'd taken to drive him away.

For ever? What a joke.

But she'd been so in love with him it had taken right up until the day she'd handed her newborn daughter over to stop hoping that it was all a bad dream, that Romano would change his mind and come bursting through the door to tell her he was so sorry, that it was her that he wanted and they were going to be a proper family, no matter what his father and her mother said.

Well, she'd purged all those silly ideas from herself about the same time she'd tightened up her saggy pregnancy belly. It had taken just as much iron will and focus to kill them all off.

'Jackie?'

It was Scarlett's voice, coming from maybe twenty feet away. Jackie smiled. She'd never quite got used to the Aussie twang that both her sisters had developed since moving away. It seemed more prominent here in the dark.

'Up here.'

'What on earth are you doing up there?'

Scarlett walked closer and peered up at her, or at least in her general direction. She'd only just left the bright lights of the house behind and her eyes wouldn't be accustomed to the dark yet.

'Come up and join me. The view's lovely,' she said.

'I know what the view looks like.' Scarlett stared up at the tree. 'You're being silly.'

That was altogether possible, Jackie conceded silently, but she wasn't going to admit that to anyone. Scarlett folded her arms and stared off into the distance.

'What? You're not going to tell me I had too much wine at dinner?' Jackie said.

Scarlett just shook her head, the movement so small Jackie guessed it was more an unconscious gesture than an attempt at communication. She had that same can't-quite-look-at-you expression on her face that she always wore in Jackie's presence. It made Jackie want to be twice as prickly back. But it became obvious as she continued to observe her sister that Scarlett hadn't taken into account that Jackie had been out here long enough to get her night vision and could see her sister's features quite clearly. After a few seconds the hardness slid out of her expression, leaving something much younger, much truer behind.

'No. I'm not going to tell you that.' Her voice was husky but cold.

Jackie stopped swinging her legs. She knew that look. It was the one Scarlett had always worn when she'd heard Mamma's footsteps coming up the stairs after she'd done something naughty. Was Scarlett…was she *hiding* something?

Just as she tried to examine Scarlett's face a little more closely, her sister turned away.

'Mamma wants us all in the drawing room for a nightcap. She says she's got some family news, something about Cristiano not being able to come to the wedding.'

Jackie swung herself down off the branch in one fluid motion and landed beside her sister. She supposed they'd better go and make peace with their mother. Mamma hadn't been best pleased when she'd returned from her powwow with the restaurant manager to find that all her illustrious dinner guests had deserted her.

CHAPTER THREE

DESPITE the lateness of the hour, Romano stripped off by the edge of the palazzo's perfect turquoise pool and dived in. Loose threads hung messily from the evening he'd left behind and in comparison this felt clean, simple. His arms moved, his muscles bunched and stretched, and he cut through the water. Expected actions brought expected results.

But even in fifty laps he couldn't shake the sense of uneasiness that chased him up and down the pool. He pulled himself out of the water, picked up his clothes and walked across the terrace and through the house, naked.

Once in his bedroom he threw the floor-to-ceiling windows open and let the night breeze stir up the room. But as he lay in the dark he found it difficult to settle, to find any trace of the tranquillity this grand old house usually gave him.

More than once during the night he woke up to find he'd knotted the sheet quite spectacularly and had to sit up and untangle it again before punching his pillow, lying down and staring mutely at the inky sky outside his windows.

When dawn broke he gave up trying to sleep and put on shorts, a T-shirt and running shoes and set out on an uneven path that ran round the perimeter of the whole island. When he'd been a boy, he'd always thought the shape of Isola del Raverno resembled a tadpole. The palazzo was on the wide end, nearest the centre of the lake, and the long thin end reached towards a promontory on the shore, only a few hundred metres away. As he reached the 'tail' of the island he slowed to a jog, then came to a halt on the very tip. He stood there for quite some time, facing the wooded shore.

Monta Correnti was thirty kilometres to the west, hidden by rolling hills.

He'd waited here for Jackie once. His father had been back in Rome, either dealing with a business emergency or meeting a woman. Probably both. When he and his father had spent the summers here, Papa's presence had been sporadic at best. Romano had often been left to his own devices, overseen by an assortment of servants, of course.

He'd hated that when he'd been young, but later he'd realised what a gift it had been. He'd relished the freedom that many teenagers yearned for but never experienced. No wonder he'd got a reputation for being a bit of a tearaway.

Not that he'd ever done anything truly bad. He'd been cheeky and thrill-seeking, not a delinquent. His father had indulged him to make up for the lack of a mother and his frequent absences and, with hindsight, Romano could see how it made him quite an immature seventeen-year-old, despite the cocky confidence that had come with a pair of broad shoulders and family money.

Perhaps it would have been better if Papa had been stricter. It had been too easy for Romano to play the part of a spoiled rich kid, not working hard enough at school, not giving a thought to what he wanted to do with his life, because the cushion of his father's money and name had always been there, guarding his backside.

He turned away from the shore and looked back towards the palazzo. The tall square tower was visible through the trees, beautiful and ridiculous all at once. He exhaled, long and steady.

Jackie Patterson had never been just a fling, but it made things easier if he remembered her that way.

She'd challenged him. Changed him. Even though their summer romance had been short-lived, it had left an indelible mark on him. Up until then he'd been content to coast through life. Everything had come easily to him—money, popularity, female attention—he'd never had to work hard for any of it.

Meeting Jackie had been such a revelation. Under the unimpressed looks she'd given him as she'd waited tables at her mother's restaurant, he'd seen fire and guts and more life in her than he'd seen in any of the silly girls who had flapped their lashes at him in the piazza each day. Maybe that was why he'd pursued her so relentlessly.

Although she'd been two years his junior, she'd put him to shame. She'd had such big plans, big dreams. Dreams she'd now made come true.

He turned and started to jog round the remaining section of the path, back towards the house.

After they'd broken up, he'd taken a long hard look at himself, asked himself what he wanted to make out of his life. He'd had all the opportunities a boy could want, all the privileges, and he'd not taken advantage of a single one. From that day on he'd decided to make the most of what he had. He'd finished school, amazing his teachers with his progress in his final year, and had gone to work for his father.

Some people had seen this as taking the easy option. In truth he'd wanted to do anything *but* work for the family firm. He'd wanted to spread his wings and fly. But his mother had died when he'd been six, before any siblings had come along, and the only close family he and Papa had were each other. So he'd done the mature thing, put the bonds of family before his own wishes, and joined Puccini Designs with a smile on his face. It hadn't been a decision he'd regretted.

He'd kept running while he'd been thinking and now he looked around, he realised he was back in the sunken garden. He slowed to a walk. Even this place was filled with memories of Jackie—the most exquisite and the most intimate—all suddenly awakening after years of being mere shadows.

Did she ever think of the brief, wonderful time they'd had together? Had their relationship changed the course of her life too? Suddenly he really wanted to know. And more than that, he wanted to know who Jacqueline Patterson was now, whether the same raw energy and fire still existed beneath the polished, highlighted, *glossy* exterior.

Hopefully, the upcoming wedding would be the perfect opportunity to find out.

'What's up, little sister?'

Jackie put down the book she was reading and stared up at Lizzie from where she was sitting, shaded from the morning sun by a large tree, her back against its bark. 'Nothing. I'm just relaxing.'

Lizzie made a noise that was half soft laugh, half snort. 'Jackie, you're the only person I know who can relax with every muscle in their body tensed,' she said as she carefully lowered herself down onto the grass.

Jackie took a sideways look at Lizzie's rounded stomach. Carrying one baby had been hard enough. She couldn't imagine what it would be like to have two inside her.

Lizzie was smiling at her. An infuriatingly knowing, big-sister kind of smile.

Okay, maybe trying to do the usual holiday-type thing wasn't such a great idea. She found relaxation a little…frustrating. She kept wanting to get up and *do* things. Especially today. Especially if it distracted her from remembering the look in Romano's eyes last night when he'd reached for her hand across the table.

He'd made her feel fifteen again. Very dangerous. She couldn't afford to believe the warmth in those laughing grey eyes. She couldn't be tempted by impossible dreams of love and romance and for ever. It just wasn't real. And he shouldn't be able to make her feel as if it were. Not after all that had happened between them.

The nerve of the man!

Ah, this was better. The horrible achy, needy feeling was engulfed by a wash of anger. She knew how to do anger, how to welcome it in, how to harness its power to drive herself forwards. Who cared if it left an ugly grey wake of bitterness that stretched back through the years? She was surviving, and that was what counted.

Being angry with Romano Puccini was what she wanted, because without the anger it would be difficult to hate him, and she really, really needed to hate him.

Jackie exhaled, measuring her breath until her lungs were empty. This was better. Familiar territory. Hating Romano for rejecting her, for abandoning her and their daughter.

How could the man who had left her pregnant and alone, a mere girl, flirt with her as if nothing had happened?

'You're doing it again.'

Jackie hurt her neck as she snapped her head round to look at her sister. She'd half forgotten that Lizzie was sitting there and her comment had made Jackie jump. 'Doing what?'

'Staring off into space and looking fierce. Something's up, isn't it?'

'Yes.' The word shot out of her mouth before she had a chance to filter it. Lizzie leaned across and looked at her, resting her hand on Jackie's forearm.

'No…' Jackie said, wearing the poker face she reserved for fashion shows, so no one could tell what her verdict on the clothes would be until it was printed in the magazine. 'It's nothing.'

Why had she said yes? It wasn't as if she'd been planning on telling Lizzie her problems, certainly not in the run-up to her wedding. She looked at her sister. The poker face started to disintegrate as she saw the warmth and compassion in Lizzie's eyes.

Could she tell Lizzie now? It would be such a relief to let it all spill out. Over the years, her secrets had woven themselves into a corset, holding her in, keeping her upright when she wanted to wilt, protecting her from humiliation. Seeing Romano last night had tightened the laces on that corset so that, instead of giving her security, it made her feel as if she were struggling to breathe. Suddenly she wanted to rip it all off and be free.

But it wasn't the time to let go, even if her sister's open face told her that she would understand, that she would comfort and not condemn. Already Lizzie was tapping into her maternal side, helped along by the buzzing pregnancy hormones. It brought out a whole extra dimension to her personality. She was going to be an excellent mother, really she was.

The sort of mother you have never been. May never be.

A shard of guilt hit Jackie so hard she almost whimpered, but she was too well rehearsed in damage limitation to let it show. Just as an underwater explosion of vast magnitude happening deep on the ocean floor might only produce a small irregularity on the surface, she kept it all in, hoping that Lizzie couldn't read the ripples on her face.

She smiled back at her sister, squinting a little as she faced the morning sun. 'It's just wedding jitters.'

Lizzie's concerned look was banished by her throaty laugh. 'I thought it was me who was supposed to get the jitters.'

Jackie saw her chance and grabbed it, turned the spotlight back where it should be. 'Have you? Got any jitters?'

Lizzie shook her head. 'No. I've never been more certain of anything in my life.' She went quiet, gazing out over the gardens, but the look on Lizzie's face wasn't fierce or hard; it was soft and warm and full of love. Jackie envied her that look.

She leaned in and gave her sister a kiss on the cheek. 'Good.' This was about as expressive as communication got in their family. But Lizzie got that. She knew how pleased her little sister was for her.

Lizzie began to move and Jackie stood up to lend her a hand as she heaved herself off the slightly dewy grass. 'Why don't you get rid of those jitters of yours by going into town with Mamma and Scarlett? They're planning to leave shortly.'

'Maybe.'

As she watched Lizzie walk away Jackie decided against the idea of joining her mother and other sister on their jaunt. A morning in the company of those two would give her grey hairs.

Going into Monta Correnti, however, taking some time to rediscover her home town, to see whether it still matched the vivid pictures in her head, now that was a plan she could cope with.

Exploring Monta Correnti was fun, but it didn't take more than an hour or so, and Jackie soon returned to feeling restless. She kept wandering anyway, and ended up in the little piazza near the church, outside Sorella.

It was late morning and Scarlett and Mamma were probably inside, having a cool drink before they decided what they were going to eat for lunch. She really should go in and join them.

But beautiful smells were coming from Uncle Luca's restaurant next door and, despite the fact she'd sworn off carbs, she had a hankering for a simple dish of pasta, finished off with his famous basil and tomato sauce.

So, feeling decidedly rebellious, she sidestepped her mother's restaurant and headed for Rosa. Uncle Luca was always good for a warm welcome and she wanted to pump him for more information on all of Isabella's brothers. This year had certainly been a bombshell one for her extended family. So much had happened already. First, there had been the shocking announcement that Uncle Luca had two sons living in America that nobody had known about. Isabella had been trying to get in contact, but she wasn't having much luck. The family had thought that sending invitations to Lizzie's wedding might help break the ice, but Alessandro had declined and Angelo hadn't even bothered to reply.

Personally, Jackie wasn't too optimistic about Isabella getting any further with that. This family was so dysfunctional it wasn't funny. But she understood the need to heal and mend, to ache to bring forgotten children back into the fold.

She also wanted news of Isabella's little brothers. She didn't know if Valentino was in Monta Correnti at the moment or not, but it would be great to catch up with him before the hustle and bustle of Lizzie's wedding. She also wanted to find out the latest news on Cristiano. Mamma had announced last night that he'd been injured at work, fighting a fire in Rome, and was currently in hospital. Of course, Mamma had made it all sound totally dramatic, even though he'd only suffered minor injuries. Jackie would have preferred an update straight from her uncle, minus the histrionics, hopefully. Cristiano wasn't going to make it to the wedding either, which was such a pity. She'd always had a soft spot for him.

The entrance to Rosa was framed by two olive

trees in terracotta pots. Jackie brushed past them and stood in the arched doorway, looking round the restaurant. The interior always made her smile. Such a difference from Sorella's dark wood grain and minimalist decor.

Everything inside was a little outdated and shabby, but, somehow, it added to the charm. There was a tiled floor, wooden tables and chairs in various shapes and styles, fake ivy climbing up the pillars and strings of garlic and straw-covered bottles hanging from the ceiling. Locals knew better than to judge a restaurant's food by its decor. Sorella, next door, was where the rich visitors and tourists ate, but Rosa was where the locals came, where families celebrated, where life happened.

At this time of day, the restaurant was deserted, but not silent. There was a hell of a racket coming from the kitchen. A heated argument seemed to be taking place between two women, but Jackie couldn't identify the voices above the banging of pots and pans and the interjections of head chef Lorenzo.

Unfortunately his fierce growling was not having the desired effect, because nobody shot through the kitchen door looking penitent. However, she heard someone enter the restaurant behind her.

Jackie had never been one for small talk. She didn't chat to old ladies at bus stops, or join in with the good-natured banter when stuck in a long queue. Perhaps it was her upbringing in Italy. When things went wrong, she wanted to complain. Loudly. So she didn't turn round and make a joke of the situation; she just ignored whoever it was. For a few seconds, anyway.

'*Buon giorno.*'

The warm tones, the hint of a smile in the voice, made her spine snap to attention. She licked her lips and frowned.

'Are you stalking me?' she said, without looking round.

Romano had the grace not to laugh. 'No. I came to see Isabella, but I won't lie—I was hoping I would run into you this morning.'

She didn't dignify the pause that followed with an answer.

'Jackie?'

She took a deep, calming breath, opening her ribs and drawing the air in using her diaphragm, just as her personal trainer had taught her. It didn't work. And that just irritated her further. She'd bet the man standing behind her didn't have to be *taught* how to breathe, how to relax.

He wasn't standing behind her any more. While she'd been on her way to hyperventilating he'd walked round her until she had no choice but to look at him.

'I would like to talk with you. I believe we have some things to discuss, some mistakes from the past to sort out.'

Now she abandoned any thoughts of correct breathing and just looked at him. That, of course, was her big mistake. The expression on his face was so unlike him—serious, earnest—that she started to feel her carefully built defences crumbling.

What if he actually wanted to acknowledge Kate after all these years? What if he really wanted to make amends? Could she let her pride prevent that?

No.

She couldn't do that to her daughter. She had to hear him out.

As always, Romano had sensed the course of her mood change before it had even registered on her face.

'Have lunch with me,' he said.

Lunch? That might be pushing it a bit far. She opened her mouth to tell him so, but the kitchen door crashed open, cutting her off.

'We have to, Isabella!' Scarlett said, marching into the dining area, looking very put out indeed. 'What if she talks to him again? What if—?'

'I don't think it is the right time,' Isabella countered in Italian. 'After the wedding, maybe.'

Scarlett, as always, was taking the need for

patience as a personal affront. 'After the wedding might be too late! You know that.'

Isabella's hands made her reply as she threw them in the air and glared at her cousin. 'You're so impulsive! Let's just wait and see how things—'

It was at that moment that she spotted Jackie and Romano, her view half blocked by a pillar, both staring at her.

'—turn out,' she finished, much more quietly, and gave Scarlett, who was still watching Isabella intently, a dig in the ribs. Scarlett turned, eyes full of confusion, but they suddenly widened.

'Jackie!' she said warmly, smiling and rushing over to give her a hug. Jackie stayed stiff in her embrace. It felt awkward, wrong. But she had to give Scarlett credit where credit was due—she was putting on a wonderful show.

'Isabella and I were just talking…'

That much had been evident.

Scarlett paused, her gaze flicked quickly to the ceiling and back again. 'We're planning a surprise hen party for Lizzie and we want to drag you out to lunch to help us organise it!'

Isabella looked at Scarlett as if she'd gone out of her mind.

Isabella voiced Jackie's very thought. 'I don't think Lizzie—'

'Nonsense!' Scarlett said with a sweep of her

hands. 'And there's no time like the present. You don't mind, do you, Romano?'

Romano didn't really have time to say whether he minded or not, because Scarlett grabbed Jackie's elbow and used it as leverage to push her back out into the sunshine, while Isabella followed.

Yep, thought Jackie, rubbing her elbow once she'd snatched it back, Scarlett was getting more and more like their mother every year.

Once they were clear of the tables and umbrellas out front of the restaurant, Jackie turned and faced them. 'You two are deranged!'

Isabella looked at the cobbles below her feet, while a flash of discomfort passed across Scarlett's eyes. 'We need to talk to you,' she said. 'Don't we, Isabella?' She hung a lead weight on every word of that last sentence.

Jackie looked towards the restaurant door, not sure if she was annoyed or relieved that her chance meeting with Romano had been unexpectedly hijacked. She looked back at her cousin and her sister in time to see a look pass between them. Isabella let out a soft sigh of defeat.

'I suppose we do. But we need to go somewhere private,' she said. 'Somewhere we won't be interrupted or overheard.'

The three of them looked around the small piazza at the heart of Monta Correnti hopelessly.

Growing up in a small town like this, you couldn't sneeze without the grapevine going into action. And, this being Italy, the grapevine had always had its roots back at your mamma's house. She'd be waiting with a handkerchief and a don't-mess-with-me expression when you got home.

That was why Jackie and Romano had gone to such lengths to keep their relationship secret once their respective parents had warned them off each other. They'd been careful never to be seen in public together unless it was when Romano and his father had eaten at Sorella on one of Jackie's waitressing shifts.

Scarlett stopped gazing around the piazza and put her hands on her hips. She fixed Isabella with a determined look. 'I know one place where we won't be disturbed.' She raised her eyebrows and waited for her cousin's reaction.

'You don't mean…?' Then Isabella nodded just once. 'Come on, then,' she said and marched off across the old town's market square. 'We'd better get going.'

A low branch snapped back and hit Jackie in the face. She lost her footing a little and gave her right ankle a bit of a twist. Nothing serious, but she'd been dressed for a stroll around town and a leisurely lunch, not a safari.

'Sorry,' called Scarlett over her shoulder as she tramped confidently down the steep hill.

Jackie said nothing.

What had started off as a brisk walk had turned into a full-on hike through the woods. Her stomach was rumbling and she was starting to doubt that food was anywhere in the near future. What kind of shindig was Scarlett planning for Lizzie that involved all this special-forces-type secrecy?

Eventually the trees thinned and the three women reached a small, shady clearing at the bottom of the hill with a small stream running through it. Jackie smoothed her hair down with one hand and discovered far too many twigs and miscellaneous seeds for her liking. When she'd finished picking them out, she looked up to see Isabella and Scarlett busy righting old crates and brushing the moss and dirt off a couple of medium-sized tree stumps.

As she looked around more closely Jackie could see a few branches tied together with twine lying on the floor, obviously part of some makeshift construction that had now collapsed. A torn blue tarpaulin was attached by a bit of old rope at one corner to the lower branch of a tree while its other end flapped free.

Scarlett sat herself on the taller of the two tree stumps and motioned with great solemnity for Jackie to take the sturdiest-looking crate. Isabella took the other crate, but it wobbled, so she stood up and leaned against a tree. Jackie suddenly wanted to laugh.

It all felt a bit ridiculous. Three grown women, sitting round the remains of an ancient childhood campfire. She started to chuckle softly, but the shocked look on Scarlett's face killed the sound off while it was still in her throat. She looked from her sister to her cousin and back again.

'So… What's this all about? You're not planning something *illegal* for Lizzie's hen do, are you?'

Scarlett looked genuinely puzzled and every last trace of hilarity abruptly left Jackie at that point. Despite the summer sun pouring through the leafy canopy, she shivered.

'It's you we need to talk to,' Isabella said. 'The party was just an excuse.'

Scarlett looked scornful at Jackie's tardiness to catch on. 'Can you imagine what Lizzie would do if we planned a night of debauchery and silliness? Not very good for her public image.'

Not good for anyone's image, Jackie thought.

Scarlett stood up and looked around the clearing. 'This was our camp. Isabella and I used to come here to share secrets.'

'I remember how close you both were—joined at the hip, Uncle Luca used to joke. It was such a shame that you fell out. I thought—'

'Jackie! Please? Just let me talk?'

The hint of desperation in her sister's voice sent cold spiralling down into Jackie's intestines.

'This is difficult enough as it is,' Scarlett said, and stood up and ran a hand through her hair. She looked across at Isabella.

'There's no easy way to say this,' Isabella continued. She pushed herself away from the trunk of the tree she'd been leaning on and started pacing. Jackie just clasped her hands together on her knees and watched the two women as they walked to and fro in silence for a few seconds, then Scarlett planted her feet on the floor and looked Jackie squarely in the eye.

'We know your secret.'

Although her mouth didn't open, Jackie's jaw dropped a few notches. Her secret? Not about Kate, surely? They had to mean some other secret—the anorexia, maybe. Her eyes narrowed slightly. 'And what secret would that be, exactly?'

The leaves whispered above their heads, and when Isabella's answer came it was only just audible. 'About the baby.'

An invisible juggernaut hit Jackie in the chest.

'You know I…? You know about…?'

Their faces confirmed it and she gave up trying to get a sentence out.

But exactly how much did they know? All of it? She stood up.

'You know I was pregnant when I went away to live with my father?'

They both nodded, eyes wide.

'You know I gave the baby up for adoption?'

Isabella nodded again. 'No one told us, but it was kind of obvious when you came home the following summer without a baby.'

Oh, Lord. They knew everything. She sat down again, but she'd chosen the wrong crate and it tipped over, leaving her on her hands and knees in the dirt. Both Isabella and Scarlett rushed to help her up. She was shaking when she grabbed onto their arms for support.

They got her to her feet again and she met their eyes. There was no point in trying to hide anything now.

'My daughter—Kate—contacted me a couple of months ago. We've met a few times—'

'Kate?' The strangled noise that left Scarlett's mouth was hardly even a word. Jackie watched in astonishment as her normally feisty, bull-headed little sister broke down and sobbed. 'You had a little girl, a little girl,' she whimpered, over and over.

Jackie was stunned. Not just by Scarlett's reaction, but by the outpouring of emotion; it must mean that, on some level, Scarlett didn't despise her as much as she'd thought. She'd always seemed so indifferent.

'I'm so sorry,' Scarlett finally mumbled through

her tears. Jackie turned to Isabella, hoping for an explanation, but Isabella wasn't in a much better state herself.

A thought struck her. 'You can't tell anyone about Kate!' she said quickly. 'Not yet.'

My goodness, if this was going to be the reaction to the news, she'd been right to decide to keep her mouth shut until after the wedding.

'It's okay,' she added, taking a deep breath. 'Things are going to be okay. Kate and I are getting to know each other. Things are going to work out, you'll see. So don't be sad for me—be happy.'

She'd hoped she sounded convincing, but she'd obviously missed the mark, because Scarlett and Isabella, who had been in the process of mopping up a little with a few tissues that Isabella had pulled from her pocket, just started crying even harder. Jackie stood there, dumbfounded, as they sat down on the two tree stumps looking very sorry for themselves indeed.

And then another thought struck her. One that should have popped into her head at the beginning of this surreal 'lunch', but she'd been too shocked to even think about it.

'How?'

Both the other women went suddenly very still.

'How did you find out? Did Mamma tell you?'

They both shook their heads, perfectly in time

with each other. If she weren't in the middle of a crisis, Jackie would have found it funny.

'Then how?'

Scarlett looked up at her, her eyes full of shame. She didn't even manage to maintain eye contact for more than a few seconds and dropped her gaze to the floor before she spoke.

'The letter.'

What letter? What was Scarlett talking about? Had Mamma written a—

White light exploded behind Jackie's eyelids. She marched over to Scarlett's tree stump and stood there, hands on hips, just as she would have done when she'd been a stroppy fifteen-year-old, and *made* her sister look at her.

'You read the letter? *My* letter?'

Scarlett bit her lip and nodded.

'How dare you! How dare you! How—'

She was so consumed with rage she couldn't come up with any new words. Not even wanting to share a woodland clearing with the other two women, she strode over to the stream, as far away from them as she could possibly get without getting tangled up in trees, and stared into the cool green tranquillity of the woods.

Another thought bubbled its way to the surface. She turned round and found them twisting round on their tree stumps, watching her.

'Then you know who…'

Isabella swallowed. 'Romano.'

Jackie covered her mouth with her hand. This was worse than she'd imagined. Hen nights involving L-plates, obscene confectionery and tiaras would have been a walk in the park compared to this.

She exhaled. It all made sense now—why they'd freaked out when they'd seen her and Romano together back at the restaurant. But why had they dragged her away? Why tell her now?

'We didn't ever tell anyone else,' Isabella added hastily.

Jackie breathed out and sat down on the crate—the good one—and looked at her sister and her cousin.

They knew. And that had been her secret mission this visit, hadn't it? To tell everyone. Did it really matter if Scarlett and Isabella had known all along? Probably not. It would just be one difficult conversation she could cross off her list. They'd actually done her a favour.

Her anger had faded now, and she even managed a tiny smile. 'I was planning on telling you all after the wedding, anyway. Kate would really like to meet her aunts and uncles and I think it's time this secret came out into the open.'

Why weren't Scarlett and Isabella looking more relieved? They were still folded into awkward positions on their tree stumps. She decided to lighten the atmosphere.

'The least you two can do after all this is help me break the news to Mamma. I think you owe me!' And to let them know she was rising above it, dealing with the past and moving on, she gave them a magnanimous smile.

'You don't understand,' Scarlett said, rising from her stump, her forehead furrowing into even deeper lines. 'There's more.'

More? How could there be more? She'd told them everything. There were no more secrets left to uncover.

CHAPTER FOUR

SCARLETT gulped and cleared her throat. 'The letter... I brought it here to show Isabella.'

Jackie felt her core temperature rise a few notches.

'You have to remember—' Scarlett shot a glance at Isabella '—we were only eleven...'

Jackie's voice was low and even when she spoke. This was the tone that made her staff run for cover. 'What else, Scarlett? You did give my letter to Romano yourself, not pass it to someone else to give to him? If someone else knows—'

Isabella, who'd been unable to stand still for the last few moments, jumped in. 'It was my fault. I wanted to tell Aunt Lisa at first...' She trailed off at the look on Jackie's face. 'I didn't!' she added quickly.

'We fought,' Scarlett said, her voice gaining volume but at the same time becoming toneless, emotionless. 'Isabella had hold of the letter and I tried to snatch it away from her. It just seemed to leap out of my hands…'

They ripped the letter a little? Got it dirty? *What*? Jackie willed Scarlett to say either of those things. *Just a little smudge. No harm done.* But she could tell from the look of pure desolation on Scarlett's face that the fate of her letter had been much worse.

'What happened to it?' she asked, and her voice wobbled in unison with her stomach.

Scarlett didn't say anything but her gaze shot guiltily towards the stream innocently bubbling over the stones, and lingered there.

'*No!*' It was barely a whisper, barely even a sound. Suddenly Jackie needed to hold something, to cling onto something, but nothing solid was within easy reach. Everything was moving in the breeze, shifting under her feet.

Tears started to flow down Scarlett's cheeks again. 'I'm so sorry, Jackie. I'm so sorry…'

Jackie tried to breathe properly. *Her letter to Romano had ended up in the stream?* Thinking became an effort, her brain cells as slow and thick as wallpaper paste. She knew it was awful, her worst nightmare, but she couldn't for the life of her seem to connect all the dots and work out *why*.

'I didn't realise at the time what I'd done,' Scarlett said, dragging the tears off her cheeks with the heels of her hands. 'I didn't realise what it meant, that

Romano was even the father... It was only later, when you and Mamma were shouting all the time.' She hiccupped. 'And then she sent you away. I knew I'd done something bad, but it wasn't until I was older, that I put all the pieces together, and understood what it all meant for you and Romano.'

Romano.

The letter had been for Romano.

Work, brain. Work!

She looked at the stream.

And then the forest upended itself. She didn't faint or throw up, although she felt it likely she might do either or both, but the strength of the revelation actually knocked her off her feet and she found herself sitting on the hard compacted earth, her bottom cooling as its dampness seeped into the seat of her trousers.

She closed her eyes and fought the feeling she was toppling into a black hole.

Oh, no... Oh, no... Oh, no.

The truth was an icy blade, slicing into her. Adrenaline surged through her system, making clarity impossible. She had to do something. She had to go somewhere.

Jackie staggered to her feet and started to run.

Romano didn't know.

Romano had never known.

* * *

There was a knock at the bedroom door. Jackie hadn't been moving, just lying spreadeagled on the bed staring at the ceiling, but she held her breath and waited. When she heard footsteps getting quieter on the landing she let the air out again slowly, in one long sigh.

From her position flat on the bed she could hear voices murmuring, the occasional distant chink of an ice cube. Mamma must have opened the drawing-room doors that led onto the terrace. She glanced at the clock. Ah, cocktail hour. Vesuvius could erupt again and Mamma would still have cocktails at seven.

But there were no Manhattans or Cosmopolitans for Jackie this evening, just an uneasy mix of truth, regret and nausea, with an added slice of bitterness stuck gaily on the edge of the glass.

A migraine had been the best excuse she'd been able to come up when she'd arrived back at the house, uncharacteristically pink, sweaty and breathless. And to be honest, it wasn't far from the truth. Her head *did* hurt.

Mamma had moaned in her sideways way about self-indulgence, but she hadn't pushed the issue, thank goodness. She was far too busy to deal with her middle daughter. Nothing new there, then.

No way was Jackie going downstairs tonight. Mamma and Scarlett would be more than she could handle in her present state of mind. No, she wouldn't leave this room until she had pulled herself together and done the laces up tight.

Now the threat of interruption had diminished she hauled herself off the bed and looked around her old bedroom. If she squinted hard she could imagine the posters that had once lined the walls, the piles of books on the floor, the certificates in frames.

Of course, none of it remained. Mamma wasn't the kind to keep shrines to her darling daughters once they'd flown the nest. She'd redecorated this room the spring after Jackie had moved to London for good. In its present incarnation, it was an elegant guest room in shades of dusky lavender and dove grey.

Jackie caught herself and gave a wry smile.

Here she was, undergoing the most traumatic event since giving birth, and all she could think about was the decor. What was wrong with her?

Nothing. Nothing was wrong with her.

It was just easier to notice the wallpaper than it was to delve into this afternoon's revelations.

Uh-oh. Here came the stomach lurching again. And the feeling she was stuck inside her own skin, desperate to claw her way out. She steadied herself on the dressing table as her forehead throbbed, avoiding her own gaze in the mirror.

Everything she'd believed to be true for the

last seventeen years, the foundation on which she'd forged a life, had been a lie.

She stood up and walked across the room just because she needed to move. She couldn't get her head round this. Who was she if she wasn't Jacqueline Patterson, a woman fuelled by past betrayal and life's hard knocks? Possibly not the sort of woman who could have climbed over a mountain of others, stilettos used as weapons, to become Editor-in-chief of *Gloss!* And if she weren't that woman, then she had nothing left, because work was all she had.

Romano didn't know.

He'd never known.

She closed her eyes and heard a gentle roaring in her ears.

Would that have changed things? Would he have stood by her after all, despite the fact they'd been so young, despite the argument that had sent them spinning in different directions? A picture filled her mind and she didn't have the strength to push it away: a young couple, awake long after midnight, looking drained but happy. He kissed her on the forehead and told her to climb back into the bed they shared, to get some sleep. He'd try and rock the baby to sleep.

No.

It wouldn't have been like that, couldn't have

been. They couldn't have lost their chance because of a few sheets of soggy paper.

She had to be real. Statistics were on her side. She was more likely to have been a harried single mother, burned out and bored out of her mind, while her friends dated and went to parties and were young and frivolous.

Yes. That picture was better. That would have been her reality. She had to hang onto that. But the tenderness in the young man's eyes as he looked over the downy top of the baby's head at its mother wouldn't leave her alone.

She walked towards the window but kept back a little, just in case any of the family were milling on the terrace with their cocktails. She stared off into the sunset, which glowed as bright as embers in a fire, framing the undulating hills to the west. Tonight the sun looked so huge she could almost imagine it was setting into the crystal-clear lake that lay behind those hills. Where Romano probably was right now.

All these years she'd hated him. For nothing. What a waste of energy, of a life. Surely she must have had something better to do with her time than that? Maybe so, but nothing came to mind.

Slowly, quietly, she began to feel the right way up again. Get a grip, Jacqueline. You're not a terrified fifteen-year-old now; you're a powerful and successful woman. You can handle this.

Romano wasn't the monster she'd needed to make him in her imagination. And he probably wasn't the boy-father of her fantasies either. The truth probably lay somewhere in between.

She had to give him a chance to prove her wrong, to find out what the reality would be. He had a daughter on this planet, one who was hungry to know who she was and where she came from.

Jackie walked away from the window and sat back down on the edge of the bed. This changed all her plans. She couldn't tell her family about her daughter's existence yet. She had to tell Romano first. It was probably a bit late for cigars and slaps on the back, but he needed to know that he was a father.

Warm light filtered through the skylights in Romano's studio, dancing across the walls as tiny puffy clouds played hide-and-seek with the sun, daring him to come out and play. That was one of the downsides of having a home office in a home like his. Distractions, major and minor, bombarded him from every direction. One of the reasons he'd accepted Lizzie's wedding invitation was that it had given him a perfect excuse to spend two whole weeks at the palazzo. The plan had been to use the free time running up to and after the festivities to think about the next Puccini collection.

Just as he'd managed to dismiss the idea that the

sky was laughing at him for sitting indoors working on a day like this, his mobile rang. He stood up with a growl of frustration.

He didn't recognise the caller ID. 'Hello?'

There was a slight pause, then a deep breath. 'Romano?'

He stopped scowling and his eyebrows, no longer weighted down with a frown, arched high.

'It's Jackie,' she said in English. 'Jackie Patterson.'

It wasn't lack of recognition that had delayed his reply, but surprise. After all these years her voice was still surprisingly familiar. It was her reasons for calling that had stalled him.

Why, when she'd been at pains to avoid him at all costs for the last couple of days—including that ridiculous show of some 'secret' lunch with Isabella and Scarlett—had she called him? As always, Jackie Patterson had him running in circles chasing his own tail. It was to his own shame that he liked it.

He smiled. 'And to what do I owe the pleasure?'

There was a pause.

'I believe you owe me lunch.'

He might be laid-back, but he wasn't slow. She hadn't actually agreed to lunch before she'd been whisked away.

He let it pass. If thirty-two-year-old Jackie was

anything similar to her teenage counterpart, the starchy accusation was only the surface level of her remark. With Jackie, there were always layers. Something that had both bewitched him and infuriated him during their brief summer fling. Her about-face could only mean one thing: Jackie wanted something. And that also intrigued him.

'So I do,' he said, injecting a lazy warmth into his voice that he knew would make her bristle. Jackie might like to play games, rather than come straight out and say what she thought and felt, but that didn't mean he was going to lie down and let her win. The best part of a game was the competition, the cycle of move and counter-move, until there was only one final outcome. 'Do you want to go to Rosa?'

'No,' she said, almost cutting the end of his sentence off. 'Somewhere…quieter.'

Romano smiled. 'Quieter' could easily be interpreted as *intimate*.

'Okay,' he said slowly, letting her lead, letting her think she was in control.

He racked his brains to think of somewhere nice…*quiet*…to take Jackie. He doodled on a pad as he came up with, and rejected, five different restaurants. Too noisy. Bad food. Not the right ambience…

He looked out of the window, at the shady lawns and immaculate hedges. 'You want to talk? In private?'

'Yes.'

Did he detect a hint of wariness in her voice? Good. Jackie was always more fun when she was caught off guard. She always did something radical, something totally unexpected. He liked unexpected.

'Come to the island, then,' he said. 'We'll have all the quiet we want. We'll eat here.'

There was a sharp laugh from Jackie. 'What? *You* can cook?' Her response reminded him of the way he'd used to tease her until she just couldn't take it any more and had either walloped him or kissed him. He'd enjoyed both.

He laughed too. 'You'll just have to accept my invitation to find out.'

There was a not-so-gentle huff of displeasure in his ear.

He waited.

'Okay.' The word was accompanied by a resigned sigh. 'You're on.'

Jackie was on time. He hadn't expected anything less. She parked a sleek car on a patch of scrubby grass near a little jetty on the shore of Lake Adrina, just south of Isola del Raverno. He had been waiting in a small speedboat tied at the end of the rough wooden structure. The gentle side-to-side motion lulled him as he watched her emerge from the car looking cool and elegant.

She had style—and that wasn't a compliment he assigned easily.

She was dressed casually in a pair of deep turquoise Capri pants and a white linen halter-neck top, which she immediately covered with a sheer, long-sleeved shirt the moment she stepped into the sunshine. Her hair was in a loose, low ponytail and the honey highlights glinted gold in the midday sun. Bewitching. She pulled a large pair of sunglasses down from the top of her head to cover her eyes and it only added to the effect, making her seem aloof and desirable at the same time. He'd always been a sucker for forbidden fruit.

There was no doubt in his mind, though, that when she'd got dressed for this meeting, she'd thought very carefully about the 'look' she wanted to create. The clothes said: *Think of me as any other woman—down-to-earth, non-threatening, relaxed.* Romano was intrigued with her choice, why she'd felt the need to dress down when most other women would have dressed up.

He stood up, vaulted out of the boat and walked towards her. She didn't smile, and he liked her all the more for it. A smile would have been a lie. He was very good at reading women, their bodies, the silent signals their posture and gestures gave off, and as he watched Jackie walk towards him the signals came thick and fast—and all of them contradictory.

Greeting people with visible affection, even if little or no emotion was involved, was part of their world and, almost out of reflex, they leaned in, he kissed her on the cheek and took her hand. He'd done it a thousand times to a thousand different women at a thousand different fashion shows, seen her do the same from across the room, but as he pulled away a wave of memories as tall as a wall hit him.

She smelled the same. Warm. Spicy. Feminine.

And suddenly the hand in his felt softer, more alive, as if he could feel the pulse beating through it, and his lips, where they had touched her cheek, tingled a little.

Up until now the idea of embarking on a second summer fling with Jackie Patterson had been a mentally pleasing idea rather than a physical tug. He sensed that afterwards he would be able to erase the niggling questions about their romance that surfaced every few years from his subconscious, only to be swiftly batted down again. A rerun now they were older and more sensible would soothe whatever it was that jarred and jiggled deep down in his soul, wanting to be let out. But this time they would end it cleanly. No fuss, no ties.

As he ushered her into the small speedboat he realised that his only half-thought-out plans had moved up a gear. Now he didn't just want to get close to Jackie again to put ghosts to rest; his body wanted her here and now. But it wouldn't do to rush it. While she was all cool glamour on the surface, underneath she was awkward and nervous. Skittish. If he wanted to take Jackie to his bed, he was going to have to see if he could peel back some of those layers first.

He smiled. Not many men would guess what warmth and passion lay behind the glossy, cool exterior. But he knew. And it made the anticipation all the sweeter.

There were several mooring sites on the island and he chose the one that gave them a walk through the lush gardens to the palazzo. Jackie didn't say much as she walked in front of him, looking to the left and right, a slight frown creasing her forehead as she climbed the sloping steps from terrace to terrace. Now and again he saw her eyelids flicker, the very bare hint of colour flare in her cheeks, and he knew she was remembering the same things he was—memories of soft naked flesh, cool garden breezes that carried the scent of flowers. Heat and fulfilment.

It was here that they'd first made love, one night when his father had been away. He'd managed to invent an excuse to send the housekeeper and cook off for the evening—making sure they'd prepared food before they'd left, of course—and he and Jackie had spent the evening eating at the grand six-metre-long dining-room table, sneaking sips of his father's best vintage wine and pretending they were older and more sophisticated, free to love each other without remark or interruption.

He hadn't intended to seduce her. He'd just wanted some time alone with her far away from prying eyes, somewhere nicer than a dusty old run-down farmhouse. She'd been too young, and he'd been holding himself back, but that night...when they'd taken a walk in the gardens after dinner and she'd turned to him, kissed him, whispered his name and offered herself to him with wide eyes and soft lips, he hadn't been able to say no. Not when she'd purposely played with fire, done things that she knew got him so hot and bothered that he could hardly think straight.

But he couldn't regret it.

It had been intoxicating, and for the rest of the summer they'd lived in a blissful, heated bubble where the only thing that had mattered was time they could spend alone together. Foolish, yes. Forgettable, no.

They reached the large terrace with the parterre and giant urns. He watched her amble round a few paths, stooping to brush the tops of the geometric hedges and leaning in to smell the flowers dripping over the edges of the stone ornaments. This time it would be different. An adult affair, free from all the teenage angst and complications. He had a feeling it would be just as memorable.

On a large patio around to the side of the palazzo a table was set with linen and silver, a cream umbrella shading the waiting food. He led her to it. Crisp white wine was chilling in a bucket of ice, a dish on a stand stood in the middle of the table. She lifted her sunglasses for a moment and he noticed her eyebrows were already raised. He knew what she was thinking.

'I had a little help,' he said, not being able to resist teasing her, even though he'd prepared most of the meal himself. He liked cooking. It was just another way to be creative, and the results brought such pleasure, if the right amount of time and precision was lavished upon a dish. And he was all for pleasure, whatever the cost.

'Would you prefer to sit in the sun? I can remove the umbrella.'

She shook her head. 'I don't do sun. It's aging.'

He shrugged and pulled her chair out for her and she sat down, her eyes fixed on the domed cover over the central dish. He whipped it away to reveal a mountainous seafood platter: oysters, mussels, fat juicy prawns, squid and scallops, all stacked high on a mound of ice. Jackie forgot for a second to wear her mask of composure. He'd remembered well. She loved seafood.

'Wow.'

'See? I can cook.'

For the first time since he'd zipped her up in her mother's dressing room, she smiled. 'You don't really expect me to believe you prepared all this?' She swept a hand across the table. 'Even the salads?'

He handed her a serving spoon and nodded towards the platter. 'Any fool can shred a lettuce or slice a few tomatoes and drizzle a bit of oil and vinegar on them.'

She fixed him with a sassy look. 'It seems that *any fool* did.'

Warmth spread outwards from his core. He'd always loved her acerbic, dry sense of humour. Jackie was funny, intelligent, and with a quirky prettiness that had fascinated him; she'd been his favourite summer fling. His last, actually. After that he'd had other things to concentrate on. Learning the ropes at Puccini Designs, proving he wasn't a waste of space. It wasn't until success had come that he'd returned to finding women quite so distracting. And by then he'd been older, and summer flings had had their day.

Lunch was pleasant. He almost forgot that he'd sensed Jackie had a secret agenda for their meeting. They talked about work and what was new in the fashion world. She listened with interest as he bounced a few ideas for the next collection off her.

Jackie Patterson deserved to be where she was. She knew her stuff. Not one person he'd ever come across in the length of his career had ever dared to suggest she was a success because her mother had once been a famous model. Quite the reverse, actually.

Lisa's prima-donna tendencies had been legendary. No one who'd been in Jackie's company for more than five seconds would accuse her of being anything but highly focused, knowledgeable and professional. He was so taken with getting to know her again that he almost forgot his own secret agenda.

'How long are you staying in Monta Correnti?' he asked as he served her second helpings of almost everything from the platter, hoping that she wasn't going to announce some urgent meeting back in London straight after the wedding.

She swallowed the scallop she'd been chewing. 'Two weeks. Mamma convinced me to take a holiday since Scarlett would be visiting.'

He nodded, too preoccupied with his own calculations to fully register the heat that suddenly burned in her eyes and died away. Two weeks would be perfect. Long enough to seduce her—it was his turn this time, after all—but not long enough to tie them together for life.

When they'd finished eating, there was a natural lull. They sat in silence, staring out at the lake, which was showing off for them, flipping its waves into frothy white crests. Out of the corner of his eye he noticed a subtle shift in Jackie's posture, felt rather than heard her take in a breath and hold it. He moved his head so he could look at her.

For a moment she was motionless, but then she pushed her sunglasses back onto her head and stared at him. He blinked and refused to let his muscles tighten even a millimetre.

'Romano…'

She broke off and looked at the lake. After a long, heavy minute, she turned to him again. 'I…I wanted to talk to you about something.'

Although they'd been talking Italian all this time, she switched into English and the consonants sounded hard and clunky in comparison. He stopped smiling.

'Would you consider an exclusive fashion shoot for *Gloss!*, timed to come out the day after the new Puccini collection is revealed?'

He opened his mouth and nothing came out. For some bizarre reason he hadn't been expecting that at all.

But that was Jackie Patterson all over. She had a way of overturning a man's equilibrium in the most thrilling manner. It was a pity he'd forgotten how that excitement was always mixed with a hint of disorientation and a dash of discomfort. Didn't mean he liked it any less.

This could be the perfect opportunity to keep close to Jackie for the next few days, easing that frown off her forehead, making her relax in his company until she remembered how good they'd been together instead of how messily it had ended.

'It's a possibility,' he said and gave her a long, lazy smile. 'But let's save the details for later—say, drinks tomorrow evening?'

[faint offset text from facing page, illegible]

CHAPTER FIVE

IT WAS just as well that Jackie knew the road to Monta Correnti like the back of her hand, because she wasn't really concentrating on her driving as she travelled back to her mother's villa. Just as well she'd only drunk half a glass of wine at lunch too. Romano had her feeling light-headed enough as it was and she'd decided she needed her wits about her if she was going to tell him what could be the biggest piece of news in his whole thirty-four years on this planet.

Only, it hadn't quite turned out that way, had it?

She'd chickened out.

Jackie sighed as she made her way up the steep hill, hogging far too much of the road to be polite.

She'd thought she'd been ready for it, thought she'd been ready to open her mouth and change his life for ever.

What she hadn't counted on was that, without the benefit of almost two decades of hate backing her up, Romano's effect on her would be as potent as ever. He'd always made her a little breathless just by standing too close, just by smiling at her. It had got her completely off track. Distracted. She'd do well to remember the mess she'd ended up in the last time she'd given in to that delicious lack of oxygen.

All the chemistry she was feeling probably didn't have anything to do with her. He couldn't help it, just exuded some strange pheromone that sent women crazy. While Romano had built a solid foundation and long-lasting reputation in his professional life he wasn't the greatest in the permanence stakes, and she'd started panicking that he'd be a bad father, that he wasn't what Kate needed.

Jackie muttered to herself as she took a hairpin bend with true Italian bravado.

What did she know? Did she have any more 'permanence' in her life? The truth was, after Romano, she'd never really let anyone get that close again. Oh, she'd had relationships, but ones where she'd had all the power. They'd dragged on for a couple of years until the men in question had realised she never was going to put them ahead of her work, and when they'd left she'd congratulated herself for having the foresight not to jump into the relationship with both feet.

Jackie slowed the car and pulled into a gravelly lookout point near the top of the hill. She switched off the engine, got out and walked towards the railing and the wonderful view of the lake.

She'd wanted to run, to get as far away from him as possible. Was that why she'd chickened out of telling Romano the truth? Was she once again thinking of herself, of keeping herself safe, of keeping the illusion of perfection intact?

No. She'd been scared, but not for herself—for Kate. She'd imagined all the different scenarios, all the different reactions he might have. Would Romano be angry? Horrified? Ambivalent?

What if she scared Romano off by dropping this bombshell? It was too sudden, too much, after seventeen years of silence. She wouldn't get a second go at this. It had to be right the first time.

She swallowed and gripped the wonky iron railing for support, but instead of staring at the majesty of Lake Adrina, she just stared at her feet.

Her heart might just break for Kate if Romano didn't want to have anything to do with her. She knew what it was like to lose a man like that. It hurt. Really hurt. And Kate might hate her for doing it all wrong and scaring him away. She couldn't have that.

Lunch had been good, but it had only been a starting point. They had to build on the fragile truce they'd started to mesh together. Whether they liked it or not, she and Romano would be for ever linked once he knew the truth.

So she'd invented a reason to keep him talking to her, to keep them seeing each other. They needed to get to know each other again. Then she could work out a way of telling him about Kate that wouldn't send him running.

She'd just have to ignore the glint of mischief deep in those unusual grey eyes, forget about the fact her body thought it was full of adolescent hormones again when she clapped eyes on him. At least Romano hadn't tried anything; he'd been the perfect gentleman, even though she was sure there'd been a hum of remembered attraction in the air. Thank goodness they were older and wiser now and both knew it would be a horrible mistake to act on it.

When Jackie finally drove through the gateposts of her mother's villa, she spotted Scarlett sitting on the low steps that led to the front door, watching her rental car intently as she swung it round and parked it beside her mother's sports car. She pressed her lips together as she switched off the engine. She knew that look. Scarlett was in the mood for a showdown and Jackie *really* wasn't.

She got out of the car and tried to ignore Scarlett, but as she neared the steps Scarlett stood up and blocked her path.

'What?' she said with the merest hint of incredulity in her voice. 'Have you been waiting for me here all afternoon?'

Scarlett returned her stare. 'Basically.'

Jackie shook her head and moved to pass her sister. Stubborn wasn't the word.

'Please?' Scarlett said, just as they were about to brush shoulders.

It wasn't the tone of her voice—slightly hoarse, slightly high-pitched—that stopped Jackie in her tracks, but the desperation in her sister's eyes. Neither of them spoke for a few seconds, and Jackie found it impossible to look away or even move.

'Okay,' she finally said.

Scarlett nodded, a flush of relief crossing her features, and set off towards the garden at breakneck pace. Instead of heading for the table and chairs on the terrace, or the spacious summer house, Scarlett kept marching downhill through the gardens. Without even glancing back over her shoulder at Jackie, she launched herself at the old tree and swung her leg over one of the thicker, lower branches.

'I thought we might as well talk on your territory,' she said.

Jackie just stared at her. This week had to be the most bizarre of her entire life.

Scarlett smiled at her—not her usual bright, confident grin, but a little half-smile that reminded Jackie of the way she'd looked when she'd stuck her head round Jackie's bedroom door and had asked her to read her a bedtime story when Mamma had been too busy.

'I can't believe I'm doing this.' Jackie hoisted herself up onto 'her' branch again. 'I thought you said this was silly,' she said, shooting a look across at Scarlett, who was now sitting quite merrily astride a branch, swinging her legs.

'It is.'

Jackie grunted and pulled herself upright and straddled the branch so she could look at Scarlett.

'We always used to come here to whisper about things we didn't want Mamma to know,' Scarlett said. She picked at a scrap of loose bark on the branch in front of her, then studied it intently for a few seconds. 'Are you going to tell her?' she said, not taking her eyes off the flaking bit of tree she was destroying.

Jackie waited for her to meet her gaze.

'I have to. It's all going to come out into the open shortly.'

Scarlett nodded.

Jackie drew in a breath and held it. 'But I have to tell Romano first.'

A look of pain crossed Scarlett's features. 'I'm so sorry, Jackie. I should have told you earlier…'

Jackie kept eye contact. Scarlett didn't shrink back; she met her gaze and didn't waver.

'Yes, you should have,' she eventually replied.

Scarlett sighed. 'It was easier to pretend it had all been some horrible nightmare once I'd moved to the other side of the world. I thought I could run from it, pretend it hadn't happened… But as time went on, I realised the true implications of my actions and I…' her chin jutted forward '…I chickened out. I'm sorry.' She shrugged one shoulder. 'What can I say? The gene for self-preservation is strong in our family.'

Jackie exhaled. She knew all about chickening out, all about desperately wanting to let the truth out but not being able to find the right word to pull from the pile to start the avalanche.

It was much harder than she'd anticipated to stay angry at Scarlett. Just yesterday she'd thought this fierce sense of injustice would burn for ever. But these weren't just pretty words to smooth things over and keep the family in its disjointed equilibrium. Scarlett's apology had been from the heart. After all that had passed between them, could they use this as a starting point to building their way back to what sisters were supposed to be?

'At least I understand why you hated me all these years.' She'd done it herself many times—made an error of judgement and turned her fury on the nearest victim rather than herself. A trick they'd both learned from their mother, she suddenly realised.

She wanted to say she was sorry too, for disappointing Scarlett, for setting up the series of events that had forced her to leave her home and live with her father, but she couldn't mimic Scarlett's disarming honesty. The words stuck in her throat.

In one quick movement Scarlett swung herself off her branch and landed on the same one as Jackie, side on, so both her legs dangled over one side. Her eyes were all pink but she hadn't surrendered to tears yet.

'Is that what you thought? That I hated you?'

Jackie felt the skin under her eyebrows wrinkle. 'Didn't you?'

'No!' The volume of her reply startled both of them. 'No,' she repeated more quietly.

'But…'

Now the tears fell. 'I didn't leave because of you, Jackie. I left because I couldn't live with myself.' Scarlett hung her head and a plop of salty moisture landed on her foot. 'When you came back from London you looked so different, so sad… I couldn't face seeing you like that. So I did what any self-respecting little girl would—I ran away and told myself it wasn't my fault.'

Jackie hadn't thought the pain could get any worse. She'd only ever thought about how she'd felt, how she'd been wronged. Emotionally, she'd never matured past fifteen on this issue, too concentrated on her own wounds to see the others hurting around her. It was as if she'd only just woken up from suspended animation, that she could suddenly see things clearly instead of through a sleepy fog of self-absorption.

Romano had a daughter he didn't even know existed. He'd missed all those years; he'd never be able to get them back.

And Scarlett had carried the scars of this terrible secret round with her all her life. It had affected their relationship, Scarlett's relationship with their mother…everything.

Jackie's eyes burned. She closed her lids to hide the evidence and grabbed at the sleeve of Scarlett's blouse, using it to pull her into a hug. They stayed like that just resting against each other, softening, breathing, for such a long time.

'I was too proud,' Jackie whispered. 'I should have gone to Romano myself, but I took the coward's way out. I shouldn't have dragged you into it, Scarlett.'

Scarlett pulled back and looked at her, eyes wide. 'You mean that? You forgive me?'

Jackie had to stop her bottom lip from wobbling before she could answer. 'If you can forgive me.'

Scarlett lunged at her, tightening the hug until it hurt. Unfortunately it caught Jackie off guard and she lost her balance. Scarlett let out a high-pitched squeak and it took a few moments for Jackie to register what that meant. Uh-oh. They clung even tighter onto each other as the tree slid away from them and they met the ground with a *whomp*, leaving them in a tangle of arms and legs.

'Ow,' said Scarlett, and then began to laugh softly. Jackie wasn't sure whether she was moaning in pain or laughing along with Scarlett. The pathetic noises they were making and their fruitless attempts to separate their limbs and sit up just made them laugh harder.

'Girls?'

Their mother's voice sliced through the late-afternoon air.

Scarlett and Jackie held their breath and just looked at each other. Unfortunately this prompted an even more explosive fit of the giggles, and Lisa found them crying and laughing helplessly while trying to wipe the dirt off their bottoms at the foot of the old pine tree.

The boy slowed his Vespa to a halt at the back of the abandoned farmhouse and cut the engine. Everything seemed still. He looked up. The sky was bright cobalt, smeared with thin white clouds so high up they were on the verge of evaporating, and there was the merest hint of moisture in the air, a slight heaviness that he hadn't noticed while the wind had been buffeting him on his moped. Now he was motionless, he felt it cling to his skin and wrap around him.

Wasn't she here? Why hadn't she come running round the side of the farmhouse at the sound of his arrival as she usually did?

Frowning slightly, he jogged round the old building calling her name. No one answered.

He found her sitting on the front step, her back against the rotted door jamb, her long legs folded up in front of her. She didn't move, didn't look at him, even though she must have heard him arrive.

'Jackie? What's the matter?'

He sat down on the step beside her and she swiftly tucked her legs underneath herself. Her long dark hair was pulled into a high, tight ponytail and combined with the coldness in her hazel eyes it made her look unusually severe.

'I'm surprised you managed to drag yourself away,' she said, looking up, her tone light and controlled. 'I thought you'd be down in the piazza still, letting that Francesca Gambardi make eyes at you.'

Romano turned away. He was getting tired of this. Ever since they'd spent the night together almost three weeks ago Jackie had been acting strangely.

Oh, most of the time she was her normal, fiery, passionate self—a fact he was capitalising on, since they didn't seem to be able to keep their hands off each other for more than a few seconds at a time—but every now and then she just went all quiet and moody. And then she'd come out with some outrageous statement. Just as she had done a few moments ago. His head hurt with trying to figure it all out.

He sighed. 'We were just talking.'

Jackie humphed. 'Well, you seem to do a heck of a lot of *talking* with Francesca these days!'

He felt unusually tired and old when he answered her. 'There's nothing wrong with talking to a friend and, besides, I was only in the piazza because I was waiting for a chance to ask you to meet me here. Which I did. And you came. So I can't see what the problem is.'

She rolled her eyes and Romano felt his habitually well-buried temper shift and wake. 'What more do you want me to do?'

Jackie's answer was so fast it almost grazed his ears. 'Tell her you're not interested!'

'I *have* told her! She keeps asking me why, wanting a reason. I can't very well tell her it's because I'm seeing you. The news would be all over town in a flash and we'd never be able to see each other again. So, until we can convince our parents to take us seriously, I'm just going to have to let Francesca talk and I will pretend to listen.'

'How very convenient for you. Sounds like you've got the perfect excuse to flirt with whomever you want and still have me on the side.'

There was a hint of grit in his voice when he replied. 'It's not like that.'

She knew it wasn't. How could she believe he'd spend every moment he could making love with her, whispering promises, making plans, and the next moment be chasing around after girls like Francesca? Did she really believe him capable of that?

Jackie's silence, the thin line of her mouth told him all he needed to know.

He stood up and walked away. Only a few paces, but hopefully far enough from her distracting presence to let him think.

'You're not being logical,' he said.

Jackie jumped to her feet. 'I'm as logical as the next girl!'

That was what he was worried about.

She put her hands on her hips, looked at him as if she wanted to melt the flesh from his bones with just her stare. Jackie always had the oddest effect on him. Instead of making him cower, it made him want to stride over to her and kiss her senseless, persuade her she was everything he wanted.

He was on the verge of doing just that when she shot his plan full of holes by marching over to him and poking him in the chest with one of her fingernails. 'I don't need your so-called logic when I've got eyes in my head. You like her, don't you? Francesca?'

He shoved his hands in his pockets and walked swiftly back towards the farmhouse and went inside, hoping the cool air would improve his mood. Jackie had fooled him.

At best the rest of the world saw him as a financial drain on his famous father, at worst a spoiled brat who knew no limits and respected no authority. He'd always thought that Jackie was the one person who credited him with more depth than that—more than he did himself even. So it stung for her to accuse him like this, it stung. It was the worst insult she could have flung at him.

It was a pity that just a few short months ago she would have been right. He'd been all those things. But that was before he'd met her, before she'd challenged him to join her in seeing who he could be if he was brave enough. But he'd obviously failed her, and that hurt.

There was a noise behind him and he looked over his shoulder to find her standing in the doorway, backlit with dust and sunshine and looking anything but penitent.

'This is stupid,' he said, sounding steelier than he'd meant to.

Instead of agreeing with him, softening and

running to him and throwing her arms around him as he'd hoped she would, she just lengthened her spine and looked down her nose at him.

'Hit a raw nerve, did I?'

He didn't even bother answering her and she took a few steps towards him. 'Francesca is a very pretty girl, isn't she?' She blinked innocently and her voice was suddenly all syrup and silkiness.

He didn't know what kind of game she was playing but he had a feeling he'd lose, whichever tack he took. She went on and on, asking him over and over again, until he began to think she *wanted* him to agree with her, that on some level his capitulation would give her satisfaction, and eventually he got so cross with her incessant prodding that he walked over to her and gave her what she wanted.

'Yes. Okay? Francesca is very pretty.'

There. That had shut her up.

Jackie seemed to shrink a little, wither, as her eyes grew round and pink.

'You like her better than me,' she said, her voice husky.

Romano ran his hand through his hair, sorry he'd let her goad him into agreeing with her. He loved her, he really did, but if he'd known that taking their relationship to the next level would have opened this Pandora's box of female emotions, he might have resisted and sat on the lid a little longer.

She hadn't been ready for this. Neither had he.

Suddenly a summer of sweet, stolen kisses and innocent eye-gazing had morphed into an adult relationship, full of complications and blind alleys.

'I see you're not denying it,' she said, her voice colder than ever.

That was it. Romano didn't lose his temper very often, but when he did...

His thoughts were red and bouncing off the inside of his skull, searing where they touched. Perhaps this wasn't all worth it. Perhaps he would be better off with a girl like Francesca—a simple girl who wouldn't tax him the way this one did. This jealousy of Jackie's...it was ugly. And he was just furious enough to tell her so.

'At this precise moment in time, I'm starting to think you are right.'

The look on Jackie's face—pure horror mixed with desolation—warned him he'd gone too far, crossed a line. It wouldn't help to tell her that he hadn't jumped over it willingly, that she was the one who'd given him an almighty shove.

'In that case,' she said, backing away, walking heel-to-toe in an exaggerated manner, 'I never want to see you again.'

And then she turned and sprinted out of the

farmhouse, leaving him only one option. It didn't take him long to catch up with her, despite those long toned legs.

'Jackie,' he yelled, when he was only a few metres away, that one word a plea to cool down, to see sense.

She stopped dead and turned around. 'I mean it. If you try to call me, I'll slam the phone down. And if you come to the house, I'll set the dog on you!'

His burst of laughter didn't help her temper, but surely when he explained she'd see the funny side and it would pop this bubble of tension. Then they could walk hand in hand to the bottom of the grove and spend the rest of the afternoon making up.

She was still glaring at him, but he stepped forward, brushed her cheek with his thumb. 'Your mother's dog is a miniature poodle,' he said, a join-me-in-this smile on his face. 'What is he going to do? Fluff me to death?'

It was at that moment that he realised he'd stupidly taken one of those blind alleys he'd been trying to avoid. Jackie was not amused by his observation in the slightest. She called him a few names he hadn't even known were part of her vocabulary then set off down the dirt track. As she passed his Vespa, she gave it a hefty kick with her tennis shoe and it fell over.

Romano didn't bother following.

There was no salvaging the situation this afternoon. He might as well get his Vespa vertical again and take off on a ride to clear his head. Jackie would calm down eventually—she always did—and then he would go and see her and they would both say sorry and things would get back to normal.

Jackie couldn't help thinking about Romano as she slid into her bridesmaid's gown. As Scarlett helped her zip it up it wasn't her sister's fingers she felt at her back, but his. Wearing his gown, knowing he had designed the ridiculously romantic bodice with her in mind, made her feel all fluttery and unsettled. And as the thick satin brushed against her skin she was reminded of what it had felt like to feel the tips of his fingers on her shoulder blades, the weight of his hands around the small of her waist, the tease of his thigh against hers...

'There,' Scarlett said as she did up the hook and eye at the top of the zip. 'I'm just going back to my room to get my bag. I'll meet you downstairs.'

Jackie just nodded. She needed to snap out of this, really she did.

There was no point in thinking about...remembering...Romano that way. Romantically, they were explosive. An unstable force. But what Kate needed right now were parents who could stand in the same room without tearing each other to shreds, and she knew from personal experience just how destructive bad parental relationships could be.

No, Kate needed security, stability. *Sensible, supportive co-parent* was the only relationship she wanted with Romano these days.

Jackie leaned towards the mirror on the dressing table and checked her make-up. It hadn't helped that in the last couple of days she and Romano had been in constant contact. But that had been the plan, hadn't it? They'd talked on the phone, had coffee together, another lunch. Conversation had mainly revolved around business, but she'd felt she'd accomplished what she'd set out to. They had the beginnings of a friendship, one that she hoped would survive the bombshell she was about to drop.

It was time to tell him.

Not today, of course. Tomorrow. She'd have to catch him at the wedding reception and arrange a meeting, somewhere far away from her family's straining ears.

'Jackie?' Scarlett yelled for her as she ran past her bedroom door and headed down the staircase.

'Coming,' she called back and grabbed both her wrap and her bag. She ran as quickly and elegantly as she could in heels to meet the rest of the bridal party, which had now assembled in the wide marble entrance hall. She slowed as she reached the last couple of stairs.

'Lizzie, you look absolutely perfect. Glowing.'

A slight blush coloured her elder sister's cheeks just adding to the effect.

'Well, it's good to know I'm glowing, especially as these two—' she paused to rub her tummy '—have been having a two-person Aussie rules football match inside me since five a.m.! I'm absolutely exhausted.'

Jackie kissed her on the cheek. 'You're not glowing *in spite* of those beautiful boys, but *because* of them.' She sighed. 'You have so much to look forward to…'

She hadn't meant to say that. Her mouth had just done its own thing. Her mouth never did its own thing. She was always in control, always careful about what she said and what she projected, and she was horrified to have heard her voice get more and more scratchy, until it had almost cracked completely as she'd trailed off.

Lizzie *did* have so much to look forward to. And it had suddenly hit her again that she'd missed all those things with Kate. Moments she wished she'd witnessed, had treasured, instead of giving them to someone else for safekeeping. Moments she would never get back.

Scarlett rested a hand on her shoulder, gave her a knowing squeeze.

'Are you okay?' Lizzie asked, ruining her 'glow' a little with a concerned frown.

Jackie instantly brightened, glossed up. 'Of course. Absolutely fine. Just the…you know… emotion of the day getting to me.'

At that her mother gave a heavenwards glance. 'Not everything is about you, Jackie.'

A couple of months ago, maybe even a couple of days ago, she would have bristled at that remark, stored it away with the others to be brought out as ammunition at some time in the future, but today she turned to face her mother and did her best to stop her eyes glinting with pride and defiance.

'I know that, Mamma,' she said quietly. 'Believe me, I finally get it.'

CHAPTER SIX

THE wedding ceremony at Monta Correnti's opulent courthouse was simple and moving. The way Jack Lewis looked at his new bride as he slid a ring on her finger brought a tear to almost every eye in the place. And then they were whisked away in limousines and a whole flurry of white-ribboned speedboats to Romano's island for the rest of the celebrations. Jackie's heart crept into her mouth and sat there, quivering, as the boat neared the stone jetty just below Romano's over-the-top pink and white palazzo.

Only close friends and family had been at the courthouse. Now a much larger guest list was assembling for a religious blessing and reception in the palace and formal gardens of Isola del Raverno.

Jackie tried not to think about Romano, but the conversation she knew they must have the following day was looming over her.

Today wasn't about that. Wasn't about her. Her

mother had been right, even if only accidentally. During the winding journey from Monta Correnti to Lake Adrina, she'd thought hard about her mother's words. For as long as she'd been able to remember, even before she got pregnant with Kate, everything had been about her. Being a middle child, she'd felt she had to fight for every bit of attention, had learned to be territorial about absolutely everything, even though Lizzie and Scarlett hadn't been treated as favourites in any way.

And she'd never let go of that need to be the hub of everything, of needing the adulation, position... supremacy.

Until she'd rediscovered her lost daughter, she hadn't realised she'd had any of those sacrificial maternal feelings, hadn't let herself remember what she'd buried deep inside. She hadn't ever let herself feel those things, not even when she'd been carrying Kate. It had been easier to bear the idea of giving a piece of herself up if she imagined it to be nothing but a blob—a thing—not even a human being. Of course, all that clever thinking had fallen apart the moment Kate had come silently into the world, in the long moments when Jackie had been helpless on an operating table with doctors and midwives hurrying around and issuing coded instructions to each other. She'd felt as if her heart had stopped, but the monitor attached to her finger had called her a liar.

When Kate had finally let out a disgruntled wail, Jackie had begun to weep with relief, and then with loss. She hadn't had the right to care about this baby that way. She'd decided to give that right away to someone else, someone who would do a better job.

And somebody else had done a better job. She didn't know if that was a blessing or a curse. Whichever way she'd thought about it, it hurt.

She'd caused all of it. All of this mess.

The boat hit the jetty and jolted her out of her dark thoughts. She grimaced to herself. So much for today not being all about her. She'd spent the ten-minute ride to the island submerged in self-pity.

Today is not the day, she told herself. You can do it tomorrow. You'll tell Romano and then you'll have plenty of reasons to feel sorry for yourself—and for him.

The wedding breakfast was held in the palazzo's grand ballroom—the late count's pride and joy. 'Ostentatious' didn't begin to do it justice. There was gold leaf everywhere, ornate plasterwork on every available surface and long mirrors inserted into the panels on the walls at regular intervals. Totally over-the-top for casual dining, but perfect for an elegant wedding. Perfect for Lizzie's wedding. And she looked so happy, sitting there with her Jack, alternately rubbing her rounded belly through the flowing dress and fiddling with the new gold ring on her left hand as she stared into his eyes.

Jackie tried to keep her mind on the celebrations, but all through the afternoon she would catch glimpses of Romano—talking to some other guests with a flute of champagne in one hand, or walking purposefully in the shadows, checking details—and it would railroad all her good intentions.

Perhaps it would be better if she just got it over and done with, went and sought him out. Then she wouldn't be seeing him everywhere, smelling his woody aftershave, listening for his laugh. Every time her brain came up with a false-positive—when she'd thought she'd detected him, but hadn't—her stomach rolled in protest. It brought back memories of morning sickness, this uncontrollable reaction her body was having. She pushed the heavy dessert in front of her away.

In the absence of dry crackers and tap water, what she really needed was some fresh air. She needed time on her own when she wasn't expected to chit-chat and smile and nod. At the very least she owed it to her cheek muscles to give them a rest.

The meal was over, coffee had been served and the cake had been cut. Jack and Lizzie were making a round of the room, talking to the guests.

No one would notice if she slipped out for a few moments. If anyone missed her, they'd just assume she'd gone to powder her nose.

But escape was harder than she'd anticipated. She was only a few steps from the double doors that led onto the large patio when her mother swept past, hooked her by the crook of her arm and steered her towards a huddle of people.

'Rafe?' her mother said.

Rafael Puccini looked very distinguished with his silver-grey hair, dressed in an immaculate charcoal suit. Even though he must be a few years over sixty, he still had that legendary 'something' about him that made women flock to him. He turned and smiled as her mother herded her into their group, and she couldn't help but smile back.

'Jackie asked me a while ago about those sunglasses of yours…you know the ones.' Her mother waved a hand and tried to give the impression she didn't give a jot about the subject of their conversation.

Jackie didn't react. Everyone knew that her mother had been Rafe Puccini's muse back in the Sixties. His *Lovely Lisa* range of sunglasses were modern classics, and were still the best-selling design in the current range.

What had surprised her was her mother's sudden mention of the glasses. She'd asked her—

oh, months ago—about finding some vintage pairs for a feature for *Gloss!* Normally most of what she said to Mamma tended to go in one ear and out the other. If anything was retained, it usually had a wholly 'Mamma' slant to it, and was often completely inaccurate.

Rafe took her mother's hand and kissed it. 'Certainly I know which glasses you mean. How could I forget something inspired by those sparkling eyes?'

If Kate had been here, she'd have made gagging noises. Jackie wasn't actually that far from it herself. She'd met Romano's father many times before, of course, and had often seen him in full flirt mode, but never with her own mother. Lisa wagged a disciplinary finger at her old paramour, smiling all the while.

Well, she'd been fishing for a compliment and she'd hooked a good one. Why wouldn't she be pleased?

Just as Jackie broached the possibility of buying or borrowing some of the vintage sunglasses, Romano materialised for real.

Fabulous. The last thing she needed was her eagle-eyed mother picking up on a stray bit of body language and working out there was some sort of undercurrent between her and Romano. Mamma was very good at that. That was why Jackie had such excellent posture. Being able to snap to attention, give nothing away, had been her best survival mechanism as a teenager. As for today, she was just going to have to extricate herself from this cosy little group and try and catch up with him on his own later.

That plan was also a little tricky to execute. Rafe and her mother greeted Romano and drew him into the conversation. Jackie had no choice but to stand and smile and hope against hope that Lizzie would send for her to fulfil some last-minute bridesmaid's duty.

As the discussion turned towards hot new designers to watch, Jackie's attention moved from the outrageous flirting on the part of the older generation to the interaction between father and son. She'd never thought of Romano as being particularly family-oriented. He didn't have those heavy apron strings most Italians had to tie them to their families. But there was a clear bond between him and his father these days. Quick banter flowed easily between them, but it never descended into insults or coarseness. They both had the same mercurial thought patterns, the same sense of humour.

Jackie became suddenly very conscious of the lack of even polite conversation between her and her mother. They didn't know how to relate to each other without all their defences up, and the realisation made her very sad.

If only she could work out how Romano and his father did it, she might be able to analyse and unpick it, work out how to reproduce it with Kate.

The need to have more than an awkward truce with her daughter hit her like a sledgehammer. She was so tense around Kate, even though she tried not to be. But the knowledge that she'd failed her daughter pounded in her head during their every meeting, raising the stakes and making her rehearse and second-guess everything she said and did. And the feeling that it was all slipping through her fingers just added to the sense of desperation every time they were together. And the more desperate she got, the harder it seemed to be natural.

She wanted her daughter to like her. *Needed* her daughter to like her. Maybe even love her one day.

Sudden jabs of emotion like this had been coming thick and fast since she'd reconnected with Kate and, to be frank, she was feeling more than a little bruised by all the pummelling she was giving herself. She'd never had to keep such a lid on herself, do so much damage control to keep the illusion of omnipotence in place.

She made sure none of her inner turmoil showed on her face, pulled in some air and slowly let it out again without making a sound.

Back in the here-and-now, she joined the conversation again, but even that was difficult. She could feel Romano watching her. She tried not to look at him, tried to let her eyes go blurry and out of focus if she needed to glance in his direction, but it was as successful as trying not to scratch a mosquito bite. Eventually she had to give in, and the more she did it, the more she needed to do it again.

Even when she managed a few moments of victory and maintained eye contact with Rafe or her mother, she could sense his gaze locking onto her, pulling her. Her skin began to warm. The outsides of her bare arms began to tingle.

She made the mistake of glancing at him for the hundredth time and, instead of the warm sparkle of humour in his eyes, they were smouldering. Her mouth stuck to itself.

How stupid she'd been to think she'd been safe from that look, that the delicate friendship they'd been threading together had wiped it from existence. It hadn't diluted its power one bit. Romano wasn't looking at her like a friend. He was looking at her as if he wanted to…

No. She wasn't going to go there.

One problem with that, though: she wasn't sure that she wasn't returning that look, measure for measure.

It was just as well he'd decided that today was the day he was going to make his move. The way

Jackie looked in that dress—his dress—made it impossible to wait any longer.

When he'd first spotted her walking through the gardens with the rest of the bridal party, he'd actually held his breath. It looked perfect on her. Exactly as he'd imagined it would when it had been nothing more than a fleeting image in his head and a quick sketch on the page. Exactly the same, but at the same time so much more.

She brought life to his design, made it move, made it breathe.

Of course he'd seen hundreds of his ideas translated into fabric and stitching before, but not one had had this impact on him. Not one. It was more than just the fit. Jackie's dress—the romantic bodice, the gently flaring chiffon skirts—brought out a side of her he'd thought she'd lost.

Jacqueline Patterson, Miss Editor-in-chief, was attractive in a slick, controlled kind of way, but now…now she was all curves and softness. So feminine. From the coiled hair at the back of her head with the soft ringlets framing her face, to the tips of her satin sandals. All woman.

His woman.

That thought snapped him back to the present pretty fast, to the conversation his father and Lisa and Jackie were having about sunglasses.

Hmm. He'd never had the desire to *own* the

women who wore his creations before, or the women who flitted through his life. They were on loan—as was he. Nothing permanent. Nothing suffocating. Nothing…meaningful.

Must be an echo. Of things he'd felt long ago. Maybe once he'd dreamed of having and holding for ever. But he'd been so young. Naive. And he knew Jackie well enough to know she was far too independent to be anyone's trophy. She'd always been that way. Seventeen years ago he hadn't been worthy of that prize, and she'd let him know in no uncertain terms. Just as well he wasn't interested in that this time around.

And, with his current agenda fresh in his mind, he immersed himself again in the conversation that had been flowing round him.

It was time. The fact he was letting his imagination run away with him only served to highlight how bright his desire for her was. But he still needed to act with finesse, with respect and patience. It was that instinct that had kept him hovering on the fringes of the wedding celebrations, holding back until he felt in control of himself, be close to her without dragging her into the garden.

His father turned to Jackie. 'Ah, your glass is empty, my dear. Let us find you another.'

Before Jackie could answer her mother piped up,

mentioning the need to have a stiff word with the head waiter, and their parents disappeared with a nod to say they'd be back in only a few moments.

Jackie smiled at him. Actually smiled. And it was real—not that perfect imitation she normally did. Once again he felt a tug deep inside him. Not yet, he told himself. Running headlong into this will only get you kicked in the teeth, and you will walk away with nothing. Play this right and you'll have a summer affair hot enough to give you your own private heatwave.

'He's quite something, your father, isn't he?' she said with an affectionate glance over her shoulder. 'I was too young and too in awe of him when I used to serve you at Sorella to realise what a charmer he is.'

He smiled back, carefully, tactically. 'I don't think that's stopping your mother from falling for it again.'

'Now that's a scary thought.' She looked behind her again to where her mother was tearing strips off one of the catering staff, while his father smoothed any ruffled feathers with a smile and a wink. It was an odd kind of teamwork, but strangely effective.

Jackie took a long look at their parents, then turned to look at him. She raised her eyebrows. 'Do you think history will repeat itself?'

A sudden burst of heat filled his belly. He didn't glance over at their parents, but kept his gaze concentrated on Jackie. 'I'm counting on it,' he said, his voice coming out all rough and gravelly.

Jackie, being Jackie, wasn't swept away by one simmering look and loaded comment, but she laughed gently. He took it as a point scored.

'I see he has taught you all of his tricks,' she said.

Although he was tempted to laugh with her, he moulded his facial muscles into a look of mock-seriousness. 'Oh, I think the old dog has had a bit of an education from me too.'

She laughed again. 'You're incorrigible.'

Now he flashed her a smile, timing it to perfection. 'So I've been told. Come on.' He looked towards the open doors, only a few feet away, that led onto the terrace *'Andiamo!'*

Jackie followed his gaze and then they were both moving, both picking up speed and heading for the delicious coolness of the shady edges of the garden. He grabbed two glasses of champagne from a waiter's tray as they made their escape, and it struck him that he hadn't needed to drag her to get her to go outside with him after all. They hadn't even touched.

Not yet, anyway.

This is ridiculous, Jackie thought, as she ignored the pain on the balls of her feet and jogged in her high heels. They fled across the terrace, out of the view of the wedding guests inside the grand dining room and down a shady path. Romano was so close behind her she could hear his breath, practically feel it in the little ringlets at the nape of her neck.

When they'd reached relative safety, beyond a curve in the path, she gave in to the nagging fire in her feet and stopped. Romano just grinned at her and handed her a glass of champagne.

'You hardly spilled a drop! That's an impressive skill.'

Romano took a step closer. 'Oh, you have no idea of the skills I've picked up since we were last together.'

A slight rumble in his voice caused her to flush hot and cold all over. Just the thought that Romano might be better at some things—other things—was not good for her equilibrium. She steadied herself on the wooden rail that followed the path downhill and looked out to where the lake was sparkling at them through the trees.

What are you doing? You can't behave like this. Not with Romano. Not now. Not ever.

She closed her eyes briefly, took a sip of champagne and opened them again. How could she have let herself start thinking this way, feeling this way? Her daughter's whole happiness hung in the balance and she'd forgotten all about that, had been too busy being selfish, letting herself relive the unique buzz of attraction that still hummed between her and the man standing just a few short steps away.

She decided to start walking again, because standing there in the shadowy silence, feeling his gaze resting softly on her, was somehow too intimate. She had to break this strange feeling that had encapsulated her. It was as if she and Romano were trapped in a bubble together, with the rest of the world far, far away. She had to find a way to pop it before she did something stupid.

Her stiletto would be perfect. She took a step away from him, hoping that the heel of her shoe would be sharp enough to cut through the surface tension and let reality flood back in. He followed her and, if anything, the skin surrounding them, joining them, just bounced back and thickened.

She kept walking and didn't stop until she'd realised her subconscious had led her to the one place on the island that she'd really wanted to avoid.

The sunken garden was as beautiful as it had always been, full of ferns, some dark and woody, some small and delicate in a shade of pale greenish-yellow that was almost fluorescent. There was something timeless about this garden. The memory of the dark, waxy ivy that had worked its way up and around every feature was still fresh in her mind. The grotto still beckoned silently, promising secrecy and shelter in its cocoon-like depths.

She tried to keep the memories, and the man she was here with, even her own desires, at bay with her next words. It was time to stop getting carried away and ground herself in reality, in the sticky, complicated present, not some half-remembered adolescent fantasy.

'I… I wanted to ask you if you were free tomorrow,' she said, without looking him in the eye. That would be far too dangerous. 'There's something important I need to discuss with you.'

She heard—no, felt—Romano move closer.

'Look at me, Jacqueline,' he said in a low, husky voice.

She licked her lips. She didn't want to look at him, but *not* looking at him would be an admission that she was feeling weak, that he was getting to her, and she needed to give at least a semblance of control. She inhaled and met his gaze.

He was wearing that lopsided smile he'd always had for her. The one that had turned her heart to butter.

'We both know that we have talked the idea of the Puccini shoot for *Gloss!* to death over the last few days.' His fingers made contact with her wrist, ran lightly up her forearm. 'We're both adults now.'

Jackie decided she had need of a fire extinguisher.

She didn't trust herself to say anything helpful, so she just kept looking at him. Had she blinked recently? She really didn't know.

'So…' he continued, 'let's not play games as we did when we were younger. If we want to spend time together, we should just say it is so. There is no shame in it.'

Jackie tried hard to deny it, but he shook his head.

'Don't lie to me. I can see it in your eyes.' He dipped his head closer, until she could almost taste him in the air around her. 'I know we both want this.'

Heaven help her, she did.

She didn't push him away when he dragged his lips across hers, so gently it was as if they were barely touching. Too gently, teasing, so her nerve endings went up in flames. More so than if he'd started off as hot and hungry as she'd half-wished he would.

Boy, Romano could kiss.

He'd always been able to kiss. But he was right. There was new skill here too. Enough to make her forget her own name.

Romano had disposed of his champagne glass—she hadn't noticed when or how—and now his hands were round her waist, pulling her closer to him. She needed to touch him, hold him, but her own glass was still dangling by its stem from her right hand. They were right beside one of the water features and she felt with the base of the glass for a flattish patch on the knobbly surface of the pool's edge. She hardly registered the plop a second or two later, too busy running her hands up Romano's chest, relishing the feel of him.

She kept going all the way up his body until she could weave her fingers through the deliciously short hairs at the back of his head. Still kissing her, he let out a gruff moan from the back of his throat. She smiled almost imperceptibly against his lips.

This was the wonder of Romano Puccini. He made her feel beautiful and feminine and alive. Not by wading in and taking control, dominating, but by acknowledging her power, meeting her as an equal, making her feel sexy and confident.

Romano's lips moved from hers. He kissed a line from her chin down to the base of her neck, then along her collarbone to her shoulder, nipping the bare skin there gently with his teeth.

Jackie just clung to him. She hadn't known how much she'd missed this. Missed him. Hadn't realised that subconsciously she'd been waiting to feel his lips on her skin again for almost two decades. How could she have denied herself so long? Why had she thrown this away?

'Jackie…' His breath was warm in her ear. 'I want you. I *need* you.'

He was whispering her name in that way that had always made her melt, but it was another name that suddenly crystallised in her consciousness, freezing out all other thoughts and sensations.

Kate.

In a split second what had been hot and tingly and wonderful between them seemed nothing more than an undignified grope in the bushes. And it was selfish. So selfish.

She pushed Romano away. Or maybe she pulled herself out of his arms—she wasn't quite sure. He blinked and looked at her, his eyes hooded and clouded with confusion.

'We can't do this,' she said in a shaky voice.

He reached for her and she was too numb to react fast enough. He breathed in her ear, knowing just what he was doing, before whispering, 'What's to stop us?'

Jackie prayed for strength, prayed for a clear head. She couldn't lose herself like that again. She needed to focus on the reason she needed to get close to Romano, and it certainly wasn't *this* reason. It was about Kate. It was all about Kate. But then his lips found hers again and she almost went under.

'No,' she said softly, firmly, and she grabbed his chin with her hand, doing whatever she had to do to stop him.

He sighed and gave her a wistful look. 'I thought we said we weren't going to play games.'

Part of her softened, found his cheeky confidence charming. Another part of her took umbrage. He was too sure of himself. Too sure he could have her if he wanted her.

'I'm not playing games,' she said, looking him in the eye, refusing to waver.

'Good,' he said, wilfully misunderstanding her.

Jackie felt like wilting. They could do this all day, go back and forth, back and forth. Romano was as persistent as she was contrary, and she feared she might eventually weaken. That would do lasting damage to her plan to build a solid relationship with him, the kind of relationship that would give Kate stability and confidence in them as parents. Unfortunately, there was only one way she could think of to shock Romano out of seducing her amidst the ferns.

'The reason we can't do this,' she said, 'is that there's something you don't know. Something important.'

He froze. 'You're not married?'

She shook her head and the smile returned, saucier than ever. '*Buono.*' And he went back to placing tiny little teasing kisses on her neck.

It was no good. Romano had obviously decided she was playing along with him, albeit in a very 'Jackie' way. He stopped what he was doing and straightened, one eyebrow hitched high, but paused when his lips were only a few millimetres from hers. She had to do this now.

'There's something you don't know about that summer we were…together.'

He was too close to focus on properly, but she sensed him smiling, felt him sway just that little bit closer. 'Oh, yes?'

'When I left for England that autumn, after our summer, I was…'

Oh, Lord. Did she really have to say it? Did she really have to let the words out of her mouth?

'I was pregnant.'

CHAPTER SEVEN

I WAS pregnant.

Those words had the combined effect of a cold shower and a slap round the face for Romano. His arms dropped to his side and he stepped back.

She had to be joking, right? It had to be some unfathomable, Jackie-like test. He searched her face as she stood there with all the flexibility of an ironing board, her eyes wide and her mouth thin.

'You mean…you…and I…?'

She bit her lip. Nodded.

Now, Romano was a man who usually liked to indulge in the elegant use of language, but at that moment he swore loudly and creatively. Jackie flinched.

He looked at her stomach. After making that dress he knew her measurements to the millimetre, had crafted it to hug them. There was no hint. Fewer curves, even, than when he'd…than when they'd…

A million questions flooded his mind, all of them half finished. And then the awful truth hit him.

'You had a... You lost it?' he said, unable to work out why a solid wall of grief hit him as he uttered those words.

She shook her head, and the sorrow reared its head and became an ugly, spitting monster. He clenched his fists, spoke through his teeth.

'You *got rid* of it?'

The look of pure horror on her face was more than enough of an answer. He didn't need to hear the denial she repeated over and over and over. But that meant...

It couldn't.

He'd never heard mention of a child...a family...in all the years he'd worked in the same gossip-fuelled industry as Jackie. She was a private person, sure enough, but could that fact have slipped by him unnoticed?

He turned in a circle but came back to face her.

Of course it could.

When had he ever been interested in colleagues' pictures of pink-faced, scrunched-up newborns? He tuned out every single conversation about their children's ballet recitals and football games, preferring to amuse himself with statistics of a different kind. Cup sizes, mainly.

He looked around his sunken garden, at the grotto,

which now seemed less like a lovers' nest and more like a crime scene.

'Romano?'

He looked back at her, confused. The soft, vulnerable expression she'd worn only moments ago had been replaced with something much harder.

'You have a daughter,' she said, voice as flat as if she'd been reading random numbers in the phonebook.

A baby? He had a baby?

He backed away, and, when he could go no further, sat down on a low, mossy wall.

No. Don't be stupid. It had been such a long time ago. She was a girl by now. Almost a woman. He stood up again, suddenly fuelled by another revelation.

'You kept this a secret from me? Why?'

There was a flicker of discomfort before Jackie resumed her wooden expression. 'I tried, but—' she looked away '—it's complicated. I'll explain in a minute, when you've calmed down a bit.'

When he'd…?

This woman had been sent to test him to the limits. All these years she'd kept this from him. All these years she'd preferred to bring up their child on her own rather than involve him. Who gave her the right to make such decisions?

And why had she done it?

The answer was a sucker-punch, one from his subconscious: she hadn't believed him ready or capable to take on that responsibility, hadn't even entertained the thought he might be able to rise to the challenge. Just as she hadn't deemed him worthy of her love. Inside his head something clicked into place.

'Is that why you ended it? Refused to see me? Or take my calls?'

She inhaled. 'No. I didn't know then. I only realised…later.'

Then why hadn't she told him later? The words were on his lips when he remembered he already knew the answer. He matched Jackie's stance, returned ice with ice as he looked at her.

'Where is she now?' He looked to the terraced garden above them, back to the house. 'Is she here?' His stomach plummeted at the thought, not from a fear of being trapped, he realised, but in anticipation.

'She's in London.'

London. How many times had he been in that city over the last seventeen years? It was a massive place, with a population of millions, and the chances of having walked by her in the street were infinitesimal, but he was hounded by the idea he might have done just that.

'Does she know about me? Does she know who her father is?'

At that question, the inscrutable Jackie Patterson wavered. 'No.'

He closed his eyes and opened them again. Even though he'd had the feeling that would be her answer, it felt like a karate kick in the gut.

'What about the birth certificate? You can't hide it from her for ever. One day she'll find out.'

To his surprise, Jackie nodded, but the words that followed twisted everything around again and sent him off in an even more confusing direction.

'I didn't tell anyone who her father was. Not even Mamma. The birth certificate has my name alone on it.'

Romano sucked in a breath. That was it, then. He was nothing more than an empty space on a form. All these years trying to prove himself, trying to get the world to understand he was something in his own right, and that was what this woman had reduced him to. An empty box.

Jackie came a little closer, but not so close that she was within touching distance. He didn't have any more words at the moment, so he just looked at her. Her hands were clasped in front of her, her fingers so tense he could clearly see the tendons on the backs of her hands.

He came full circle again. 'Why?' he whispered. 'Why have you never told me?'

'I thought I had.'

Her answer turned his pain into anger. And when he was angry his usual good humour became biting and sarcastic. 'That's funny,' he said, aware that the set of his jaw was making it blindingly obvious he was anything but amused, 'because I think I would have remembered that conversation.'

Jackie walked over to a low stone bench and sat down, staring at the floor. Reluctantly he followed, sensing that keeping close, pushing her, would be the only way to uncover more facts.

As he sat there staring at the fountain bubbling away she told a ridiculous story of lost letters, secret rendezvous and missed opportunities. She told him she'd waited at the farmhouse for him. Waited for him to turn up—and dash her hopes, he silently added, because, surely, that was what she'd expected.

'Why didn't you try to reach me again when I didn't show up? You had no way of knowing if I'd been prevented from meeting you there.'

Jackie leaned forward and covered her face with her hands. For a long time the only sound she made was gentle, shallow breathing.

'I wondered about that at first,' she said through her hands, and then she sat up and looked at him. 'I waited for hours, way past when I should have been back home. Just in case you were late. And I would have come back day after day until I saw you. I wanted to believe you were coming.'

The look of exquisite sorrow in her eyes tugged at him. It felt as if she were pulling at a knot of string deep inside him, a knot that was just about to work itself loose. He refused to relax and let it unravel.

'I thought you knew me better than that, Jackie. If I'd got the letter, of course I would have come.'

She made a tiny little noise and he couldn't tell whether it was a laugh or a snort. 'And you would have done…what?'

'I don't know.' He frowned. 'We would have worked something out.'

Jackie stopped staring straight ahead and turned her whole body towards him. 'You're not saying that you would have stood by me?'

'Yes.'

'No!' She blinked furiously. She spoke again, softer this time. 'No.'

'You can't know that!'

He would have stood by her. He would have. At least that was what the man he was now wished he would have done.

'Think about this, Romano! You're saying you would have wanted to keep her, that you would have put a ring on my finger and we have had our own little teenage Happy Ever After?'

He looked deep inside himself, saw a glimmer of something he'd hoped he'd find. 'Maybe.'

Instead of her laughing in his face, Jackie's eyes

filled with tears, but she didn't let a single one fall, not even as her hands shook in her lap. 'Don't be ridiculous. You're just daydreaming.'

He jumped up, started pacing. All this sitting around, keeping everything in, was far too British for him. He needed to move, to vent.

'Is that so hard to believe? Am I that much of a disappointment?'

Jackie opened her mouth to answer, but there was a sudden rustling and the sound of voices further up the path. Without thinking about how or why—maybe it had been the memories of all that sneaking around in the past—Romano grabbed Jackie by the arm and manhandled her into the shelter of the grotto, silencing her protests with a stern look. This was one conversation neither of them wanted to have overheard.

He was close to her again now, pressed up against her, her back against the wall of the grotto. If they stayed in exactly this position they couldn't be seen from most of the sunken garden. She was rigid, all of the soft sighing, the moulding into his arms, over and done with. Just as well. Any desire to *fling* with Jackie Patterson had completely evaporated.

But how much worse would it have been if she'd told him afterwards? She'd been right to put a stop to what had been going on. However, that one small mercy in no way balanced out her other sins.

'It's Lizzie and Jack,' she mouthed at him, obviously recognising the voices.

He nodded and tilted his head just a little to get a better view, hoping that the happy couple weren't looking in his direction. He was lucky. Bride and groom were too wrapped up in each other to spot an inconsistency in the shadows at the far end of the garden.

Lizzie laid her head against Jack's shoulder and let out a loud sigh. He stroked her back, kissed her hair. Romano and Jackie weren't the only ones who had needed a bit of fresh air. He hoped, however, that the newly-weds' walk was going to turn out better than his had done.

Jack and Lizzie wandered briefly round the sunken garden, hand-in-hand, stopping every now and then to kiss, before moving on down the path towards the small beach.

Romano stepped out of the grotto as they disappeared out of view and stayed there, staring at the spot where he'd last seen a flash of white dress.

They seemed so happy.

From his short observation of the bride and groom, they were a wonderful complement for each other. They had so much to look forward to: their honeymoon, starting a new life together, raising the twins Lizzie was carrying and building their own little family.

He realised he was outrageously jealous, which surprised him. He'd never expected to want all of that. He'd got on quite well since the death of his mother without feeling part of a traditional family, and he'd never guessed he'd harboured a longing for it, preferring to keep his relationships light, his ties loose.

How ironic. He could have had it all along. *He* could have been the man in the morning suit looking captivated by his fresh-faced bride. *He* could have been the one looking forward to seeing his child born, to rocking her when she cried and, when she was older, scaring the monsters away from under her bed. But now, when he realised how much he wanted those things, those moments were gone, never to be salvaged. They'd been stolen from him by the woman steadying herself against the grotto wall with wide-spread hands, looking as much like an out-of-her-depth teenager as he'd ever seen her.

The sight drew no pity from him. He wouldn't allow it. Instead he looked away.

Marry her? Have a Happy Ever After with her? Right at this moment it was the last thing he wanted to do. In fact if he never saw her again he'd be ecstatic. But that wasn't an option. She was his sole link to his daughter. A daughter he could still hardly believe existed.

He spoke without looking at Jackie. 'What's her name?'

'Kate,' she said blandly.

Kate. Very English. Probably not what he would have chosen, given the chance. But he hadn't been given the chance—that was the point. He wanted to shout, to punch, to…do *something* to rid himself of this horrible assault of feelings. Normally he could bat negative things away, dissolve them with a joke or distract himself— usually with something female and pretty—but this just wouldn't go away and he didn't know how to handle it.

Facts. Stick to facts.

'Kate,' he echoed. 'Short for Katharine?'

She didn't answer. He let out a rough sigh. How could she still be playing games with him after what she'd revealed? How did she have the gall to make him work for the answers?

Because she's Jackie. She sets tests. You have to prove yourself to her over and over and even then she'll never believe you.

He swivelled round and looked her in the eyes, knowing that the lava inside was bubbling hard, even though he was desperately trying to keep a lid on it. Instead he let its heat radiate in his stare, let it insist upon an answer.

She swallowed. 'I suppose so. I'm not sure.'

Was a straight yes or no so hard to come by? Suddenly, it was all too much for him. He couldn't do this now. He needed time to think, to breathe. One more of her cryptic answers and he was going to lose it completely.

'Fine. If that's the way you want to play it, I'll go.'

She looked shocked at that. He didn't care why.

'But don't think you've heard the end of this,' he added. 'You owe me more. And you can start paying tomorrow with answers. Facts. Details. Call them what you want, but I will have them.'

Jackie got over her surprise and pushed herself away from the wall of her grotto with her hands so she was standing straight. She fixed him with that flesh-melting stare he remembered so well. He refused to acknowledge the ripple of heat that passed over him in response.

'Don't you dare act all high and mighty about this, Signor Puccini! You and I both know you weren't ready for fidelity and commitment back then.'

That lid he'd been trying to keep tightly on? It popped.

But he was aware Lizzie and Jack might well still be within earshot and he didn't have the luxury of using the volume he would have liked to. He did the next best thing and dropped his voice to a rasping whisper.

'You have no right to judge me. No right at all.

You don't know what I would have done, how I might have reacted. Who do you think you are?'

Jackie marched out of the grotto and for a moment he thought she was going to leave him standing there, all his anger unspent, but she got halfway up the garden and then turned back and strode towards him.

Of course. She always had to have the last word. Well, let her. It still wouldn't make what she'd done right.

'Who do I think I am? I'll tell you who I think I am!' Her face twisted into something resembling a smile. 'I'm the poor, pathetic girl who waited at the farmhouse all afternoon for you, scared out of her wits, feeling alone and overwhelmed.'

She wasn't making any sense.

'You know I didn't get your letter,' he said. 'You can't blame that on me.'

She took her time before she answered, her eyes narrowing, faint glimmer of victory glittering there. 'I saw you, Romano, that afternoon.'

Saw him? What was she talking about? He'd thought the whole point had been that he *hadn't* turned up.

'When I finally gave up waiting, I walked back up the track towards the main road, and that was when I saw you.' She waited for him to guess the significance of her statement, but all he could do was shrug. 'I saw you drive past on your Vespa with…*her*. With Francesca Gambardi!'

Ah.

He'd forgotten about that.

So that was the afternoon he'd finally given in to Francesca's pestering, had agreed to take her out on his *bella moto,* as she'd called it, because he'd hoped her presence would make him forget the crater Jackie had left behind when he'd finally got the message she'd wanted nothing more to do with him.

It hadn't been one of his finest moments. Or one of his best ideas.

And it hadn't worked. Francesca hadn't been enough of a distraction. Every time she'd looked at him, every time she'd brushed up against him, he'd only been plagued by the feeling that everything had been all wrong, that it should have been Jackie with her arms around his waist as they whipped through the countryside, that it should have been Jackie sidling up to him as they'd stopped to look at a pretty view. In the end, he'd taken Francesca home without so much as a kiss. A first for him in those days.

Jackie was way off base, thinking he'd had something going with Francesca, but he remembered how insecure, how jealous she'd been of the other girl, and he knew how it must have looked to her. But if she'd only asked, only would have deigned to talk to him, she would have known the truth. He'd acted foolishly, yes, but she hadn't behaved with any more maturity.

'And that was why you didn't bother telling me you were carrying my child? Because you saw me with another girl on the back of my Vespa? Jackie, that's a pathetic excuse.'

The smug look evaporated and she looked as if she'd been slapped across the face with the truth of his statement. Her jaw tensed. It didn't take her long to regroup and counter-attack.

'But I thought you'd read my letter, remember? I thought you knew I was pregnant, that I was waiting for you to discuss our future. And when you rode past the farmhouse—our special place— with that girl pressing herself up against you... well, it sent a message loud and clear.'

Okay, things might not be as black and white as he'd thought.

It was all so complicated, so hard to keep track of who knew what and when. Jackie had always been hot-headed and quick to judge and while he didn't like her reaction to the situation he could understand it, understand it was the only way she could have acted in that moment. What he didn't understand was why that one, unlucky coincidence, when he'd driven past with Francesca, had decided everything, had defined both their futures.

'But you didn't think to ask me? To find out for sure? Maybe not right then, when you were still angry, but what about the next month or the one after that? What about when the baby was born, or when you registered her? On her first birthday? On *any* of her birthdays? Hasn't she asked questions? Doesn't she want to know?'

Jackie just stared at him.

Maybe his daughter took after her mother. Maybe Jackie had brought her up to be as hard and self-obsessed as she was. Unfortunately he could imagine it all too easily. The elegant flat in one of the classier parts of London, the two of them being very sophisticated together, eating out, going to fashion shows. What he couldn't imagine was them laughing, making daisy chains or having fun.

He sighed. Jackie had always been such hard work, had always kept him on his toes. What would it be like if he had two such women to placate? It would leave him breathless.

He'd drifted off, almost forgotten Jackie was there. Her voice pulled him out of his daydream... nightmare...whatever.

'I did think of you when she was born, in the days following...' She paused, made a strange hic-cupping noise. 'And don't think that every birthday wasn't torture, because it was. But by then it was too late. It had already been done. And I wouldn't have turned back time if I could have done. It would have been selfish and wrong.'

His first reaction was to stoke his anger—she was talking in riddles again—but the weighty sorrow that had settled on her, making her shoulders droop, diluted his rage with curiosity.

'What do you mean "it was too late"?'

Jackie looked up, puzzled. 'She'd gone to her new family—the people who adopted her.'

The words didn't sink in at first. He heard the sounds, even knew what they represented, but, somehow, they still didn't make sense. He walked away from her, back towards the grotto and stuck his hand—shirtsleeves and all—into one of the chilly black pools, just because he needed something physical, something to shock his body and brain into reacting.

It worked all right. Suddenly his brain was alive with responses. Unfortunately, the temperature of the water had done nothing to cool his temper. He flicked the water off with his hands and dried them on the back of his beautifully crafted, mortgage-worthy suit.

'You're telling me that, rather than raise our daughter yourself, rather than telling me—her father—of her existence, that you gave her away to *strangers*? Like she was something disposable?'

He marched up to her, grabbed her by the shoulders.

'Is that what it was like, Jackie? She didn't fit into your nice, ordered plans for your life, so you just put her out of sight...out of mind?'

Jackie's jaw moved, but no sound came out. She had gone white. And then she wrenched herself free and stumbled out of the garden on her high heels, gaining speed with every step.

For a man who lived his life in the shallows, Romano experienced the unfamiliar feeling of knowing he'd gone too deep, said too much, and he didn't know how to deal with that. There wasn't a quip, a smart remark, that could save the situation. He was in open water and land was nowhere in sight.

Jackie had disappeared along the path and into the small patch of woodland that hid the sunken garden from the island's shore.

The path. The one that led down to the beach.

Oh, hell.

He sprinted after her, even though he couldn't rationalise why stopping her from bumping into Jack and Lizzie was so important. In his mind she deserved all she got. He told himself he was speeding after her to stop her putting a huge dampener on the wedding and ignored the pity that twinged in him every time he thought of how much she would hate anyone—especially her adored older sister—to see her in such a mess.

It didn't take long to catch her up, only twenty steps away from where the trees parted and she would have a full view of the shingle beach.

'Jackie!' It wasn't quite a shout, wasn't quite a whisper, but a strange combination of the two.

She faltered but didn't alter her course. He was closer now and put a restraining hand on her arm, spoke in a low voice. 'Not that way.'

All of her back muscles tensed and he just knew she was getting ready to let rip, but then they heard a rumble of low laughter from the direction of the water's edge and she jolted in surprise.

'This way,' he said, as quietly as possible, and led her through the trees in the opposite direction, heading for the narrow tip of the island, away from the house, where they would be less likely to be disturbed by wandering wedding guests. They reached a clearing with a soft grassy bank and she just seemed to lose the ability to keep her joints locked. Her knees folded under her and she sat down on the grass with a thud.

'It wasn't like that at all,' she said, enunciating each word carefully. 'You don't know…'

It took Romano a couple of seconds to realise she was continuing the conversation she'd walked out on as if no time had passed. And that wasn't the only strange thing that had happened. He no longer wanted to erupt. He didn't know why. Maybe he'd experienced so many strong emotions in the last half-hour that he'd just run out, had none left. He sat down beside her.

'So tell me what it *was* like.'

He knew his request didn't sound exactly friendly, but it was the best he could do under the circumstances.

She kicked off her shoes and sank her bare feet into the grass. Even the shade of her toenails complemented her outfit. So *Jackie*…

She hugged her legs, drew them up until she was almost in a little ball, and rested her cheek on her knees. Her face was turned in his direction, but her eyes were glazed and unfocused.

'I wanted to believe you'd come,' she said in a voice that reminded him of a little girl's. 'I wanted to believe that it would all turn out right, but I truly didn't think it was ever going to happen.'

Another nail in the coffin. Another confirmation from her that he was a loser. He ought to get angry again, but there was something in her voice, her face, that totally arrested him.

Honesty. Pure and unguarded.

It was such a rare commodity where Jackie was concerned that he decided not to do anything to scare it away. He needed answers and she was the only one who could provide them.

'Mamma was so cross when I told her I was pregnant that I thought she was going to break something.'

One corner of his mouth lifted. Yes, he could well imagine the scene. It wouldn't have been pretty.

'She insisted that adoption was the only way. How could I argue with her? I couldn't do it on my own.'

'What about your father?'

She snorted. 'He might be a blue-sky-thinking entrepreneur, but he's smart enough to do what Mamma tells him to do.' She blinked, looked across at him as she lifted her lashes again. 'I don't think he knew what to do with me. He's good with big ideas and balance sheets, but not so great with the people stuff. I think he wanted the problem to just go away. It was as much as he could manage just to let me go and live with him until the baby was born.'

Romano didn't say anything. He'd always thought of Jackie as being just like him—a child of a wealthy family, secure in the knowledge of her place in the world. He'd even envied her the sisters and the multitude of cousins compared to his one-parent, no-cousin family. His father hadn't been perfect, but he'd always shown him love, and that had made Romano too sure, too cocky, when he'd been young, but he realised that Jackie had never had that.

One loving parent—however unique he might be—had to be better than two clueless ones. His father would never have forced him to do what Jackie's parents had made her do. Yes, her mother had been the driving force, but her father had to take responsibility too. He'd let her down by omitting to stand up for her, to fight for her, to do anything he could to make her happy. That was what fathers were supposed to do.

That was what *he* was supposed to do now.

Jackie lifted her head from her knees. 'Once I was too big to keep it a secret any more, Mamma packed me off to London to live with Dad, and you know what?' She rubbed her eyes with the heels of her hands and took a long gulp of air.

'What?' he said softly. No longer was he trying just to keep her talking, aiming to get dates and times and details from her. He really wanted to know.

'When I went to live with him, he never even mentioned my pregnancy, even though I was swelling up in front of his face. He just…ignored it. It was so weird.' She shook her head. 'And when I came home from the hospital without…on my own…the only emotion he showed was relief.'

She hugged her knees even tighter and rested her chin on top of them. He could see her jaw clenching and unclenching, as if there were unsaid words,

words she'd wanted to say to her father for years, but never had.

She'd been so young. And so alone.

He didn't have a heart of stone. He would have been a monster if he couldn't have imagined how awful it must have been for her. And she'd only told him bare details.

There wasn't anything he could say to change that, to make it better. For a long time they sat in silence.

'What was it like?' he finally said. 'The day she was born?'

Jackie frowned. 'It rained.'

He didn't push for more, sensing that the answer he wanted was coming, he just needed to give her room. The sun had started to set while they'd been in the clearing and, through the trees, the sky was turning bright turquoise at the horizon, and the ripples on the lake glinted soft gold. The temperature must have dropped a little, because Jackie shivered.

Not a monster, he reminded himself, and pulled his jacket off and draped it around her shoulders. The sleeves hung uselessly by her sides.

When she spoke again, she went on to describe a long, complicated labour that had ended in a distressed baby and an emergency Caesarean section. All the half-formed ideas of cute newborns sliding easily into the world were blown right out of the water. Real birth, it seemed, was every bit as traumatic as real life. And she'd done it all on her own, her father away on a business trip and her mother still in Italy keeping up at the façade, lest anyone suspect their family's disgrace.

'What was she like? Kate?'

Jackie's face softened in a way he hadn't thought possible. 'She was perfect. So tiny. With a shock of dark hair just like yours and a temper just like mine.'

He wanted to smile but he felt strangely breathless.

A single tear ran down her cheek. 'She's amazing, Romano. Just so…amazing.'

He sat up a little straighter. 'You've met her?'

She nodded. 'She started looking for me a few months ago and we've been meeting up, trying to establish a bond.' She pulled a face. 'It's not been going very well.'

Well, if she had Jackie's temper, that was hardly surprising.

He watched Jackie as she stared out into the gathering dusk, not sure he'd ever seen her like this before, with all the armour plating stripped away.

'I was going to tell my family after the wedding,' she said. 'She wants to meet them, find out where she comes from. And then Scarlett told me about the letter and I realised I had to tell you too—tell you first. But I was going to do it after today, to avoid all…this.'

You stupid fool, he told himself. All this time you thought she was coming on to you and all she was doing was paving the way for the truth to come out.

'What are we going to do?' she said, with equal measures of fear and uncertainty in her eyes.

He stood up and offered her his hand. She took it, and he pulled her to her feet and waited while she slid her feet back in her shoes.

He stared at a cluster of trees, looking for answers.

Honesty deserved honesty.

'I don't know,' he said, 'but it's time we went back to the party and faced everybody.'

CHAPTER EIGHT

JACKIE felt as if her skin were too thick, as if sensations from the outside world couldn't quite get through. She was floating and heavy all at the same time. The details of the walk back towards the terrace were fuzzy; she didn't remember which path they took, or any of the sights and sounds. Just before they emerged from the trees and into the open, she stopped, pulled at Romano's shirtsleeve.

'Here. You'd better have this back.'

She started to slide his jacket from her shoulders, but he hooked the collar with a finger and pulled it back up. 'Keep it. You look cold.'

She *was* cold. Ever since Romano had said those things to her in the grotto, she hadn't been able to ignore the shivering deep, deep inside. Sometimes it worked its way outwards and she had to clench her teeth to stop them rattling, but it all felt a little disconnected from her, as if it were happening to someone else.

'But—'

'What's the point, Jackie?'

'I…'

She didn't know. Just that it seemed the right thing to do, to hide the fact she'd been in the garden with Romano. The need to keep everything about their relationship under the radar had become a habit she'd never thought to break.

'We don't have to keep it a secret that we went for a walk in the garden,' he said, taking her by the hand and leading her forwards. 'Who cares if anyone sees us together? Your family will know all there is to know soon.'

Jackie nodded, because she recognised the need for response of some kind. Her brain wasn't working fast enough to keep up. Romano's words seemed to make sense. Why hadn't she thought about this before? Somehow in the confusion of recent days she hadn't connected the fact that telling her family also meant that they would know about Romano, that they would all know the secrets she had kept to herself for seventeen years.

Seventeen years.

That was more than half of her life. She'd hated Romano, believed him to be heartless and superficial, for all that time. But now the truth was out. Her secret had been revealed. Wasn't she supposed to feel free? Lighter? But she was too numb to feel anything but the pressure of Romano's fingers on her hand and the warmth spreading all the way up her arm.

In their absence the party had spilled outside. The tall glazed doors that led from the ballroom onto the patio had been thrown open and guests were wandering through the upper terraces, champagne flutes in hands. The large paved area where she and Romano had lunched the other day had been cleared of furniture and planters, and a swing band played while couples danced.

She tugged on Romano's hand, not really knowing why. Just that she didn't want to throw herself headlong back into the party. She didn't know what to do now, how to behave. How could she just go and rejoin her family as if nothing had happened?

He squeezed her fingers lightly and nodded towards the palazzo.

Good idea. Perhaps there was somewhere quiet inside where she could sit and recover.

Despite the fact she was still wearing his jacket, nobody took any notice of them as they weaved their way through the neatly clipped bushes. Romano walked slightly ahead, his face serious but not forbidding.

He'd surprised her by taking her news incredibly well. Too well—he was handling it much better than she was, even though she'd had more time to adjust to recent revelations. Under normal circumstances, doing better than Jackie Patterson at anything simply wasn't allowed, but at this moment she was heartily relieved.

They were only a matter of steps from one of the entrances to the ballroom when she spotted her mother inside, heading their way. Jackie suddenly veered in another direction, following the curve of one of the low hedges. Their hands were still joined and she took Romano with her. He let out a grunt of surprise, then muttered something about quick thinking. Jackie was looking directly ahead but with all her attention behind her as she strained to pick out her mother's footsteps, as she waited to hear her name in that shrill voice.

Just as they reached the edge of the dance floor it came.

'Jackie?'

She kept going. There was no way that she could deal with her mother in her present state. The only fireworks planned for this evening were the ones that Jack and Lizzie had arranged, and she'd very much like to keep it that way.

'Jacqueline!'

She should have known that she'd need a more sophisticated plan than just trying to outrun Mamma.

'Sorry, Lisa,' she heard Romano say beside her as he slipped his jacket off her shoulders and pulled it away. Jackie didn't see how he disposed of it. '*Jacqueline* promised me a dance. You don't mind, do you?'

And then he took her in his arms and spun her away. When the motion had taken her one hundred and eighty degrees and they were disappearing into the crowd, she looked back to see her mother standing there, holding Romano's jacket, with her mouth open.

'I can't believe you just did that!'

Romano smiled his twinkly smile. 'What was it that you called me? Incorrigible?'

A soft laugh escaped her lips. 'I never thought I would say this, but I'm very glad that you are.'

He turned again with some nimble footwork and her mother disappeared from view.

'Glad to know I have a redeeming feature,' he said softly so only she could hear. 'I've been trying very hard to develop one.'

She smiled and laid her head against his shoulder. It hadn't been a conscious decision, but something she'd done on autopilot. How strange that after all this time being in Romano's arms felt as easy and comfortable as it always had done. She really ought to put some distance between them, try to maintain a little bit of self-respect, but she couldn't quite bring herself to reverse her mistake. It was too much of an effort to pull away from him and balance on her own two feet again.

Romano wasn't helping. He slid his arms around her waist and pulled her close, rested his cheek against her temple.

The song changed. In fact it might have changed more than once, but Jackie didn't notice. She just moved side-to-side, round-and-round, enjoying the luxury of having someone to lean on, if only for a few snatched moments. She'd spent her whole life making sure she stood high and lonely on her self-created pedestal, and now she realised that it had left her unspeakably tired.

Romano didn't say anything as they danced; he just held her. There was something wonderfully comforting about a man who knew how to be strong, solid…still. They silently danced like that for what seemed like hours and she was grateful for the chance to have time to absorb and assimilate the afternoon's events.

She tried to pack it all away neatly in her brain, but one question refused to be properly silenced and stowed.

Why hadn't she made more of an effort to talk to Romano about the fact they were bringing a new life into the world? Just one attempt in all that time seemed juvenile. Had she really believed him to be the villain of the piece, an evil seducer of young girls, who cared for no one but himself and never faced the consequences of his actions?

Yes and no.

She'd believed it because she'd needed to believe it. Not believing that had been far too dangerous an option. Hatred had helped her shut the door on him, pull up the drawbridge and keep herself safe. Second chances would have meant giving him access, giving him the opportunity to hurt her all over again, and she couldn't have had that, because any further rejection would have involved Kate too. Self-righteous anger had been the path of least resistance—the coward's way out. She'd taken it without a second thought, without even really understanding her own motivations or the long-term consequences.

But you were fifteen...

No excuse.

She'd been old enough to make a baby and that meant she'd needed to accept the responsibility that went with it. And despite her best efforts she'd failed, had chosen a course of action she wasn't sure now had been the right one.

Could she have made a go of it with Romano?

The truth was she'd never know. They might have survived. They might have been awful teenage parents—children trying to bring up a child of their own. Perhaps it was better for Kate that her adoptive parents had been so stable and sensible. They obviously loved her a great deal.

More than you?

She shut her eyes against that thought. Whichever way she answered it, it made her stomach bottom out.

'I think it's safe now.'

Jackie raised her head from Romano's shoulder. She felt so lethargic. 'Huh?'

'Your mother. She's gone. I think I saw her talking to your uncle.'

Well, that didn't make sense. Mamma and Uncle Luca were hardly on chatting terms.

Romano stopped moving and Jackie looked up at him. 'That means we can stop now,' he said, looking down at her.

Was it wrong that she didn't want to stop? That she wanted to stay here, warm in his arms, and not have to face the world again?

She knew the answer to that one.

Of course it was wrong. It was weak. She let her hands slide from where they'd been resting against his chest and stepped back. All the easy warmth that had flowed between them suddenly evaporated. She didn't know what to say, how to leave gracefully.

In the end she decided to do what she did best and attack the practical angle. Inter-personal stuff was so much harder. She brushed herself down, straightened her hair. 'I think we should talk tomorrow, once we've both had time to think.'

Romano gave her an odd look. 'I agree,' he said slowly. 'Jackie? Are you okay?'

She straightened her shoulders. 'I'm fine. Just tired. You know…'

His mouth creased into a sort of combined grimace and smile. 'I will call you in the morning.' And then he nodded once and walked away.

Jackie blinked. What had she done to Romano? He'd lost all his charm and polish. She'd never seen him take leave of a woman without kissing her on the cheek, or saying something witty to make her laugh and then watch him as he walked away.

Jackie decided to find somewhere quiet to sit and fend off the migraine she felt developing before it took hold.

As she made her way through the wedding guests in the ballroom, heading for one of the smaller rooms, she spotted her mother and Uncle Luca deep in conversation, just as Romano had said. She passed behind her mother, but stayed out of her peripheral vision so she could slip by unnoticed. As she did so she caught a snatch of their conversation.

'I appreciate your honesty,' her uncle was saying.

She heard that little intake of breath her mother made when she was finding a subject difficult. 'I mean it, Luca. I am truly sorry I ruined your birthday dinner by causing a scene. It was extremely bad manners.'

Jackie paused, hovering on the balls of her feet. She'd heard all about her mother's outburst from Lizzie—how Mamma and Luca had got into a terrible fight and then she had told the whole of his unsuspecting family of the twin half-brothers they'd never known had existed. What was it with this family? Surely life would have been much easier for them all if they could have put their pride aside and just accepted each other, *loved* each other. Wasn't that what families were supposed to do?

And then her mother's words actually registered. *Holy*…something or other. Had her mother just apologised? Wonders would never cease! Or maybe it was just the prosecco talking. Mamma had knocked plenty back this afternoon.

'What's done is done,' Luca said, his palms upturned in a gesture of resignation. 'I didn't like the way the news came out, but it was well past time for my family to know about Alessandro and Angelo. It needed to be said. There are too many secrets in this family.'

Jackie wanted to laugh out loud. You don't know the half of it!

But you should. You all should.

Jackie filled her lungs with air and moved slightly to the left so her uncle could see her, but he was too deep in conversation to register her presence at first.

'How can we be strong as a family if we are splintered like this?' he said, taking Lisa's hands in his. 'It's time to put the old grudges to sleep, time to stop the fighting.'

Her mother sighed. 'We've been warring for so long that sometimes I forget how it all started.'

Uncle Luca laughed and kissed her on the cheek, much to her mother's surprise. 'We have war, yes, but that is because we have passion. Let us use that to build rather than to destroy.'

Jackie smiled. Uncle Luca always did get very flowery with his speech when he'd had a few.

'It is a new era,' he added. 'Valentino and Cristiano and Isabella now know about their brothers and I am feeling the need to mend things instead of fortifying them. There is a subtle difference, you know.'

Much to her surprise, her mother nodded. 'I know. Having my girls together again has me feeling that way too, even if I am not convinced we can learn to do things differently. There are some wounds that just don't want to heal, no matter how well we bandage them up.'

Uncle Luca shrugged. 'We can but try.'

Her mother gave the smallest of nods and began to look around. This was Jackie's cue to scuttle away before she was noticed, but she did the unthinkable and took a step forward to stand beside her uncle, putting herself right in the firing line. Uncle Luca gave her a kiss and hug.

'Beautiful as always, *piccolo*.'

She smiled and shook her head. 'Uncle Luca, you're full of it, but I love you anyway.'

'We've been talking about family,' he said. 'Talking about coming together, all Rosa Firenzi's children and grandchildren—as it should be. We need to unearth the roots of the secrets that have grown within us and choked us.'

There he went again. But this time Jackie didn't smile. There was too much truth in what he said.

'I agree,' she said, and turned to face her mother. 'And in this new spirit of unity and openness, I have something I really need to tell you.'

Even though Jackie slept hard and deep that night, she still woke up feeling as if she'd been clubbed about the head with a cricket bat. She crawled downstairs and found Scarlett in the kitchen.

'You're looking fabulous this morning,' Scarlett said with a broad smile on her face.

Jackie just grunted. As always, Scarlett was looking perfect. 'I told Mamma,' she added, by way of explanation.

Scarlett grimaced. 'And you survived? How did you manage that?'

'I don't know,' she replied, shaking her head

slightly. 'It wasn't at all what I'd expected. She was very calm, which was worrying, because either she's had a complete personality transplant or it means there's going to be a delayed reaction.'

'Good luck with that.'

'Thanks.' Jackie walked over to the coffee machine and kept her voice matter-of-fact. 'And I told Romano.'

Her sister didn't say anything.

'Sorry,' Scarlett said from behind her. 'But I thought you just said you'd told Romano.'

Jackie turned round. 'I did. Yesterday. At the wedding.'

'At the…? Wow!'

Jackie nodded. 'I know. I hadn't planned on it, but it was the only way to stop him…never mind.'

Scarlett's eyebrows had almost disappeared into her hairline. 'Oh, really?'

'Let's not go there,' Jackie said, trying her best to make her cheeks cool down. 'Let's just say that things took an…interesting…turn. I hadn't planned on letting it all out on Lizzie's wedding day, but situations arose that warranted full disclosure.'

Scarlett burst out laughing.

'What?' Jackie said, a little cross after her great efforts to remain dignified about the whole thing.

'Just listen to yourself!' Scarlett said. 'As soon as anything becomes remotely emotional, you start getting all wordy and businesslike. You're just like—'

'Don't you dare say it!'

But it was too late. The word had slipped out while Jackie had been ranting.

'—Mamma,' Scarlett finished.

'I am nothing like Mamma. You're the one who looks most like her.' Jackie countered.

Scarlett shrugged. 'What can I say? I've come to terms with the similarities between us. Doesn't mean I like it, but at least I'm not in denial.'

Jackie steadied herself by taking a sip of coffee. 'Don't be ridiculous!' she muttered. 'I'm nowhere near being in denial—about that or anything else.'

'Darling,' Scarlett said before sauntering out of the room, 'denial is your middle name.'

'Rubbish!' Jackie called out after her. 'You haven't a clue what you're talking about.'

She couldn't have.

Jackie wasn't wrong about this. She was rarely wrong about anything.

Oh, yes? Or is it just that you've made sure that you're top of the heap, that yours are the opinions that count, so you never have to deal with being wrong? It's too difficult.

Rubbish, she repeated to herself. One mistake. That was all she'd made in her life. Sleeping with Romano when she hadn't been old enough for that kind of relationship. Okay, and there was the letter. She should have talked to Romano herself. She'd been big enough to admit that to herself—and him—already. And, of course, there was the whole thing about her not getting in contact with him ever since. She knew that was wrong now.

See? Scarlett didn't know what she was talking about. She was capable of admitting her mistakes. She'd just unearthed an extra two. Denial? Hah!

She'd matured since she'd met Kate again. She was ready to turn around and face the past she'd been running away from for so long. That didn't sound much like denial, did it?

What about Romano?

What about Romano? she asked herself in a haughty tone. Things are going well there, too. He hasn't disowned Kate. Early days, but it's all good.

What about how you feel about him?

She closed her eyes, but the question just reverberated round the inside of her head, so she opened them again. I don't love him, she told herself. I'm attracted to him, yes, I can admit that, but that's all there is to it.

See? No denial at all. She was being brutally honest with herself.

But that attraction wasn't a factor in her plan. The only relationship she wanted with Romano was as co-parent. No time for distractions or repeating any of the silliness of yesteryear. They would have to work as a team, think up strategies, come up with a plan for blending their lives with Kate's seamlessly.

You're getting all wordy and businesslike again.

Oh, shut up, she told herself.

The only place they could think to meet nearby where they wouldn't be interrupted was the old farmhouse. Jackie drove her rental car as far up the dirt track as it would go, then walked the rest of the way.

On the surface, it was exactly the same. But then she looked more closely. The olive trees looked even knottier and had grown tall and spindly. Some had fallen or been damaged in storms or high winds and had never been repaired or cleared away. The roof of the farmhouse had almost gone completely and every window was broken. In the cracks in the masonry, weeds and wild flowers had found sanctuary and were busy pushing the stones apart as they anchored themselves better.

She found Romano sitting on the low step by the front door. He was looking at the ground, shoulders hunched, his elbows rested on his knees and his hands hanging limp between his bent legs.

She'd always thought Romano untouchable, capable of dissolving anything negative with a wink or a dry comment, but he looked...broken.

She'd done this.

Why hadn't she tried harder, told him sooner? It all seemed so stupid now, her reasons—her justifications—for keeping their lives separate. She hadn't been thinking of Kate at all, even though that had been a big part of her rationalisation. She'd been selfish, keeping herself protected and pretending she was being altruistic.

But you were fift—

No. No more excuses. You were wrong. Live with it.

'Romano?'

He looked up, smiled. But the eyes didn't twinkle the way they ought to. They were cold and grey and still.

'I want to meet her.'

Jackie nodded and sat down next to him on the step, mirroring his pose. 'Of course you do.'

Of course he did. Why had she expected anything else? This was Romano. Didn't she remember what he was like? Yes, he was full of froth and bluster, but underneath there was so much more. The boy she'd known had carefully hidden his softer, more sensitive side from the world, but he'd revealed all of it to her. Yet she'd only chosen to remember the surface. The lie.

And she knew all about lies. For the first time, she wondered why Romano stuck with his, why he persisted in letting everyone think he was shallow, feckless. Even in a few short days she could see that he'd surpassed the man she'd hoped he'd become. Oh, he'd never lose that infuriating charm—and she wasn't sure she'd want him to—but he was honest and caring, committed and trustworthy. A man worth knowing. A man worth—

No. Co-parents, remember? Focus, Jacqueline.

'When? I'll have to talk to her parents—'

'*We're* her parents.'

He sounded cross. She could understand that.

'I know. But this is complicated.'

He looked across at her, one eyebrow raised. She put her hands up in the air, palms out.

'Yes…okay! *I* made it complicated. I accept that.'

Romano snorted, the kind of snort that said: *What's new…?*

'But it doesn't change anything,' she added. 'We'll have to tread carefully.'

Romano stood up and walked away. 'To hell with treading carefully.'

'For Kate,' she added softly. 'Don't do it for me. Do it for her.'

He turned and nodded, and his expression softened a tad. 'Okay. For Kate.'

He walked back towards her and offered her a hand. Jackie looked at it. He'd done the same many times before. Then she looked at the half-dilapidated farmhouse and the neglected olive grove. Some things could never be the same. She mouthed her thanks, but pushed herself up on her own. He shoved his hand in his jeans pocket.

'I have booked us flights back to London in the morning.'

Jackie's eyes bulged. Tomorrow?

'That's too soon! I need to talk to Sue—her adoptive mother. I thought we said—'

'And I agreed,' he said, his brows bunching together. 'But if I have to wait, I would rather be in London.'

She could understand that too.

'Okay.' She exhaled. It seemed to have been an awfully long time since she'd done that. 'What time do we fly?'

CHAPTER NINE

THE sun drifted softly between the leaves of the olive tree Jackie was propped up against and tickled her cheeks. Her lashes fluttered and then she opened her eyes. It was a perfect afternoon. A gentle breeze flowed round her occasionally and she felt utterly relaxed.

'Hey there, sleeping beauty…'

She shifted against the warm body underneath and behind her and smiled gently. 'Yeah, right. If "beauty" means "the size of an elephant".'

He leaned forward, placed his hands, fingers spread wide, on the curved mound of her stomach. 'You're beautiful…both of you.'

She sank back into him and sighed. 'What did I do to deserve you?'

She waited for an answer, but none came. After a few minutes she realised she wasn't as comfortable, that something hard was sticking into her back, just below her left shoulder blade. She sat up, all the sleepy languor gone, and turned around. The only thing behind her was the twisted trunk of the ancient tree.

Carefully she hoisted herself to her feet, resting a hand on the trunk of the tree when things got dicey, when the seven months' worth of baby growing inside her made it too difficult.

'Romano?'

Nothing. She heard nothing save the sound of the clouds bumping by and the sun warming the dry grass in the meadow.

'Romano!' Louder now, with an edge of panic to her voice.

She began to run—well, waddle—as fast as she could, every step making her feel heavier and heavier. She called his name once more and listened for his reply.

Silence.

No…wait!

She could hear something. Just at the edges of her range of hearing, a familiar rumble…

A Vespa!

She began to half waddle, half run again, supporting her stomach underneath with splayed hands, searching, calling…

Soon it got dark and it began to rain. Not the warm, heavy drops of a summer storm, but cold, icy drizzle that chilled her skin and sank into her flesh. There were no meadows and olive trees now, only grey paving slabs and narrow brick alleyways. And the rain, always the rain. She began to shiver.

Where was he? Where had he gone?

She kept looking, no longer running, just loping along as best she could, putting one foot in front of the other, through dirty puddles and potholed backstreets. It seemed to take hours to find somewhere she recognised.

Did she know this street? The trees reminded her of the ones near her father's house, but the buildings were wrong—too small, too dirty. And not a single one had a light on.

Another shiver ran through her and she instinctively reached for her bump, a habit she'd developed in the last few months, a form of self-comfort.

But her fingers found nothing but fresh air.

Now she was grabbing at her stomach with both hands, but it was saggy…empty…the hard, round proof of the life inside her gone.

'No,' she whispered as her legs buckled under her. And then the whisper became a scream.

'*No!*'

Jackie, although her eyes were still closed, breathed in sharply and tensed. Romano lowered the paper he was reading and turned to watch her, lying rigid in the half-reclined seat.

'It's just turbulence,' he murmured, watching the movement below her closed lids and guessing she'd just woken up. 'The captain mentioned a while ago that the descent into Gatwick might be a bit bumpy.'

While he'd been talking she'd opened her eyes. She looked very sad, almost on the verge of tears. 'I'm sorry it hasn't been a smoother journey.'

Jackie nodded. And then she looked away, turned to the window.

Romano straightened in his seat and stared straight ahead. He sensed that Jackie was finding his smooth composure irritating. Even he was finding it irritating, but he didn't seem to be able to snap out of it. What was the alternative? Lose his temper? Have a breakdown? He would be meeting his daughter for the first time in a few days and the last thing he needed was to be a nervous wreck. What good would that do anyone?

On the other hand, he wasn't sure he wanted to be the same old, skating-on-the-surface Romano. He wanted to change, be better. Learning he'd been a father for the last sixteen years had caused him to look back on that time with fresh perspective.

He'd been successful professionally, yes. But the rest of his life? Full of ugly holes, a waste-land—which was odd, because he'd always thought he'd been having so much fun. Why had he never seen this desolation before?

Ah, but you saw it a long time ago. Jackie showed you.

He shifted in his seat and frowned.

But he'd done something about that, changed since then. He'd matured, hadn't he? He'd stopped living the life of a poor little rich kid and had learned how to work for a living.

Work. Is work life?

Oh. Now he got it. He'd channelled his new-found sense of responsibility into his professional life, but not much had spilled over into his private life. True to form, he'd been so shallow that it had taken him seventeen years to see that. And once again, it had been Jackie Patterson that had held the mirror up to his face.

He turned just his head, the leather of the headrest squeaking against his ear, and looked at her.

It was Jackie who had caused him to look deep inside himself as a teenager. At first he'd been horrified by the casual arrogance he'd seen, but she'd not let him stop there, she'd brought out the nobler virtues that had been rusting away in the dark—honesty, courage, love. Things he'd thought he had lost for ever after the death of his mother.

He'd cried right up until the funeral, but after that he'd become numb. When he'd thought of her, he'd been unable to produce a single tear. He'd been so upset about that he'd just stopped thinking of her, worried he was a bad person for not being able to feel anything more.

It had been a horribly short time before his father had started disappearing regularly, being photographed with one woman after another, but Romano hadn't judged him. He'd known that his father had adored his mother, and that this had just been his way of distracting himself from the grief he'd been too afraid to feel.

A cold churning began in his stomach, nothing to do with aeroplane food. *Like father, like son,* Lisa Firenzi had once said to him. She'd meant it as a compliment, but suddenly another layer of his life was ripped back, exposing the unflattering truth.

He'd let his guard down once, briefly—for Jackie—and when she'd walked away without a backward glance, so he'd thought, he'd done what he'd always done. Instead of asking himself why, of being brave enough to keep trying until he'd made her listen to him, he'd given up, run from those awful feelings of not being good enough to stay around for. And he'd kept himself busy with pretty young things like Francesca Gambardi, distracting himself.

He'd been seen out and about with the cream of the fashion world, A-list celebrities. Women who had everything. And yet he hadn't wanted *everything* from even one of them. Where Jackie had been high-maintenance, abrasive, complex, he'd chosen to date bland, interchangeable blondes who would sit at his feet and worship. No threat there. He'd been safe.

He'd also been incredibly bored.

At the time he'd told himself not to be so stupid, told himself he was reaching for a fantasy that didn't exist, and that he might as well enjoy the moment. Despite his best efforts, he'd never been able to convince himself he was in love.

Jackie sighed softly and pulled her seat belt a little tighter. The plane was rocking now as they descended through a thick layer of cloud. She glanced across at him and when she found him looking back at her she averted her gaze and pulled the duty-free magazine from the pocket on the back of the seat in front of her.

Only her.

He'd only ever loved one woman.

Did that mean she was the love of his life? The one he was fated to be with?

He let out a gentle huff of a laugh. His friends would never let him live it down if they knew he was thinking like this.

He really hoped he was wrong. If Jackie had been 'the one', then his chances of finding anything close to a fulfilling love life in the future with someone else were zero. And that was a scary thought. He couldn't live his life looking over his shoulder, believing his one chance was behind him, getting farther and farther away with each passing year. No wonder he'd not wanted to consider this before. It had been much more comfortable to pass her off as a fling and kid himself that the chance to have what his mother and father had had was still in his future.

She'd become a speck in the distance, a grain of sand that irritated and niggled now and then. Not any more. They were slap-bang in the middle of each other's lives now, joined for ever—but not in the naïve way they'd imagined when they'd been young and in love.

What did it mean? Was this a second chance or a cruel joke? He was slightly terrified by either option.

Getting involved with Jackie again would be…complicated. But if that wasn't his fate, it didn't seem fair that he'd been woken up to the truth only to make him ache for chances lost. He'd have preferred to stay happy and ignorant in the shallows if that were the case.

No. No, he wouldn't.

Somehow he knew the mix of emotions that was finally breaking through the crust of numbness was necessary. Kate didn't need a father who would only provide money, status and a million opportunities to have too much too soon. She needed a man who could be there for her, who could communicate his love without flashing his credit card. And he wanted to be that man.

Love.

Normally that word made him itchy.

But when he thought about the girl he was yet to meet, who didn't even know he existed, warmth flooded every vein and filled his chest to bursting point.

He loved his daughter. He always would. Strangely, the realisation didn't bring panic, but relief.

The captain announced it would be another twenty minutes before they were able to land. A collective sigh of frustration travelled through the cabin.

Jackie held hers in.

She held everything in.

She felt very similar to how she did when a bee or a wasp was buzzing round her. She knew she needed to be still, calm, but the effort of doing so made her feel as if she were going to implode. Even in the wider business-class seats, she felt crowded. Romano was too close and she couldn't switch her awareness of him off, no matter how hard she tried to ignore it.

That stupid dream was lingering in her sub-conscious, flavouring the atmosphere, making her want things she shouldn't, ache for things that were impossible.

She'd dreamt about him every night for the last week, ever since he'd done up her zip and given her the tingles. Had that only been a week ago? She felt as if she'd aged a decade since then.

She turned that thought around and made it work for her.

Act your age, Jacqueline. You're a mature woman in control of your emotions. You're too old for silly fantasies and fairy tales. You've got to stay focused, strong. For Kate's sake.

Think of Kate.

She shifted her hips slightly under her seat belt and angled herself to face Romano. 'I got a text from Kate's adoptive mum, Sue, before we boarded. She was responding to the message I left.'

Romano looked completely relaxed, even with his feet planted squarely on the floor and his arms on the arm rests of his chair. Most people would look rigid in that pose, but Romano just looked as if he owned the world and was slightly bored with it. If there hadn't been a spark of interest in those grey eyes, she'd have wanted to slap him.

'Kate's finished all her exams,' she continued, 'so she doesn't have any school at the moment. Sue's going to see if she wants to meet up with me tomorrow, but she stressed it was totally up to Kate and she wasn't going to push it if Kate had other plans.'

Romano blinked and his lids stayed closed just a nanosecond longer than they needed to. 'What about me?'

Jackie cleared her throat, tried to make herself sound as neutral as possible. 'I think we need to minimise the shock factor.'

No, the overwhelming first meeting loaded with fears and expectations hadn't gone brilliantly for her and Kate. Too much pressure on them both. And it had set the tone for subsequent meetings, a tone that was doing its best not to fade away. She wanted to spare him that. After all she'd done, it was the least she owed him.

'What does that mean?'

'I don't think we should tell her straight away. I'll take her out for the day. You can come along, and she can get to know you a bit first.'

Romano still lounged in his seat, but there was something about the set of his shoulders now that gave him away. That spark in his eyes had turned cold.

'So…who do you introduce me as? Your boy-friend?' His eyebrow hitched ever so slightly, making an innocent suggestion sound all rakish and inappropriate. Jackie felt the familiar slap-or-kiss reflex and her cheeks got all hot and puffy. He was doing it on purpose, to get a rise out of her, making her pay for her unwanted suggestion.

'No. Of course not.'

'No,' he said, a dry half-smile on his lips. 'Stupid idea. Who would believe anything so…what do you always say? Ah, yes. *Ridiculous.*'

The eyebrow dropped and his mouth straightened as the ever-present lopsided quirk evaporated. Her breathing stalled for a heartbeat and then kicked in at double speed.

This man was the darling of the gossip mags for his seductive charm, his devil-may-care attitude but, when the devil *did* care, he was twice as devastating. Knowing this, seeing what everyone else usually missed, was what had got her into trouble the last time. She didn't want to see it now.

'What about us? What are *we*, Jackie?'

His voice was all soft and rumbly. Her throat suddenly needed moisture. She reached for the glass of water perched on the arm of her chair and then remembered that the stewardess had cleared it away.

'There is no *us*,' she managed to say after swallowing a few times.

His eyelids lowered a fraction; the shoulders bunched a little further. 'We have to have some kind of relationship,' he said. 'We have a daughter together.'

'I know that. Don't you think I know that?' She heard the shrewish tone in her voice and made herself breathe, consciously relaxed her vocal cords before she tried again. 'We're…co-parents. That's all.'

The infuriating smirk was back. 'That sounds very formal. This isn't a business merger. You know that too, yes?'

She folded her arms across her stomach. 'It's the best I could come up with,' she snapped. 'Stop making fun of me. This isn't easy for either of us, and you're taking this out on me by being all…by making me feel all…' She shook her head, gave a half-shrug. 'You know what you're doing, Romano.'

He dismissed the whole thing with a slight pout of the bottom lip and an imperious wave of the hands.

They both straightened in their seats and stared straight ahead. For the longest time, as the plane circled and circled, he didn't say anything then, just as the jet straightened and began to lower again, making her ears feel full and heavy, he spoke. His voice was quiet, all the bravado gone.

'Do you think she'll like me?'

With just that one question, walls inside Jackie that had been built and firmly cemented into place years ago crumbled like icing sugar. She'd never heard such self-doubt in his voice before, such sadness. It broke her heart.

She didn't have to force the smile that accompanied her next words. 'Of course she will.'

He looked across at her without moving his head

much, just his eyes. That hooded, sideways glance reminded her so much of the boy who had made it his mission to be cool, no matter what. The boy she'd lost her head and her heart to. The air turned cold in her lungs.

'Everybody does,' she added, keeping the smile in place, even though her mouth wanted to quiver.

He broke the moment with a subtle shift of his features and she knew he had his mask back in place while hers was still sliding.

'That is true,' he said, pretending to be serious, but covering his real vulnerability with a twinkle and a smile in his eyes. 'I am me, after all.' But what he said next just confused her further, because she couldn't tell if he was mocking her or in earnest. 'You don't.'

She didn't leap to agree with him the way she knew she should have done and, for the life of her, she didn't know why. The only option was to follow his lead and descend into razor-sharp humour.

'Maybe that's because I'm a world-class bit—'

He covered her mouth with the tips of three fingers, leaned in close enough to make her pulse race and shook his head.

'You might be able to fool the rest of them,' he said, glancing over his shoulder and then locking his gaze back onto hers, 'but you can't fool me.'

* * *

Waiting. He'd never liked it. Now he absolutely hated it.

He wanted to meet Kate.

His every waking moment was spent anticipating this moment, and the more he waited, the more he started to think he'd be the worst father in the world and should probably just get back on a plane to Naples and do the kid a favour.

But he couldn't leave.

He sat down on the edge of the hotel bed and stared at his shoes. It should have made him laugh that he could actually see tracks in the carpet from this angle. Not that he'd worn it away. It was just his pacing had brushed the pile into a wide stripe.

When Jackie had first told him about his daughter he'd been furious. It had been easy to be angry; everything had been black and white, right and wrong, but now he'd been living with the knowledge for a while he was only too aware that anger had been the first of so many emotions he'd experienced.

He stood up again. It was all so complicated. Multi-layered. Confusing.

Jackie's actions—her choices—that had seemed so wrong to him, now were much more understandable. He knew the same gut-wrenching fear of rejection, the same awful sense of impending failure, had pushed and pulled her too.

He'd forgiven her.

That might seem odd to some, especially as revenge and retribution were coded into his genes, but from the moment she'd collapsed onto the grass and told him of the rainy day when Kate had come into the world in that strange monotone voice of hers, he hadn't been able to stop his heart going out to her.

At the moment his generosity annoyed him. He wanted to be cross with her, cross that she'd scuttled back to her house and had left him to his thoughts while he'd booked into a nearby hotel. He needed her to distract him.

Because distracting him she was.

The phone rang and he was relieved to hear her voice on the other end of the line. Meet up for dinner to finalise plans for tomorrow? Sure.

He filled up the hour before dinner by having a shower and at eight o'clock sharp he met Jackie at some overpriced restaurant close to both her flat and his hotel in Notting Hill. One look at the menu told him he was going to order an unpromising appetiser just so he could send it back and vent some of this nervous energy that was eating him alive.

As soon as they'd ordered, Jackie got straight down to business. It was as if the London air had breathed fresh starch into her.

'I thought we could either go to this new art gallery I've heard good things about, an exhibition on Chinese music or a walking tour of Churchill's London. What do you think?' she asked without even cracking a smile.

'That's the sort of things you do with Kate when you take her out?'

Jackie nodded, but was distracted by a movement near the kitchen, which heralded the arrival of their appetisers.

'How about I pick the venue?' he said. 'It's the least you can let me do, if I am going to ride shotgun.'

Jackie's mouth tightened and her eyebrows puckered. 'But you hardly know London—'

'I know it well enough,' he said, refusing to blink or even look away. 'I've been here plenty of times—for business and pleasure.'

'Oh…okay.' She kept scowling as the waiter placed a dish of seared scallops in front of her. Romano studied his calamari with disappointment. It looked much better than he'd expected.

The waiter had only retreated a few steps when Jackie called him back. 'I can't possibly eat these,' she said, shoving the plate back at him. 'They're horribly overdone. Bring me something else.'

That was when Romano began to chuckle. All the tension rolled out of him in wave after wave of laughter. Jackie just stared at him as if he'd lost his mind. Perhaps he had. Tomorrow was the most important day of his life and he was acting like an idiot.

'You are not as English as you make out,' he finally explained when he was able to get a word out.

'Of course I am,' Jackie said, lifting her chin. A tiny twitch at the corner of her mouth gave her away.

As they continued their meal Romano realised he hadn't watched Jackie eat in the last week. Once she'd attacked her food with passion, now she measured it out with meticulous cuts, removing any trace of fat or sauce or flavour. He eyed the steamed vegetables she'd requested to go with her plain grilled fish suspiciously. Why did he know she was going to order nothing but black coffee for dessert? How had he guessed that she'd leave half of her meal picked over but not eaten?

Because he'd seen this behaviour before.

Suddenly it all made sense.

He could see it so clearly, as if he'd known her during the time when she'd punished her body, when she'd denied herself life and pleasure. It didn't take much imagination to fill in the blanks of the years he'd missed. He could tell she wasn't in the grip of it any more, but the ghosts of old habits lingered.

He wanted to tell her that she hadn't needed to do it to herself, that she was the bravest, strongest, most maddening woman he'd ever met. That she ran circles around the doe-eyed, physically interchangeable *girls* that seemed to be everywhere these days. Her sharp humour, her quick mind—and, yes, her giving heart—set her apart, but he doubted she'd believe him.

And that was when it hit him like a steel-capped boot to the solar plexus.

It didn't matter what had happened in the past. He still wanted her.

No. He wasn't ready to admit that yet.

He focused back on her half-finished food. This was her coping mechanism. So what was she coping with? What was she finding hard to deal with?

'You're nervous,' he said as the waiter cleared away their plates.

She'd been folding up her serviette and she paused. Without answering, she carried on, folding it into perfect squares—once, twice, three times. And then she laid it on the table and smoothed it flat.

He pushed harder. 'Why?'

She looked up at him, moving only her eyes and keeping her head bowed. 'Tomorrow.'

'About me? You think I'll blow it? That I won't be up to scratch?'

She exhaled and everything about her seemed to deflate a little. 'I don't want to think that way, but I'd be lying if I didn't say I'd worried about it once or twice.'

Thanks, Jackie. That's the way to put a man at ease.

She shook her head. 'I'm more worried about me than I am about you.'

He frowned. 'I don't understand.'

'It's not been going well, Romano. Kate and I...' She gave a hopeless little shrug. 'We can't seem to find any common ground. I'm worried that she's slipping away from me. Again.'

Just the panic at the thought of the same thing happening to him was enough to erase any lingering indignation that her less-than-subtle but totally honest answer had caused. They didn't need coffee. He signalled for the bill.

'*Andiamo*,' he said.

Jackie just nodded.

A few minutes later they were walking down the street, the warm, slightly humid air of the summer evening hugging them close. Jackie didn't seem to be thinking about where she was going, but her feet were taking her in the direction of her tall white house and he kept pace beside her.

He took her hand and she let him.

They were the only two people in the world who felt this way at this precise moment. Both of them waiting, fearing, dreaming of what might happen in the morning, their fate resting in the hands of a stranger. Yet that stranger was their daughter.

Somehow the skin-to-skin contact, their fingers intertwined, communicated all of this. They didn't need to speak. The silence continued until they were standing on Jackie's doorstep.

She turned, her back to the door, and looked somewhere in the region of his chest. 'I can't lose her again,' she whispered. And then the tears fell.

Romano was momentarily stunned. He'd seen Jackie cry before, of course, but this was different. Each bead of moisture that slid down her face was alive with heartbreaking desperation. Until a few days ago, he wouldn't have understood that, but now he did. She couldn't give up now. He wouldn't let her.

He rested his hands on her shoulders, pulled her a little closer. 'You won't.'

She looked up into his face, eyes burning. 'You don't know what it's been like.'

He wanted to say something, but the words weren't in his head yet. He knew what she was like deep down inside, how she loved freely and passionately and completely. He knew she had it in her to win her daughter's heart.

He moved his hands up her neck, held her face gently and stroked her cheeks with the sides of his thumbs. 'You can do this, Jackie. You have so much to give—if only you'd let yourself.'

She blinked another batch of tears away and stared back at him. *Do you think so?* her eyes said. *Really?*

He started to smile. *Really.*

This was the Jackie he'd missed all these years, this unique woman full of contradictions and fire. Finally she'd peeled the layers back and he could see the woman he'd loved. The woman he still loved—God help him.

He sealed the realisation with a kiss, bending forward, pressing his lips gently against hers. It reminded him of their first kiss ever: tender, slightly hesitant, as if they both could hardly believe it was happening. This kiss was far sweeter than the hungry ones they'd shared in the grotto, because it joined them. They weren't just 'co-parents' any more; they were Romano and Jackie—nothing more, nothing less—two souls that were meant to be together.

Full of romance and drama as teenagers, they'd seen themselves as a modern-day Romeo and Juliet. Now, as he held her close against him, as he felt her warm breath through the cotton of his shirt, he hoped with all his might that their tragedy would end up better. He wasn't sure he could lose either her or Kate again.

He kissed her again, losing himself in her softness, in the feel of her slender frame within his arms.

Every soft breath from her lips pulled him deeper. He knew he was lost now. He might as well admit it.

She broke the kiss and shifted back a little to look at him. He just drank her in, letting his eyes communicate what his mouth was on the verge of saying.

'I—'

She quickly pressed her fingers to his lips, mirroring the gesture he'd made on the plane.

'Don't say it,' she whispered, looking not angry but very, very frightened.

'I want to,' he said plainly, unable to keep the beginnings of a smile from his lips.

Jackie just looked pained. 'Then you're more of a fool than I am.'

He knew this wasn't going to be easy; he'd been prepared for that, but something in her tone made his insides frost up.

'You feel the same way. I know you do.' The smile uncurled itself from his mouth and left.

She shook her head. 'It's just chemistry, Romano. Echoes of long ago. We couldn't make it then, how are we supposed to make it now?'

He threw his hands upwards in lieu of an answer. He didn't know how or why; he just knew.

'We were kids back then,' she said, stepping to the side and walking back down the garden path a little. 'We weren't ready for that kind of relationship.'

'We're not kids any more.'

'I know. I know.' She clasped her hands in front of her and straightened her back. 'But I don't think we're any more ready for it now than we were then.'

'What you mean is—*you're* not ready.'

'Neither of us are ready. I don't want—'

'Save it, Jackie!' Unfortunately, he knew only too well what she didn't want. Him.

'It wouldn't work,' she said, looking and sounding infuriatingly calm. 'You know that, deep down.'

'Then what was all this about?' he said, walking up to her and invading her space, reminding her of just how close they'd been a few moments ago.

'Like I said—chemistry.'

Oh, she really knew how to send him skyrocketing.

He clenched and unclenched his fists. 'So what you're saying is, I'm good enough for a—' he was really proud that he managed to find a milder English idiom than the first that had come to mind '—for a roll in the hay, but I'm not good enough for anything permanent? And you call *me* shallow?'

Jackie got all prim and prickly on him. 'I'm not saying that at all!'

Somehow the fact he had her all flustered too made him feel better, but the glow of triumph only lasted for a few seconds and then he was feeling as if he needed to burst out of his skin again.

He moved closer and closer to her, walked round her and kept going, so she backed up until she was pressed against her front door and had nowhere to go.

'Then maybe I should be the man you think I am and give you what you want,' he said with a devilish twinkle in his eye, his lips only millimetres from hers.

If she'd looked fierce, or frightened, he would have walked away as he'd intended to, but he saw her pupils dilate, heard the little hitch of breath that told him he wasn't entirely wrong, so he kissed her instead. Hard and long and hot. And he pulled back before she had a chance to push him away, while her fingers were still tangled in his hair and her chest was rising and falling rapidly.

The name she called him wasn't nice.

He shrugged. The contrary kid in him rejoiced in having her confirm her assessment of him, even if he knew it was no longer the truth. If she couldn't see it, then it was her loss.

He walked back down the path and swung the black iron gate wide. 'I'll be here at nine with a car to pick you up,' he said. 'Wear comfortable shoes.' And then he strode away into the falling darkness.

CHAPTER TEN

JACKIE opened the lock with fumbling fingers and crashed through her front door. Once she'd run up the stairs and shut herself in the sanctuary of her bedroom, she sat on the end of the bed, knees clamped together, back straight, and stared at the warm angled patterns the street lamp was making on the wall through the plantation shutters.

She had not seen that coming.

She *should* have seen it coming.

Ever since she'd told Romano about Kate, he'd changed. She'd thought he'd stopped thinking about her that way, had thought that the way the air fizzed every time he was close was a totally one-sided thing.

Why? Why did he want this?

Why did he want *her*?

She didn't get it, really she didn't. She'd just been grateful that they'd been getting along, while she tried to puzzle out why he didn't hate her more.

She closed her eyes.

Had he really been going to say what she'd thought he'd been going to say?

Her head automatically started to move side to side. That couldn't be right. He couldn't feel that way after all she'd done to him. It had to be the emotion of the moment. He was caught up in a whirlwind of feelings about meeting his daughter for the first time, and she'd got sucked in by accident. When he came back down to earth, he'd realise it was all a mirage.

And yet that kiss...

Her insides felt like ice cream that had just met with a blowtorch. It had been much more than chemistry. She'd lied about that. But she'd had to. She'd had to push him away.

It was the right thing. For her. For Romano. For Kate. She was certain of that.

She opened her eyes again and forced herself to move, forced herself to switch on the light, close the shutters and take a shower. And as she stood there under the steaming jet she asked herself one more question.

Why did doing the right thing always have to hurt so much?

She was giving him the silent treatment. Frankly, he didn't blame her. Things always went wrong when he lost his temper. Why else had he spent most of his life making sure he didn't care too deeply about anything, if not to save himself from these extremes of emotion? It never ended well.

Look at what he'd done: Jackie was sitting on the opposite side of the limo's back seat, almost pressed against the door.

And they'd been making such progress. They'd begun to enjoy each other's company again. Now she thought him an insensitive idiot.

She was right.

All he wanted to do was crawl back under his security blanket of quick wit and smooth banter and forget the whole thing had ever happened. He was nervous enough as it was and he didn't need his heart jumping about as if it were riding a pogo stick inside his chest.

His gaze dropped to her shoes and he felt a familiar tickle of temper down in his gut. Four-inch heels in fire-engine red. They looked fantastic with the skinny jeans, a floaty bohemian top and coloured beads—a look he hadn't expected to ever see her in, but was working for her. Why the change?

Ah, yes. It was part of her costume for today, just as she'd dressed down to come to lunch on the island. She was making sure she looked fun and funky and carefree, dressed in the sort of thing that might appeal to a teenage girl. When was

Jackie going to learn that wearing the right accessories didn't change anything?

They travelled out of central London, past some really grotty areas and then into the leafier suburbs. The car slowed then stopped down an ordinary road filled with semi-detached houses. He glanced over to where Jackie was easing herself elegantly from the car.

And then his heart stopped.

Standing on the doorstep of the house they'd pulled up outside was a young girl with long dark hair and eyes just like his mother's.

Jackie stepped out of the car and smiled. Kate gave a half-wave and a grimace and turned to shout inside that she was going. As Jackie reached the garden gate Sue appeared and gave Kate a kiss and a hug. Jackie ignored the squeeze of her heart as she saw how easy they were with each other.

'I hope you don't mind, but I brought a friend with me.'

What Romano was to her couldn't exactly be quantified, but that was as specific as she wanted to get. She glanced over her shoulder and frowned. Where was he? She could have sworn he'd been right behind her.

She gave Kate and Sue a nervous smile. 'I'll be with you in just a second.'

She turned round just late enough to see Kate roll her eyes and give her mum a weary look.

Romano was nowhere to be seen. She walked back down the path and opened the limo door. It was empty.

Where—?

On instinct she straightened and looked down the road. He was twenty feet away, staring at a neatly clipped privet hedge. She opened her mouth to call him over, but then she noticed the way his hand shook as he turned his back to her and leant on a fence post. He ran his spare hand through his hair then dropped it to his face. Even from the back she could tell he'd just dragged his palm across his eyes.

The wall of ice she'd built that morning disappeared into a steaming puddle.

She walked forwards until she was hidden by the next-door neighbour's hedge, called his name softly and held out her hand. His shoulders shuddered as he took a breath and then turned round. The brave smile he'd forced his face into was her undoing.

Of course she loved him too.

How could she not?

But that didn't change the fact that it was the worst possible thing in the current situation. He walked towards her and she bit her lip, nodded. She understood. Right from the bottom of her heart she felt his pain, because it was her pain too.

He took her hand, kissed her knuckles, placed it back down by her side and looked in the direction of Kate's house, hidden as it was behind a wall of green shiny leaves. She admired his courage, knew why he'd chosen not to hang onto her. Everyone had their pride.

Side by side they walked back to the limo. Kate had ambled down the path and now was staring at Romano with open curiosity.

Jackie took a breath. 'Kate? This is Romano—a friend of mine. He's coming with us. Is that okay?'

Kate tipped her head on one side. 'Suppose so.'

As they climbed into the car she turned to him. 'Are you her boyfriend?'

Jackie held her breath.

Romano made a rueful face. 'No. I am not her boyfriend.' And then he smiled. 'She won't let me be.'

It was probably the most mortifying thing he could have said, but he had such a way with him that it seemed light and funny. Kate even gave a one-sided smile in return.

'So where are we going?' Jackie asked, eager to be included in the conversation.

Romano looked very pleased with himself. 'The zoo.'

Both Jackie and Kate spoke at the same time, an identical note of incredulity in their voices. 'The zoo?'

Inside Jackie wilted. Kate was sixteen, not six! This was going to be a disaster.

'Everybody loves the zoo,' he said, the trademark Romano confidence now completely back in place. Jackie folded her arms and gave him a *'we'll see'* kind of look.

As they drove through the London streets, back in the direction of the city centre, Kate yabbered away to Romano, obviously deciding he was a safer option than her biological mother. Jackie willed her to keep going. She wanted Kate to like him. Wanted her to accept him.

Which was most unlike her. Normally, she wasn't that generous.

Every now and then she caught Romano's eye over the top of Kate's head. If she'd thought there'd been a sparkle before, it had only been a foreshadowing of the light she saw there now.

Isn't she amazing? his eyes said. Look what we made!

She couldn't help but sparkle back in agreement.

Jackie rested against the solid glass of one of the enclosures in the ape house and took the weight off her feet. She looked down at her shoes. Stupid choice. She'd known it when she'd put them on. They'd been payback for that last kiss, the one that had left her both angry and pulsing with desire.

She'd wanted to show him that it hadn't meant anything, that he couldn't tell her what to do.

As always, her hot-headedness had backfired on her. Romano was having a blast of a time with Kate, running all over the place, while Jackie hobbled along behind them. She was the only one smarting from her so-called defiant gesture. She sighed as she eased her hot, slightly swollen foot from its patent leather casing and wiggled her toes.

A sudden pounding behind her made her jump so high she left her shoe behind as she propelled herself forwards and away from where the glass had reverberated behind her. She spun round to see a large black chimpanzee glaring at her and baring its teeth.

Of course Romano and Kate fell about laughing. But she couldn't work herself up to quite the pitch of indignation she'd have liked to. Not when those two laughs sounded so similar and so infectious that she almost joined in.

Romano walked across to where her shoe was lying, picked it up and handed it to her. She jammed it back on her foot. It complained loudly.

'I'm hungry,' Kate said.

'I think it is time to eat,' Romano said, looking at his watch. He looked down at Jackie's feet. 'I saw picnic tables under some trees over there. Why don't you two sit down and I'll get us something?'

Jackie sent him a look of pure worship. How she was going to get through the rest of the afternoon, she didn't know, but at least half an hour or so off her feet might help.

Kate pointed out a free picnic table and jogged towards it while Romano headed off in the direction of one of the zoo's cafés. Jackie trailed behind her daughter and plonked herself down with very little elegance when she reached the rough wooden structure, so desperate was she to shift weight off her feet and onto her bottom.

Kate played with the table, tracing the ridge of some blocky graffiti carved into it with her fingernail. 'He's okay, isn't he?' she said, without looking up.

'Yes,' Jackie said, a little too wistfully for her own liking.

Kate kept her head bowed slightly, but raised her eyes to look at Jackie from under her long fringe. 'And he's definitely not your boyfriend?'

Jackie glanced over her shoulder towards the café. She couldn't make out Romano in the crush inside.

'No.'

'Why not?'

Jackie didn't really want to answer that, but she was aware this was the first conversation Kate had initiated with her all day and she didn't want to jinx that.

'It's complicated,' she finally said.

Wrong answer.

Kate's expression hardened. 'You always say that.'

'Normally because it's true,' she answered with a sigh. 'Life *is* complicated.'

Kate went back to running her finger over the graffiti and the silence congealed around them. Then the finger stopped and Jackie heard Kate inhale.

'Mum—I mean Sue—says things are usually simpler than I make them.'

Jackie just smiled. Maybe there was some common ground here after all. When Kate looked up and saw her smiling, she looked shocked at first, but then the beginnings of a curl appeared on her lips too.

Oh, what Jackie wouldn't give to just vault over the table and pull that girl into her arms. But she was painfully aware that any such gesture might be rejected, so she made do with smiling all the wider.

There had been another first. Kate normally always referred to Sue as 'Mum'; the fact she'd adjusted that, had used her name as well, was a tiny concession to Jackie that she hadn't missed. Maybe Romano would be good for the two of them. If he and Kate got on, it might help somehow. For the first time in weeks Jackie thought her relationship with Kate was starting to go in the right direction. She had hope, and she clung onto it as if it were a life raft.

Romano returned with a tray of ominous-looking foodstuffs. He placed it in the centre of the picnic table. Jackie looked warily at the cardboard cartons and cups that didn't look like skinny, decaff, no-foam lattes. Something cold, fizzy and sweet seemed to be lurking inside.

'Burgers and chips?' she said, trying to sound unfazed.

'Cool.' Kate dived right on in.

Jackie didn't do burgers and chips. In fact she couldn't even remember the last time she'd eaten junk food. She almost said as much, but she managed to stop herself. A comment like that would probably earn her another black mark from Kate.

'Not hungry?' Romano said, with just a glimmer of mischief in his eyes.

Ah. She got it now. Payback for the shoes.

She grabbed one of the square cartons and flipped its lid open. A waft of warm meat hit her nostrils. Romano and Kate were already making great inroads into their lunch, loving every bite. Jackie, however, felt as if she were on one of those high-diving boards, teetering on the edge.

She looked into her carton again.

As fast food went this wasn't too repulsive. The bun wasn't soggy. The lettuce and tomato looked crisp and fresh. She picked the burger up with both hands and held it in front of her, elbows resting on the table.

She'd show Romano Puccini she wasn't afraid of a bit of meat and a few carbs! Without hesitation she sank her teeth into it, taking as big a bite as she could. Now all she had to do was keep it down. She chewed and took another bite. Actually, this was okay—she'd forgotten how nice a little bit of fat with her meat could be.

After a short while, she became aware of someone watching her.

'What?' she said to Romano, mouth still slightly full.

He shook his head and smiled, then pushed a container of chips her way. Jackie wavered for a second. Oh, well, might as well put on a good show. She grabbed a handful and put them in the lid of her open burger box. She'd regret this next week when she saw her personal trainer, but at the moment she just didn't care.

Just so Romano didn't think he'd had a complete victory, she shoved the sticky, fizzy drink back in his direction. 'I draw the line somewhere,' she said, but couldn't help grinning afterwards. He just laughed.

It wasn't long before they were clearing away. Unfortunately the end of lunch meant she was going to have to stand up again. Something she was not looking forward to. Romano went to dispose of their rubbish and then disappeared. She and

Kate just looked at each other in bewilderment when after five minutes he hadn't returned.

'Do you think he's been eaten by a lion?' Kate asked, a little hint of sarcasm in her voice.

Jackie laughed. 'No. I reckon he could sweet-talk most creatures out of having him for supper, especially the female ones.'

Just as she said this Romano appeared round the corner of the café, a brown paper bag from the zoo gift shop in his hand.

Kate stood up and put her hands on her hips. 'Where have you been?'

Jackie shut her mouth. She'd been about to say and do exactly the same thing.

'On an errand of mercy,' he said and produced an ice cream for Kate, which she eagerly accepted. But then he reached into the bag and pulled something else out—the ugliest pair of flip-flops that Jackie had ever seen. They were luminous turquoise and had plastic shells and starfish all over them. He handed them to her.

She kicked her shoes off and slid them on. Heaven.

'I could kiss you,' she said as she plopped her heels into the waiting paper bag and took it from him.

Kate paused from licking her ice cream. 'Why don't you? Sue says it's rude not to say thank you when you get a gift.'

The look on her face was pure innocence, but

Jackie wasn't fooled for a second. Still, Kate was actually talking to her, joking with her, and she wasn't going to spoil that now, and she was ridiculously grateful for the garish footwear. She stood up and gave Romano a quick, soft kiss on the cheek.

'Thanks.'

Kate smiled.

Jackie didn't miss the way his arm curled round her waist and how it didn't seem to want to let her go when she tried to step away again.

'What's next?' she said brightly. 'Snakes or elephants.'

'Both,' Kate and Romano said in unison.

Jackie couldn't remember when she'd enjoyed an afternoon as much. They wandered round Regent's Park Zoo, pointing things out to each other and having increasingly inane conversations that made them all laugh. She wondered how they looked to other people.

Could people tell they were a family? Did they blend in and look like the other adults and children? It would be wonderful if they did. Maybe, if they looked like that on the outside, they could feel like that on the inside too one day.

She and Kate hadn't got along this well in weeks—if ever.

And Romano…

Jackie was starting to anticipate the moments when he'd move closer to get a better view of something, when their hands would 'accidentally' brush. He'd been so wonderful, so…perfect. He made her believe she could be that way too—at least when she was with him. She needed him. Needed him for herself and for Kate. If only she could snap her fingers and have him appear out of thin air every time she met with her daughter. It would help their relationship mend so much quicker.

And maybe, when things were finally on a better footing with Kate, they could revisit the idea of being more than just co-parents. She hardly dared hope it would work between them, but she wanted to believe it might, that maybe second chances existed after all.

Just as the heat bled out of the day Romano called for the car and they all piled inside. After the initial chatter about the day out, they fell into silence, then Kate began to ask Romano about where he lived, who his family were. Jackie listened with a smile on her face as she gazed out of the windows.

Kate was sitting in the middle seat, between her and Romano, and Jackie was suddenly aware of a lull in the conversation. She turned to find Kate looking at her, brain working away at some complex internal question. Without saying anything she transferred her gaze to Romano.

'You're my dad, aren't you?'

Jackie held her breath. Why on earth had she thought they could keep this anonymous? A girl as sharp as Kate was always going to guess, was always going to be one step ahead. She too looked at Romano, willing him to give the perfect answer, even though she was pretty sure there wasn't one.

Romano's face split into the biggest grin yet. It was totally captivating. 'Yes,' he said simply. 'And I'm very proud to be so.'

There *was* a perfect answer! And it wasn't so much in the words as in the delivery. Kate rewarded Romano with a matching smile. 'Cool.'

But over the next few minutes the smile faded, more questions arrived behind her eyes. She turned to Jackie.

'So why didn't you tell me about him right at the start? Why did you say all those things about not needing to know, about how it wasn't the right time?'

Uh-oh. She needed an injection of Romano's effortless charm. Quick. Jackie sent him a pleading look. He gave a rueful smile, and she knew he'd have helped her if he could have done, but this was her question and hers alone. She only hoped she could pull her answer off with as much panache as he had done.

She frowned. How did she say this? She didn't want to tell Kate that she'd thought Romano hadn't wanted her—that would be too cruel. So she started to tell a story. A story about a girl younger than Kate who had unexpectedly found herself pregnant, and her sadly inadequate attempt to deal with the situation. Kate's eyes were wide and round as she listened and as she got deeper into the story Jackie found she couldn't look at her daughter, that she had to concentrate on the fingers endlessly twiddling in her lap instead.

Before she'd finished all she had to say, they arrived at Kate's home. None of them made a move to get out of the car. Jackie kept talking, afraid that if she stopped, she might never have the courage to start again. And then finally there was silence. All was laid bare. She held her fingers still by clasping her hands.

The air in the back of the limousine was thick with tension. Jackie's heart thudded so hard she thought she could feel little shock waves reverberating off the windows with each beat. She looked up.

Kate was crying. Large fat tears rolled down her cheeks. Jackie reached for her, reached to brush them gently away. 'Sweetheart—'

'Don't!'

Kate sprang away from her, back against Romano, her mouth contorted in a look of disgust. Jackie would never, ever forget that look.

'Don't you dare call me that! Don't *ever* pretend

that you care! You couldn't even be bothered to name me. You left that up to Sue and Dave!'

Jackie dropped her hand. Her mouth was open, but she was frozen, unable to close it, unable to do anything.

'You! This was all your fault! All of it!' Kate broke off to swipe at her eyes. Her voice dropped to a whisper. 'You ruined our lives. All of our lives. I…'

Don't say it, Jackie silently begged. Please, don't say it.

'I hate you. I never want to see you again.'

She made a move for the door and Romano clambered out of her way. He reached for her, laid a hand on her arm. 'Kate, please?'

She shook her head. 'Sorry, Romano.'

And then she marched up the garden path and disappeared past a shocked-looking Sue into the house.

Jackie just sat there, numb. Just like that, her whole world had caved in around her. She really, really wanted to blame Romano, but she knew she couldn't. Kate had been speaking the truth. It *had* been all her fault. How could she foist the blame on anyone else?

'She doesn't mean it,' Romano said as he climbed back into the car.

Jackie's eyes were fixed on the back of the driver's seat. 'Just like I didn't mean it when I said I didn't want to see you again? I think you'll find she meant every word.'

'Then you do what I didn't do. Keep trying. Never give up. Don't be a coward like I was and take the easy way out.'

The tiniest of frowns creased Jackie's forehead. She smoothed it away with her palm. 'The easy way out?' she echoed quietly.

Romano nodded. 'Pretending you don't care. Distracting yourself with other things so it doesn't hurt so much.' He let out a dry, short laugh. 'In my case, distracting myself with other girls.'

Jackie felt her shoulders tense. 'I don't want to know how many girls you had to sleep with to get over me, especially not as Francesca Gambardi was first in the queue.'

Romano's arm shot out and he captured her face in his hand. 'Look at me.'

The tension worked its way up from her shoulder and into her jaw. Reluctantly she let him manoeuvre her face until she was looking at him.

'I *never* slept with Francesca. I didn't even kiss her. How could I have? After all that we had?'

She wanted to spit and shout and tell him he was a liar, but the truth was there in his eyes. She nodded and tears blurred her vision.

'You changed me, Jackie. Knowing you made me a better person.'

She started to laugh. That had to be the funniest thing she'd ever heard. As if she had that kind of power! Why, if she could do such miracles, she'd wave a magic wand and make her mother love her, she'd wiggle her nose and Kate would come skipping into her arms.

'Stop it!'

The laugh snagged in her throat. She'd never heard Romano speak that way before and it shocked the hilarity right out of her. She'd never seen him look so fierce.

'You were wrong about me and Francesca. Just allow for the fact that you might be wrong about this too?'

She nodded. Mainly because she knew it was the expected response. She was such a liar. Even when she kept her mouth shut she kept on lying—to him, to herself, to everyone.

'Can you take me home?' she asked, sinking back into the seat and kicking the stupid flip-flops off so they disappeared under the passenger seat. 'I'm starting to get a headache.'

Once again, because of her own stupid decisions— the same stupid decisions—she'd lost her daughter.

Kate refused point-blank to have any contact with Jackie. Texts went unanswered. Calls ignored. If Jackie got creative and dialled from a number Kate wouldn't recognise, she put the phone down on her.

At least she was still in contact with Romano.

Apparently the whole drama had only served to increase the bonding process between father and daughter. They'd been calling each other every day. Romano had even been to the house to see her again.

Jackie knew this because she demanded daily updates. Each evening they'd meet up to pick apart what had happened that day. Romano was unswerving in his belief that Kate would come around eventually. He was deluding himself. He'd even told her he was staying in London until it was all sorted, to which she'd replied that he'd better find himself a nice flat, because the hotel bills would bankrupt him.

By Sunday of that week she'd had enough of torturing herself. A call had come in from the office to say there was an emergency meeting of all the different editors-in-chief of the various international *Gloss!* editions in New York that Monday and Jackie had no reason to tell them to take a hike. Her job wouldn't exactly be on the line if she didn't go, but it wouldn't look good. And with her personal life flushed down the pan, she might as well hold onto the one area that *was* working out.

She was busy throwing things into a suitcase when the doorbell went. She heard her housekeeper let someone in. Moments later there were footsteps on the stairs, then Romano appeared at her bedroom door. She flipped the lid of her case closed, bizarrely ashamed of her haphazard packing, and turned to face him. 'How did it go today?'

He did one of those non-committal gestures that involved both hands and mouth.

'That good, huh?'

'She is a fiery young woman, not too different from another young woman I used to know.' He raised his eyebrows. 'Give her time. All her life she's wanted to know who we were, and it's nothing like the fairy tale she invented for herself. It's been a shock.'

Jackie marched over to her wardrobe and threw the doors open. She didn't know what she was looking for.

'Well, it's all worked out rather nicely for you.'

Romano ran a weary hand over his face and said something gruff in Italian before he answered her properly.

'With two such women! I should be sainted.'

'You do that,' she said, then pulled a black suit from the rail, only to throw it back in again two seconds later.

Romano sat down on the armchair near her dressing table. 'Jackie?'

She peered round the wardrobe door at him. 'Yes?'

'I have something to tell you. Good news, I think.'

She clutched the blouse she was holding to her chest and walked towards him. 'You do?'

'Kate has asked to come with me back to Italy to meet my father, and Sue has agreed—as long as she comes too.'

Of course Sue had agreed. With Jackie she'd been like a Rottweiler, but with Romano…

'She thinks it will help Kate come to terms with all that has happened recently,' he added. 'She hopes that meeting my family—and yours—will help Kate put it all in context. I agree.'

Jackie crushed the silk blouse so hard she feared she might never get the wrinkles out again. 'You want to take her to meet my mother?'

Romano nodded.

A short, hard laugh burst from her mouth.

He dropped his voice, laced it with honey. 'I was hoping you would come too.'

Oh, yes. That would be really popular.

'It's impossible.'

He stood up and walked towards her, and his easy, graceful stride momentarily mesmerised her. What would it be like to just walk into a room and have people react that way…to love you, to adore you? She'd never know. And in truth she really didn't care. There was only one person she wanted to impress and she doubted very much that walking anywhere, anyhow, was going to accomplish that.

He tugged the blouse from her claw-like hands and put it on the bed, then he ironed her fingers out with his and closed his hands round hers. 'Nothing is impossible. Look at us. For years… nothing. And now—'

She began to shake her head.

'No, Jackie. I know you feel it too. What we thought was dead is very much alive.'

She pulled her hands away. 'You're starting to sound like Uncle Luca. Pretty words aren't going to solve this, Romano.'

Jackie opened her case up again and threw the crumpled blouse inside. Romano started to say something, but then stared at her and closed his mouth.

'What are you doing?'

She went and picked the black suit up from the floor of the wardrobe, then folded it clumsily into the case. 'Packing.'

He frowned. 'But you were packing *before* I came in. Why?'

'I'm going to New York. Work. Tomorrow morning.'

CHAPTER ELEVEN

WAS she insane?

Who was thinking of work at a time like this? This was family! And if Jackie handled this badly now she might never be able to repair the damage. Wasn't she even going to try?

He had the feeling that Kate was testing her mother, stretching the fragile bond between them to its utmost. The worst thing Jackie could do now was to disappear. He needed to persuade her to change her mind—and not just for Kate's sake, but for his own.

He'd never expected to want a family, had never been sure he'd know what to do with all that permanence, all those expectations. But now he had one, he'd found himself rising to the challenge. The idea of loving someone, of pledging himself to one woman, come what may, didn't scare him any more. He wanted that adventure.

'You can't go.'

Jackie paused from collecting together an armful of products from a drawer in her dressing table. 'I have to.'

He walked over to her, took each item out of her hands one by one and put them on the dressing table. 'No. You need to come with me, with Kate, to Italy. You need to come home.'

Jackie had her weight on the balls of her feet, rocking backwards and forwards slightly, as if she was getting ready to run. 'There's no point. Not now.' She didn't add the words *not ever*, but Romano heard them inside his head.

She was giving up. Locking herself up tight inside her pride.

But Jackie wasn't arrogant, or full of hot air. Quite the opposite. Pride was her life jacket, her air bag—emotional bubble-wrap. She used it as protection, and as such it was extremely effective.

Even if there hadn't been a trip to New York, she'd have found an excuse not to come with him. And it was this mindset that was dangerous. He had to shake her out of it, show her that there was a better way. He wanted her to learn how liberating it could be to knock down the walls, to feel the breeze on her soul and be *seen*.

But Jackie wasn't thinking about breeze and walls and souls. She was packing.

Romano knew of only one sure-fire way to claim

her full attention, so he decided to play dirty. He waited until she brushed past him on her way to putting more 'stuff' into her case, pulled her into his arms and kissed her.

When he finally felt the tension melt from her frame, he pulled back and looked at her. 'I still love you, Jacqueline. Come with me.'

Jackie went white. Instead of reassuring her, his words only seemed to spook her further. He kissed her forehead and drew her back against him, letting her ear rest against his chest so she could hear the steady thump of his heart. And then he just held her.

'Be brave,' he whispered. 'There is still a chance for you and Kate. And for us. Be patient. There will be healing.'

Jackie, who had been breathing softly against him, went still, and then she wriggled out of his embrace and stepped away. On the surface she was all business and propriety, but he could see the war inside shimmering in her eyes.

'You're going all Italian on me again, saying things you don't mean, getting caught up in the moment…'

A corner of his mouth lifted. 'You know that's not true.'

She moistened her lips by rolling one across the other. 'It doesn't matter if it is or if it isn't—' she shook her head and backed away further '—because I don't love you back.'

The words hit him in the chest like a bullet, even though he knew they were only blanks, empty words designed to scare, with no real impact, no truth to them. She must have seen this in his eyes as he gathered himself together, ready to make another assault of his own.

'Don't flatter yourself,' she said, raising her chin and looking at him through slightly lowered lids.

So this was how it was going to be. Once again Jackie was going to abandon everything that was real in her life in order to keep herself safe.

He wasn't going to beg, but he wasn't above one last attempt at making her see sense—for their daughter's sake.

'Don't do this,' he said.

Jackie picked up the items he'd put back on the dressing table and placed them in strategic points in her half-full case. 'I have to.'

Her voice didn't wobble, but he knew that was only down to supreme effort on her part. He knew this was breaking her heart, but he had to keep pushing. He wanted her to believe in Kate the way she hadn't been able to believe in him all those years ago.

It was useless. As each second passed he watched her use all her strength to board herself up. His compassion for her evaporated in a sudden puff.

He walked away from her, right to the bedroom

door, and back again. 'I never thought you a coward, Ms Patterson, but that is what you are.' He shook his head. 'She deserves more than this from you. A lot more.'

Jackie met his gaze, jaw tense, eyes narrowed. 'You think I don't know that? I can't believe it's taken you all these years for you to work out I'm just not up to it.'

His hands made an explosive gesture, like lava gushing out of a volcano. What was it with this woman? She was so stubborn! So blinkered! It was so…familiar. He took a moment to assimilate that thought. So very familiar.

'If it makes you happy to pretend that's the way it is, fine! Why bother risking anything when you have your wall of denial to hide behind? You know, sometimes you are just like your mother.'

'Get out!'

Jackie was holding a shoe in her right hand. Her fingers were tensing and flexing around the rather sharp heel and he sensed he might need to duck at any second. He kept himself ready but folded his arms across his chest.

'I am not going anywhere until you agree to come to Italy with me.'

'Fine!' She tapped the heel of the shoe on her upturned palm, then tossed it on the bed. Then she pivoted round and headed for her bathroom. The door slammed hard enough to get an answering rattle from the hefty front door downstairs. 'I'm taking a shower,' she yelled through the door. 'And if you are here when I get out, I'll be calling the police!' The sound of drumming water drowned out anything he might say in response.

Impossible woman! He let out a huff of air and scratched his scalp with his fingertips. Think, Romano. He was loath to beat a retreat, but if he stayed and fought Jackie would just dig deeper trenches, hide herself in her iron-clad excuses.

So he would go. But he wasn't giving up entirely. A good soldier knew that when frontal assault wasn't possible, guerrilla tactics were occasionally necessary.

First, he tore a page from a pad by the telephone and wrote down the details of the flight to Naples in the morning. There was still a ticket with her name on it. All she had to do was check in at London City Airport and the seat on the plane was hers. Secondly, he took a moment to retrieve a couple of items he'd spotted in the bottom of Jackie's wardrobe and placed them in her case.

With one final look at the bathroom door he walked out of the room, out of Jackie's house and back to his hotel. He had some packing of his own to do.

* * *

Jackie had such a migraine coming on by the time she emerged from the shower that she took a couple of tablets and crawled into bed, not even bothering to move the case that filled half of it. She'd work round it.

But sleep wouldn't come.

The accusation Romano had flung at her ran round her head, screaming, making her temples throb.

Why, when anyone wanted to get close, did she push them away? It was a reflex she didn't have any control over. Where had that come from?

It didn't take long for her subconscious to provide a clue. She saw herself as a child, sitting halfway up the old pine tree, shivering in the dark. The memory of the cold air on her skin, the prickle of the needles against her arms was very clear. What was less clear was the reason for the tongue-lashing Mamma had given her, but she recalled the look on her mother's face, the one that said once again she hadn't lived up to expectations, that her best just wasn't good enough.

She'd sat up in that tree for hours and had promised herself that whenever she got told off in the future, she wouldn't cry and try to cuddle Mamma again, because that only made her crosser. No, from then on she'd decided she wouldn't make a sound, wouldn't shed a tear. She'd show Mamma she could be a good girl. Even if Mamma didn't believe it, she'd save herself a few smacks for 'making a fuss'.

So when her mother had finally found her late that evening, Jackie had calmly climbed back down to the ground and had taken her punishment without even a whimper.

Somewhere along the line—probably not long after her father had been kicked out—Mamma had decided she was 'difficult'. The label had stuck, even though Jackie had tried a hundred times to peel it off and prove her mother wrong. Why could she never see that? Why was she always so sure she was right?

How did you deal with someone like that? Trying to change their mind was like trying to stop the earth and start it spinning in the other direction.

With these hopeless thoughts in her head, Jackie set her alarm for six-thirty and drifted off into a tense sleep. But the spinning didn't stop. It carried on through her dreams, shaking loose everything she held to be true, turning her over and over until she wasn't sure which way was up.

Kate came and stood next to Romano as he helped the driver load cases into the boot of the car.

'She's not coming, is she?'

He put an arm round his daughter and squeezed her to him. 'I don't know.'

Kate sagged against him. 'It's all my fault. I

shouldn't have said those things. I was horrible and I don't even know why I did it! It's just sometimes, all this stuff is boiling up inside and it all comes out.'

He placed a hand on each of her shoulders and turned her towards him. 'Family…' he said, and added an arm gesture that encompassed the English he couldn't remember. 'This is not easy for any of us. Family is so…so…'

What was the word he was after? It was right there on the tip of his tongue.

A small wry smile curled the edge of Kate's mouth. 'Complicated?'

Romano nodded. '*Sì. Complicato.*'

He shut the boot of the taxi and opened the door for his daughter. What more could anyone say?

An hour before the alarm went off Jackie opened her eyes.

Oh, hell. Romano was right. She was just like her mother.

Why her brain had processed this unfortunate realisation during the night and had decided to wake her with it was a mystery. She rolled over onto her other side and kicked something hard.

Ouch.

Her case.

It was a sign. She might as well catch up on the packing she'd forgone last night. She didn't have to be at Heathrow until ten, but it always made her feel better once her case was all zipped and pad-locked and sitting obediently by the front door.

Coffee first. She slid on some dark pyjama bottoms and an old T-shirt.

Once her coffee was made she went back upstairs and decided she would have to completely redo her case. She didn't even remember what she'd chucked in there last night while she'd been rowing with Romano.

As she walked back into the bedroom she noticed a scrap of paper on the dressing table. She didn't remember leaving anything there so she leaned over to get a better look.

Flight number and time. Destination. Airport.

But not her flight. Not her destination.

She turned her back on the note and walked over to the bed, took a large slurp of coffee, then rested the mug on the bedside table.

Unpacking and reorganising the emotions that were fermenting inside her would just have to wait until later. After New York, probably. There was no way she was going to risk breaking down at the airport or on the plane. Right now she needed something mundane to keep her distracted. Packing a suitcase sounded like the perfect job.

She flipped the lid of her case open and squinted at the contents.

Really?

What had she been thinking packing that blouse? It was so last season.

She tugged it out, intending to get it back on a hanger as soon as possible, but something underneath it in the case caught her eye.

The ugliest pair of flip-flops she'd ever seen.

Eye-piercing turquoise with plastic shells and sea creatures on them.

Gingerly, she reached out and traced a bright orange seahorse with the tip of a nail. It wasn't enough. She picked the flip-flops up and hugged them to her. The soles pressed against her T-shirt, stamping zoo dirt onto her chest.

She didn't cry; she wouldn't let herself.

Unravelling was for later, remember?

So she peeled the flip-flops away from herself and placed them neatly on the floor, a good distance from the rest of her packing, just in case she was tempted. Then she stared straight ahead.

She needed to order a taxi.

It had slipped her mind last night and if she didn't get on the phone soon, she'd have a terrible job getting to the airport in time. Mechanically, she reached for the phone.

* * *

Romano stood with Kate and Sue at the check-in desk. For the first time in his life he envied the people flying economy. There were no queues to delay his party at the business-class desk and he'd gladly have put up with non-existent leg room and a snotty kid kicking the back of his seat if it meant just a few more minutes before they went through security.

He knew he was being stupid, but he'd made a silent bet with himself that she'd appear before they passed through the metal detector and X-ray machines. It was getting closer and closer to their flight departure time, and once they went through into the interior of the airport he knew the chances of Jackie appearing were slim.

The check-in clerk handed him back his passport and boarding pass and he felt the last shred of hope slip from his grasp. Kate glanced towards the entrance, then pursed her lips slightly.

And then they were going through security, flinging their bags into little grey plastic trays and removing their shoes. Romano forbade himself to look back, both physically and mentally. He had something *really* worthwhile to live for now, much more important than seeing his family name on a label in someone's clothes. Now he had a family to pass that name on to, and it mattered in a way he'd never thought possible.

Just as he was helping Sue wrestle her hand

luggage off the conveyor belt, there was some kind of commotion behind them. He ignored it at first, too drained to spend any emotional energy on anyone but his little party, but then someone yelled, 'Do I *look* as if I'm carrying any hand luggage to you?' and all the hairs on the back of his neck lifted and tingled.

He dropped the bag he was holding and spun round.

Right there, giving the female security officer at the metal detector the evil eye, was Jackie. At least, he thought it was Jackie.

This woman had no make-up on, her hair was half hanging out of a ponytail and she was wearing an old lilac fleece and a pair of… What were they? Jogging bottoms? And on her feet were the ugliest pair of flip-flops he'd ever seen.

Kate froze to the spot beside him and Sue crowded in protectively. Jackie stopped waving her passport and boarding pass at the woman in the uniform—he didn't want to think about where she had her money hidden in that outfit—but then she looked up and saw them standing there, watching her. Multiple emotions flickered across her face. Relief. Frustration. Joy. Panic. When the woman officer nodded to indicate she could pass through, Jackie pulled herself to her full five feet six and walked through the arch with her head held high.

Even though his overriding instinct was to laugh out loud, Romano kept his face under control. She'd done well by turning up, but she still had a way to go before it was time for hugs and celebrations.

'Sorry I'm late,' she said, and brushed a tangled strand of hair out of her face. She turned to Kate. 'I need to talk to you.'

Kate was so tense, he thought her over-long teenage body would snap if she moved. He knew she was desperate for some show of emotion from Jackie, but the need to put on a good front must be genetic, because right now she was looking as approachable as...well, as Jackie usually did.

Kate folded her arms. 'So talk.'

Jackie's face fell. 'Here?'

Her daughter just pressed her lips together and nodded.

Jackie took in a breath and blew it out. 'Okay. Here it is, then.'

Where did she start? There was so much she wanted to say, so much she'd left unsaid. Which of the hundred possible speeches she'd rehearsed in the taxi did she pull out of the bag?

Then she remembered how Romano had talked to Kate. *Not so much in the words as in the delivery.* And she knew she had to start right back at the beginning. She wanted to pull Kate into a hug, take hold of her hands, but Kate's body language told her she'd better not try. The best she could do was look her daughter in the eyes and tell her the truth. No varnish. No *gloss*.

'I did name you,' she said, and discovered her knees had just gone all cotton wool-like. 'Right after you were born.'

Kate's eyes widened. 'You did?'

Jackie nodded furiously. 'But I didn't tell anyone. It was a secret name, one just for me.'

Oh, hell, her voice was cracking and she really, really needed to sniff. Kate did it first, and Sue produced a couple of tissues from her capacious hand luggage and offered one to each of them.

'I knew I had to—' her face crumpled and she struggled to get the next few words out without completely going to pieces '—give you away.' Nope. That was it. The tears fell. Her throat swelled up. Kate was staring at her, as if she were a being from outer space. Jackie decided to keep going while she was still able to croak. 'It seemed selfish to tell anyone. It wouldn't have been fair to your new parents…'

She glanced at Sue, expecting to see her normal guard-dog expression, but instead found a warm smile and a look of compassion.

Kate stepped forward and her arms dropped to her sides. 'What…what did you call me?'

Jackie had never babbled in her life. Not until now, anyway.

'That first day, when they let me hold you in the hospital…' She took a great gurgling sniff. 'It would be healthy for me to say goodbye, the social worker said. She was nice…' She paused as a mental picture flashed in her brain and she smiled in response. 'I swear her arms were as thick as my thighs. And she smelled of peppermints and talcum powder. Sorry… I seem to remember every silly detail of that day.'

The four of them were like statues. Passengers coming out of the security checks were pushing past and muttering about people getting in the way, but they didn't move.

Jackie sniffed. 'You can't laugh or hate me for it. I was sixteen and had very funny ideas about things…'

Sue nodded and glanced across at her adoptive daughter. 'Tell me about it.'

Kate blushed.

Jackie wanted to cry and laugh and smile all at the same time. She managed two out of three. 'I called you Adrina, after the lake near Romano's home. It means "happiness".'

Sue nodded. 'That's beautiful.'

'Well, she was.' Jackie looked Kate in the eyes. 'You were. And it tore my heart out to give you away. Don't ever think that I didn't care. I did. But I only let myself feel it for that one day. After that I had to make myself not care, or I never would have survived. And that's why I struggle sometimes…'

Kate frowned. Jackie could see the disbelief in her eyes. 'Because you don't care any more? Because it worked?'

'No!' Here came the tears again. It was just as well she wasn't wearing any mascara. 'Because I *do* care! I love you, Kate…so much. And I've wanted to tell you so many times, but I've taught myself to bury it deep and hide it well. And, even if I do say so myself—' she gave a weak smile '—I'm an excellent teacher. I'm sorry. It's going to take me some time to unlearn all those hard lessons and I'm afraid you are just going to have to be patient with me. One day I'll be a woman who'll make you proud.'

She held her breath and waited, then Kate, who had been looking fiercer and fiercer all through her speech, launched herself into Jackie's arms and held her tight. Jackie, who had never held her daughter since that day in the hospital, wept freely, making the most unattractive noises, and hugged Kate back.

Eventually they separated themselves. Kate reached for the tissue that she'd stuffed in her jeans pocket and decided that it had no more uses left in it. She looked hopefully at Sue.

Sue shrugged. 'I'm all out. Let's go and find some more.' And discreetly she led Kate away in the direction of the Ladies'.

Jackie turned to Romano, who had been standing slightly to the side, and had been silent all through her outburst. He smiled at her.

'Where did you get that lovely jacket?' he said, with a twinkle in his eye.

'It belongs to my housekeeper. I found it by the front door.'

'It's a well-known fact that what a person wears says a lot about them. What do you think your clothes are shouting about you right at this moment, Ms Patterson?'

Oh, help. By the time she'd decided to try and catch them it had been too late to do anything but jump in the cab and tip the driver exorbitantly so he'd make it to London City Airport in time. What must she look like? She was standing here in front of the man she loved in cheap flip-flops, her housekeeper's dog-walking fleece and her pyjama bottoms. Whatever that was saying, she wasn't sure anyone wanted to hear it.

'That I was in a hurry?' she said optimistically.

Romano just threw his head back and laughed out loud. And then he wrapped his arms around her and lowered his head until his lips were almost touching hers. 'No,' he said quietly. 'This is the most beautiful I have ever seen you.' And he kissed her, softly, tenderly, deliciously, to drive the point home. 'Today, your clothes say that you are on the outside who you have always been on the inside—a woman of great courage, great strength and great love.'

Jackie smiled against his lips. 'Really? You got all that from an old lilac fleece? I must wear it more often.'

Romano kissed her once more. Or she kissed him, she wasn't sure which, and then he took her passport and papers from her and tucked them into his bag.

'I don't think the New York fashion gurus are ready for this look yet, so it's just as well you are coming home with me.'

ELISA HADEN

EPILOGUE

NOT long after there was another wedding at the courthouse in Monta Correnti, followed by a small reception for family and friends. Tables and chairs from a restaurant in the piazza outside the church were rearranged to accommodate the bridal party and their guests.

Musicians appeared and serenaded the bride and groom, and wedding guests and locals began to dance in the piazza and the air was filled with song and laughter.

Late in the evening their youngest bridesmaid tottered over the cobbles on her new high heels and handed the bride and groom a medium-sized, slightly wonkily wrapped present.

Jackie gave her daughter a kiss on the cheek. 'You didn't have to get us anything! Just the fact that you came was enough.'

Kate just smiled shyly. 'Open it.'

Romano slid it across the table to his brand-new

wife and she carefully peeled off the bow and wrapping paper. Inside was a big scrapbook. Jackie opened the cover, then instantly covered her mouth with her fingers. On the first page was a picture of a dark-haired baby, grinning toothlessly at the photographer. And after that was page after page of memories—photographs, programmes from school concerts, certificates and badges. It left the bride and groom completely speechless.

'Sue helped me put it together,' Kate explained.

Jackie picked it up and hugged it to her chest. 'Thank you,' she whispered. 'You don't know how much this means.'

'I think I do. I just wanted to say that I understand now, and that I'm sorry I didn't share these moments with you...' She paused and scrunched her face up. 'But I can't be sorry you gave me to Dave and Sue, either.'

A look of sudden horror passed over her features, and Jackie reached out and took her hand. 'That's how it should be, sweetheart,' she said. 'Of course you love them.'

Jackie stood up and pulled her daughter into a hug.

'I love you too, Mum,' Kate whispered in her ear, and by doing so she gave the bride a wedding present beyond price and compare.

They held each other for the longest time, until Kate tugged herself gently away. 'I'm going to go now.' She glanced at where people were dancing in the piazza. 'A really cute boy asked me to dance.'

Romano straightened in his seat and started to look around. Jackie just patted him on the arm and told him to 'stand down', and then they kissed their daughter again and watched her wobble her way back across the cobbles towards where the dancing was.

Later that evening, Jackie and Romano left the town partying and crept away to a little island on a nearby lake for the start of their stay-at-home honeymoon. They walked out onto the terrace, a glass of champagne each, and stared across the lake as it winked the stars back to them.

'I can't quite believe the pair of us managed to produce a human being quite as perfect as Kate is,' Jackie said softly.

'I know,' Romano replied, in that mock-serious voice of his. 'It would be a terrible waste if we didn't do it again. It's practically our duty to the world…'

Jackie turned to look at him. 'Are you saying what I think you're saying?'

Romano took the glass out of Jackie's hand and placed it on the stone balustrade with his own, then pulled her close and kissed her.

'I certainly am.'

She looped her arms around his neck and pulled him close, kissed him in a way that showed just how much she agreed. 'I love you, Romano.'

'You know what I love?' he said, surprising her by pulling back and giving her a cheeky grin.

She shook her head.

'That, although you wouldn't allow me to design your dress—and I was cross about that at first.'

Jackie let out a shocked chuckle. 'Cross? You pouted like a two-year-old!'

He shrugged her comment off. 'No matter. My father has outdone himself. I have never seen you look so breathtaking.' He pulled her close and started to kiss her neck, bunch the silk taffeta up with his hands. 'What I really love, *Signora* Puccini,' he whispered in her ear, 'is that tonight, I get to *undress* you.' His fingers toyed with the top button on a row down her spine that seemed to go on for ever.

Jackie just laughed softly and wiggled closer to give him better access.

'You're incorrigible,' she whispered back.

'Oh, yes,' he said as he gently bit her ear lobe. 'And that is just the way you like me.'

ROMANCE 2-in-1

Coming next month

DOORSTEP TWINS
by Rebecca Winters

Strangers Gabi Turner and powerful Greek Andreas Simonides
are thrown together to care for their baby twin nephews.
Just as they start to feel like a family – the twins'
real father arrives!

THE COWBOY'S ADOPTED DAUGHTER
by Patricia Thayer

Hired to run a quilting course at the A Bar A ranch, Allie is
appalled when brooding cowboy Alex Casali accuses her
of trespassing. Then her little daughter utters her
first words in months – to him...

SOS: CONVENIENT HUSBAND REQUIRED
by Liz Fielding

May Coleridge has one month to find a husband and save her
home. Adam fits the bill, but he's been left holding his sister's
baby! May loves babies...can they make a deal?

WINNING A GROOM IN 10 DATES
by Cara Colter

Geeky Sophie is all grown up when her childhood crush
returns from the army. She still dreams of winning Brandon as
her groom but she's only got ten dates to do it!

On sale 6th August 2010

Available at WHSmith, Tesco, ASDA, Eason and all good bookshops.
For full Mills & Boon range including eBooks visit
www.millsandboon.co.uk

MILLS & BOON®

NEW VOICES

Do you dream of being a romance writer?

Mills & Boon are looking for fresh writing talent in our biggest ever search!

And this time…our readers have a say in who wins!

For information on how to enter or get involved go to

www.romanceisnotdead.com

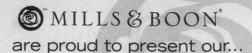

MILLS & BOON

are proud to present our...

Book of the Month

Time Raiders: The Protector
by Merline Lovelace
from Mills & Boon®
Nocturne™

Cassandra's psychic skills are the reason she's been sent to seventh-century China on a dangerous mission. Soldier Max is supposed to protect her, but when the crusade turns deadly, Max and Cassie are powerless to fight their growing attraction.

Mills & Boon® Nocturne™
Available 18th June

Something to say about our Book of the Month?
Tell us what you think!
millsandboon.co.uk/community

0710/01a

MILLS & BOON
MODERN

The Drakos Baby

An enthralling linked-story duet by best-selling author

LYNNE GRAHAM

A Greek billionaire with amnesia, a secret baby, a convenient marriage…it's a recipe for rip-roaring passion, revelations and the reunion of a lifetime!

PART ONE
THE PREGNANCY SHOCK
On sale 16th July

Billie is PA to gorgeous Greek billionaire Alexei Drakos. After just one magical night together, an accident leaves Alexei with amnesia and Billie discovers she's pregnant – *by a man who has no recollection of having slept with her…*

PART TWO
A STORMY GREEK MARRIAGE
On sale 20th August

Billie's baby has been born but she hasn't told Alexei about his son's existence. But her return to Greece and their marriage of convenience will lead to a shocking revelation for Alexei…

Available at WHSmith, Tesco, ASDA, Eason and all good bookshops
www.millsandboon.co.uk

DESERT HEAT...

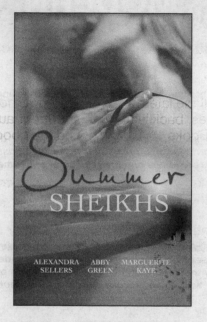

Three sheikhs are sending
temperatures soaring in:

Sheikh's Betrayal by Alexandra Sellers

Breaking the Sheikh's Rules by Abby Green

Innocent in the Sheikh's Harem
by Marguerite Kaye

Available 16th July 2010

www.millsandboon.co.uk

WEB/M&B/RTL2

Discover Pure Reading Pleasure with

**Visit the Mills & Boon website for all
the latest in romance**

◎ **Buy** all the latest
releases, backlist
and eBooks

◎ **Find out** more
about our authors
and their books

◎ **Join** our community
and chat to authors
and other readers

◎ **Free** online reads
from your favourite
authors

◎ **Win** with our
fantastic online
competitions

◎ **Sign** up for our
free monthly
eNewsletter

◎ **Tell us** what you
think by signing up to
our reader panel

◎ **Rate** and review
books with our star
system

www.millsandboon.co.uk

 Follow us at twitter.com/millsandboonuk

 Become a fan at facebook.com/romancehq

0203 455 X

2 FREE BOOKS
AND A SURPRISE GIFT

We would like to take this opportunity to thank you for reading this Mills & Boon® book by offering you the chance to take TWO more specially selected books from the Romance series absolutely FREE! We're also making this offer to introduce you to the benefits of the Mills & Boon® Book Club™—

- **FREE home delivery**
- **FREE gifts and competitions**
- **FREE monthly Newsletter**
- **Exclusive Mills & Boon Book Club offers**
- **Books available before they're in the shops**

Accepting these FREE books and gift places you under no obligation to buy, you may cancel at any time, even after receiving your free shipment. Simply complete your details below and return the entire page to the address below. You don't even need a stamp!

YES Please send me 2 free Romance books and a surprise gift. I understand that unless you hear from me, I will receive 5 superb new stories every month including two 2-in-1 books priced at £4.99 each and a single book priced at £3.19, postage and packing free. I am under no obligation to purchase any books and may cancel my subscription at any time. The free books and gift will be mine to keep in any case.

Ms/Mrs/Miss/Mr _____ Initials _____

Surname _____

Address _____

_____ Postcode _____

E-mail _____

Send this whole page to: Mills & Boon Book Club, Free Book Offer, FREEPOST NAT 10298, Richmond, TW9 1BR

Offer valid in UK only and is not available to current Mills & Boon Book Club subscribers to this series. Overseas and Eire please write for details.. We reserve the right to refuse an application and applicants must be aged 18 years or over. Only one application per household. Terms and prices subject to change without notice. Offer expires 30th June 2010. As a result of this application, you may receive offers from Harlequin Mills & Boon and other carefully selected companies. If you would prefer not to share in this opportunity please write to The Data Manager, PO Box 676, Richmond, TW9 1WU.

Mills & Boon® is a registered trademark owned by Harlequin Mills & Boon Limited.
The Mills & Boon® Book Club™ is being used as a trademark.